MAGEBREAKER 3

DECLAN COURT

CONTENTS

THE STORY SO FAR

Book One – *Magebreaker*

Davik, known as **Darkshire**, narrowly escapes a final job in Swinford. After a long, bloodstained career as an adventurer and conscripted magebreaker, he retires to Oakshire, where he takes a quiet job at a tavern run by **Sariel**, a beautiful Embriel battle-elf who once fought against him in the Summoner War.

There, Davik meets **Elina**, a halfling cleric of the Mistress, goddess of love. She charms him—literally—with a spell that alerts Sariel if he kills or steals. Though they share a bed, **Elina's** true goal is to guide Davik toward a new life.

Over time, **Tyra**, the Faen cook helps introduce him to town, and **Karley** the dark elf bartender barely tolerates him. He takes notice of **Vorga**, a shy book loving waitress that he slowly befriends.

As he adapts to tavern life, Davik grows closer to Sariel, though her war guilt—and the knowledge that he nearly starved in a prison camp—keeps her distant. Meanwhile, his firewood business draws danger, and when it comes, Davik answers with violence.

Later he travels with Elina, Brim the gnome dishwasher, and Vorga to Trinth, securing a heating system for a the tavern. But on their way out, Vorga is falsely arrested by **Sheriff Searlus** and taken by **Bellick Bloodgums** the jailor.

Injured during the confrontation, Davik plummets into the river—then climbs back into the city. With help from his old thief partner **Rushe**, he dons the mantle of Darkshire again and storms the jail, freeing Vorga, a pale woman named **Lyra** (a fallen paladin turned thrall), and a young girl Davik later learns the father of.

That night, Davik and Rushe murder Searlus in his bed and burn his home. In his chambers Davik finds the mace he was struck with, with an enchantment that somehow slipped past his runes. Rushe escapes the city with the ransom gold. Davik, near death, returns to Oakshire, confesses to Sariel, and collapses.

He awakens in her home. Elina healed him with divine magic—his runes now accept her. He later takes Vorga boar hunting, where their bond becomes undeniable and intimate. He welcomes Lyra to Oakshire, but warns her: if her cursed bloodline ever threatens them, he'll end her.

At the autumn festival in Tawney, Davik sees old war comrades. One, **Alain**, had shared a prison camp with him. Learning that Sariel their former enemy is nearby, **Alain** lies to his men that it isn't her, and gives Davik the potato he has carried for years for fear of hunger, remarking it might be time to put it down.

In the epilogue, **Vilas**, a vengeful elven mage, comes to the tavern. He claims the sword Davik gave to the two surviving members of his crew in Swinford belonged to his brother

Venthren—an elf Davik killed. Vilas casts dice, each a taunt targeting one of the women Davik now protects.

"Imagine," he says, "a tavern full of lovely girls. Their own little stories. Guarded by a great warrior..."

One die for an old Embroil betrothed. Another for a coven looking for a dark elf like Karley. A third for a vampire seeking his thrall. A fourth—for a **Faen King**.

But Vilas didn't know Davik is a Magebreaker when he attacks him. Davik caves in his skull with a table leg imbued with the spells he tried to cast on him.

∾

Book Two – *Magebreaker 2*

After Vilas' death, Davik travels to Daggar. There, he meets his old friend **Devan Redscale**, now a beggar beneath the statue the city built in his honor. Glowing red-eyed and addicted to bright-drop, Devan refuses to leave and tells Davik never to return.

In a tavern, Davik meets **Limlas**, Vilas' former apprentice, now voidsick and crippled. He admits he knew little of Vilas' plans. The Embriel ignored his warnings, the vampire who turned Lyra already knows where she is, and Karley's enemies remain unnamed. There are no Faen kings—there never were. Davik gives him Vilas' spellbooks and leaves.

Back in Oakshire, a funeral procession arrives. Davik, **Kardak** the minotaur constable, and the rider bury a corpse marked by Neytha. The body tumbles out and scratches Davik.

Meanwhile, Tyra inadvertently imbues the tavern food with grief, until it becomes inedible. Davik falls deathly ill, succumbing to a fever because of it.

In his fever dreams, Davik sees Rayleth, Trith, and memories of guarding **Elyse Sewell**—a princess he once protected, and later widowed after killing her abusive husband. He also sees **Allie**, a young child that used to sit on his shoulders during the defense of Rochdale who died when the city fell.

After Elina helps heal him, Tyra reveals her secret: she's from a line of Faen winemakers whose soul-linked trees produce sacred wine. Her mother's tree—and Tyra's sapling—are being sold by her deadbeat father at Floraison, an underground wine festival on the edge of the Lowlands.

The group promises to help. As Tyra recovers, Davik teaches her to ride a horse. She names Vilas' warhorse **Polly**, calming her with faen magic. As they spent more time together, their bond deepens.

Meanwhile, Elina devises a method to store healing spells in Davik's runes, allowing him to heal—but at the cost of his magical resistance.

At the summer festival in Oakshire, a knight named **Sir Eralt** and his squire **Puris** arrive. Eralt reveals that Elyse Sewell's sister was the girl freed from the dungeon in Trinth. Her father, **Lord Sewell**, is dying and wants Davik to come to Windpeak. Davik refuses. The two men share a bitter history: Eralt once besieged Rochdale, only to later fight beside Davik under Prince Jame.

On the road south, the group finds a ferry town empty and a storm forces them into a ruined tower. When Karley falls into a goblin tunnel, Davik dives in. Sariel, Eralt, and Puris follow. Brim collapses the tunnel behind them with pyrocrystals.

Later, they reach Hollyhead, a faen cider village. There, Davik meets Aunt Aubrie and Silvus, a fellow veteran. The group prepares for Floraison, where Tyra's tree and sapling is up for auction.

At the festival, Tyra's father **Grane** plans to sell the tree, now dying from over-harvesting to make Brightdrop. **Fenner**, a former Rochdale comrade who ran out on Davik, reveals that he's using Grane to pay off debts—and brewing Brightdrop on his ships.

Despite Tyra's mother's will, the auction won't pull the tree. Tyra imbues a glass of wine. When Grane drinks it, he awards her the tree, betraying Fenner and dooming himself to death.

To secure Grane's reprieve, Davik offers Fenner his elven sword and a gnome stone from Brim. Fenner, now gloating, reveals he opened Rochdale's gates to enemy forces, sacking the city and selling captives.

That night, Fenner's men attack Hollyhead—but the group is ready. Sariel, Eralt, Puris, and faen veterans repel the assault. Davik captures a mage and forces him to cast until voidsickness kills him. Using the stored arcane energy, he splits Fenner's ship, *The Faen King*, in half, then defeats him and takes his head.

Tyra's mother's tree is buried. Tyra plants her sapling, and she and Davik finally embrace.

As they prepare to head home, Puris the squire begs Davik to reconsider Windpeak. He reveals that his sister, Allie, the girl from Rochdale, is alive—raised by Eralt. Moved, Davik agrees, asking them to meet him in Stroudsburg, where he'll call on an old friend. He also demands a hostage for their journey.

But that night, Karley goes missing. Davik finds her outside, unresponsive, her eyes black. Beneath her: a spellbook Vilas had given her. His runes confirm she just tried to cast and is now void sick.

The book ends with Davik carrying her to a horse, racing to Stroudsburg to save her life.

In the Epilogue, we are shown the POV of a necromancer investigating a coven of warlocks. It is revealed that he was the corpse in the casket, infecting Davik with a disease. While he controlled his fever, he saw Davik's past and grew interested in his runes more than serving the clients who sent him there to kidnap someone. The man interrogates one of the surviving assistants who engraved Davik's bones, which the man now wants.

The book ends with the necromancer commanding the undead ferrymen he took from near Oakshire to go north, where he will find a fallen comrade of Darkshire to torment him and rip his soul from his body.

DRAMATIS PERSONAE

Main Characters

Davik of Darkshire

Former Magebreaker engraved during the Summoner War, prisoner of war, then famed mercenary known as Darkshire.

Sariel

Embriel battle-elf and former enemy, now Davik's lover and tavern owner. A war veteran trying to protect a quiet life.

Karley

Sharp-tongued drow bartender. Karley was an orphan from the Severing, when the dark elf kingdoms of the underdark sealed off their entrances to limit the mage collegiate influence.

Tyra

Redheaded Faen cook for the tavern, sparkling skin, wingless. Tyra is able to imbue food and drink with emotional properties, as well as briefly share emotion and receive it with touch.

Vorga

Most-orc waitress, quiet, inquisitive. Loves hunting and reading. Open in her affection for Davik.

Elina

Halfling cleric of the Mistress. Gentle, spiritual, fiercely protective. Uses rare divine magic to heal and shield. Ascended in her powers from book 2, her moon-ink tattoos grow with her and Davik's relationship and bond.

Brim

Dishwasher, pyrotechnical hazard and psionic gnome.

Lyra

Fallen Paladin of Selene, Goddess of Justice and Fairness. Vampire, known as sun-cursed or crimson-touched.

Trith

Wood elf sorcerer and spellslinger. Longtime mercenary and adventurer, retired years ago after the Rochdale rebellion. Davik's closest living friend.

The Necromancer

Also known as the "Man who isn't a Man." Nameless, corpse-like spellcaster with a soul dungeon inside him. Wants to wear Davik's body and end magic at its source.

Returning Characters

Sir Eralt

Aging knight of Windpeak. Former enemy who laid siege to Rochdale, later served Prince Jame for Lord Avelmont when Darkshire was there.

Puris

Young squire raised by Eralt. Brave, sincere, once fought with Davik at Rochdale as a youth.

Elyse Sewell

Former betrothed to Prince Jame. Widowed by Davik many years ago.

Mara Sewell

Elyse's younger sister, unknowingly rescued by Davik from the Trinth dungeon in book 1. Her capture sparked Eralt's task to find Darkshire.

Rayleth

Also known as Rayleth Half-Heard due to his missing ear. Elven exile and Davik's fallen comrade. Revered swordsman.

Deiga

Rayleth's sister. A scarred, bitter mage who once taught mage generalists. Dislikes Davik deeply.

Knightly Houses & Allies

Windpeak – Seat of House Sewell.

- *Allie* – Puris' sister, used to sit on Davik's shoulders during the siege of Rochdale. Thought dead.
- *Luka* – Axe-wielding son of a Rochdale leatherworker
- *Ekyll* – Broad squire and friend of Puris

Drakemoor –

- *Silas* – Tournament entrant
- *Renrick* – Eldest brother.

Bronzefell – Young house in bronze

- *Sir Hewer* – Lead suitor
- *Helmed* – Silent monk-trained warrior.

Springdall / Highblade – Competing banners

- *Ettimer Highblade* – Noble, soft-handed son

Avelmont (Destroyed)

Once the dominant banner in the Lowlands, led by **Lord Elrick Avelmont**, known as *Ironclad*. Ruthless and unyielding, he brought the region to heel. His death from illness loosened his grip—and chaos followed.

- Prince Jame Avelmont – His only child, betrothed to Elyse Sewell. Hired Davik after the Rochdale rebellion. Murdered by Davik the morning after their wedding.

PART ONE

THE CITY

CHAPTER

ONE

I rode as I had a thousand times. Whether through a battlefield or a city street with guards firing from rooftops after me. The terrain had changed, but the circumstances hadn't. I was out of time, out of luck, and trying to ride faster than Karley's slowing heartbeat.

The bartender's moans echoed with voidsickness. The stain of her soul tormented the runes in my body. When her eyes did open, reeling at some unseen horror, they were as black as oil.

"Stay with me," I whispered through clenched teeth. Karley shivered against me.

Sariel and the girls and Brim had fallen far behind me once we left Hollyhead. I couldn't wait for them. I couldn't wait for anything. I took Polly, the destrier, and the nag from Trinth. A dying mage and a single waterskin along with the contents of one of my packs.

It was all on me. Her life was in my hands. The question was how much could I push, how much could I withstand, to save a girl from her foolishness? I had grabbed the spellbook she had nearly killed herself with in case it helped.

It was a day's ride to Stroudsburg, and the dark elf in my arms wouldn't last that long. So I pushed it. I rode. I rode until my thighs bruised and then bled, caking the saddle with rivets of blood. I rode until the muscles in my arms cramped from holding her. Then I kept riding. I rode until the thunder in Polly's heart nearly gave out, and then I switched to the nag.

"Stay with me." I pulled on the reins, racing towards a city I hadn't been to in years. Filled with memories, most of them bad. And I didn't want to add one more.

Something like fever swept into me. Any water we had, I would sip at a gallop and then lift Karley's murmuring lips, spurting what she needed in our first kiss.

Hours passed, lit by moonlight, until the road smelled like ghosts, and I couldn't tell if it was sweat or blood in my eyes. A fever came over me, born of horse flesh and the hypnotic trample of hooves. Friends smiled at me as I rode past, waving with ghostly arms.

A memory clawed at me. I'd done this before—and I'd failed. A dying comrade in my arms. A temple spire on the horizon. My smile at finally reaching it. The relief when I looked down to tell her.

We made it. You're going to be alright.

Terrible thing, realizing you're suddenly alone when you hadn't been a moment before. She had died just before we arrived. I sold that horse. Couldn't be reminded of when I hadn't been quick enough. I used the money to bury her next to the temple I had failed to reach.

That couldn't happen, not now. This wasn't my adventuring days. There were no grand quests. This was a foolish bartender in my arms, not someone who had entered the game knowing what was at stake.

"Stay with me," I whispered to Karley.

I might've slung her over the follow-horse. But in that frantic fear of life and death, maybe I thought I could keep the dark rider at bay if I held her. And I didn't want her to fall.

Or die with no one holding her.

I felt the spell warring with her soul inside her. Elina hadn't been able to help. No cleric would unless their deity dealt with the arcane. If their gods were the gods of magic, they were my enemy.

I'd have to go to the collegiates in Stroudsburg. Among the many there, none held a warm place in their hearts for me.

But there was one man who would help me. The collegiate had no real name, no proper title. And the man who ran it had been behind the death of more mages than I.

We crested over the hill, deep past midnight, and I stared at Stroudsburg nestled before the sea like a dying man in the desert. There were harbors and spires of sorcery. Winding streets thick with buildings. Bells from faraway ships and music flittered over the wind. A place that never slept.

The city had never truly fallen under the control of the Lowlands. But the coin that flowed here brought tolerance from the southern feudal lords who hated outsiders. The kind of men who would take your bribe and deride you for it.

The kind of men who would conscript you into a war.

I raced to the western entrance. It had been years, but there shouldn't be any charge to enter the city. A half-elf guard walked to me, bearing the emblem of the towered city.

"She sick? Is it plague?" He walked forward, raising a torch at Karley.

"Voidsick." My throat was a corpse, gasping for air. "I need to find a mage."

He raised a hand, motioning for me to show him. I hefted

her down and opened her eyelids. When he saw how black her eyes were, he waved me through.

"Hurry then."

No shit.

I swung the reins in my hands, pushing through the cobbled streets in the dead of night. The sea air smelled of kelp mingling with the trash piles of the streets. Polly's clop swung into the whine of steel horseshoes on stone.

Even after not being here for many years, I still knew the streets with my eyes closed. I glanced up at the mage towers, curling my teeth. They would be my last resort. And I'd probably have to fight my way out.

The man I needed wasn't easy to find. That was the nature of his entire order. He was a predator supreme. An alley cat, watching the robed rats scurry where he wanted. He owed me. If you want to find a hunter, you stalk what it likes to eat.

So it was time to find a rat.

"You sure it'll work?" the red-robed mage inspected the scroll. It was a prepared spell, for single usage. Meant to disintegrate the moment it was utilized.

"Work?" Lukyll the Bright Eye smiled at her, pushing his oily hair over the side of his head. "Of course it'll work, dear Tessa. Lukyll wouldn't steer you wrong." For a drow, he was sallow-skinned. Too much time in the sun; too many years below. The small wine house was near the edge of the collegiate district.

The girl looked down at the scroll again. "It's just, they said if I can't ascend I'm out. And my father won't send more money for my tuition."

Lukyll tutted. "Parents can be so misunderstanding. You're a grown woman. What are you, nineteen?"

The girl blushed. "Nearly twenty-two."

He leaned over the table. "Well, you don't look a day over twenty!"

She giggled. "Debra said you were—"

"Said I was what?" Lukyll leaned back into his chair with a grin, his eyes sliding down to the cleavage spilling out of her robe. The winehouse was one of his regular bastions of dealings. "Handsy? Well, you can judge me guilty on that."

The mage blushed. Then she withdrew the coins from her purse. "I have the forty gold..."

"Ah." Lukyll shook his head sadly, snatching the scroll gently away. "It's fifty, my dear. I have another buyer, didn't you know? I held this for you. You should have told me if you were short on coin."

Her face fell. "But you said forty."

"That was last week. You have to understand, I didn't sell it. But I can't take ten less just for you, Tessa, you understand?"

Her eyes welled with tears. "But my ascension test... it's tomorrow."

"Listen. We can work something out. Would you like that?" Lukyll slid his hand forward, grasping hers. "I keep a room upstairs..."

When she tried to pull away, the dark elf gripped her wrist.

Her face flashed with fear. "Let go of my hand."

But Lukyll was enjoying this. He liked reeling in a good fish, and the best ones wriggled before they slid into the basket. The illicit sneer rose from him like a sickness. "Do you know how *hard* I am right now, just sitting here? Just an evening, little Tessa."

I slid my hand over his wrist, squeezing until the bones clicked together. "I'm fucking hard, too."

Lukyll's eyes were wide, not believing the nightmare over him. "No!"

I grinned murder at him. "Yes."

The collegiate student rose from her seat, causing heads to snap over at the commotion.

I turned my head. "Don't forget your scroll."

She looked down, weighing saying something, then she snatched it and walked away.

"You always had bad manners, Bright Eye." I gripped the back of his neck. "You still taking severed Drow down into the caves, promising them a way into the underdark and abandoning them?"

"Darkshire!" He hissed. "What can I do for you?"

"I need to find *him*. I know you sell spellbooks and information on your collegiate. Where are they now?"

Lukyll shook his head. "I don't know. I stopped—"

I squeezed harder. "You always were a cunt, Lukyll. I remember when you ran in Daggar. If you don't know, then you're no use to me." I curled my fingers into his skin. It was time to show the world he had a spine.

"Okay!" Lukyll gasped when I released him. "I'll tell you!"

"Show me." I stood slowly, pulling him up. "I've got a friend in the alley out back. When I pick her up, if you run you better hope I don't catch you."

I walked the kidnapped mage out the backdoor. When the owner saw my face, he looked quickly away, finding better things to do like polish glasses.

The night air welcomed us. I moved a barrel, releasing him and picking up Karley. Then Lukyll made a break for it. My dirk hissed into my hand, and I barreled him against the alley walls.

"Hold still," I sneered. Then I shoved the dirk through his forearm, stapling it to his hip.

Lukyll's mouth opened in a silent scream. His dark eyes slid down to the blade protruding from him. Hip bones are dense, like a stump. You'd be surprised what you can anchor into one. "You cunt, you miserable—"

I uncovered Karley and lifted her over my shoulder, then drew my sword and motioned him. "Let's go."

Lukyll limped slowly, and I moved his cloak to cover the dagger sticking out of him. A thin line of blood trailed after him as we walked towards the collegiate towers.

"You better hurry, Lukyll." I hefted Karley. "Only so much of that stuff in you."

The drow cursed under his breath as we walked. No one gave us much mind. It was late night. A time for drinkers and those on the underhanded side of life. This had been my city once, in more ways than one.

We walked for ten minutes, circling around the edge of the collegiate tower district. Lukyll stopped, panting. Behind us, a procession of dark elves held banners in silver script, bells chiming lightly on a neighboring street.

"What's that about?" I nodded. I wasn't used to seeing such a late-night crowd.

Lukyll was doubled over in pain. He bit off each word. "It's the returned. The drow in the city. Underdark is having negotiations to reopen."

I snorted. Those negotiations never went anywhere. "Won't happen." Then I reached out and twisted the dagger, causing him to scream. "Break's over."

"Fucking... up... *there*. The bakery."

I looked up, and I felt it. A lot of mages were behind those doors, simmering with power.

Lukyll pushed the cloak aside, wincing as he stared at the dirk jutting from his hip. "Get it out."

I glanced down. Karley was still unconscious in my arms, burning up with voidsickness. Time was short, but sometimes you make time for little indulgences.

Lukyll had always slithered around the edges—too cowardly for the Unseen, too useful to ignore. They wouldn't take him. Just use him.

But tonight, he'd led me true.

I lowered Karley into a sack of flour, carefully. She moaned once, weak and barely there.

Then I turned to Lukyll. "Come on. I'll do it."

He tried to grin through his pain, teeth red. "Like old times, eh?"

I grabbed his shirt and popped the dirk free. Old times indeed.

"Fuck," Lukyll breathed. "We done?"

I glanced at Karley. The truth was, Lukyll had always had it coming. He had a habit of disappearing whenever Trith, Rayleth, or I had been in town. Hadn't liked the way he grabbed that girl in the bar, nor his words for her. Never liked the rumors about those lost dark elf families dying of thirst, abandoned underground, just trying to find home.

"Yeah." My voice was iron. "We're done."

Lukyll gasped as I pulled him onto me, hefting the spike through his ribs, digging for that weak heart of his. His hands clasped on my back, the wheezing hiss of his last breath filling my face.

"This was a longtime coming," I hissed into his ear.

I wrenched up, making quick work of it, before dropping him behind some shrubbery for the guards to find. I blessed his passing into the underworld with a gobbet of spit, wiping the needle blade on his pants.

I grabbed Karley and carried her up to the bakery. The windows were covered in dust.

8

I banged on the door five times.

I could feel powerful mages turn to regard me.

I knocked again, four times.

"Come on," I grunted, hefting Karley's limp body up. "Come on, you fucking—"

The door opened. A young human girl regarded me, dressed like a commoner. "Do you need something, sir?"

I cleared my throat and spoke the words clearly. "I left my flowers in Runethor."

She considered me, then spoke the counter-challenge back. "Why did you water them?"

A dozen protective wards locked onto me—heat like the breath of a dragon. They wouldn't touch me. But Karley? She'd burn to ashes in my arms.

I eyed the mage. "They forgot to grow."

She nodded, and in a blink, the glammer burned away. The baker girl was gone. In her place stood a tiefling in blood-red robes, her chipped horn catching the dim light. She sized me up, slow and deliberate. "What do you need, Magebreaker?"

"Tell him I've come for my favor."

The horned mage laughed, nonplussed by the dying girl in my arms. "Who's *him?*"

"Him," I repeated.

A cart rumbled behind me, and she shook her head. "He isn't here."

"He's everywhere," I growled. "You tell him the hand that freed him is here, and it's open. My friend needs help."

"You don't have friends, Darkshire." The mage shut the door in my face.

That was abundantly clear. But I felt her communing behind the door. I glanced behind me at the six different mage collegiate towers, each a worse option than the last.

A wizard's soul approached the door. My runes screamed

9

from his raw power. And beyond that power, I could feel tendrils of absolute control. When the door opened again, a half-elf regarded me in a set of simple leathers. His hip glittered with a warlock's blade, and one silver eye flashed as he scanned me up and down.

"Hello, Davik."

"Hello..." I reached for a name to call him.

"Evior will do, today." He bent forward and felt Karley's wrist. "An initiate? Voidsick?"

"Can you save her?" I held her up.

He regarded me as if there was time to burn. "Not your usual, Darkshire. Saving mages."

"Saved *you* once."

The half-elf nodded. "Twice, actually. But I doubt you remember." Most would take him for a drow. But he was half Seavori sea-elf. It was all in the eyes.

I watched the tattoos on the side of his shaved scalp shift for a moment. Under certain circumstances, this was the most dangerous mage alive. You could feel the air learning how to lie around him, becoming what he wanted. I was one of several people who knew what his real face looked like.

"You'll need to wear this. It'll block your runes." He held out a cloak I hadn't seen a moment ago. The old joke of Runethor, that damned city of sorcerers, came back to me.

There is no school of illusion.

"No," I told him.

Evior smiled. "You can take it off, Davik. But a lot of work went into what's behind these doors. Can't have you stomping through the sandcastle."

"Take her," I told him. The collegiate master held Karley in his arms. He was strong, bigger than most half-elves. And I knew the markings of some of his tattoos that shifted around him, moving like writhing ink. Iceland barbarian tribes.

I pulled the cloak on, smothering my runes.

"So graces your presence, Darkshire." The wizard shouldered the door open, welcoming me inside. "Welcome to the Collegiate of the Unseen."

CHAPTER
TWO

We stepped into a grand tower that shouldn't exist, the weight of the illusion pressing against my cloak like unseen hands.

Through a window, sunlight streamed at midnight, from Runethor, a city almost a thousand miles away.

"We have time," Evior assured me. "The wards within have stilled her affliction until we can cure it. She isn't the first to come here with dire wounds or poisoning."

Karley felt better in my arms. The war of temperatures had receded inside her. A sliver of relief penetrated my weary mind.

Almost there.

"I'd ask how you've been," I ventured as we walked through the corridors. Their length defied the logic of the size of the bakery outside.

"I know you would. And I'd answer if I could." Evior continued walking. Mages passed us, all in differing robes of multiple collegiates. I expected furious looks from them but received none. If they were surprised I was here, they didn't show it.

"They can't see me?" I asked him.

Evior shrugged. "They see what we allow them to. Blinders keep the horse on target."

"Glad you won your war," I offered.

Evior laughed. "Victory is an illusion. Wars rarely end. They just change."

The spies continued past me. Or maybe they were simple assets of this dangerous school, thinking they were somewhere else. We passed by a small library, and I saw a masquerade mask turn on a pedestal, made from mirrors, watching me with no one to fill it.

Some reading areas were bathed in the light of soft elven grottoes. Other armories housed priceless enchanted items in rooms that looked like orc fortresses.

A pretty human girl walked past me, her eyes ablaze with sorcery. As she passed Evior, her dress flickered to nothing for a moment, giving us both a view of her nude body.

"Sorry," Evior said. "She didn't know you were there."

"So all the students have a crush on the teacher?"

Evior laughed. "That was my teacher, once."

History, vision, and maybe even time were malleable things to certain wizards. It was a world I wanted to know less about than I did. Leave paradox to the robed fools who cracked the world open for power.

"Here." Evior motioned to a room without a door. As we walked in, a woman with a grisly set of facial scars turned from a shelf of potions and tinctures. Her nose was mostly gone. She reminded me of Aella, the scarred halfling I had known once when Rayleth, Trith, and I had traveled with Brightplate.

"You didn't tell me, love." The woman murmured something, and in the twist of a second, she was beautiful. The illusion clung to her face before I could tell her species. "I'd have put on my face. Hello, Magebreaker."

I looked at Evior, waiting. He held up a hand. "My associate will take care of your friend."

"What's your name?"

"We don't do names here." She gently opened Karley's eyes. "Your friend summoned something strong for an ascendant spell. It's stuck in the channel of her soul."

My heart slowed in my chest. "Did we make it in time?"

"Yes," the woman whispered. "What did she cast? What school?"

I reached for my pocket. "I have the page here. Or what the book was opened to."

I handed it over to the woman. The room was well-lit, but from where I couldn't tell. The wizard ran her thumb down the page. Arcane words glowed through the page, pulsing like mushrooms in the underdark.

"Oh." The woman set the page down. "You foolish girl. Lay her down on the table."

I did so, and then Evior motioned me towards him. "Stand back, Darkshire. Even with that cloak, I don't want those runes interfering."

His associate waved her hands over Karley, fingers sifting through invisible sand that I couldn't see. The human's eyes took on a green haze, the color of trampled grass. Then she found whatever was within Karley.

"*Keva,*" her voice echoed. "*Aleith tera, linus linus.*"

Strands of black ether rose from Karley's body, pulling her chest upwards.

"*Reyka til nurud,*" the human muttered.

Karley gasped, the loudest noise she had made in hours. The mage pushed her chest back down to the table, wrenching a pool of black shadow from her.

"*Antem!*" The woman threw the spell from her, casting it

into a glass contraption nearby where it teetered over and rolled onto the floor.

Karley coughed. It was the first noise I'd heard from her, and not just her body, in a day. She gripped the table in fear.

"Where am I?" she asked.

"*Noctum.*" The woman waved her hand, and Karley fell unconscious.

"The fuck did you just do?" I snarled and ripped the sword from my scabbard.

"Davik," Evior said with a raised hand. I saw the pulse of witchfire swirling in his palm. "She's just asleep. She can't know she was here. You know that."

"She won't remember anything." The woman stared at Karley's sleeping form, ignoring my blade that I now sheathed. "Wish that could go for all of us. But she needs to rest."

Evior waved at me. "Come on, she'll look after your friend."

I stared at the collegiate master. "I have a choice?"

"Of course you do."

"We don't hurt people here, Darkshire," the woman said. She stared down at Karley, smoothing her hair in an almost motherly way. "Despite what you might think."

I walked forward and put my hand on Karley's forehead. Her fever had vanished. She murmured as she slept under the touch of the spell.

We made it. You're going to be alright.

"Take her to that cot." The woman motioned to me.

I carried Karley to the bed. Her clothes were soaked from sweat and the grime of our ride here. In a day and a half, the girls and everyone else would catch up. They'd meet us at the *Dragon's Nest*, the yellow-painted inn towards the East Gate.

"I'll stay with her," the wizardess whispered.

"She's safe, Davik," Evior called to me from the hallway. "Come on. I'll buy you a coffee. Just keep that cloak on."

I walked from Karley. Coming here had cost me one of the most valuable favors any man could have. If my name hadn't been drenched in the blood of wizards, it would have been ten gold pieces. But the world has its own pricing system for men with their histories.

I looked back again at the woman.

"She'll be okay," she assured me without turning.

I turned to Evior in the hallway. He opened a door across from us, where the landscape of the Icelands greeted us both. Soft glaciers and pale violet dusk stood under an unsetting sun.

I shook my head. "Fucking wizards."

IF THIS WAS AN ILLUSION, it was a powerful one. The coffee in my hands was warm, but the cold around me felt muted. The snow didn't seep into my armor or the clothing beneath it. The Icelands were a place I had only been to several times, but the aching beauty of that deathscape was one that you never forgot. The sun seemed more like a distant star as it rose above the edge of the horizon, touching everything and warming nothing.

Narwhals swam in a pod ahead of us, circling one another with echoing warbles. In the distance of the glacial shoreline, a white direbear prowled the snows, waiting for one of his prey to get close.

"Do you miss it?" I asked Evior. We had no crackling fire. The Iceland tribes wouldn't waste something as precious as wood on fires. Those barbarians had other ways to heat themselves. They used runes, shamanic magic, or burned oil and blubber from the beasts they hunted.

The collegiate master watched the narwhals, his silver eye

muted in his socket. I noticed here that his tattoos didn't shift on the sides of his shaved head, and his hair was braided in the fashion of some tribe. Around us was nothing but ice and the occasional peak of rock. Somewhere in the distance, seals yelped.

"Sometimes. I miss hunting." Evior's coffee sat next to him, the tin cup creating a perfect circular pocket of molten snow. He wore furs now. Adorned with tusks and bones that hung on leather straps. He was less of a wizard and more of a hunter. "And those who taught me."

Evior whittled something with a spike of metal. When I looked closer, I saw it was a small tusk. The ivory was a nicotine brown, gleaming white where he carved his scrimshaw.

"Your drow friend is going to be okay, Davik." Evior set his tusk down and picked up his coffee. "But some doors can't be shut once they're opened. Only she'll be able to tell if it can be closed."

"I know." The breath from my mouth turned to plumes of steam as I spoke. "Any suggestions?"

He didn't answer me. Evior leaned back a bit, settling into the snow. "It's a paltry thing, saving a mage compared to what I owe you. A balance remains, Darkshire. So tell me—what else do you want?"

I appreciated that. Some people knew how to conduct business properly, and Evior was one of them. Of all the payouts and favors he tallied, blood had been his first currency. The genesis of this collegiate was born in revenge and all the things that came with it.

"You know a Vilas?" I asked.

Evior grinned. "The elf you murdered? No one knows him any longer."

When he saw the expression on my face, he smirked.

"Come now, Darkshire. Who are you speaking to? How do you enjoy Oakshire? It's quite pretty, isn't it?"

My hand crept very slightly towards my dirk. "You sell someone information about me?"

Evior *tsked* and shook his head, causing his braids to swing. "We don't sell information, Davik. We *buy* it. And we control it. And we distribute something close to it but not quite. Vilas was well-known in some circles. Powerful circles. But a circle isn't a circle once it's been broken." A devilish smile crept across his mouth. "He was brother to Venthren, by marriage. A stronger mage than he." His eyes swept over mine. "And Venthren shared a nurse-maid with Rayleth Half-Heard, your great friend. But you knew that."

I sighed and leaned back. "All elven royals have two dozen brothers and sisters—all those political marriages."

"Price of living forever." Evior nodded. "Speaking of, Deiga has been here awhile."

"Shit." I sipped my coffee. "I would almost rather deal with you."

"Elves do know how to hold a grudge."

I considered what I could ask him. "I'm looking for an enclave that might be after Karley."

The mage shook his head again. "That's bigger than what remains of your favor. Now that you're in town... if you wanted, there are some people you could say hello to for me. That would buy you what you seek."

"I'm not in that business any longer."

"I imagine Fenner and Lukyll would disagree. But it's nice to think so."

The half-elf reached into his pocket and pulled out a very small scroll with a hard wax stamp. He held it out to me. It was a collegiate contract scroll. The thing that had surged the ranks of mercenaries and adventurers after the war. Opening it was the first step toward an agreement.

I didn't move to take it. "Didn't hear what I just said?"

"In case you change your mind." Evior shrugged. "What else would you ask?"

"What do I do with her?" I slid the scroll into my vest, planning on never opening it.

"What do you think you should do?" Evior replied.

Mages.

Nothing was straightforward with them.

Evior sipped his coffee again, and his left eye gleamed like a molten star. For a moment, I saw a claw battering on the cage of his iris, like something was trying to get out. "You'll need Deiga's help with your friend."

"I know," I told him. I didn't want to know what was trapped in his eye... or who. Ahead of us, a narwhal lifted its horn like a knight preparing for the joust, before spraying saltwater into the air. "I'll get to it."

"They've changed." Evior regarded me. "Trith is in town, too, you know."

That I did know. And in the cold of this place, and the upcoming journey and wedding, it warmed me. "Where?"

Evior laughed. "Take one guess, and you'll be right."

That settled that. "What should I ask you for?"

"I wouldn't want you to think I'm leading you astray. Might end up with that dirk in me."

It was my turn to laugh. "That's if you're really here. Maybe you're a spell."

The mage stifled a smile. "Always were smart, Davik. Kept you alive. Kept the quill scratching out your story. Was it worth it?"

I stared at the snowy expanse, imagining the green hills of Oakshire. "For me, it was."

"Your friend will have a decision to make. Her ascension didn't work. It could. The void will seep into her now, and she'll need to purge it. If it's small spells, and she ignores the potential, the tear in her soul will eventually heal. If she pushes further... it can't be closed."

It was what I was afraid of. "Will she ever..."

"Not have it?" Evior slid his scrimshaw into his furs. "Maybe."

"That scarred woman with you... who is she?"

Evior's face looked like a man who had just fallen on a spear. "Someone who loves me too much and maybe shouldn't have. She's a good woman. And I am a bad man."

I turned to see figures on the far horizon. A rowboat of some kind drifted to a bank. Now I was certain this was an illusion. You didn't see such small boats in the Icelands, nor men not wearing furs. Maybe Evior was losing his touch.

Evior regarded me. "You think about it, Davik. If you want to know about that enclave, open the scroll. You do what it says, the answer you want will be yours. Just like the old days. And I'll owe you an entire other favor."

The high mage stood and dusted the snow from his furs. By the time I pushed myself up, they had changed back to his leathers, complete with his sword on his hip.

"The names on that scroll, are they guilty or innocent?"

Evior pulled on a door I couldn't see, opening the collegiate hallway back into existence.

"Yes."

～

"Do you know what this is?" The female wizard held up Karley's spellbook when we walked back into their medicae. It should've surprised me to see the entirety of my saddle and the contents laid out on the table, but in this collegiate, nothing surprised me.

I nodded. "A spellbook."

The woman regarded me, driving the point home. "A drow spellbook. Proprietary."

That surprised me. "She can't read drow."

"My love," Evior said softly. His eye flashed again.

She sneered at him. "Don't look at me with that eye. You know I hate it."

Karley dozed in the corner. Must be nice to sleep your troubles away while someone else took care of everything. Then again, I had a higher count of that with the girls than anyone.

"Tell me about the spell?" I offered.

"It's starfall," the woman said with a shake of her head. "Far beyond her level. Far beyond a third-year's level. But, she nearly did it."

Evior didn't smile. His tone was informative and a little wary. "You have someone with a lot of potential on your hands, Davik."

"What school?" I turned to both of them. "What school was it?"

"Light." She shrugged. "Drow witch magic."

"You just said starfall."

She looked at me. "All natural light comes from stars, in one way or another. This isn't just a spellbook, it's a journal."

Evior stepped back and waved in two members of his order. "Pack this up, and put it back on his horse." As he turned, he stopped, transfixed by Searlus's mace that I had in my saddle.

"Where did you get this?" Evior held it up. I saw the light around him crackle. The room's illusion broke like someone smearing their palm on a fresh painting. He held up the weapon, inspecting its mark.

"In Trinth." I walked towards him. "Why?"

The woman looked over. "My word."

"What?" I asked them both. "It's enchanted, isn't it?"

Evior set the mace down. "More like disenchanted. Who owned this?"

"Some human," I said, waiting to see if he knew what had happened in Trinth. "What do you mean?"

"This mace shouldn't exist," Evior explained. "The more you try to deny it, the more it asserts itself."

I was surprised to be getting this information for free. "What does that mean?"

Evior looked up at me. "Magic changes reality, Davik. It borrows from other planes, shaping this one. This weapon was made to exist. It's *undeniable*. The more something wants to counteract its effect, the stronger it becomes."

"Sounds familiar..." I found myself saying.

Evior glanced at the long incision scars along my body. "Similar, but not the same. Be careful with that, Davik. You swing at a shield of enchanted protection with this. It might shatter your arm."

"So it's a spellbreaker?" I ventured, trying to enter their arcane nomenclature.

"In a way..." The female mage changed subjects. "Your friend... she needs rest."

I nodded. "Let's wake her."

Evior murmured something under his breath. The room shifted around us, and I felt a burning sensation in the cloak I wore. Evior looked like a portly baker, and Karley now lay upon sacks of flour instead of a bed. The woman didn't change.

Karley coughed. She looked around wildly, and I raised a hand to calm her as I walked forward.

"Where am I?"

"Where you were." The woman stared at Karley, playing

the role of the lone wizard. "Was the verge of death. Where you are is Stroudsburg. That spell was too strong for you. Too strong for an awakening spell. The void was stuck in the tears of your soul, poisoning you."

"I just..." Karley began, and then her gaze fell on me. It was like she could read our journey there.

I was too tired and relieved to give her more than an exhausted stare. But I saw the shame in her face, and the story plain across it. The secret she had been reading in the dark of the tavern's cellar in Oakshire. All those hints I missed while I was focused on getting us to Hollyhead.

It's easy to be angry with people who nearly bring their own ruin. And shame is a terrible shadow when you stand in it. There are times to be angry and times to take someone into consideration.

"Davik..." Karley whispered.

"Hey." I walked towards her. Her face softened as I put my hand reassuringly on her back.

"I just... thought I could handle it."

"You didn't."

Karley stared me in the eye. That same look. That teasing defiance when we were in the bar together. "I almost did..."

"It's okay," I told her. "It's okay."

The smallest smile broke on her mouth until I spoke my next words.

"You're just an idiot."

CHAPTER
THREE

The man rides.

The bear is white, stained red. It weighs over a thousand pounds, but the might of its enslaved soul is so much grander than its meek form. The glow of its risen eyes tints the icy terrain in emerald light.

He is here to find the tomb where Darkshire left his friend, Rayleth. What was his name?

Rayleth the Half-Heard.

Rayleth will hear him. When the necromancer speaks, the dead listen.

Most of his dead oarsmen wait miles behind him. Their corpses are small blots on the landscape as they hold the boat steady. Only the dead are strong enough to row here. Several servants pursue him, stumbling as they carry his effects.

The cold here is tolerable, but its severity slows his tendons. He has not been feeding enough. His form withered too long in Oakshire. He didn't feed enough in the thaumaturge's coven.

I should have devoured that entire warlock village of cringing cowards.

Twin reins of spectral control shine in ghostly incandescence from his hands, looping into the brain of the dead dire bear. He opens the valve of instinct in its mind. Its soul is powerful, and he cannot let it gain too much control. If the beast ever remembered itself fully, the consequences would be... not ideal.

His dead eyes slide over the horizon. They are far north of Daggar but more inland. If the coastline was a skin, he is the knife puncturing under the dermis, sliding into the fat under the body of the world.

The white bear growls again. The smell of blood drives his furred mount forward. The beast is almost entirely instinctive, built from its environment over thousands of generations. It does not *need* to eat. But it does not understand this.

The scent it catches is unusual to it, and the necromancer allows it to pursue, releasing the reins slightly to rock back and forth as it crawls over crag, over peak and gully, and takes them both closer to their buried prize.

IN THE DEEP NIGHT, he needs a break. It is too cold; his movement is too stiff.

This is a desolate place. Nothing grows, so nothing can die. There is no wood. He coaxes a fire into existence, a fever of energies burning and crackling under the starred sky. The dire bear sleeps, forced into its slumber by the soul he has wrestled into submission. The fire warms him, and he dislikes this. It reminds him he is all too alive and still all too dead.

The frost carries more than silence. He pauses, listening, but there is only the crackling fire and the bear's slow breathing. Still, the feeling lingers. Something else lives in this place. Something that watches him but is too afraid to call out.

Not every mystery should be explored.

He can feel the Darkshire moving across the world to some distant land. The faintest touch of the disease is still within him. But there is time. Time to capture those bones and the lost daughter of the underdark.

He grows excited. He pictures a legion of dead marching, armored in the Darkshire's bone runes. Cracking open mage towers like husks—devouring the whimpering eggs within.

He could slaughter every mage in Runethor if he wished. To see an army of dead choking those streets, tearing mages apart, would be a welcome sight. Surely their spells would find ways, but not for long.

When I choke their magic from the world, the only art will be the profane. All will study the veil.

And after?

Cities of dead, moving alongside the living. Such wonders await the world once the mages perish.

There is a pulsing inside his chest. At first, he thinks it may be his heart. But upon further query, this is thankfully not so. His client is tugging at the bonds of the world, pulling the strings of the arcane that the man despises.

If his eyes had enough moisture, he might roll them in annoyance.

The man casts the misshapen soul into the body. It is not a proper soul; it has been morphed, tethered, and stretched between two points: one stationary, and one that travels slowly in him.

Selling a soul is a sin, and sharing one seems unfaithful. He rarely speaks with clients once a task is taken, yet this one has what he wants. They hold the keys to the doors the man wants to open, so he has made an exception.

Like all exceptions, it is likely a mistake.

"Speak," the man commands.

The body twitches as the new soul takes root. "Are you close?"

"I am," the man says. He feels like he is, so it must be the truth.

"You... don't feel close," the voice cracks. "I can barely hear you."

If you truly heard me, you would go deaf from the sound of it.

The man stares at his corpse servant. "What do you desire?"

The body twitches, cocking its head to stare at the man. "It has been almost a year since we contracted you."

Contacted or contracted may have been said; things get lost in the tethering through the veil. And the accent of the dark elves doesn't help.

The man stops smiling.

A year?

Is this true? It doesn't feel true.

But he has done this before. He is prone to distraction. Once he had delivered a man to an employer, dragging the screaming retiree. By the time he arrived, his employer had died from the pox two years past.

He gets distracted... there is much to study, much to explore. When dealing with the living, it's easy to forget how important time is to them.

"You must hurry..." the corpse growls at him. "Negotiations begin soon. Is he dead?"

It is tempting to lie, simply so this conversation can end. But such things rarely work out for the best.

"He still lives. He survived my first probing. He will not survive the second. I am close."

It is and isn't the truth. It will suffice.

The corpse twitches again. "You are not in the Midlands... there is ice and rock around you."

The man shrugs. For a moment, he thinks about reaching through the soul conduit and doing something terrible.

"I will deal with your matter soon," he says.

The corpse considers this for a moment, placing a finger on its own chin, adding humanity to the marionette show of strings and souls. The man finds he does not like other people using that which belongs to him.

Yet perhaps I have been too patient, too distracted. The girl is a tool, nothing more. But their value of her is high.

The man stares at the speaker through the eyes of his corpse slave. "I will have her to you soon. Then I will have the lore you promised."

The key to the void is made of arcana. I need the wizards who know its shape.

His client nods. "We are pleased to hear that. Safe travels to you, veilwalker."

Veilwalker. The man does not like this; it is not the right word.

The corpse goes limp as the man summons the tethered soul back to the dungeon in his chest.

The criticism from his client irritates him because it is valid. He decides to feed even more. To power his step and body again. There will be more sensation. He has hung onto the world with the last vestiges of flesh for perhaps too long. There are liches in the deep caverns that take a year to move across the room. He understands their choice.

He does not respect it.

Work ethic is important. Very important. Three more of his corpse-slaves bring his supplies for the camp. Some crates have not been opened in years. He beckons one of them forward and commands it to be opened.

28

Tomes are packed within, covered in rotten straw that crumbles to dust. The profane fire nearby flickers, powered by his will, draining and warming him at the same time.

The man picks a journal treatise written by an occlumency sadist. He beckons forth two of his corpse slaves and replaces their souls with two others from his chest dungeon.

Rise, he commands the sleeping dire bear. The beast growls.

Go bring down something large, keep it alive, and drag it back here.

The bear lumbers off. The control command will sit in his brain until dawn.

The two souls he selects from his dungeon inhabit the bodies of the two rivermen. They stretch their arms and legs in wonder. They have been alone for some time.

He opens the grimoire, scanning the jagged handwriting.

"What do you want?" the first corpse growls at him in irritation. It is one of his peers from long ago.

Not laughing now, are you?

The man holds up a ghostly finger as he reads.

The other corpse sneers at the man. "Again?"

"It is my hope," the man says, "that you continued our last debate in the chambers while we took a pause."

"It's been three years," his former peer states. Then he laughs, emitting a throaty sound from the corpse as he looks around. "Where are we? What *are* you, now? Do you remember my name, or has your brain dehydrated fully?"

The man blinks and looks up. "You are..."

The author of the journal chuckles. "He won't know."

He forces the blood into his brain, willing it to remember. He points to his old peer. "Ebrir. And you are Vabres the Harvester."

Vabres shakes his head. He is speaking too quickly for the

29

mouth he powers. There is a dry clicking sound as he rushes the words out. "He cheats. My name is on the treatise."

Ebrir squints at him. "It is a journal, at best."

"That *journal* pushed the studies of flesh archiving by centuries."

Ebrir snorts. "Decades, if we're generous."

"Here we are." The man finds the passage they last spoke on. "The pages are unnumbered. *The plasticity of necrotized flesh once re-surged with blood degrades over time, but this can be offset or even stalled by proper storage in airtight containers. This opens new pathways for transport and resurrection.*"

"Nonsense," corpse-Ebrir says. "Airtight does not mean sterile."

Vabres the Harvester jerks his head back. "You have to lend some allowance to the narrative."

"Now we deal in allowances?" Ebrir laughs with a clicking sound.

In the distance, he feels his bear-ward bring down something large. Something with tusks and brown leather skin, thick enough to stave off a spear. The combat lights his nerves on fire as the bear severely wounds the animal.

Easy, my friend. I must feed on its grey matter.

It is surprisingly pleasant to have company again. The necromancer leans back, suddenly wishing for wine and a tongue with enough blood to taste it. The debate devolves quickly into dry-throated shouts and accusations. There won't be much progress in the discussion this evening. At least it will be entertaining.

The man casts a favored soul into an oarsman and commands it to sit next to him.

The fungal scholar looks at the man, blinking his dry eyes. He glances at the two arguing corpses. "Do I have to be here for this?"

"Yes, you do," the man says.

CHAPTER

FOUR

"*Stay with me.*" The whisper drew my eyes open.

I blinked, feeling along the floor. The memory of booking the suite atop the *Dragon's Nest* vaguely came back to me. The words of the manager after I paid him.

Welcome back, Darkshire.

As befitting my life, I woke up on the floor of one of the finest suites in the city. A place for adventurers, mercenaries, and those in the life to spend frivolous coin.

The bed squeaked gently next to me as Karley shifted in her sleep. I rolled my eyes up, seeing the glow lights of Strouds-burg. We had slept through the entire day, waking in the evening.

A rhythmic shifting, which I had mistaken for my dream, made me turn my head. The sound of soft flesh on silk.

I arched my neck and saw Karley sprawled face-down in the bed. At first, I thought her void fever had returned. But then her hips rolled—slow, deliberate, teasing the air. Not fevered. Hungered.

I stared in that strange waking state, trying to see if she had fallen back into sickness.

Her thonged ass flexed, high and perfect—teardrops swelling from her narrow hips. A rear that defied gravity when she stood and beckoned when she was prone. Her thighs shifted, and the heart-shaped gap between them gleamed with the twirl of her black-lacquered nail over silk. She moaned, low and ragged.

It wasn't just waking lust—not entirely. Magic changed things. Made you more.

I cleared my throat. She froze.

"Uh..." Karley's voice was muffled by a pillow.

"Glad you're up." I stood, hearing my bones click. "Meet me outside when you're finished."

Karley pulled a sheet over herself, and I'm sure she was blushing. "Where are we?"

"Inn."

After several minutes, she met me in the hallway.

"Where are we going?" Karley glanced around.

"Everyone will be here by tomorrow. Come on."

"Sorry about... that." Karley blushed. "The spell, I can feel it. Just makes me antsy."

I handed her a light cloak and didn't say anything else as we left. Her footsteps fell behind me, trailing my longer strides. She pulled the cloak tighter around her and followed me down the stairs.

The inn floor was empty, and a small draconic—or drake as they preferred to be called—manager nodded to us politely as we exited into the night.

"City never sleeps," I said to myself more than her. Karley fell in beside me, squinting at the cold air. She was far from her makeups and powders, but she was still a looker. Slim, tight, and as dangerous as a falling knife. Especially to herself.

It was the rainy part of spring, and the cobblestones were wet. I reflexively tracked the tall buildings we passed, noting which ones would shelter the alley enough if you had to sleep in them.

Childhood habits never die.

I took her along Bayside, where the view of the sea was blocked by small shops and stalls that trailed us uphill. In the distance, the palace that once belonged to nobility sat like a small fortress. More dangerous people than kings ruled there now.

I took Karley along the streets and into Pruren to visit the night market. I bought two horns of hot wine and handed her one.

"You like lizard?" I stopped at a rotating spit of reptiles. The coals under them pulsed from the wind.

"Uh, no." Karley laughed. "Not really."

"Too bad." I slid my hands into my pockets and kept walking. Lizard was always cheap. The ships that returned from far lands were infested with them. Meat vendors climbed aboard when they docked to hunt and sell them to the poorest of the city. My sword shifted under my traveling cloak as we slowly stepped through the night market.

We saw steamed barrels of silkworms that made anyone want to retch from their scent. Several bugbears roasted something that looked like a pig. Karley held her nose as we passed it.

I looked around the night market. Between dozens of sailors and merchants perusing wares and spices and cheap meats, you could see the flit of small urchin feet prowling the shadows.

I pulled Karley close. "Watch."

She opened her mouth to say something but stopped.

"But don't look like you're watching. That boy there is going to grab something."

"Where?" Karley leaned over past my shoulder.

"With the straw-colored hair." In the reflection of a shop window, I saw him make his play, stealing towards the bugbear butchers. It was a bad move. Too sudden, and his prize was too large to hide.

A furred fist backhanded him from the stall without so much of a glance.

"They hit him," Karley breathed the words.

"What's he doing now?" I watched the reflection. I saw the boy slink away, rubbing a sore jaw.

"He's..." Karley stood on her tiptoes. "Sitting down. He looks like he keeps swallowing blood."

I turned around now and watched him, sitting on a perch near the street while the world walked by. "Not blood. He's trying not to vomit; otherwise, he'll lose what he stole earlier."

Karley nodded, not saying anything.

"Come on." I pulled her along. We bought one of the more tasteful things the night market had to offer—several bread pastries filled with cheese.

"A silver." The old baker held his hand out, taking us for tourists. He was uglier now than when I had been a boy. "Local delicacy."

I pointed the rolls at him. "There are yester-rolls. They go bad by morning. Try again."

He glowered. "Ten coppers."

I gave the cunt exact change and turned away.

The boy recoiled a bit when we approached him. A beggar wants to be seen. A thief, the opposite. He looked like he'd failed at both.

"These are for you..." Karley held out the cheese rolls.

The boy didn't move to take them. He glanced at my sword, and even though he looked at me, he wouldn't meet my eye.

I crouched down and set the bread next to him. "You need to be quicker and steal smaller." It was up to him to take them or not.

The boy was maybe ten. He looked farm-raised, and I couldn't tell you why I knew that. The ghost of a healed bruise shadowed one eye. His clothes were still fresh enough. Likely new to the city.

I reached into my belt and pulled out three gold pieces. His eyes danced on them, but he didn't move to take them. Not everything offered in a city was a gift.

I placed them in his dirty palm and closed his fingers around them. "You from the Lowlands?"

The boy nodded.

"Do you want to go back?" I asked.

Karley shifted next to me. This wasn't the warmth of the Oakshire tavern. This was the world, raw and real.

Karley cleared her throat. "We'll take you back home if you want?"

The boy looked up at her in alarm. Then he sprinted away from us.

I watched him vanish into a line of visitors to the night market. My words were as soft as a prayer. "Stay alive."

Karley went to take the rolls, but I stopped her. "He'll come back for them when we leave."

I put my arm around her and continued out of the night market. Away from its spices and smells and the movement of drinkers looking for a late-night snack.

"Hell of a thing, being an orphan," I mused aloud as we walked. "Alone. Hungry. Finding your way in a world that didn't want you."

Karley stayed silent. I took her through the gold district

where jewelers worked in the deep hours, and for every pound of gold, there were ten hired guards watching us.

"Get caught stealing here, you'll die." I pulled her along. I heard her breath falter when we walked into Underhollow.

"Always gets busiest at night, here." I motioned towards the dark elf neighborhood.

Karley walked ahead of me, drawn in fascination at her people. Cloth was stretched between every rooftop to protect the citizens from the sun. But here in the deep night, small violet lanterns lit the walkways. Gardeners tended to glowing mushrooms and plants that shone in fuchsia pink.

"They only speak Drow here. You'd have to improve if you lived here."

"I had heard..." Karley murmured. She turned, taking it all in. "They're refugees from the Severing."

"That's right. They made a little piece of their world here." I didn't comment further. Maybe to her, it was wondrous. But Underhollow was a neighborhood that looked like a deadened dream in the daylight.

"You want to look around? Look for work?" I asked her.

Karley looked at me. "What do you mean?"

I gestured. "Close as it gets."

She regarded me with vibrant eyes. There was no tavern bar for her to hide behind. We were in my world.

Karley shook her head slowly. "No, let's keep walking."

I shrugged and led her out of Underhollow.

"Did you live here?" Karley asked after a moment. I had seen her vulnerable this evening. Maybe she was trying to even the score.

"I wouldn't have called it living."

The towers of the arcane area wavered ahead of us. I had taken her on a long loop, and we walked boldly into the small district.

Even after all these years, standing in the presence of the Collegiates made me clench a fist. This wasn't Runethor, but they had a real presence here all the same. The streets were rain-wet, mirroring the towers next to them in shadow and light.

"What do the flags mean?" Karley stared at the tower of Collegiate Ignis. This was one of their many schools across the realm.

And we helped you win those early days, didn't we? I'd never forget which robes weren't present at Daggar when it counted most.

"Declarations of war."

Every shop here was arcane in nature. There were stores with heavy wards. A large sentinel of stone, summoned from the depths, stood guard.

I pointed to a tower that had seawater trickling from it and kelp growing on the sides. "If you go there, you'll spend a year at sea. If you survive, you can enter the collegiate."

Karley shifted beside me. I didn't think she meant to, but she pressed closer to me. There was iron in my voice as I pointed to the Ignis tower.

"Heat, and fire. Made to shape the world. You'll study for six years before you're even apprenticed. Then you'll duel your student body. You survive, you get a mentor. Those not chosen..." I shrugged. "Find their work elsewhere. Paying off the tuition."

Karley looked at me. "You pay for tuition even if they don't admit you?"

I nodded.

"What about that one?" Karley pointed to a sapphire tower. It was beautiful, lit with an otherworldly ether. Several blue-robed wizards entered it, speaking amongst themselves. I felt their souls like sparks against my bones.

"Stormcallers." I stared at the tower, feeling the hair on the back of my neck stand. "Blue mages. But they abandoned rain long ago. Now it's lightning.

"They put it in weapons?"

I spat on the ground. "Mostly put it in people. They'll open a storm in your soul. Choking you from any other type of magic."

"Why are you showing me this?" Karley asked.

The question surprised me. "Thought you might want to know."

As we stood, Karley turned, looking at a tower behind us. It was plain, and raucous sounds came from within it. "What about that? Which collegiate is that?"

"Everbound." I stared at the limp yellow and black flag. "They rip creatures from another plane, house them here. Call upon them when needed."

A few low-caste mages, those without a tower, watched us as they passed. Two men and a woman. My runes whined, tracking their movement and the spells loaded in their souls.

I gave them a blank stare. When they stopped, Karley slid next to me.

I pulled my cloak back, gripping my sword with my left hand. "Help you?"

There was good money in dragging an initiate into one of these towers. Press-ganging a mage was now illegal in Stroudsburg, but the lore a group of lowly wizards might receive made it worth the risk.

Where my name was whispered in some cities, and spoken in Daggar, it had been shouted in Stroudsburg once. Usually accompanied by upheld hands begging for their lives.

I was still under protection from the Council, but the weight of my name didn't need their bolstering.

"*Darkshire*," one whispered in warning. They pulled their friend away, dragging him as he stared back at me.

"Come on," I said to Karley and pulled her along, off towards the citadel and the harbor. "Never liked this place."

When we passed a tower of black shadow, I stopped, staring up at it. Their flag floated in the night air.

"What's this one?" Karley asked.

"Not a good place," I whispered.

The door to the tower opened, and a black-robed wizard walked out slowly. I stared up at him from the street. His soul felt like a knife in the world that carved as he moved. Eyes as black as hell, and I remembered when they had been brown.

"Davik?" Karley gripped my arm.

More mages exited. Initiates and acolytes, each wearing their shadowy robes. They fanned down the steps cautiously, looking back at their master for guidance. But our eyes never left one another. Karley's soul was so meager in power compared to the ones approaching us now. But like a tide touching an immovable cliff, they kept a careful distance.

The night felt heavy with the weight of spells. The collegiate master didn't move. His face was passive—curious, almost. Our eyes were two lances pointed at one another. I didn't grip my sword in threat. I didn't need to. He had seen its work before.

"Davik..." Karley murmured again.

The collegiate master never looked away, even as he nodded once, slowly touching his chin to his chest. Not a threat; not a promise. Just an acknowledgment of history. When most of your friends are dead, sometimes your enemies know you best.

I returned it, and several mages exhaled in relief.

Then we turned and left.

· · ·

40

WE SAT on the sea wall near the harbor. Dozens of ships waited in line to get to the crowded docks. There was a northern gate to the city for the dock alone, keeping the already crowded streets as free as they could be. Even in the night, gulls cried above us like demons. The harbor was lit by slow flares from mages, lighting the sky with soft comets.

"No home," I said, staring at the ships. "Can go wherever they want. Take you wherever you want to go."

Karley slid her hood back, revealing her violet ears. She turned to me. "Which would you pick, a city or a sea? Seems easy to get lost at sea."

"People say you can get lost in a city. But nobody talks about how you can stay lost."

Karley gestured to the horizon. "Maybe they're looking for something out there."

"Girls will be here by tomorrow." I slid one of Vilas' gold bars from my belt. "Was planning on dividing one of these up for everyone. You want yours now? If you want to slip away before they come, it might be easier."

Karley's voice grew heavy. But she didn't move to take it. "Do you want me to slip away?"

Behind all the jokes, and the interrupted dances in Tawney, there was a question between us. One I could answer right now if I wanted. But Karley was a lost and confused soul, ready to cling to anything. To offer myself in that would be lower than robbing a lost traveler trying to find their way.

"Doesn't matter what I want," I replied. "It's a shit thing, you know."

She blinked. "What is?"

"Being an orphan."

"That's not it. I..."

"Yeah, it is. It's in everything." I held her look and smiled softly. "First, it's sadness, then fear. And then you spend the rest of your life looking for a place that doesn't exist. Or in a mirror, wondering why you couldn't have what everyone else seemed to."

Karley didn't say anything.

"I don't have an answer for you or any advice, Karley. All I can tell you is that it isn't fair. But maybe, just know you weren't the only one."

The drow's voice crept towards me. "How old were you?"

I paused. But if I was asking, I may as well be telling. "Old enough that I remembered them. Young enough that it almost killed me. What about you?"

She looked down. "I was... six, maybe."

"I'm sorry."

"It's not just that..." Karley whispered, and I could hear her trying to hold back years. "They're all going to hate me."

That surprised me. "The girls?"

Karley wiped her eye with the back of her hand. "Especially Tyra. You two just... you know. Then I run in the middle, and it's all about me."

"She won't hate you. Not for that. But don't be surprised at how angry they are."

Karley pulled her knees to her chest. "I took you away from her."

I laughed. "They're going to be angry because you almost died."

She fidgeted with the cloak I'd given her. "Are you?"

That was rich. "Karley, I could kill you right now. Do you know how dangerous that was?"

"Yeah." She sighed. "No. I don't know. I just... I knew I could be one, you know? My parents were. I never thought about it until you came."

"Do you want power?" I asked her. "You want to walk into one of those towers?"

Karley shook her head. "I don't know. That's not why I read it. Just..." She looked at the harbor. "They threw us away, Davik. In the Severing. *Not enough food to go around when the gates close.* I was sent to a human orphanage. I was just this confused dark elf. They split so many of us up. The only thing I was ever good at was our school play. When I put on a mask, I wasn't afraid. I didn't feel ashamed. I saw all those people clapping for me..."

It dawned on me now—that tavern brawl and those brats from Tawney. "That's why you wanted to act with Carsta and those girls?"

Karley looked at me. "Nobody ever picked me, Davik. Not to adopt me. Not to be their child. My parents didn't want me. They sent me from the Underdark. I barely spoke common. Then I forgot Drow. I was this quiet girl who squinted all the time from the sun. But every year we put on a play. A *real play*. I studied so hard. I thought if I performed well enough, I'd be picked."

"And nobody ever did?"

Karley shook her head. "When I was eighteen, I had to leave. I was more of a teacher by then than a resident. They told me I could stay. The owner liked me, or so they said. I left and wandered around. Tried acting... and I did well. But the first time I acted in a real play, someone sent me flowers after."

Her voice sounded harsh. When I was a boy, my mother told me what actresses were expected to do when the play ended.

"The playmaster introduced us." Karley clenched the hem of her cloak. "I thought he would be a patron... I thought actresses made their money that way. Fans gave you coin. He was wealthy, and he tried to corner me in the dressing room. When I shouted for help..."

"Nobody came," I answered her.

Karley nodded. Her eyes grew more serious as the memory burned through her. "His face just changed when we were alone. He called me a dirty shitskin. He hit me, but then when he tried to lock the door, I smashed a vase of flowers over his head. I was so scared. But I was lucky it didn't go further."

Listening to her story felt like someone pouring a tea kettle into my gut, filling me with boiling hate.

"Karley..."

She shook her head like I wasn't even there. "I must've cut him. There was so much blood. It wasn't just fear. It's like—I realized that plays were different for adults. I didn't know. I was so angry." She looked up at me. "I ran screaming out of there. I ran out of the city. I ran for years."

"It's alright." I almost said he deserved it. But that changed nothing. It's a hell of a thing, killing someone when you don't mean to.

"I always ran after that," Karley whispered. "It's what I do. Sariel never pried. Not really. Felt like I could stop running in Oakshire. Then I saw you and Elina and Sariel...and then Vorga. I don't know. I tried to meet someone, even in Oakshire. But I'd just run every damn time."

"You didn't run in Hollyhead. You saved those kids. I saw it."

"Only time I ran towards something. But when I got to that rooftop and fumbled the crossbow with that faen." She sighed and leaned back, staring at the sea again. "Only had my hands. We were about to die until you came."

I put a hand on her shoulder. "You were brave that night."

"Better than the alternative, right?" Karley smiled softly as she brought my words back to me. She had me there.

I pulled at her cloak, freeing it from her fist. "I get it."

"Do you?"

"Sure." I sighed. "Ran for years. Couldn't stand being still."

"Then Vilas came into the bar that day..." Karley trembled. "And I *knew* what he was. I fucking knew it. How he walked like he could kill everything around him. I ran, but then he called me by my name."

"What did he say?"

Karley looked at me. "He said *your parents wrote this*. And he put the spellbook on the counter. I stopped. I was halfway to the back door, and I heard you outside. I grabbed it and threw it behind the woodpile before I found you."

"I understand."

"Do you?" Karley asked. "How?"

"You wanted to know where you came from. Wanted to know why they got rid of you. Did you?"

Karley shook her head. "Its hard. I had to translate it, and Helena at the bookshop had some dictionaries for me. It's more like a diary. But my parents wrote it, Davik. It's real."

"What do you want?" I asked her.

Karley sighed. "No fucking idea. What happens to a half-dead girl who opened a spellbook and failed?"

"You have to learn to cast. Bleed the void as it enters you. Maybe it closes, and maybe it doesn't. Or you run."

The gold bar I could give her would buy a lot. A new city, a new name, tutors to prepare her or even get her entrance into a less sinister collegiate.

Maybe one day she'd look back and remember Oakshire and the people she once knew.

Karley watched the harbor, the lights of falling stars reflected in her eyes. "Little tired of running. Did that ever happen to you?"

"That's why you met me." I stood and offered her my hand.

She took my hand, and I pulled her up. Maybe it was the flex of my runes or the sight of her earlier in that bed, but I pulled her a little too hard.

Karley pressed against me, and for a moment, her hips shifted into mine. The question that slid from her lips was a blank page, waiting for me to turn it into a map. "Where to now?"

I felt the pull and told myself it was just my runes hungering for another mage. I stepped back and steadied her. "We'll stop and leave a note for a mud mage who hates me. Get you a lesson or two before we leave."

We turned and walked back towards the inn, leaving the departing ships to their business.

Karley sighed. "I'm really in for it when they come tomorrow, aren't I?"

I grinned. "Good thing you like being spanked."

Karley socked me in the arm. As we traveled back towards the inn, the sky bruised with the approaching sun.

CHAPTER
FIVE

"Focus."

When Deiga repeated the word, it snapped me out of my daydream. Rayleth used to say that to me when he first trained me. I wondered for a moment if she had gotten it from him.

We were three hours into Karley's first lesson with Deiga, an elven mud mage. Our arrival had been costly, but Deiga had a soft spot for new initiates. She wasn't the fondest of me, but she was talented, and more importantly, she hated the collegiates.

Karley nodded. The drow and elf were seated on the third floor of her tower, facing one another in the shadow of a broken observatory telescope the size of a small battering ram.

"When you study the spell," Deiga said, her voice measured, "the arcane pours into you, taking form. Yours to command. But when the time comes, you have to release it, or it'll devour you. Do you understand?"

"Yes," Karley whispered, beads of sweat gathering on her brow.

Deiga stared into her eyes. "Good. Now—tell me the first word."

"*Ignis...*" Karley's voice echoed, causing my runes to hum in response. Offensive spellfire was about to enter the room, and that old kill-twitch ached.

"The moment you say it, it burns from your mind as it comes into existence." Deiga leaned towards her new student. "Feel the fire, but don't let it consume you. Don't be like those fools in the towers."

"I feel it." Karley's voice was somewhere between agony and the heavy breath of lust. "Where?"

"Point your hand." Deiga guided Karley's trembling wrist. "And finish it. Slowly."

Karley's voice echoed with power. "*Et Consurge.*"

Flames sputtered from her hand. The heat flared into the room. Deiga grabbed her hand to steady it, pointing the flames toward a series of chalk runes that absorbed her spell.

Deiga nodded. "Good. That's enough for now."

Karley smiled, but the exhaustion in her face looked like she had just tilled a field by hand. For a moment, her irises glowed a vibrant violet. "It hurt, but I feel lighter."

"Inside you?" Deiga looked at her for clarification. "That's what we're doing. Low-level spells. Just bleeding the void as it trickles into your soul. Think of it as baling water in a sinking boat. We're trying to stay afloat. You're not a mage. Not yet at least."

"So it'll close?" Karley looked at her unburned hand.

"Perhaps," Deiga replied. "Sorcerers are born tethered to the void. Wizards are different. Their souls begin as pinpricks, tiny openings carved wider by study and willpower. But you... you've ridden a horse-sized breach through yours."

"Nice to know I have a soul." Karley stretched. "So, how many times a day?"

"I would say two more lessons, then cast for the next week. Only when you feel the void filling. If the tear closes, the spell should be weaker." Deiga turned her scarred face to me. "We're going to study another, Davik."

"I have time." I turned back to the window. The sun was sliding up into the day, and somewhere on that eastern horizon, the rest of our group would be making their way here. If they didn't show up today, we'd go out and find them.

Despite my career, I had rarely seen someone learn magic. The mages I had traveled with weren't keen on sharing their secrets with a man designed to slay them dead. But I did know that one mage showing another a spell quickened things exponentially.

It took another hour and a half of translation, explanation, and learning about an elemental source. It felt voyeuristic to watch Karley. I saw the eager tension in her body.

Slowly, Karley prepared a frost spell inside her. I knew when she had done it. I could feel it locked in her soul.

"It's there," Karley whispered. Her hand trailed down her flat chest. "I feel like I could cast it right now."

Deiga watched her. "How does it feel?"

"Cold, but good..." Karley glanced at me and then lowered her voice. "I feel... *lively*. Does that always happen?"

Deiga smirked. "There's raw power inside you awaiting your command. It's a stimulant. Trust me, you wouldn't be the only mage to study their morning spells with one hand."

"Always?"

"In the beginning, it can feel like that." Deiga patted her shoulder. "Tell me the first word."

Karley shut her eyes. "Kryos."

"Good, now try to hold it. If it gets too much, cast it, but make sure you're alone. Or throw it at him." Deiga cocked a thumb towards me.

I shook my head at Karley. "Don't do that."

Deiga stood and pulled Karley up. The scarred mage wore her brown robes today, a mark of a caster belonging to no collegiate. "Remember, this is to save your life."

"Thanks again." Karley smiled.

"Wait for me downstairs," I told Karley.

"She's talented," Deiga said once she left, wiping the runes from the floor. "Most like her are."

"What do you mean?" I asked.

Deiga moved her supplies to an old table. "Doesn't belong with a mud mage. She belongs with a drow enclave."

The word enclave piqued my interest. Vilas had said that. "Enclave?"

"You know what a witch is?"

"Sure," I said. "Curses. Woodsy women in a forest. Dark powers." And I had dispatched a few, many years ago. Best way was to put their hut to the torch and wait with your steel drawn.

Deiga shook her head. She was a shorter elf, never as tall as her brother Rayleth. "That's what *you* would call a witch. For drow, witch is a rank, not a pejorative. *Wvytch'ya*. They're still mages who study, but they feel magic. It's intimate for them. You saw her eyes light up?"

"So?"

"So, nothing. They have an affinity, is all. Drow track their bloodlines closely. It's why the collegiates wanted them."

"Okay."

Deiga sighed. "How's it feel, being back?"

"It's fine."

Deiga snorted and moved a spellbook to a shelf. "Darkshire, Darkshire. Murdered Prince Jame and never came back to the Lowlands once his father Ironclad called for his head." She looked over. "You really taking that girl to a Lowland wedding for Elyse Sewell?"

"Maybe, haven't decided."

Deiga smirked, but it was all poison. "Ironclad died, so you're free to move about the Lowlands, is that it?"

"I have safe passage." I shrugged and turned to the window. "He never had pull in the city anyway."

"You have to watch out for Karley. You know anything about mages, other than killing them?"

I knew plenty, and she knew that. Deiga had little love for me, and the feeling was close to mutual. Rayleth had adored her, but she had never been a killer. Never been one to sit around the campfire. She belonged in libraries and shops in the cities of the world.

And she never forgave us for burying Rayleth so far from her when he died.

I didn't answer. "What do I owe you?"

Deiga shook her head. "Already told you, Davik. Don't want your coin. Even when you pay, it seems to cost something."

You want to learn about grudges? Surround yourself with elves. Those long ears are there to hear you apologize for eternity.

"Your brother wasn't alone."

Deiga spun, snarling at me. "Rayleth thought the world of you, you know. And in the end, he died for *nothing*."

"You weren't there." I shifted my sword out of habit. "You would never understand."

Her eyes lingered on the blade on my hip, and she snorted. "You still carry it?"

"Was his." I touched the handle, remembering him. "Then Venthren. Gave it to some kids, but Vilas found them." My eyes lingered on her. "Never knew Venthren had a blood brother."

Deiga almost flinched at his name. "Now there was a cunt. My father married his mother and it brought ruin. You two would've gotten along."

"You still use that?" I nodded to the giant telescope behind her. Once upon a time, she had taught students with it.

Deiga glanced at the giant contraption. "You mean since you broke it?"

I gave her a stern look. "I'd say *you* broke it. Or that thing you summoned that threw me out the window."

Deiga shrugged. "Needs new brass fittings. New lens."

"Can't fix it with magic?"

"I wouldn't want to. Bring Karley tomorrow, Davik. I'll show her what I can."

As I turned to descend the stairs, Deiga called after me.

"When you find Trith," she said, "tell him I know it's him."

"Him, what?"

Deiga hid something close to a smile. "Tell him to stop breaking that window I threw you out of. Bring her tomorrow."

WE LEFT DEIGA'S TOWER, and I felt younger, in a bad way. Like every choice I'd made still echoed in someone else's voice. Karley showered when we got back to the inn. I could feel the spellfire in her through the door. Every mage feels different. I had traveled with some so long that I barely noticed them, like Trith.

But she was different. On the walk to the inn, she had strode shoulder to shoulder with me, the frost spell readied inside her. Her smirk matched the swagger in her hips. Violet hipbones peeked from the gap between leather and skin. So different from the sashay some women had. She didn't glide through the world. She cut her way in.

Fucking wizards.

"How are you feeling?" I asked when she settled on the railing next to me.

"Strange. Feel it inside me." Karley smoothed her wet hair back. "This inn is nice. How do you know it?"

"Tradition for crews, way back. Spend some good coin to enjoy yourself, since you might not know if you make it back."

Karley squinted in the morning light. The smell of soap lather on her permeated my senses.

A group of dark elves with moon-ink banners came up the street, causing both of us to lean over. They beat a slow drum, calling out. When they saw her on the balcony, they called up to her.

"*Sister! Come to the parade!*"

"Uh." Karley looked at me.

"The shadow calls!" Another dark elf woman smiled up at her. "Meet your people near the Citadel!"

Karley sank away from the railing. The Stroudsburg guards near the eastern gate waved the procession along, directing them towards the capitol building.

"What's that about?" Karley looked at me.

"Severed are protesting to go home. Underdark ambassadors are here in town for talks."

"How do you know?"

Lukyll's surprised face flashed in my mind. "Some asshole told me."

Karley shook her head, leaning over the railing to watch them. I grabbed the back of her belt. "Easy there. Don't think your frost spell will save you from a fall."

"Are they with the collegiates?" Karley asked.

"They used to riot outside their towers. Blaming them for the Severing. The Underdark representatives have agreed to sit down again."

"You think they'll open it?"

I shrugged. "I don't know. Collegiates put up bases in the Underdark before the war. Pilfered arcane bloodlines, putting them in their schools. Once the war happened, they filled their ranks with them."

"You met some?" Karley asked. "Kidnapped drow?"

I nodded. What's the difference between being kidnapped and conscripted? The kidnapped get to go home. The memory wasn't a pleasant one—as few were during the war. Her anger, whether she knew it, was well warranted.

We had captured a drow mage once in the war. He hadn't even spoken Common. But one of the clerics spoke a little Drow. We got a bit of his story out before the Lowlanders got their hands on him.

"Damn," Lonnie had said. "He's a conscript, too. Imagine you're sitting in your home in a cave and one of these collegiate bastards snatches you? Next week you're facing down Magebreakers."

"Shut up and dig." I wiped the sweat from my brow. I wanted to finish this and get next to a brazier. "And get that rope off his neck."

Lonnie bent down to untie the noose. "Nothing like a Lowlander necklace."

"I did." I leaned against the railing. "Drow who had never even seen the sun were thrown into battle. Collegiates used them as fodder. Called them *squints* because they were half-blind from the light."

"How can they stand with the collegiates now?" Karley watched the procession leave.

"Lot of those collegiates are gone. And they want to go home. But the drow kingdoms have a long memory."

"Bastards." Karley spat.

My heart did a somersault when I saw Sariel's silver and black armor in the morning light. The bright red of Tyra's hair and the green of Vorga's skin as they sat on the wagon, driven by Brim. Elina was speaking to them from the rear of the wagon, and all of them craned their necks to see how far the line into the city was.

When I waved to them, the wind carried their shouts back to us. I could feel Karley's nervousness next to me.

"Fuck," she said.

I continued waving. "Yep. You're in for it."

Sariel led them through the gate. Brim puffed on his pipe, steering the wagon into a hard left to settle far beneath us. Even from here, I could see the dark circles around his eyes.

"She's okay!" Vorga shouted.

"Karley!" Elina yelled and stood on the wagon before she fell back down from the shift of the cobblestones.

Brim's growls filled the air as he parked the wagon. I leaned over the balcony, meeting Sariel's eye. My elven lover's face filled with relief, and she looked up at me with a weary smile.

"You want to stay here?" I asked her as I walked to go downstairs to greet them all.

"Yeah..." Karley turned from the railing. "Better get ready for this."

I raced down the stairs, eager to fill the salon with the people who were dear to me.

"Good morning, sir," the inn attendant said from his desk. "Are those your guests outside?"

"They are." I walked past him and the small dining bar of eating patrons. "We'll need the stables for the wagon and horses."

"Right away." The elf turned to go convene with several inn attendants.

Sariel climbed down from her horse. The look on her face

told me how hard their journey was to catch up to us. When she threw her arms around me, I felt her strength sag a bit.

"Thank you, Davik. Thank you." A sob crept into her voice. Underneath that miraculous plate armor was a trembling elf who expected the worst for Karley.

"She's okay," I whispered. "We made it. I'd have turned back to find you all, but I figured I might have ridden past you."

Sariel stood up and wiped her eye, giving me a small smile. "Thank the gods you didn't. It was rough getting here. Almost lost our way."

"I've got us a set of rooms on the top floor." I leaned over and saw the girls climbing down from the wagon, grabbing their packs. "Leave it! The inn will take care of it all."

Brim climbed down from the wagon and walked up to me. His eyes were bloodshot.

How is she, ugly-man?

"She was real sick," I told him. "Sorry you didn't get the chance to head home."

I come wedding. Sent word to Oakshire from Silvus.

Smart, that move. At least Rober and Lyra would know we'd be delayed another week. I felt bad at leaving Tyra's Aunt Aubrie so suddenly, taking her niece so soon.

Elina came next, walking slowly in her silken robes. Attendants of the *Dragon's Nest* walked down and began to unload the packs and several other items.

"I'm so glad you two are okay," Elina said as I bent to hug her. "I'll go check on Karley."

Vorga jumped down from the wagon, smiling as she hefted her spear. "Hey, you."

"Hey, yourself." I broke from Elina and gave Vorga a quick kiss. "We're on the top floor. Quite a few beds and a bath."

Vorga peered at me as if suddenly realizing something.

"What?" I asked.

"Nothing." The most-orc smiled, holding onto her secret. Then she pressed her pink lips to me again. "Just figured out the ending to something I'm writing."

Her hand trailed off me like she didn't want to let go as she walked up the steps. I turned to watch her, puzzled by her jovial mood after such a long journey.

Tyra came to me last. I felt a pang of longing as she approached. Her hair was a red mess. Dirt smudged her sparkling skin. We had hoped to enjoy Hollyhead and each other before leaving.

"Davik," she whispered.

I pulled Tyra into my arms. The emotion boiled off of her and into me. I didn't need words to know how she felt. Waves of anxiety and fear whipped into my flesh, along with relief.

"Are you okay?" I asked her.

"I knew it was a matter of time before you ran off with another woman." Tyra smiled. Before I could respond, the faen grinned. "Polly has that effect on people."

"You caught me." I laughed. "Sorry we couldn't stay longer with your aunt."

"I've got to check on Karley," Tyra said and kissed me again, before sliding her hand across my belt. "But I want to see you later. We need to make up for lost time."

"There're no orchards here." I kissed her again.

"Mmm." Tyra gripped my arm, flashing a jolt of lust into me. "We'll see about that."

Brim rolled his eyes. Vorga and Tyra followed Elina into the inn, where the attendants were carrying their belongings up to the penthouse.

Sariel looked up at our accommodations. "Nice place, my love. I think Brim might need his own room. He's had nothing but women prattling in his ear for two nights."

"Rahh." Brim nodded.

"I'll see you up there." Sariel kissed my cheek and walked up the steps of the inn.

"How was the journey?" I asked him while the manager got his key.

Brim shut his eyes. *Strenuous. Much worrying.*

"You did well." I took the key from the manager. "Can you have some food sent up to his room?"

I gave Brim his key, and we walked up the steps to the top floor.

The top floor was quiet, save for the muffled shouts coming from behind the salon doors. Brim grinned as he unlocked his room. *Good luck in there. You'll need it.*

He wasn't wrong. When I walked into the salon, everyone was in the living area.

"You could have killed yourself!" Vorga screamed.

"What I do isn't your business!" Karley shouted back.

That threw Vorga over the edge. "What did you say? Not my *business*? Are we just roommates? Is that it?"

Sariel wrenched Vorga back. "Vorga, take a minute."

Elina was the only one sitting on the couch. If there were prayers that stopped women who lived together from fighting, she didn't know them. "Karley, we're just glad you're okay." The halfling looked around. "Right?"

I noticed Tyra was oddly quiet, staring at them in front of a weapon rack.

"You need to pull your head out of your ass!" Vorga hissed as Sariel pushed her back. "Do you know how worried we were?"

"Oh please!" Karley snapped, struggling not to cry. "Just go into the woods with your boyfriend! Stop pretending to give a shit about me!"

Vorga couldn't believe what she had just heard. It wasn't a

common thing to see her temper flare. Her gentle face contorted with rage. "You stupid—"

"Enough," Tyra declared as she walked forward. She stepped slowly between all of them. At Tyra's approach, Karley's defenses withered.

"Tyra..." Karley murmured, locking eyes with her. "It wasn't because of you and Davik. It was just—"

For a moment, I thought we were about to see a repeat of the fistfight in the tavern. It seemed Elina did as well, pushing herself from the sofa. Vorga's anger was a boiling kettle. Sariel was too exhausted to be anything but grateful.

But Tyra was ice. She hadn't said a word until now.

Karley didn't step back when Tyra walked up to her. She held her chin up high as if waiting for the strike that would punish her.

Tyra shook her head softly. Then she put her arms around Karley, pulling her into a hug. "You have no idea, Karley." Tyra held her close. If Karley didn't want to believe she meant anything, Tyra was going to show her. I saw Karley's face clench in anguish as Tyra poured all that worry into her.

"Tyra..." Karley whispered. "It's too strong."

"Of course it's strong. We thought you died. You aren't going anywhere," Tyra vowed. "You're our sister. Stop looking for something you already have."

Karley sobbed. Vorga broke from Sariel's grasp and joined them in a clasp of arms.

Sariel walked towards me. "I could kill her," Sariel said as she turned to look at the three girls embracing. "But Vorga beat me to the attempt."

Elina wrapped my arm around her. "You protected her, Davik. All of us."

I bent down and kissed the cleric on the lips.

"Are we safe here?" Sariel met my eye.

I nodded. "Safe as could be. Nothing moves without the Council's go-ahead here."

"Come on, idiot." Vorga pulled Karley towards the open bedroom. "You can borrow my clothes. We left most of our things in Hollyhead to race after you."

"I think a shopping trip is in order," I called to them.

Tyra turned with a smile. "That sounds nice. We should wash up. I don't think I can sleep."

Elina cleared her throat. "After a quick rest, we might do with a splash of fashion for the wedding."

Even with Karley's transformation, and the bloody night in Hollyhead, it would be good to see Stroudsburg as so many usually did: a place to spend money, not earn it.

Vorga looked at me, a plea in her eyes. "We're still going, right? To see Mara and the castle?"

Everyone looked at me.

"We're still going."

CHAPTER
SIX

"So Karley's tear can close?" Sariel asked me as we walked behind Vorga, Karley, and Tyra. Elina flanked my other side. Brim had been asleep when I knocked on his door, so I left him a note we'd be back this evening.

"That's what my friend said," I answered. Deiga wasn't exactly my friend, but I didn't feel like explaining.

"Was this your wood elf friend?" Elina looked up at me.

"No, it's—She's a mud mage we used to know. Trith's a sorcerer—it's a little different."

Sariel squeezed my arm. "If that's what Karley wants, I hope it closes."

"Me, too."

We strode near the city square, sometimes called Silken District due to all the garment vendors and dressmakers.

"I can't believe we're going to see a wedding in a *castle*!" Vorga laughed. "The girls of Oakshire tavern are world travelers now."

"And to see a bunch of knights hammer the hell out of each other," I reminded her. "Should be quite the time."

"Are you fighting, Davik?" Tyra turned around. "We never had gown tourneys near Mirrimer's estate."

"No dear," Sariel answered. "His is a ceremonial position. As gown champion, his say is final on who takes her hand."

"But if they take issue, he duels?" Karley asked.

I shook my head. "I won't be dueling."

It wasn't just my hope, it was what I'd decided. Puris and Eralt begged me to assist Windpeak in this, so I would. The prize of seeing Allie alive was enough for me. But I only planned to wield my reputation at Windpeak, nothing else. I had spilled enough blood for Elyse Sewell and other Lowlanders.

"Davik is doing a good thing, especially for Sir Eralt," Elina chimed in, reaching back to squeeze my hand. "No one will contest with him as the champion. Eralt can save face."

I watched Karley, somewhat separate from the group. Tyra noticed, too, and grabbed her by the arm, linking the two of them. "Come on, this shop has robes. If you're going to be a caster, I bet you'll need some."

Sariel shook her head. "Never understood how armor stifles a mage from the void."

"Speaking of," I said, turning in the street, "the blacksmiths aren't far from here." I was in sore need of a refit on my leather armor. But more importantly, I wanted mail for the girls to wear under their clothing.

Sariel raised her eyebrow. "You might be overestimating how strong they are. Vorga maybe, but Tyra and Karley might fall over with thirty pounds of chainmail. Elina will crumple to the floor."

That was true. But there had to be something. Ringmail even.

"Girls!" Vorga waved from a dress shop. "I think we have some coin to spend in here."

"I do need new linen wrap..." Sariel gazed at the shop. "You want to come inside?"

"You go ahead. Watch them, alright?"

Sariel laughed and walked into the shop. "We'll see what's fashionable for visitors to the Lowlands for a wedding."

Elina lingered as the others funneled into the shop. "I'll come with you. Let's go."

I took the cleric's arm and walked her toward the armorer's district. Even from here, you could hear their hammers.

When Elina gripped my hand, she murmured her prayers under her breath. Divine healing flooded into me. Where I used to have to concentrate to draw them into my runes, now they drank her power in easily. By the time she finished, she had filled four of them, the icy sensation making me shiver.

The halfling squeezed my hand. Once, a single rune's worth of healing would have drained her. Now she didn't even look fazed.

"Are you growing more powerful?" I asked.

"I don't know about that. But after Hollyhead... I feel *more*."

"Sounds exactly like what it is."

"Tell me again," Elina whispered and pulled me towards her. "What you said in the temple grotto."

I bent and kissed her. "I love you, cleric of Oakshire."

As we broke our embrace, Elina blinked up at me with those amber eyes. "Many love you, Davik. And I'm proud to be among them."

I grinned. "Worse problems to have."

Elina held my gaze, shifting against me in her silken robes. "Many things move right now. Closer to you... farther from you. Stay watchful, lover. You protect the garden, but it thrives on you."

"Same goes for you." I took her hand. "You have the habit of looking after others before yourself."

"I'm looking forward to meeting your friend, Trith. How can you be sure he'll join us?"

I smiled at that. "Because I'll ask him."

"That's true loyalty," Elina mused. "Not many are fortunate to have that."

Before we even made it to the edge of the square, Elina turned to another store.

"Oh! What's that?"

She stared at a shop filled with dresses. In the front window, a mannequin stood clad in a battle dress—regal and fierce, the kind a warrior queen might wear. Above it, the shop's name stood out in bold, confident letters:

The Practical Girl

"Yes, please!" Elina laughed and pulled me towards the shop. There's little stronger than the grip of a woman pulling you into a store. When we entered, it was empty save for an older woman behind the counter.

"A cleric of the Mistress!" she declared and shut a heavy ledger. "You are most welcome!"

"Hello!" Elina grinned around the store. "I'm also a practical girl. What do you sell here? It looks very interesting."

The shop owner smiled and walked towards us in a beautiful gown. "This is for practicality in a dangerous world... and introducing the downfall of a partner in the bedroom."

Elina giggled. "My facet is curious."

"Are these costumes?" I looked around. Women I had worked with in my past wore ill-fitting armor usually made for men. If they had real coin, they could get it tailored. But aside from some decorative breastplates on gowns and verbose shoulder pads, I didn't see armor.

"Not at all." The shopkeep smiled. "We straddle the blacksmiths district and the fashion square for a reason. We sell weapons and armor." She beckoned us towards a hanging green dress. "Come feel. This has ringlets woven through it."

Elina and I touched the sleeve, feeling the chainmail within. Thinner stuff.

"It's so light." I held it up. "What's it made from?"

"Cold glass tempered beads, woven into soft chain."

I shook my head, letting the sleeve go. "Might be fine for a small knife, but a crossbow would go right through it."

"Ah," the human woman said with a smile. "You need something else. Spidersilk."

Spidersilk was used in some armor, but it was extremely tedious to harvest. I had a chest piece once that had it woven within, and it had cost a pretty penny. It also flamed up like a oiled rag the second a candle touched it.

The shopkeeper pulled out an elegant white dress. "This is spidersilk."

"It's so lovely." Elina ran the back of her hand down the gown.

When I held the fabric, I felt it underneath the linen.

"That's thicker than I've seen," I admitted.

The older woman grinned. "That's because it's from a drider."

I dropped the sleeve. "What?"

The older woman smiled as if this was a piece of delicious gossip. "Scandalous, isn't it? We have a contract with some drow who raise them outside of city limits in the crags of mountains. The ropes are as thick as rigging lines. It isn't cheap, but it's three times as strong as spidersilk."

"What's a drider?" Elina asked.

The woman waved any worry away. "Oh, it's just a big spider that lives underground."

"A big spider that eats people." I resisted the urge to shudder. I'd seen them before. Even after the Severing, there were ways into the Underdark—and good money if you were brave enough to go there. You needed the right guide to get you through the alternate paths. Untamed paths. If you've ever seen a drider, you know why it's best to carry a spare pair of pants in your pack.

"It's woven throughout?" I asked.

"Of course," she answered. "This isn't for ostentation. This is elegance and safety."

I looked up at her. "Crossbow?"

The older woman smiled. "Only one way to make a believer out of you. We can fire it in the back if you like. And before you ask, it's treated to be fire resistant."

Elina looked at me. "Would you feel better if we all wore this?"

"If it does what she says, yes." I looked at the shopkeep. "You sell undershirts and leggings made from that?"

"We do and can make more." The shop owner counted something in her head for a moment. "But it wouldn't be flame resistant. A blade would have a tough time getting through this. But this isn't a breastplate. A crossbow wouldn't puncture the cloth, but the force will still shatter the bones beneath it."

Elina stared at it. "How much is this dress?"

"Eighty-five gold pieces." The shopkeep held her head high.

I whistled. More than twice the cost of a steel breastplate in Trinth and not as reliable. Still, it was exactly what we were looking for.

The shopkeep had a look on her face, one you learn to recognize when you haggle often. Stroudsburg was much safer than it used to be. I didn't know many adventurers who would want to wear this kind of fashion while traveling through the wilderness. There were more practical things to protect yourself with. The highborn had guards, and the strange upper middle class this store targeted wasn't large.

"That's okay, Davik." Elina smiled at me. "We can keep looking."

As Elina walked towards the exit, I saw the flicker of defeat on the shop owner's face. She moved to put the dress away until I asked her a question.

"What about bulk pricing?"

THE SHOPKEEP'S name was Aida, and once I filled her store with the excited exclamations of multiple customers, she shut the front door and popped a bottle of sparkling wine.

"Hold still!" she said to Karley. The dark elf rolled her eyes as Aida measured her from every angle.

Karley stared at me, begging me to rescue her. "Davik."

I raised my hands. "You need a dress for the wedding."

"You have a wondrous figure, like a dancer. Dridersilk will look fabulous with your complexion." Aida pointed to Vorga who was digging through a selection of waist-corsets that went over a tavern dress. "Those are four for the price of three!"

"Amazing!" Vorga laughed.

"Davik!" Sariel poked her head out of the dressing room she shared with Tyra.

"Everything okay?"

"This is going to take a while." Sariel grinned.

"I'll go find my friend." I nodded to her. "Stay awhile; enjoy yourself."

"Oh, I will." Now that we were all back together, she seemed full of life. "Aida's done measuring Vorga and Karley, if you want company."

"Sure."

Aida leaned back to call to Sariel. "How are you finding those weapons?"

"Weapons?" I looked around.

"Of course," Aida said with a laugh. She pointed to a dress set for tailoring. "Armor."

Then she marched towards Sariel and reached for the dressing room door. "Do you want the sturdy swordsman's opinion, my dear?"

Sariel grinned and pushed the dressing room door open. Soft blue stockings ran up her supple thighs. Her cleavage poured from soft blue lace, barely restrained by pearled clasps. For a moment, I was the man coming out of the wilderness to her bar, astounded by her.

"What are a good set of silks but weapons?" Aida looked away with a practiced glance. "Made to fell any man."

Sariel raised an eyebrow at me. "What do you think, Davik?"

Tyra turned around. Where Sariel was wrapped, Tyra was half-hidden. An unbuttoned blouse showed her sparkling skin, barely covering the edge of a nipple as pink as a brightberry. Her skirt was as red as her hair and thin as a whisper, reaching to cover her cheeks—and failing magnificently. Plaid stockings ran up her thick legs.

"Do you like it, Davik?" Tyra's voice dripped with silk. She turned, tugging her skirt higher by an inch, showing me what I'd be sliding off later.

"Bedwear is always sold in a set. They're optional, of course..." Aida said.

The faen cook and battle elf stared me down, in a shop that smelled of powdered roses. Twin sets of silver and blue eyes smoldering like I'd stumbled into their lair.

"No." I cleared my throat. "Weapons are good."

"I couldn't agree more." Aida shut the door slowly, cutting off my view.

"Davik! What do you think?" Elina called to me from the next stall. When the halfling stepped out, she looked like the Mistress come down from the heavens.

It was a simple nightgown, showing off her short stature. The cloth was the same hue as her tattoos, and it made the amber in her eyes pop.

"Beautiful," was all I could manage to say.

You'd think being surrounded by beautiful women might make you dull to their charms. But thank the gods we can be so very, very wrong.

When a beautiful halfling wears a nightgown like that, you know certain things are true. That beds are better shared. And that going to bed early is good for your health.

Behind her, I spotted a pile of darker clothing and a silver chain. Elina noticed and blocked my view. "That's a gift for someone! No peeking!"

I bent down and kissed Elina, and she grabbed my ruined chest armor. "Mmm, I can't deny how you seeing me in this makes me feel."

"These have locks, you know..." I gripped the dressing room door, inching her back within.

"Out you go!" Elina laughed and pushed me away. "Dangerous beast! I have to get fitted for my dress robes."

I knocked on Sariel's dressing room again. "Meet you back here?"

"Yes!" Sariel giggled through the door. *"Help me with this. It's locked itself."*

"Look at this, it's riding up! Now I have to buy it!" Tyra laughed.

I walked to the front of the shop.

"You two want to come with me?" I asked Vorga and Karley.

"Absolutely," Karley said immediately. I noticed she had hidden a pile of cloth to the side, out of my view. Was she hiding a surprise or just not ready to share her new taste yet? "Let's get out of here."

Vorga turned from a rack of dresses. "Yes! Thank you for this."

Aida unlocked the door to let us out.

"What was your friend's name, Davik?" Vorga asked as we stepped outside.

I stared towards Temple Street.

"Trith."

CHAPTER
SEVEN

Stroudsburg bustled like it always had, filled with every race that walked the realms. The shock of it in the daytime after being in the Midlands was a strange homecoming. I remembered when the first guilds were little more than gangs fighting to ply their trade. Slaying each other with the tools they made a living from.

Each street was a makeshift market. Coils of cloth and canvas shielded us from the hard Lowland sun. Half-orcs carried barrels of wine, and Tieflings shouted and beckoned us forth to their stalls of glittering water pipes. The sweet smell of tobacco drowned in fruit pectin filled the air.

A drake warlock smiled as I passed, recognizing me. The scales along his body were etched with the contracts of the demons who owned his soul. He raised two red claws in a mock salute, daggered teeth flashing. Half of his scales had fallen out. Whatever patrons had flushed him with power would soon come to collect.

"Stay close," I told Karley and Vorga. "Keep your hands—"

"On your purses," Karley groaned. "We heard you the first hundred times. *The Silver Hands are everywhere.*"

"Why are they called the Silver Hands, Davik?" Vorga rushed to catch up next to me. A kobold slid past us, carrying a half-carcass of meat and jabbering to his fellows.

"It was how you got in." I shouldered past two stinking gnolls. Their chittering howl-laughs screamed of intoxication. "It was a pick-pocket gang when it started. You got one chance to lift something off someone. If you did, they used to say you had silver hands."

"And if you got caught?" Karley held her hand over her nose from the onslaught of smells.

I looked around the bisecting street. "Then you stayed a beggar. Come on, this way."

The streets of my old home had changed, but my feet remembered running and hiding down them when the city had been far less crowded.

Stroudsburg was a melting pot that had cooked for a hundred years, the flavor shifting with famine, then war, and then new owners. It was like one of those cauldrons above an inn's fire that never emptied. Lowlanders down south were wary of too many outsiders. The human lords owned the coast to the forests and functioned as the food basket for half the world.

It was why villeinage and their strict hierarchy of vassals, knights, and heraldry were enforced. It was also why they had fought so hard against the collegiates, aside from the insane power they had wanted to drench the world in. When a group of people could make crops grow where they shouldn't, markets were at stake.

We walked until the crush of bodies opened up. A gnome tripped in front of me, steadying his hand on me to break his fall.

"Apologies sir!" He looked at me with a smile, then his face fell as my hand closed around his collar.

I held my other hand up, and the pouch he had lifted from my belt was placed back into it.

"Sorry, didn't recog—"

I let him go. "Tell your friends the girls are with me as well."

The gnome nodded, then scampered off.

"Did you know him?" Vorga turned back as he slipped into the crowd.

"Oh yeah. Best friends."

I took the girls by the shoulder and marched them up to what we used to call Temple Street. Beggars stayed clear of here, as did most thieves.

"Look! A Temple of Selene!" Vorga pointed. "Do you think Lyra has been there?"

"What's that? There's no name." Karley stared at a hovel of a temple that shimmered with profane magic. A large dagger above the entrance continually dripped blood without a source.

I grabbed her and turned her away. "Don't look at that."

As we walked, half a dozen sailors rose from an altar of Tidemor, each bearing the yellow thumbprint of the sea priest who had blessed their next voyage. His driftwood facemask followed us as we passed, eyes swirling like tides behind it from his deity of the deep.

"This sure isn't like the Midlands," Vorga murmured.

We passed more temples. A battlemaster in a suit of engraved armor opened a sack, pulling wet orbs to place on the pillar of Strivor. I covered both of their eyes, dragging them up the street. The warrior stacked the skulls of the stone pillar before clasping his bloody fist over his breastplate.

"Sariel is going to kill me," I muttered and released my hands over the girl's eyes.

I got us to the top of the hill and spotted the three-story tavern down the street. The last temple on the street bore the markings of a red sun, and you could hear the slow, lilting chants of the fanatics within.

"Wow! What's that?" Vorga smiled at the lush green tavern, seemingly unbothered by Temple Street. "It's a tree!"

"Kind of," I said and pulled them along. "He should be in here."

"Your friend?" Karley asked.

"Yeah."

The old, familiar tension crept over me—the need to have eyes in the back of my head. Even though the Council ruled here now, some things never left me. Being here made me ache for Oakshire. Stroudsburg had always been too relentless.

"Don't touch anything that moves in here," I told them as we approached.

The tavern was out of place. A spike of nature in a city of red stone and trade coming from across the seas. Everything in Stroudsburg was booming again, and they pushed the crops from the Lowlands in tight crates, feeding the world from the Ironwood Forests of the Embriel to the Feytha High Elves and all the way down to those warm tropical reaches, where mages captained ships on dead waters, fueling them with makeshift wind.

The Quinx had been here a long time. Unlike the shrines of deities on Temple Street, where a begging boy might find himself press-ganged into a new religion, this had been a refuge for druids.

The doorwoman was a redheaded girl with copper wires in her hair. She smiled lazily, drifting on the pipe's touch. Her dress was made of leaves as she moved aside to let us enter.

"Have fun." She smiled.

"Wow," Vorga murmured next to me as we entered.

Greenery draped the walls and ceiling, filling the tavern with moist cool air. The bar—a twisted mantle of driftwood, now polished clean—served both as counter and trophy from their war with the Tidemor Temple.

I walked Vorga and Karley to the bar.

"Take a seat." I fished a silver out of my belt.

A tiefling woman with dark grey skin and too little clothing stared at me expectantly. "What'll it be?"

"Give them some juice," I told her, "and some fruit, and keep an eye on them."

The Tiefling tucked the silver into her blouse. One of her arms ended in the gnarled talons of an eagle. "No problem."

"Look, Karley!" Vorga waved at a cat that walked on the bar, reaching out to pet him as he meowed loudly. "We should get a cat."

"Is every bar made out of trees?" Karley looked around as Vorga whisked up the cat and nuzzled him.

An older half-elf woman leaned from the corner of the bar. "That's my husband."

"Sorry!" Vorga set the cat back down. "I didn't know he was a husband-cat."

"Get out of here." The bartender waved the cat away. "Keep him at your seat, Eleanor! How many times do I have to tell you?"

As I was about to walk to a set of tables in the back, four monks of Vex walked towards the exit. Skull medallions hung from their necks behind the platters of food they had purchased. Every eye in the place avoided them. Three kobolds in white robes of Selene made it a point to stop their conversation as the monks slowed and inched closer to them.

The Tiefling bartender clacked a claw on the driftwood bar. "Hey! Keep it on Temple Street."

Karley and Vorga both turned from their stools at the commotion, but I turned them around. "Don't look at them," I ordered.

The monks wore soft smiles, each bearing the same serene, patient expression—uniform and unchanging, as though it had been issued alongside their robes.

They turned to walk out of the bar, sliding between me and the table. They stank of their profane god, and in their eyes boiled a hate stoked by a religion bent on making the world blind from vengeance.

There were stories when we were kids, about the monks of Vex. If your husband stepped out on you, spending all your money on some harlot on dockside, they would whisper in your ear to give you the strength to turn yourself into a widow. Their clerics were rare but were terrible forces on the battlefield. The most esteemed of them had died long ago, near Daggar, put to death. I had known him well.

The monks stopped as their leader smiled up at me. "Darkshire."

We had never met, but it was said Monks of Vex spoke to those who had died sealing their sworn vengeance.

I nodded slowly. He gazed at my clenched fist hanging at my side, as if pleased to see it. "Blessings be upon you, Darkshire. We will speak to the shade of Blackplate at seeing you. The order never forgets you were there in the end."

The words were dry in my mouth. "Thanks."

"Hey!" The bartender knocked on the bar. "That name's not allowed in here! You've got your food. Time to go."

The monk bowed slowly. "Thank you, Deidre. But Blackplate's name is never forgotten."

The tavern sighed collectively as the monks left. The

bartender cast me a scowl but went back towards the kitchen to fetch the food for the girls. Silver always triumphed over offense.

"Stay here, don't move," I repeated to the girls and walked towards the back.

In the back, several mages crowded around one of the tables, playing dice. I saw a flash of wild copper-blond hair, causing a smile to break on my face.

A wood elf with tanned skin sat in a sleeveless leather vest, tattoos etched down his arms to the elbow in the mimicry of the jagged roots on a tree. He always got on well with druids. Most wood elves did. A dozen wands littered his chest bandoliers. He had one boot up on a chair, for an absent player, and a long halfling knife was sticking out of it.

A young mage in red robes slid a pile of coins forward, and he smirked. I stood back, watching him for a moment, remembering all those years together when I had started adventuring again. Of all the living friends I had, you only needed a single finger to count them, and if you did, you pointed it at Trith.

"Big bet," Trith said to the mages. He smiled with the ease of an elf who took everything as it came, sometimes unnervingly so. It used to drive me crazy.

"Just call it," the mage snarled. "Or lay it down."

Trith tapped a finger on top of his dice cup, hiding what lay within. Behind him, his short spear-staff leaned against the wall, its crystal tip dull against the green ivy. The wood elf leaned forward, peering at the mage.

"Sounds good to me." Trith smiled. "I'm out of coin. Shall we cap it?"

The mage's eyes slid over to his spear. "Throw that in, and we'll call it even."

Trith tsked slightly, and I felt my grin spreading from where I watched him next to the pillar. "Can't do that, friend."

"Two wands then." The mage's friend was practically licking his lips, eyes sliding over Trith's collection. "Make it two wands."

"These?" he clasped his chest. "Oh, boys, now you're trying to rob me."

"Pony up." The player stared at him.

Trith sighed and slid the wands from his chest. The spell-slinger placed them down on the pile of silver dotted with gold. "Tuition rates rising? Never understood why you pay men to read a book yourself."

"We've got him now." The friend laughed.

It was Bear Pit, a simple game normally made for quick drinks at a tabletop. One man rolled a set of dice and saw how high he set the bet or folded. The other player wagered on if he was higher or, if you were crazy, the same number.

The mage leaned back, grinning. He lifted his cup, and several onlookers leaned forward.

"Eleven." He smiled at Trith.

Trith peered at him. This was the part of the game where you could take half your bet back upon seeing the trap. "Nicely done."

"You folding?"

Trith grinned, tapping his own dice cup. "I'll see the bear."

"Show it," his friend growled.

The sorcerer lifted the cup, and everyone leaned over.

"Two squads!" someone exclaimed. "Twelve!"

The onlookers broke into a gasp. Trith grinned and leaned forward to rake his winnings in, but the mage stopped him by slamming his hand down on the pot.

"Cheat!" he spat.

Trith's face fell. "You've got your hand on my money, friend."

My runes thrummed, feeling the spells ease forward from

both the player and his robed friend. "You can't cast for shit without those wands, Trith. We all know it."

Trith didn't blink. "That so?"

A hobgoblin onlooker broke the silence. "Gents, it's a bet. Trith's no cheater, come now. Part of being a man."

Trith leaned back, taking his hand from the pile. "If you think it's yours, go ahead."

"Thought so." The collegiate mage bent over the table and grabbed a fistful of coins. Trith stared at him, clenching his fists as his sorcery snaked out.

A terrible searing sound filled the air, punctured by the scent of cooking metal and meat. The coins shimmered in the mage's hand. Then he screamed.

"*Oh shit!*" someone yelled.

The silver dripped down his hand, coating it in swirls of molten metal. He fell to the ground in agony, rolling like he was trying to put a fire out.

His friend rose and stretched his hand to cast. "Bastard!"

I slid from the pillar, pulling my dirk.

Trith beat me. He whipped a wand from his chest and stuck it in the young man's face.

"Don't even try it, Ian." Trith's voice was a gentle warning. "Unless they taught you how to resurrect yourself."

The dice player rolled on the ground, his groans turning to whimpers. The bartender cursed and started coming over. I saw Vorga and Karley standing, trying to see what was happening.

"Don't do it, kid." The hobgoblin put a hand on the collegiate student. "That's Trith. You know who he rode with. He blew a paladin's leg off last week."

Trith's copper eyes flashed in warning. "Listen to your friend, Ian. This was just a friendly game. No use making it unfriendly."

Ian lowered his hand. His face promised this wasn't the end of it. "You're a cheat, spellslinger. One day, you'll get what's coming."

Trith's face grew serious. "I knew men who'd filet you for words like that." Then he smiled, softening the blow. "You're lucky I'm such a nice fellow. Why don't you be a good friend and take Davey here to the clerics?" Trith tossed a gold piece onto the edge of the table. "On me."

The student shook his head, but the older hobgoblin hurried him away. "Pick that other one up! Come on!" Several men reached down and grabbed the whimpering student. His hand was hardening with metal.

Someone laughed. "Boy's fittin' to join the Silver Hands with that!"

They carried the two wizards out the door. The crowd around Trith clapped him on the shoulder, but I could see how irritated he was. He had never liked violence.

But not liking a thing doesn't mean you're not good at it.

"A silver for you, friend." He didn't look up from the pile as I approached. "Saw you try to stop him."

"You were always too sentimental, you know that? You don't look very retired."

Trith froze. He stared at his hands, shaking his head ever so slightly. When he looked up, his face looked like he saw a miracle.

"Davik?"

I grinned. "Hey, you."

Trith shook his head, not believing what he saw. Then he walked around the table and grabbed me, holding me tight.

"Where you been, Davik?" Trith murmured as I rocked him back and forth. It was beyond good to see him again. He slid back from my hug, smiling at me. "I thought you bought it in Swinford. Everyone said so."

"I retired, so to speak." I motioned to the table. "Got a minute?"

We sat, and I took a chair to keep Karley and Vorga in my sights.

"What have you been up to?" I asked him.

Trith drank a mug of spring water. "Oh, you know, this and that."

"You seen Rushe?" I asked.

Trith looked surprised. "That old rat? Last I heard, he was giving out gold in the Midlands. Must've found religion or something."

"I saw him in Trinth," I admitted. "He helped me with a job."

Trith's face fell a bit at the mention of business. "Didn't like leaving you, Davik, after Rochdale. But... just didn't have the stomach for it anymore, you know? Job was done."

"You don't owe me anything. You did your time, Trith. More than anyone."

Trith shook his head. "Still eats at me. Just couldn't follow where you kept going. Nothing felt the same, after Redscale and all that, and Rayleth."

I held up my cup. "To Rayleth."

Trith smiled. "To Rayleth."

I noticed his ear was blank of its usual earrings, except for one. "What happened there?"

"Oh." Trith smiled. "Guess I finally found one that made me take off all the others. It ended badly. Haven't had it in me to start putting more on."

"How badly?"

Trith shrugged. "She stabbed me, but, you know. These things happen." Trith shifted the coins around. "I'll send these to Stirr. I'd ask if Devan is still around, but there'd be cities on fucking fire if he wasn't..." Trith looked up at me. "What do you need, brother? You need coin?" He motioned at his winnings. "I've got more than this nearby. Say the word and it's yours. What's happening?"

It had been a long time since someone offered me something without anything in trade. After Rochdale, Trith had gotten out of the life, while I had stayed to wage war on the Lowlanders. He had tried to get me to come with him, but I just couldn't let it go.

Once our old troupe met its demise, his heart hadn't been in it any longer. Loyalty had sent us to Rochdale, and it had almost killed us.

"It's not business," I told him. "I know you don't really... work any longer. But I have to go into the Lowlands, and I've got some people with me."

"Is this a job, Davik?" Trith's face fell. "I thought you said you retired."

"I am. This is personal. There'll be a reward, and half is yours if you come with."

Trith pointed at me. "Knock it off. When have you ever needed to offer me coin?"

Another chord struck deep in my heart. Before Oakshire, he was the only person I could truly count on. That's why I never sought him out once he left the life.

"I need someone to watch my back and the people with me. Get them out if something happens."

"Done," Trith declared. "Suppose if I stick around here, there'll be a few mages outside tomorrow, anyway." He leaned over, looking at Karley and Vorga eating fruit at the bar. "They with you? What are they, rookies?"

"They're my friends. So to speak."

Trith grinned. "Shit, Davik, I'm your only friend. You know that."

"That you are." I leaned back in the chair. We eyed each other, trying to make sense of what we saw.

"What?" he asked.

"Gambling again?" I raised an eyebrow. "You?"

Trith grinned. "Got a little bored when I came back from home. So where we going?"

"Windpeak."

"That princess you guarded? The wedding? That was how you lifted our warrants."

I nodded.

Trith shook his head. "Didn't you murder her husband? Ironclad's brat?"

"Well, yes. She's getting a new one. I'm there to make sure it goes smoothly."

Trith raised his hands, begging me to explain. I sighed and gave him the recounting all the way from Oakshire to Hollyhead.

Trith's face grew dark when I told him it had been Fenner who had the Rochdale gates opened. "You're sure?"

I nodded. "Oh, he couldn't help but admit it."

"Swore he just ran." My old friend shook his head. "We could've fucking *held* it. Where is he now?"

I gave him a look.

Trith nodded slowly. "That explains why there's no brightdrop in the city. People been real sick since it stopped."

Fenner had mentioned something to me in that Floraison auction. *I should thank you for taking out the Silver Hands. You opened up my territory.*

"Noticed there haven't been any Silver Hands around," I said slowly, watching him. "Council always wanted that to happen."

Trith shrugged. "Guess someone moved on them. Folks

said it was you. Darkshire came back from the dead when they butchered his crew in Swinford."

"I was in Erast, after that."

Trith changed the subject. "This wedding?"

"It checks out. Elyse is having a gown-tourney. Two knights who helped me out in Hollyhead are bringing her or her sister as hostage. Then we ride out."

"Knights helped you?" Trith laughed. *"You?"*

"One of them is Allie's older brother."

Trith looked perplexed. "The little girl with her doll? The one on your shoulders? "

"That's right. She's alive." I leaned forward, wanting to drive the point home. "Listen, Trith. These women with me, I wouldn't risk them. But this could be dangerous. It might be a trap or—"

Trith cut me off. "When are we leaving?"

I smiled. "Knights will be here in a few days. We're at the Dragon's Nest. Where are you staying?"

Trith shrugged. "Over near the Citadel. Been there almost a year."

"I need to get a bit of gear in town. Who's good now? Got a little gold. But I want to make an impression on these Lowlanders. Little bit of theater in case they get any brave ideas."

Trith started laughing.

"What?"

He drained the rest of his cup and pulled on a long necklace around his neck. When the key finally emerged, a splotch of black iron, I couldn't believe it.

"You kept it?"

My old friend winked at me. "I'm sentimental like that."

CHAPTER
EIGHT

This is not ideal, the necromancer sends to his bear-ward. They have tracked this scent for days. The rattle of decayed vocal cords is his only response.

Three horses shift as he approaches. Southern beasts—not suited to this climate. When the man gazes up at the spire peak next to them, three figures in glittering steel make slow progress up the mountain. He can feel their divine power even from this distance.

He leans from his mount to inspect the horses. They don't skitter much. They are war destriers and well-trained.

You could learn much from them.

The ice bear growls in irritation. It's taking a good amount of his control to keep him from attacking the horses.

He moves the furs until a lancing pain scorches his hand. That's surprising. When he inspects the leather throng, he squints against the glare of the emblem.

Selene.

The necromancer grins and gazes back at the spire. Three Justicars of Selene, this far into the Icelands? Only powerful and dark prey would draw these hunters so far. He considers it for a moment. There is no taste like the blood of the heroic.

Tempting, but discipline must be maintained. He steels the bear forward, a thousand pounds of rippling dead flesh, controlled by loops of pain and guidance.

The debate last evening had been lively. He quiets the two warring souls in his chest, still arguing in the covens down there. In an unusual act of cruelty, he housed them together in his chest dungeon. Perhaps tonight they will continue the debate. It did feel good to be social again.

They travel for another half day towards the bastion of a fallen keep. He can feel numerous souls under the landscape. Lost souls too tortured and fanatical to find their way in the Veil.

As he holds his hand over the ground that they travel, he can feel the taint in many of them. Some strange disease brought their end.

And fire.

He cocks his head, tasting the dreams of the dead. Rivers of fire had scorched the land here, before the snow covered it again.

You cannot do much with fanatics. Even in death, they are insufferable.

There. The man steers his bear-ward up the hill, climbing towards the fortress. The memories of the Darkshire match this place. Rayleth is what he seeks. With him at his side, the Darkshire will falter.

And I will open him like a book for those runes before I drape myself in the very pages.

The tower has been swallowed by ice. There are soul-voices at its peak, hissing to him of a scaled god. He ignores them, climbing.

The cairn is here.

He slides down from the white bear, walking to press his ear to the tomb.

Rayleth's soul is distant. It is nearly to its afterlife, but a life of blood and vengeance causes him to falter.

Good. This is good.

He could find better warriors, better swordsmen. But how do you defeat a man that profane magic cannot touch? You maim his soul.

The greatest pugilist in the world will drop his hands when his dead father walks into the ring to do him harm. It's better to storm a small castle with the fallen friends of the archers who defend it. It brings hesitation, and hesitation is time.

Hear me, Rayleth. Come and serve.

The necromancer beckons the dead paladins forth. Once mighty warriors, now they will be his laborers. But something slithers through the tendrils of the world, coring into the portions of his revived brain flesh.

Aid me...

The man freezes. His eyes circle in their sockets, seeking the tone. There is nothing.

He continues his work. Nine dead paladins rise from their icy graves. Their souls are too defiant to stray into an afterlife they weren't promised. Hypocrites often linger.

Aid me...

The psychic voice carries an ancient weight resonating through him like a whisper in the night. He turns slowly, searching.

The spire.

Somewhere on it, the Justicars make their high climb toward their quarry. He respects such hunters. It will take them another day to surmount where they need to go.

Whatever they hunt calls to him. The man grins.

Everything must die.

The necromancer gestures as his nine slaves begin to disassemble the cairn. A shifted slab releases a gust of air that is not poison but not *not* poison. The red paladins are just bodies. If he willed it, they would duel like drunken children, waving swords like sticks at each other. Their minds and bodies are too ravaged to accomplish anything but the simplest of movements.

He creeps forward and gazes at his prize.

The elf is untouched. There is no decay. No decomposition. Bless the never-aged and their flesh. Bless the dry, cold climate of this place, and bless the seal the tomb has made.

Rayleth's body is massacred by wounds, but it is fixable. It is very fixable.

He presses on the cold flesh. The corpse looks like he is sleeping. His ear is mangled down to a nub. There are death wounds. But the rest of his flesh is immaculate.

Royalty. Elven royalty.

Fate, or luck, which he does not believe in, is with him. But Rayleth's soul is resistant. It will not come easily. Nor will it be simple to control.

The man commands the corpses to build him a table. He will need to work all night.

PREPARING Rayleth's body for his soul's return takes another day. The man turns the citizens of his chest dungeon into a marketplace of struck deals.

A bonewright sees to the knee in exchange for true death. The same for three other fleshwrights, reviving his nerves and matching the muscle tissue. He watches Rayleth's flesh change to a sickly golden pallor. Small protective wards are woven into the skin by a bard who lulled courts to sleep with his magical voice before cutting their throats. He believed there was no point in living after someone heard his masterpiece.

My final song. The bard grins as the man banishes him to the Veil. Artists can be so fickle.

The body is ready. The vessel can house him now.

Vabris's voice is the first to break through.

"You think you can shape a soul like clay, like some novice artisan? The elf won't bend easily."

The man's lip curls. "Shall I remind you of how malleable you were in the end?"

Vabris falls silent. His shade falls back.

Others are there, including his old teachers before the black citadel fell. Many call for his attention, seeking their release to aid him in this craft.

One voice climbs above the others. It is filled with the cruelty of eons. One of the few mages he has ever kept.

Theris the Red. The blood mage whose cleverness had once undone kingdoms. Once an arcane healer, until the cruelty of the battlefield drove him to power. In the end, his harem had held captured queens and trembling maidens, but they said the arcane was his only true mistress. The malevolence in his voice is soothing... almost.

"The sadist is right, you know." Theris smiles from his dungeon. *"The elf won't be bound by force. His heart must be coaxed. He dreams, so you must craft his dreams."*

The necromancer pauses. Theris has never spoken. No matter the machinations or cruelties placed upon him, the blood mage has been unbreakable. Too powerful to release; too valuable to destroy.

"What would you suggest? A song of homecoming?"

Theris chuckles. *"Give him what he craves most, and he'll rise willingly. Until the truth tears him apart."*

The man sighs. "And you would offer his insight for what? A moment of starlight?"

Theris's voice darkens. "*When you choke the void, cast me into it first. I would drown in the arcane before it is sealed forever.*"

That... that the man could do. But would he? Perhaps. Perhaps not.

"I cannot promise that, yet." The man looks down at Rayleth as he weighs the bargain. To grant Theris even the smallest amount of control is dangerous. But there would be no one better suited to his next task.

He nods. "So be it. Now guide me."

Theris grins and leans forward. "*You consume memories and dreams, little necromancer. But you're so mistaken. Souls do nothing but dream. Life is a dream.*"

The man ignores Theris's words. He feels almost every denizen of his collection shrink back. They fear him, even in the fortress of his soul.

He places his hand on Rayleth's icy brow. When he focuses on his soul, the elf resists.

"*Start with his victories.*" Theris hisses. The man does not like him being this close. "*Make him believe he is needed again.*"

Theris pushes the man into Rayleth's wandering soul. Together, they enter Rayleth's memories.

"*Now.*"

They dive within. Even the necromancer is awed at Theris the Red's skill. The dark elf did so much in his short life.

They see duels in Rayleth's early life. The tutelage of a blade from many masters. He has an affinity for it. A natural talent, honed and prepared for years. There are elven courts and blood feuds and champions. He is his father's favorite, and Rayleth honors him greatly.

In the crowds, his brothers watch him. And a sister. Some applaud loudly at his victories. Others stare in secret jealousy.

One step-brother wears a red cloak from one of the elven mage enclaves.

His step-brother, Venthren, claps proudly when Rayleth defeats another duelist. But there is something worse than jealousy in his eyes. His father has woven an intricate knot of marriages and alliances, and Venthren seeks to pull at it.

He was a duelist. These victories mean nothing to him. Theris waves the memories away, driving deeper into the tomb-cold memory.

There is a campfire found after escaping his homeland. Rayleth is welcomed by the first humans who are not vassals he has met. He is young, for an elf, and filled with folly.

They welcome him with warmth and with wine. They tell him stories of mages that grow with power and the adventures they have been on. He likes them.

The wine is drugged, and soon the wineskin falls from his limp hand.

Here. Theris urges. *This must be used.*

He screams when they hold him. For all his training, he is but one man against many. He is not strong enough to fight off six who hold him down.

They are clumsy butchers. They carve too much of his ear away. If they only knew who they held, they could have had a great ransom. Rayleth sees his own ear and feels the hot wet sensation of it now missing. The sounds of the world are as raw as his gaping wound.

"*Let's get that other one.*" A man sneers and bends forward.

Rayleth escapes, striking out and grabbing the knife that maimed him. With a blade, he is beyond formidable. He sees his sword leaning by a log, like stars wrapped in steel.

That will do. Theris raises them from the memory. *That is the kindling.*

The necromancer takes the memory and crafts it into a

dream. A dream without a beginning or an end, placing it back in Rayleth's body. He feels the swordsman's soul stop its thrashing, gazing back at it.

"More is needed," the man says aloud.

Theris chuckles. "*Indeed.*"

They see a storied career. They see distaste and distrust grow. Rayleth wanders into a town, and he is robbed at an inn. The more he understands the world beyond his kingdom, the more his heart blackens. He falls to bloodshed and challenge.

For years, he imagines Venthren in his opponent's eyes until their bodies are nothing but carcasses.

"*His hatred is magnificent,*" Theris remarks.

Until it isn't. The world, the many lands and people he meets, prove to be his greatest teacher. The hate is refocused, pointed only at Venthren.

He meets the Darkshire and wishes to help him. He sees how lost the man is after his war and what he wasn't taught. There are quests and adventures. Until a final one.

"*Oh, this one will be quite the bladeward.*" Theris strains against his chains as they watch Rayleth cut down red paladins like chaff. "*Do you feel it, fleshcrafter? Look to see who he protects.*"

The necromancer strains, trying to focus in the whir of bladed combat. He isn't used to moving this quickly, and Rayleth is faster than most. Finally, the elf pivots, spinning his blade. He sees the Darkshire and several others in the grunt of combat.

"*Yes,*" Theris says. "*That will do. The campfire as well, where he trains the engraved man. His soul will need a place to rest, lest you wish to find those eyes on you next.*"

The man takes the memories and crafts them into dreams that will circle Rayleth's skull. A small house with only several rooms.

Theris clatters against his chains. *"He still resists his home-coming! You have tempted him with things completed. But what will move him?"*

"State your meaning."

Theris the Red cackles.

"You drape yourself in flesh, but you have completely lost what it is to be alive. The heart, necromancer! The heart, bonethief! What moves the heart?"

"Amorous affection..." the necromancer murmurs. It is growing very cold on this peak, and he wishes to put Theris away deep into his soul. "Called love, by most races."

Love! Theris laughs. *Did you see love in his life? No... no... it is what is left undone.*

They do not have long. He needs Theris to aid him pull Rayleth's soul from the veil. He is tethered, but soon the tether will break.

"His brother..." the man realizes aloud, remembering that face in the crowd of an elven court.

Theris nods. *"He hides something from us. It must be delicious."*

The man concentrates, traveling back into Rayleth's memories. What he wanted... what he never did.

Venthren.

It is the first time he hears Rayleth's voice. Even after so many years dead, there was one name he never drenched in blood. His eldest brother.

"Yes." Theris sneers. *"Now you have it."*

The man finds Rayleth's memory. Stumbling into the bedchamber of their father, a mighty elven lord. Rayleth cannot believe what he sees. His own sword, blue and gold fili-gree, drenched in the blood of their father.

Venthren smiles and tosses the blade at Rayleth's feet. He takes it up immediately. Venthren is no duelist. He is more dangerous than that. He plucks at the strands of court intrigue.

Guards burst into the room as if signaled. They wrestle Rayleth to the ground as he screams. He never stops screaming as they take him away. Only his sister's words will trade his execution for exile. Venthren gives him the sword as a mark of shame. No one expects him to live long. *May your shame cause you to sheathe it where it belongs.*

"Perfection." The necromancer grins and molds the memory into a dream.

Rayleth stops struggling. Vengeance calls to him, and he follows the tether towards the dreams.

The soul houses itself, like a crab moving from shell to shell, sure this is its home. He tethers his control tightly.

Theris chuckles. *Loyalty is fickle in the dead. You know that better than anyone.*

Rayleth rises from the platform, eyes burning like emeralds. The elf turns his head, awaiting his command.

The man gazes at the spire where the Justicars hunt their dark quarry. They would make fine sport for his new bladeward. The recently raised ought to be tested. He is eager to see their creation in action.

Theris laughs from his chains. *"You didn't bring a sword for the swordsman?"*

CHAPTER
NINE

We all have friends that are meant to be a single ingredient. They don't mix well when you introduce them to the wider broth of your life.

That had been me.

Trith was the opposite of that. He could mesh with anyone. Even when we took captives after Rochdale to ransom them, he was friendly with them. He was always sincere. I don't even think I've ever seen him tell an outright lie. Yet, there was one person I was loath to introduce him to.

When Trith met us in the tavern of the Dragon's Nest, Brim was the first one up. And by up, I mean standing on top of the table, hand on his knife, growling.

Trith walked forward, locking eyes with the dishwasher. "So you're Brim."

"Rahh." Brim held his head up in challenge.

They stared at each other.

Sorcerer vs. dishwasher.

Wood elf vs. Gnome.

Psionic vs Sorcery.

"Wood elves know how to deal with gnomes." Trith squinted at Brim.

"Pretty boy," Brim spat.

Trith slid his hand slowly into his pack, never taking his eyes from Brim. The girls looked at me, not sure what to make of it.

"Davik?" Sariel asked me. I held up my hand to give it a second. I wondered if this was going to be the first time Trith met someone he couldn't befriend.

Trith pulled out a large glass jar stuffed with sweetvine. Silver chrysalis shimmered on the green buds. Brim's eyes instantly locked onto it.

"Friends?" Trith shook the container at him.

Brim grabbed the jar, unscrewing it. When he had given it a good sniff, he smiled. "Elf friends."

"Oh, that's nice!" Elina looked at everyone.

I gave Sariel a look. "What the hell?"

Sariel smiled. "Guess you should've come to Oakshire bearing gifts."

"Hello, everyone!" Trith made a quick bow. "Davik told me all about you."

"Everyone"—I motioned to the sorcerer—"this is my friend, Trith."

Trith cleared his throat. "*Best* friend."

"Best friend," I added.

Sariel laughed. "Well met, cousin. We have lots of questions for you."

"Let's get going." I looked around the table. "Everyone ready?"

The girls nodded and stood. It was time for a night on the town.

The first request was for stories, of course.

"He's so quiet about his past," Tyra said. "How long did you two travel together?"

"Oh" Trith passed the pipe back to Brim as we walked. "Many, many years. I met him right after the war."

"What was he like?" Elina asked.

Brim coughed, and Trith stopped walking to clap him on the back. "Scary."

"Still scary." Karley bumped my shoulder as she walked past me. "Guess that hasn't changed."

It was another night without rain and the Stroudsburg crowds were out in mass to enjoy it. We walked along Bayside, the same path I had taken Karley.

We ate deep-fried fish served in wax paper and drank cups of cold beer.

"This is pretty good!" Vorga raised her fish at me.

Trith grinned. With such a large group, we fell into the habit of fanning into a circle when we stopped somewhere. Tyra held my hand as we walked, and Vorga stuck close by, each of them eager to be close to me. But every time I looked at Karley, I saw her turn away.

"This was Davik's favorite." Trith finished his meal and rolled the wax paper into a ball. His fist glowed for a moment, burning the paper and casting the ashes harmlessly behind him. "Every time we came back to Stroudsburg, we had to go here first thing."

"Fried fish?" Tyra gave me a smile and sent a pulse of illicit need into me.

Vorga released the grip on my arm. "I felt that!"

Tyra giggled.

Sariel finished her beer. "Fried fish is the way to this man's heart?"

"Every time." Trith laughed. Then he looked down at Brim next to him. "How we doing?"

97

"Rahh." Brim was red-eyed and silent, his eyelids half-hidden above a lazy smile as he mechanically put more fish into his mouth.

I pointed my fish at Trith. "Not sausage sandwiches, though."

A grin broke across my old friend's face.

"What's that mean?" Elina looked at us.

"Just an old joke." I winked at her.

When you're young, the night moves, and you chase after it.

I've known rangers who can track from a fallen feather and druids who can sniff a man a mile away. But if you can't chase the night, you're destined for a dull evening. Rushe would always slip away between the bars, off to steal something or someone. Trith was alright, but I was better.

Rayleth had been the best.

The brooding warrior prince walked with authority in the daytime. He was disciplined. Reserved, almost. I rarely saw him rattled or even surprised. Angry—only once. And four men had clutched at their severed throats for their folly.

Elven royals can be like that, even exiled ones. He always shook his head in protest when we dragged him to a tavern before or after a job. We lured him with the spell all men knew. *Just one. Just one quick cup, and we'll call it early.* But once he wet his whistle, he found the night.

I had been talking up a sad redhead one night, making her smile in a little winesink. It was a dirty place. A brawl broke out, of course. Violent men are too eager to pick up the tools of their trade when they are "relaxing."

We had two bottles of wine in Rayleth by then. He could hear the night, like a song wafting away. He'd point his finger in the air, dictating where we needed to go. That night, someone threw him onto a table, crashing next to me and the redhead. We both looked down at his hanging head. He only said one thing.

Davik, we need to get sausage sandwiches.

Sounds strange, but we always listened to him. I'm not superstitious, but as we used to say, I'm a little stitious'. We followed him through Runethor that night, foregoing two sausage vendors.

Leth! They sell sausages! They sell bread!

But the drunk swordsman was already stumbling up the street. *It's not the same!*

Finally, we found a bar that served sausage sandwiches. We swapped his wine for a pitcher of bitter juice, hoping he wouldn't notice the taste of our trickery. Then Trith had nudged me.

The mage we had been hunting for weeks sat in the corner, talking to his apprentice.

Trith had shaken his head. *Forget that sword of his. We should put a leash on him. He'll find us gold.*

Then the arcane shouts came, the running, the screaming, and the spark of spells. Once we captured the old wizard, we even gave him one of the sausage sandwiches, before we dumped him at the collegiate who had put a contract out for his return.

I caught Tyra looking at me, and I realized she must have felt a bit of that memory as it came through me. But there was no sadness in it. I watched Trith's eyes, knowing he was remembering the same night as I did. He gave me a soft nod.

"Where to next?" Sariel asked.

"Call it, Davik." Trith opened his hands to the city.

"Low Lantern." I grinned. "We'll make our way there."

I led the group through the familiar streets of Stroudsburg, giving a quick tour of our old haunts. After a day of shopping and tailored dresses, everyone moved with that easy, content fatigue.

Brim lagged behind, yawning, so I hoisted him up onto my shoulders.

"Horsey," he giggled, his small hands gripping my head.

"Don't get used to it," I said as we rounded the corner.

The Low Lantern came into view, a quiet stone hollow with warm lanternlight spilling across the steps. I set Brim down gently.

"It's beautiful," Sariel said, sliding up beside me.

"Always liked this place," I murmured, slipping my arm around her waist as the others fanned out behind us, voices softening like even they knew—some places deserved quiet.

Sariel rested her head on my shoulder. "Wish I had known you sooner, my love."

"I do, too." I took her by the hand and descended the steps to the cobblestone hollow. At an outdoor stall that looked like a potion stand, we bought glowing drinks, taking them and walking with the flow of the crowd.

Tyra slid next to me as we slowed. "You didn't get one, Davik?"

"I did." I held my glass out for her to take. When I released it into her fingers and stepped away, the soft amber color flickered to life.

Her blue eyes softened. "Your runes... they won't glow for you."

I ran a strand of her red hair behind her ear. "I've got enough magic for a lifetime."

Tyra kissed me, pressing her body against me. "And more."

When we caught up with the group, Karley held her glass out in front of her, squinting against the bright light of the wine.

"Too bright, dear?" Elina turned to her. "It might be because of the magic in you."

"Yeah..." Karley looked around for a place to set the glass down.

"Here." Tyra pulled me towards Karley. "Davik can help."

Before either of us could protest, Tyra placed my hand around Karley's. The wine darkened like a blown-out candle. Tyra slid her hand down Karley's arm, and I felt the quick heat of her sharing something with the dark elf before she slipped away with a grin.

Karley and I stared at each other, a pocket of shadow in a river of glowing glasses.

"That better?"

"Yeah," she exhaled. "Do you want some?"

"Is there enough?"

Karley smirked. For a moment, her finger trailed down mine, soft as a burglar on a deadly lock. "There might—"

"Karley!" Vorga turned around with a grin. "Come look!"

The dark elf slipped from my grasp, the glass illuminating her face as she broke from my touch. I felt the pull of her. That old reflex to pursue a mage flooded me—but with such a different intent now.

Everyone joined the crowd to watch the illusionists put on a show. Their faces lit with the flash of leaping flames. The grateful crowd clinked coins in appreciation as the mud mages bowed with smiles. Their brown robes were a youthful defiance from the collegiate towers they had absconded from.

As the women of my life pressed closer, standing on their tiptoes to see the dance of the illusionists, Trith drifted close to me. We were shoulder to shoulder, both of us pretending to watch the show.

I squinted against the glare of a seadragon whipping through the air in a spray of sparks. Six mages concentrated, spells flying from their palms like sand as the mythical beast roared in the night.

"Happy for you, brother," Trith said without looking at me. "They're good people. You deserve that."

As the seadragon circled the crowd, something caught in my throat. "Missed you. Just never wanted to drag you back."

Trith followed the dragon as it circled into the sky, spreading into a shift of colors. "I know."

I wanted to ask him in that moment if he had been to Swinford. But the moment was too soft, even between brothers.

Claps came as the show ended. Brim applauded louder than anyone, growling his approval at the display. Then he marched forward to ask questions of the mud mages.

Sariel turned around with a knowing smile. She whispered something to Elina. The halfling laughed, glancing at Trith and me. "You're right, they do."

"What is it?" I raised an eyebrow at them.

Sariel's silver eyes settled on me. "You two look like brothers."

"We've got dresses now." Vorga looked at both of us. "Let's go see that treasure you spoke of."

Trith glanced at me. "Grab some gear?"

I nodded. "Let's."

TRITH UNLOCKED the glyph wards to the storage vault. We were in the tunnels of the Bank of Stroudsburg. A place that never closed. It held half of the merchant inventory that flowed into the city. That old thieves guild, the Silver Hands, had been the reason for this place.

"This place is something," Vorga whispered as she glanced

around the tunnel. Mage guards and other specialists walked slowly on patrol. Down the hall, several merchants moved a late-night delivery into a vault.

"It is." I slid my arm around her. "You know, I might have some books in here."

Vorga grinned. Then she nuzzled her head against me and scratched my jaw with a gentle tusk. "You still have to show me the library here before we leave."

Before I could respond, trapped air gushed forward as Trith pulled the door open. Arcane lanterns along the ceiling flickered to life, illuminating the twenty-foot room.

Sariel whistled as she walked forward, giving me a playful nudge. "You have writs of purchase for all of this?"

I grinned. The truth of adventuring is the finest of items and gear are all war tokens. Bards sing hearty songs about the sword on your hip and the beautiful battle you waged to get it. They leave out where you pull the items from a corpse. Or search for a river to wash the blood from it, staring at the red tendrils, wondering if someone else will clean your gear the same way one day.

Guess it doesn't do well with the tavern crowd.

"Wow," Tyra said as she walked next to me. "This is your orchard?"

"In a way." I surveyed the room without stepping in. It looked exactly the same as when we had left it. I peered at Trith. "Whoever made it out of Rochdale was supposed to sell all this."

Trith shrugged. "Didn't get around to it."

Our group wandered inside. Brim made a beeline for a collection of powders and crystals. Several weapons glowed with arcane energies on the tables, and one axe glowed blue as it shimmered.

"What's that?" Karley stared at it.

Trith grinned. "Barbarian Chieftain Davik... bested. We always thought it was too pretty to sell."

Karley didn't respond. She moved among the collection of weapons and armors, of trinkets and other items.

I turned back and saw Sariel and Elina inspecting a traveling trunk with runes of containment etched on it. A long time ago, I had kept a sorcerer in there.

Trith looked around. "Half of this is yours, Davik. Don't know if you remember it all. We can get you a vault if you want. Move it now."

"I do plan on putting on a show in Windpeak." I looked around the room, then at Tyra. "Want anything other than a crossbow?"

Tyra laughed. "I'm a cook! You have a magic oven in here?"

Trith shared a look with me, raising his eyebrows.

I shrugged. "Sure."

"Did you ever hear of Linlock the Minstrel?" Trith walked deeper into the storage area.

"No, what did he play?" Tyra stood on her tiptoes.

Barely anyone had called Linlock a minstrel. He had been a lute player and was terribly deadly with a flip-knife. He used one talent to get him close enough to use another. He had been twenty when he died in Daggar.

Good cook, though. That was always welcome.

"Oh, he played many things." Trith bent over, his short spear bobbing on his back as he rummaged. "But this was his favorite."

Trith turned and held up a frying pan. As he held it, small gleams of veined mineral shimmered in the metal.

Tyra looked at me. "What is it?"

"Doesn't need a fire," I told her. "You can just cook on it."

"Linlock left it to Davik since he hated sparks." Trith

handed her the skillet. "Though it's useless when he touches it. Linlock thought that was the funniest thing."

"Go ahead," I told her. "Swing it through the air."

Tyra gripped the metal handle, and as she waved the frying pan, streams of orange light trailed after it. "Oh, my!"

"Gives a little burn if you smack someone with it. Just be careful." I kissed the top of her head.

"I've got Embriel arrows in here." Trith turned back around. "Lady Sariel? How many do you need?"

Sariel left the trunk and walked forward. "As many as you can spare."

Trith handed three quivers full to me. Sariel inspected them when I gave them to her and raised an eyebrow at me. "These are Demtha Sect's. They don't part with these easily."

"They were very rude," I promised her.

Sariel laughed and slung them over her shoulder. "I suppose there are boons to being your woman."

On the table, Trith unrolled two leather surgical kits he had repurposed. Two dozen wands of differing colors, lengths, and shapes slid over the table to Karley and me.

"These'll do." Trith looked at me and Karley. "Deiga's teaching you?"

Karley nodded. "That's right."

"Have her show you how to use one of these." Trith slid a wand over the table. "You know what that is?"

"A wand?"

"It's a spell." He grinned. "No morning studying needed. That's a flare—she'll be able to tell. Lights up the room. Might as well know how to do it, and it'll take a tiny amount of your power. When you're out of stored spells and there's no time to stick your head in a spellbook, they come in handy."

Karley held up the wand. "How do you know which is which?"

"Very carefully." Trith's warm laughter bounced off the walls. Then he nodded to my sword, already knowing the answer. "You bringing that?"

"I am. Got a small mace, too, but it's a little untrustworthy."

Trith grinned, turning back to the weapon rack. With a quick tug, he pulled a long blanket off a gleaming rod of steel I had forgotten about. The sight of it sent a memory ringing through me—heavy plate crunching, screams muffled by helms.

"Remember this?" Trith held out the warhammer. Three and a half feet long, its grip was thicker than most, the head a jagged, serrated edge. The opposite end curled downward like a cruel fang.

"Eight-pound head..." I murmured as I took the familiar weight in my hands.

"Ten pounds of nightmare," Trith finished with a grin. "That smith was a real salesman."

I tilted the hammer, letting the liquid flow back into the head. A momentum weapon—deadly against heavy armor. Swing it and the mass shifted, ringing a man like a temple bell. The spike gleamed in the low light, freshly sharpened.

It felt a little too right in my hands.

"Davik," Vorga called to me from behind. "Can I borrow these books?"

"Sure." I set the hammer on the table.

"Ah." Trith's voice was flat, and I saw why.

High Houses of the Lowlands. Volumes one through three. We had taken them from the rulers of Rochdale to learn about our enemies. Seeing Vorga hold them made my mouth go dry.

Vorga flipped one book open. "They have their histories! Hey... someone wrote in them?"

Vorga turned the book to me, and I saw hard stenciled

handwriting over the illuminated texts. Monks of the Sword had drawn coats of arms and small vignettes of the Lowland houses. We had used them to figure out who we captured, where their homes were. It hadn't been a history book to us; it had been a map of vengeance and ransom.

"Someone crossed this one out." Vorga's voice was sad as she showed me a coat of arms, three wolves on a red field with a brutal X marked over it. The mark of an ended bloodline. Then her voice lifted, and she grinned up at me. "I can clean it up, I bet. These okay?"

"Sure," I said with a dry throat.

Vorga noticed me. "You okay?"

"Never better," I lied with a smile. "You hold on to those. They don't belong here, all alone."

Vorga giggled and kissed me on the cheek.

Trith walked back to the open area of the table and set down three wood-elf tents. "Right. Tents, rope. Caltrops, chains. Got some red-weed for wounds." He glanced up at me, taking in my armor. "You can't wear that, brother."

I pulled at one of the leather ribbons hanging from my armor. Several of the metal slats in the chest had fallen out during Hollyhead. "I'll get it touched up."

Trith shook his head and motioned us to follow him. "Over here."

Tyra, Karley, and Vorga slid behind me as we went deeper into the end of the storage vault.

"Brim!" Sariel yelled behind us. "Don't drink that! It may not be wine."

"Rahh," came a low growl.

"I'll take these bandages," Elina said behind me.

Everyone walked after Trith towards the end of the armory. The collection of items slowed from haphazard piles to the strict order of a museum.

Then I realized what we were looking at. I saw Valek's boots, stamped with the sigil of his dark deity. The only thing we could get back from his body.

I turned, seeing one of Ella's feathers. It had been the druid's favorite form.

Blackplate's mace lay wrapped on the table, bundled inside a blanket. When Karley reached to inspect it, I stopped her.

"Don't touch that." I had been the only one able to carry the cursed weapon here.

"Why?"

"Trust me," I told her.

An armor rack stood at the end of the armory, holding a full kit. The armor seemed to stare at me, like an enemy who had been waiting a long time to see me.

It was black leather, reinforced with steel so rigid it looked like a ghost filled it. The left arm was full-sleeved and ridged to catch swords. Below it hung a matching armored set of pants, boots, and greaves. Spikes ran along the tip of the right boot, for climbing or killing.

Mostly killing.

The gloves were reinforced. The left held a shift of black chainmail around the palm for half-swording. The right was fingerless, with studs of dented metal along the knuckle. The right pauldron was the only thing breaking the shift of dark leather. It bore loose metal scales: one white, one red, and one twisted piece of metal—dark as shadow. People used to say the armor was adorned with the trophies of enemies I'd slain. But the realms make up their own stories.

A white scale for Brightplate. A red scale, gleaming like a dragon's eye, from Devan. A twisted black metal fragment from Blackplate after he was killed. And several more. Each one belonged to a friend or a comrade we had lost.

I looked around slowly.

This wasn't an armory. It was a museum of Trith's grief.

At the base of the armor stand were almost thirty crossbows, stacked like an offering. I remembered them well, they had been pointed at me and my crew on that ship in Swinford. My last job.

I picked up one crossbow. It was melted, ruined by spellfire. Others were blackened or broken.

What had Trith said in the Quinx about the Silver Hands?

Guess someone moved on them.

A quietness settled around the group as they looked at the collection.

I slowly looked up at Trith. "Did you stop in Swinford, Trith?"

The elf's usually mirthful face was hard as stone. There was no shame, nor pride. His voice dripped with the finality you hear when a man stands over you. "I had business there."

Business. The business that calls a wood elf out of the forests of retirement. The business that comes when a friend destined to die by the sword finally does, but it eats at you too much to leave it be. The slow work. The grudge too sharp to sleep on, so you pick it up and put it in someone.

The group stared at my old armor. I had given it to Trith when he left the Lowlands.

Karley stepped forward, reaching out with a violet hand. "What is that?"

Trith's voice was low, almost reverent. "That's Darkshire."

CHAPTER
TEN

The remaining days in Stroudsburg were lovely but short as our departure loomed. I saw the city I had known for a long time through the eyes of the women in my life, and in that way, it was new to me.

Tyra and I made up for our lost time in Hollyhead. Exploring bakeries, often finding ourselves in the public gardens that had been little more than rubbish dumps when I was a youth. My mornings smelled of cinnamon and tasted like the lips of a faen.

"You're my favorite, you know," Tyra said to me one morning as we ate in a garden.

I laughed. "Favorite what?"

Tyra slid her hand over mine. "Everything."

Ever since I had planted her sapling, something opened up between us. Tyra had tasted hardship in the world and never let it poison her outlook, but she suffered no foolish ideals, either. The feudal Lowlands didn't hold the romantic allure it did for Vorga, but for me, she would brave them. She had a fighter's heart, stout as any I'd known. But her hands grasped pots and pans, and the world was better for it.

I walked through bookstores, smelling pages and leather bindings—always punctuated by the scent of coffee. And between those stacks of books, Vorga's brown eyes smiled at me. She played a game, where she would go into the store before me and leave a note in a book. I had to find it, guessing which one drew her eye. On our final trip, I found it on the first try. A book on Lowland legends.

"What's my prize?" I asked when I showed it to her.

Vorga took it from my hands, smiling at me. "You'll see, soon enough."

After we bought her a book, we would sit on the bench outside, and she would read the first pages to me. Her voice was like a net, keeping me in place as the city drifted by. My mother had taught me to read. But it was only through Vorga that I enjoyed stories because when she read them to me, I listened to the rise and fall of her voice. Her delight was better than any tale.

In the evenings, Sariel and I walked along the beach, even in the rain. She searched until she found a seashell to add to her growing collection. We would stop and stare at the horizon. The edge of the world.

"I love you," she would always say, gripping my hand tighter.

"I love you, too."

When I pulled her into my arms back at the inn, undressing her until the only thing on her was the scent of sand and salt, those silver eyes drank in my soul. Her hands locked around my back, and we were two warriors morphing into lovers. In those silver eyes sat the question as she shuddered against me. The same question she had asked in the forest. The start of a different game. A child.

Before dawn, I would shower with Elina. The two of us scrubbing and tending to one another, speaking of soft things. Afterward, I would lie behind her in bed while she studied her prayers, her head resting on the crook of my arm while I was inside her. This ritual was our own, somewhere between love-making and meditation.

She would imbue me with healing spells as her power grew, her moon-ink tattoos fluttering as the sun rose. In that way, she changed me. Turning the runes from violence into restoration. The same she had done with me. When we finally gave in to what we waited for, it was with a fiery tenderness.

Then I would walk Karley to her morning lessons with Deiga. The elven mage didn't soften to me, which I never expected.

"You keep watching," Deiga told me one morning, "and there'll be an accident."

"My runes?"

Deiga rolled her eyes, the burn scars stretching on the bottom half of her face. "You're distracting her."

So I took my coffee on the second level of the tower while the floor above me thumped with spells. Karley was a quick study. Even if her soul closed, that wouldn't mean her taste for power would vanish.

When Karley finished her lesson, she practically prowled down the stairs.

I turned, taking in the sight of her. Violet skin that almost gleamed with sensuality. And when she stared at me, she looked like she had the day I had her over my lap behind the woodshed, a defiant eye meeting mine.

Maybe you should punish me.

As we walked back to the inn, she asked me, "Don't like watching me practice?"

"Deiga says I'm distracting you."

Karley laughed. "Right. You prefer to be on stage, not in the audience." Before I could cut into her with her own history of watching Sariel and me, she continued, "Does it bother you, being near me?"

"Not at all."

"Liar." Karley smirked. "What's it feel like?"

"I've worked with plenty of wizards..." But when I looked at her, I saw she wasn't buying it. "It feels like... I can *find* you."

She stopped walking, leaning back to stretch out a hitch. Her tank top trailed up her violet abs. "Find me, huh?"

"That's right. Find you." I turned around, confused. Karley was backing into the morning crowd. "What are you—"

The drow's face broke into a devilish smile. "Prove it."

I shouted her name as she ducked into the crowd, weaving through hundreds of people in the blacksmith's district. The arcana in her spurred her on.

She flitted back and forth like a predator, and my runes howled to chase her. Just as Karley wanted.

"Gods fucking—"

And I was off, shouldering my way through the crowd.

I fell into old, hard instincts. Early in the war, it had been simple. Feel the mage, find the mage, and kill the mage. Afterward, I had tempered that bloodlust, learning to work with them, and eventually for them. Every caster's soul was different. If I was around them long enough, I could recognize and tolerate them.

I felt Karley in the crowd. She moved east towards the center of the city. Moving fast. I saw a blur of violet flesh, her face turning back in a grin as she squinted in the sun. Then she was gone.

Karley ran towards the garment district, and my boots pounded cobblestones, leaping over carts and sidestepping merchants under a veil of covered streets. For a very real moment, anger coursed through me. She was being foolish. Impulsive. Downright dangerous was what she was.

Then why the hell am I smiling?

I cornered her in *Underhollow*, the dark elf neighborhood I had shown her, running faster than I had in a long time, driven by the seething need to capture her. To dismantle her.

I caught my prey in an alley.

Karley backed against the stone walls, looking left and right with a grin. My heart raced, but not from the run. In the shadows of this place, her eye flickered violet for a moment with a prepared spell.

"What happened when you caught them, Davik?"

I closed in on her. "They died."

My runes howled for her demise. But more than that: for her supplication. That bratty attitude was back, mingled with something new.

"Are you going to punish me?" Karley snickered in the near darkness. Then her voice grew heavy. "Tell me how foolish I am?"

"No," I said. The same as when she would tease me in the tavern, this wasn't bait I'd rise to.

But things were different now. The drow grinned, the whisper of a spell on her lips. "What if I wanted to see it? Would you show it to me?"

I raised an eyebrow. "See what—"

A blast of cold crashed into me. Compared to a war mage, it was low-level power. But three of my runes were filled with Elina's healing spell. Three runes that didn't do what they were designed for. Pain lanced through me. It would have dropped a normal man. For me, it was like being hit with a dozen snowballs. The ice coiled off me in steamy wisps, boiled away by my rising wrath.

She yelped when I surged towards her. But that surprise

turned quickly into a wicked grin. My hand was around her throat, closing in a creak of leather. Karley didn't struggle. She pleaded with me, those dark eyes begging for more. Begging to be chased. Begging to be caught.

I loosened my grip, but she held my arm. "Don't... stop."

My runes demanded her death for striking me. My heart thundered to hear that silken voice change under my grip. To hear her teasing turn to begging.

Her throat tinged with frost from my fingers. Had I held my dirk, it would've been coated in her spell. I wanted to vanquish her, conquer her... own her.

I traced my hand down her chest, spreading my fingers over her flat stomach. She shuddered from the cold of it.

"What you did was very dangerous." I slid my hand to the edge of her pants.

Karley stared at me invitingly. The defiance was a challenge in her smirking voice. "Prove it."

I unbuttoned her pants, spreading the soft black leather. If her soul aligned with mine, it was a jagged fit. One where we cut into each other. I could give her what she wanted. I could have her now.

But what fun would that be?

Karley melted into my arms as I spun her against the alley wall. The arcane darkness that covered *Underhollow* shielded us, making it more illicit. I pulled her leather pants down, taking my time as she writhed against me.

What I denied her would mean more.

Her plump little ass was soft in my hands. Frost caked her flesh as I trailed my hand up her cheek. She shuddered, pressing back into me. When I slid my ice-caked fingers between her thighs to tease her, moist heat welcomed me, melting the frost until it ran down her legs.

"Davik..." Karley groaned. "Fucking punish me."

But I wasn't caving to any demands. I ran my fingers over her thonged ass, feeling the cloth harden from the frost spell pouring out of me. "You forgot something..."

Karley ground against my waist. When she tried to reach for my fly, I denied her with a pull of her hair.

"Please," she groaned.

I spanked her, violet cheeks rippling with a frosted hand-print. It was different now that she had the void in her. It was more. Karley moaned something that may have been my name. I reached up, trailing my cold hand up her spine.

She bent forward, trying to push herself onto my hand.

"You going to run again?" I asked.

"That depends." She looked back at me. "You going to chase me?"

I spanked her again, the swift smack echoing in the alley. Karley's pants looked perfect tangled around her calves. She was panting. Waiting for me to decide.

"Do you want me to teach you a lesson?"

Karley groaned, pushing against me. "Yes."

I teased the edge of her panties like I was about to pull them down. Then I stepped back, leaving her shivering against the wall.

Karley sucked in a breath. This wasn't rejection, it was a delay. And I saw in her eyes, behind the awe of me shrugging off her spell, that I had won in the way she wanted. "What lesson is this?"

I smirked, knowing she could see it in the darkness. "That not everything comes easy."

CHAPTER
ELEVEN

S ir Eralt of Windpeak came that next morning. The wagon was packed, the horses saddled and readied. We rode out quickly to meet our hostage. As Stroudsburg trailed behind us, I felt like I was on a new type of quest. There was no one to kill, no loot or organization to get our hands on. It was a journey to see Allie brought back from the dead and another girl married. The end of stories, not the beginning.

To say it was strange to head out with the girls as well as Trith would be an understatement.

"This is something, brother." Trith drank from a waterskin as he rode a small trotter next to me. "Back to these feudal lands."

"That it is." I pulled the reins on the nag Rushe had given me. When I leaned back in the saddle I winced; something pressed me in my rear pocket. I withdrew it, staring at the scroll Evior had given me.

"Oh, brother, don't tell me you went to him." Trith shook his head.

"I put it in my saddle bag." I leaned over and slipped it away.

"Contract scrolls have a way of ending up where they want. You didn't open it, right?"

I rolled my eyes. "No, I didn't open it."

"Good." Trith gathered his reins. "Because only one collegiate uses those anymore. And that shapeshifting fuck is slippery."

"Quit your barkin'." I laughed when he snapped his head over to me. "Old *man*."

"Davik, I am prettier than you."

"Let's hope you stay that way."

The warhammer tapped steadily on the side of the saddle. The liquid metal—some miracle of alchemy—slid back and forth as we rode.

Eralt led our party south, breaking off from the main merchant's road. It was another half hour of riding, the hills shifting to the long green grasses of the Lowlands, until we came across Puris.

The squire held the twin reins of horses, along with our hostage.

"That her?" Trith stood in his saddle. "Seems young for a twice-bride."

"Her younger sister, the one I pulled out of that dungeon in Trinth."

Sariel, Trith, and I rode up to join Eralt, who climbed down from his horse.

Puris smiled at me. "Davik."

I nodded. "How are you, squire?"

"Well enough. Glad to see you all."

Eralt walked towards Mara. "I present, Lady Mara Sewell of Windpeak."

Mara was a homely girl. But now that she wasn't a starved

and terrified girl from a dungeon, I saw the resemblance to her sister Elyse.

She smiled at me, but there was hesitation behind it. She had seen me in that Trinth dungeon. I wondered what she thought now—if she tried to make sense of the man who had killed her sister's husband but saved her. "Hello. Good to see you again, Sir Davik."

Eralt cleared his throat. Both Trith and Sariel sported small grins. "Dark—Davik is not a knight, Lady Mara. He is your captor-ward. You remember what we spoke of on the way here?"

Mara stepped forward, bowing. "I am your hostage. Windpeak extends its protection and hospitality to you." Then she glanced through our collection of shifting horses at the wagon. "Vorga? Elina?"

Vorga leapt up from the wagon. "Mara!"

Mara ran towards Vorga until they gripped in a hug. Vorga hefted her off the ground. "It's so good to see you again! You look fabulous!"

"So do you!" Mara giggled. Then she looked at the wagon. "Elina! I never thanked you properly for tending to me. And Brim! All of you! Is that minotaur here?"

"Rahh." Brim shook his head.

Elina smiled and leaned over the wagon, hugging Mara from above. "You're looking so well, Mara."

"Real threat of danger," I said to Sariel as we watched an exchange of hugs given all around.

"Oh, yes." Sariel steadied her horse. "Right group of cutthroats on that wagon."

Eralt coughed and walked up to my horse, his features reddening in the sun. "Lady Mara is under your protection. But I'd remind you, propriety demands—"

"I have a separate tent for her," I assured the old knight. "One of the girls will share it with her."

The last thing I needed was any accusation of stolen virtue. The Lowlands were still feudal. Being caught in a room alone with the wrong woman without an escort might lead you to the gallows. The faith of the Sword was still followed here, though it was waning.

"Can I ride with you?" Mara asked Vorga, who was already helping her up to the wagon. "Oh, what are these books! Have you read them all?"

"Come on," I called to the group. "We've got daylight to burn."

Eralt and Puris led the way, while Mara, Elina, and Vorga fell into rushed conversation on the back of the wagon. Tyra kept a watchful eye from Polly's horseback, with Karley behind her. Of our group, she wasn't enamored with highborn titles.

"Sariel?" I looked at my elven lover.

"Yes, love?"

"Keep that girl the hell away from me."

Sariel laughed. "I think you have a different admirer right now."

I gave her the side-eye as we rode. "That so?"

The battle-elf shrugged, biting her lip. "She might have an admirer, too. With dark armor." Before I could respond, Sariel leaned over her horse and tugged on my breastplate, kissing me. "I love you, my river."

Her words from the tavern, the day I had nearly bled out in the booth. As I glanced around the Lowlands, the high cliffs and the flat plains leading to the sea, I was ready to head to Oakshire after this.

Used to take contracts from princes...

Trith rode up to Puris. "You looking at my friend's women, squire? You better be careful. You know he eats people, right?"

Puris looked shocked. "No, sir! I did—"

"Leave the kid alone, Trith," I called up. "He's alright."

Trith laughed and clapped Puris on the back. "Tell me about your battle at Hollyhead. I want to hear what I missed out on."

"I like your friend, Davik." Sariel watched the same conversation I did. "He's nicer than I thought he'd be."

"Yeah." I watched Trith joking with Puris. "Always was the most easy-going of us."

"Seems sad, though," Sariel noted. "Elves have deep feelings. Die of shame, of grief."

I reached over and grabbed her hand. "Love, too?"

"No silly." Sariel kissed my knuckle. "That's why we live forever."

WE MADE GOOD TIME. The luster of the road began to whittle at the group. Hands waved at horse flies. Bathroom breaks were requested.

Brim looked back at me by mid-afternoon. *Ugly-man. The women haven't stopped talking for hours. Please kill me.*

"We'll stop soon!" I called up to Brim.

I'll drive this wagon off the cliff. I'll kill us all. With cliffs.

"You're doing great!" I shouted.

"I'll give Brim a break," Sariel said. "Put him on my horse and tether it."

"We need someone to watch Mara tonight," I told her. "Best it's one of you."

Sariel winked at me. "Your pick, my love. Though... I might like a little tent time tonight. Before you go off romancing someone else."

I laughed. "You're greedy, you know that?" When she stood in her saddle, I gave her a quick spank as she rode up.

Once Sariel left, Tyra pulled Polly over to me with Karley sitting behind her. "Hey, Davik, I think Polly might need a break. She's tired from the ride to Stroudsburg. I can feel it."

"Alright." I leaned over and grabbed Karley, lifting her from the saddle. Tyra watched me with a grin. I sat Karley in front of me and handed her the reins.

"Mmm, that's better." Tyra reached out and touched my hand, sending a pulse of emotion that felt like approval.

"I knew you needed another day in the city."

Tyra winked at me and pulled Polly off. "Going to go chat with Mara. See if our hostage has any juicy gossip."

I watched Tyra gallop away. She had become a great rider. Polly tolerated me when I rode her, but she molded to Tyra.

"Needed a break from being wrapped around Tyra. Every time she looks at you, I get a pulse of emotion." Karley settled back against me. "That okay?"

She was sitting on my lap, the soft pants on her like a second skin. "That's fine."

"What were you and Sariel talking about?"

"Just figuring someone to watch Mara tonight. Vorga may—"

"I'll do it," Karley cut me off.

I leaned over. "Yeah?"

Karley shrugged. "She's our hostage, right? Won't exactly be afraid if it's Vorga or Elina."

We continued riding, and Karley shifted against me. It reminded me of all the times she had pressed against me in the bar. The day continued like that, the stamp of hooves as we traveled the roads into the Lowlands. The sun eventually slipped away behind distant clouds, promising rain.

"You cold?" I asked Karley after a moment. "You shivered. Is it—"

"Just a chill." Karley leaned back against me as we traveled up a narrowing cliffside. The wide fan of our group became a single file. "I haven't had to cast. I think it's closing. The frost spell eroded."

"How do you feel about that?"

Karley shrugged. "Might make things easier. Back to being a bartender." But her voice held the weight of disappointment. *Everyone wants to be special, especially if they're not.* That's what she had said to me in Hollyhead. I still felt her in my runes.

"You know, it's not—"

"So this girl, Elyse, you were her guard or something?"

I sighed. It's amazing you can have someone sitting on your lap and never be further from them. That was Karley. Close, then far. Then missing. "More like bodyguard. It was a contract." I held the reins tight.

"Did you two ever, you know..." Karley blurted out.

"No. I was there to guard against that."

I leaned over in the saddle, taking a dagger I had in there in a leather sheath and handing it to her. "For your watch tonight. I want you to keep this on you when we're in the Lowlands."

Karley took it. "Not sure I know what to do with it."

"Hard to block a knife. Most people grab and swing."

"What about you?"

I laughed. "Not something you want to know."

Karley's tone grew edged. "I'm here, aren't I?" That same edge that always seemed to be between us. "Show me the real way."

Maybe it was the ember of soulfire in her, coaxing me forward. If she asked, I'd show her.

Karley yelped when I grabbed a fistful of her hair and

yanked it back, pressing a single finger against the side of her neck. "You take 'em by surprise, like this."

But she wasn't scared. A grin broke across her lips, and I noticed how close my mouth was to her ear. She had picked up a new fragrance somewhere in Stroudsburg. Smelled like rain on stone in a garden.

"Not across?" Karley whispered, pressing back against me.

"Through." I pressed my finger against her neck. "Until you're halfway in. Twist and then push. Less cutting, more gutting."

"That's... specific."

I let go of her hair. "You asked. But not something you need to know. Don't hurt Mara. She's a hostage, but it's more a formality."

Karley cocked her head from side to side. "I think I get it. Some Lowland ritual?"

"For enemies seeking peace."

"So..." Karley squinted against a break of sun. "How many dates are you taking to the wedding?"

I watched Sariel ahead of us. "Well, if we're going to make an impression... I have an Embriel warrior."

"True."

"A faen cook and imbuer. Maybe Tyra's some girl I kidnapped. She imbues me to keep me from attacking innocent people. Vorga is obviously another bodyguard who writes down my dark deeds, thus the paper."

"Obviously." Karley kept her tone flat like she was bluffing in a dice game. "Elina might be a nice touch."

"Obviously, Darkshire needs healing. But if I want to put on a bit of theater, I'd need an actress. You know any?"

Karley shut her eyes as we navigated the top of the cliff. "I might. What's the part?"

"Dark sorceress. Evil witch."

"One you captured?" Karley shifted as I steadied her hips, pulling her back as we descended. "An old enemy? You going to keep me in a trunk?"

I couldn't see if she was smiling, but it sounded like she was. "I think Darkshire's lover bathes in blood. It helps her spells."

"You and baths." Karley wiped her lip. "What's this witch like? Other than blood baths, of course."

"Deadly. She can see through walls. Turn men into sheep. Makes a decent cocktail."

"Ah, the sheep. Anything else?"

I kicked the nag into a trot. "Beautiful, of course."

WE MADE camp with our back to high stone peaks. I remembered camping near them once, maybe, after conscription and on our way to war. The stones were like the scales of a great stone dragon, long slain.

Tyra handled dinner, whipping a stew up from our wagon of ingredients.

"Davik, be a love." The redhead smiled at me. "Fetch us some local meat? Take Vorga."

I bowed. "As the cook commands."

I took Vorga hunting for Lowland rabbits that were out in the spring. Knights hunted wolves often, as did farmers here. But as a youth, you could make a good bit of copper trimming rabbits from a field. Young boys dreamed of being knights, defending castles of carrots from long-eared invaders.

"What do we use?" Vorga asked me.

I held up several tree branches I had broken and whittled smooth. They were about a foot in length and solid. "Try to throw it side-arm."

In the end, among those moving hares, we bagged three of them. With Vorga's strong arm, they died or were stunned quickly and dispatched even quicker. I showed her how to push-gut a hare, which made her squeal.

"Oh my gods, Davik!" Vorga stared at me as I shook the entrails out. "It all came out!"

I laughed. "You're not this squeamish when we clean a boar."

"Yes." Vorga stood closer to me. "But it isn't so... explosive."

We walked with a string of rabbits for the pot, stopping at a small stream to wash our hands. The wind blew the long grasses, curling her brown hair over her face.

"Excited for the wedding?" I asked.

"I am." Vorga kept stepping. "I know you worry. But I think it's a brave thing you're doing."

I stopped walking. The wind swirled around us, whipping the grass like soft sheets. Vorga stood shoulder-to-shoulder with me.

"Such a pretty land." Vorga reached out to hold my hand.

It was. It always had been. When I turned to Vorga, her tavern dress flapping like some lost maiden on the moor, I was captivated by her. Even after all this time, all the nights in her room, she could take my breath away. Seeing her run and hunt, seeing her soft smile. She took life as it came. Same as she had taken me, keeping a piece of me in her pocket.

"Wrote you something," Vorga whispered.

When she said it, it felt important. It felt like we were the only two people in the world. The sea in the distance, below the flat cliffs. The rocks behind us were like the shadows of giants, whistling softly as the wind cut through them.

"Did you?" I asked, feeling the softness of the moment. And it should feel soft, I decided. Even with the armor of my past on, and holding onto this girl, that was my future. A most-orc who had a big heart and brown eyes so deep you could drown in them.

"Took me a long time to write it." Vorga pulled a small notebook from the back of her dress like she had been keeping it there.

Her face was the same expression as it had when she arrived at the Dragon's Nest, as if seeing some new part of me she hadn't realized was there.

It was a small vellum, something she had bought herself. Small enough to fit in your pocket. I untied the long leather string. When I held the leather between my fingers, I looked up at her for confirmation. She nodded. Boar leather, from one of our hunts. Not something she had bought, something she had made.

I opened the first page, shielding it from the wind. In her flowing script, three words greeted me. Bold in their truth, with nothing else on the page.

I love you.

My heart climbed in my chest. "It's perfect." When I flipped the page, the same thing was written again.

I love you.

I let the pages go, turning in the wind. Each one marked by three words. As if they were the only ones that could be said.

Vorga's eyes glistened, and her tears might have stayed, if the wind hadn't slid them away. They streaked across her face, traveling like comets across the freckled stars of her green flesh. Her voice was a shouted sob in the wind, trying to reach me. "You know I'm in love with you, right? I don't think I can ever not be."

I slid the book into my pocket, feeling the power of her words. But they were just words, trying, but never truly capturing, what I felt for her. Somewhere along those evenings, as more women and more days and nights came into Oakshire, I was given another gift.

And like most things in life, the gifts you don't deserve mean the most.

I stepped towards her. "I love you."

We kissed in a new way. Not the slow lust of our first hunt together or the frantic need in the tavern when we stepped off somewhere. Even here, in this union, she had ventured something.

When we fell into the grass, the wind swirled past us, and we embedded into the earth like a cocoon. Vorga said my name as we kissed, running my hand over her heart.

"It's yours," she whispered. I felt the heat of her, of us, as the wind crept past. Flowing from the hillside down towards the sea, only to be pushed back in its eternal struggle. I parted her thighs, feeling her welcome me, drawing me forth with her hand until I entered her.

When we made love, it was in agreement. Pinned to the soft rich soil of this place, two people in search of stillness inside one another. The words of her book protruded from my pocket, shifting as we writhed in heat. Written in ink that couldn't be denied.

WHEN VORGA and I walked back to camp, Tyra grinned at us from between two campfires. "My favorite hunters. What did you bring?"

I held up a string of rabbits. "I'll get to work cleaning them."

Trith wandered down from his own bedroll, situated high above the camp. He always liked to sleep outside, save for the severest of elements. "I'll give you a hand."

When Tyra looked at Vorga, the most-orc nodded.

"Yes!" Tyra squealed and jumped up and down, holding Vorga. "And you were worried!"

Mara wandered over, eager to be included. "Worried about what?"

Vorga grinned over Tyra's mass of red hair. "Nothing. Just something I made for someone."

I bit into the rabbit's back, making a hole before peeling the skin off. Sariel smirked, seeing Tyra and Vorga jump up and down. In the distance, the swing of practice steel sounded as Eralt and Puris trained together.

"Feels like old times." I crouched next to Trith and handed him a rabbit.

The wood elf laughed. "The hell it does. People are happy."

Tyra did wonderfully for dinner. She used Linlock's frying pan to sear the rabbit, stewing it with garlic before chopping and adding it to the pot. Bowls were handed around once the stew simmered for a few hours. Trith and Brim walked off to share a pipe.

"Enough for everyone?" I asked Tyra. When I bent down next to her, I slid my hand over her rear.

She bit her lip and looked at me. "More than enough... What about you? Did you bring enough for everyone?"

I kissed her cheek, and she held my face there for a moment. "You'll find out."

As night came, we stoked the fires higher.

"We have hardtack," Eralt offered when we ladled a bowl of stew for him.

"I'd say we're fine to share a meal together, don't you?" I looked up at him. Here I was, serving my former enemy.

Eralt nodded slowly, taking the bowl. "Aye, I'd say that."

"Thanks, Mister Davik." Puris smiled when I served him.

We sat around the two campfires in one circle, watching the flicker of the flames on the high boulders around us.

"This is delicious, Tyra." Mara raised her bowl. "Truly wonderful. I've never had faen cooking. But you might have just converted me."

Tyra smiled. And I could see her make the effort to be kind to the same highborn who she had once been indentured to. "You're always welcome to stop in Oakshire again."

Vorga settled next to me. "Just no kidnappings this time."

Mara laughed. "Oh, believe me, I was visiting friends in the Midlands. My father won't let me go anywhere without an escort now."

Sariel swirled her bowl, reaching forward to the fire to grab a small loaf of bread. "That's good sense these days. Eralt says the bandits have been driven from your lands. Is that true?"

"It is." Mara smiled at Eralt. "Though he's too modest to say it was he who did that."

Eralt bowed his head. "It is my duty, nothing less. But much honor goes to the squire corps that Puris leads. He has done very well."

Elina walked back from the privy we had dug, her soft robes sliding as she stepped through the grasses. "Got room for me?"

I raised a bowl I had ready for her. She hopped down and sat between my legs, leaning back. Mara grinned at the sight of it. "Midlanders are pretty casual."

"Blame the Mistress," Karley muttered from her bowl.

Elina ate in my lap, leaning back into me. "This is nice."

"That it is," I said and kissed the top of her head.

Eralt and Puris both stood, thanking Tyra for the meal. They gathered several bowls to go wash. I had to give it to them, they fit into a camp quite well.

"The watches?" Eralt asked me.

"We'll take first. Then we'll grab you two."

The knight and his squire bowed. Mara looked at Karley. "If it's not too much of a bother, could we go to sleep? I'm not used to traveling like this."

Karley looked around until she remembered she was in charge of Mara. "Oh, yeah sure."

Mara stood. "You've all been lovely captors. Thank you."

"Goodnight," Elina said with a smile.

"Let us know if you need anything." Sariel gave her a small wave.

"So, Trith"—Tyra pointed at him—"what embarrassing stories do you have about Davik?"

Trith grinned across from us. Even Brim looked interested, turning next to him. "Oh, I can't remember any."

Tyra laughed. "Now I'm really interested!"

Trith shook his head. "Awful memory, I'm truly sorry."

Elina leaned back into me. "Boys and their secrets. Good for you two." Then she glanced at Sariel with a grin. "Though I bet some here would love to hear of former exploits."

Sariel laughed and threw a hunk of bread at the halfling.

"Did he ever date any humans?" Vorga asked, perking up.

Trith's smile froze, and he shared a look with me. Some stories weren't meant to be shared or revisited. They're meant to be buried with the person you built them with. "Not... that I can remember."

Sariel picked up on the look and stepped in to shift the mood quickly. "Tell us about your homeland. The girls here haven't met someone from the Copper Forests."

"Gladly." Trith leaned back and withdrew his pipe, offering it to Brim. "If anyone likes to partake, this is from my home."

The girls shook their heads. Brim eagerly reached for the pipe.

We stayed up another hour until the girls rose and

announced they were off to bed, one by one. One of Trith's woodland tents was ours, and it was large enough to house five of us. Brim's eyes grew redder and redder as the stories went on until he growled he was going to bed and went to the separate tent.

"Davik," Trith asked as the girls finally stood to go to bed, "walk the perimeter with me?"

"Ah," I said, understanding. "Of course."

As we walked from the stamped-out campfires, Trith and I went towards the rear boulders where we had dug the latrine. "Thanks."

I shrugged. "No problem."

"When I'm on my own, it's fine. Just. I know it's *not* a job, but it feels like a job."

"Hey," I told him. "Don't have to explain anything to me."

I drew my sword and turned my back to the latrine while he did his business. Trith could never go unless someone was standing near him. Not since we had found two men traveling with us, dead with their pants down in the latrine, their throats cut by cultists of the red paladins. Ever since then he always needed someone near.

Trith whistled a tune. The nameless song brought me back to the thousand times I had done this. Any sign of it being interrupted would tell me to turn around and invade his privacy. I heard the rustle of the waterskin and scrub of soap we had set up after he filled in part of the latrine.

"Thanks." He dried his hands with a pulse of sorcery, making his soul flare against my runes for a moment. "I was dying around that campfire."

I laughed as we walked along the boulders, stepping along one that came out of the hill like a platform. We looked down at our camp from twenty feet away.

Warmth waited for me in a tent, but for my brother, I'd

brave the cold and dark. Always. And I saw in the sag of his shoulders that he needed it. "Thanks for coming."

Trith settled down next to me. "You've built a good thing, Davik. I'm glad."

"What about you?" I looked at him. "Who's this mystery woman who knocked all the other earrings from your ear?"

Trith smiled softly, laying his spear staff across his legs. "You'll need wine to get that one out of me."

I raised the waterskin to him. "To Eron."

"Eron."

We sat there for a time, not talking about our fallen friend. A man I had once despised. If I shut my eyes, I'd feel his bloody hands on my chest.

Funny how men you hate turn into ones you miss. The silence was heavy, and we were together in it. As present as the ghost we thought of.

"You've got a good life now, you know. Those are good women," Trith said after a time.

"Just following your lead."

The wood elf laughed. Far beyond us, cattle moved among pens near the towns along the sea. "None of the rings on my ear ever met each other. Even I wasn't that crazy. What's Oakshire like?"

I leaned back, both of us swinging our legs gently off the edge of the boulder. "Peaceful. Warm, even in the winter. House full of women, tavern full of people."

"You know I always—" Trith began.

"You didn't leave me." I turned to him. "After Rochdale. It died before that. I left you. Left you to chase knights and a doomed rebellion and blood. Just didn't know how to want anything else."

"I know." Trith was quiet a moment. "Still hear those city bells in my dreams."

"I do, too."

"Felt like I fucking left you," Trith muttered. "Went home to my family in the copper forests. Thought the leaves and the rivers would soothe me. Stayed for years, just trying to... trying to fucking..." he trailed off.

"Breathe?"

Trith laughed without a sound. "Yeah. A decade of campaigning, and after Daggar? We should've called it then. But Rochdale... for Eron. We had to. But what did it change?" Trith gestured to the fields beyond us. "What did any of it change? At least you got Fenner. But he's one bastard out of ten thousand."

"Why'd you leave home, Trith?"

Trith picked up his spear and leaned his head against it. "Heard the Silver Hands did you in. All I could think was it wouldn't have happened had I been there. So I went to Swinford. Brought everything. Every scroll, every wand. When I was done, I was still standing." He sounded disappointed. "So I went to Stroudsburg, another ghost slinking through the streets."

I put my hand on his shoulder and pulled him in. "You're crazy, you know that?"

Trith glared at me. "You'd have done the same. You'd have done worse."

He had me there.

Trith shook his head. "Couldn't go home after that. My old man called me *Quinamir* when he first saw me. Copper-tainted. Bloodstained. That old hypocrite."

"Woods didn't help?"

Trith laughed. "The silence drove me crazy. It took me a year to figure out why I was so wound up. No sound of a horse or a man marching. No tavern. No laughter around a campfire."

"It's alright now," I told him.

Trith inhaled. "I keep looking at you, Davik, making sure it's real. It's like I don't get to give up anymore. Was figuring on going back to Daggar, just sitting next to Devan."

We stared at the valley we had once waged a guerilla campaign in. Not for armies or for gold. Just for blood. All around us were the spaces between the boulders, giving form to what wasn't there.

"Miss the hell out of them, sometimes," Trith breathed out the words. "Wish Rayleth were here."

"Me too."

CHAPTER
TWELVE

The man watches the camp of the Justicars, so close to their quarry. A small flame flickers between the rocks they use for shelter. His dire bear is silent behind him.

The psychic power is nearly nauseating, this close to the fiend the paladin's target. The man extends his senses out, feeling along the dark cavern walls where it hides. His presence is welcomed. The red souls of lower vampiric thralls cry out in betrayal, recently devoured by their master.

The vampire grins psychically. *I'm all out of friends.*

The voice is ancient, tinged with the depravity that grows too often in the deathless.

These three will sever your head tomorrow. The necromancer sneers.

Think of the paladins. These Justicars. I know you, fleshcrafter. Their vessels will serve you. I can turn them.

He considers this. The flesh of the Justicars will be imbued with the strength of Selene. The heartiness of divine touch. Much is lost when casting a soul into a fine vessel. But if the soul is bendable?

Impossible.

Not... impossible. The fiend is frantic. *Their goddess is fickle. Aren't all gods?*

A vision comes to the necromancer, and he accepts it. He sees a beautiful pale woman, black of hair, trapped under the grip of crimson-touched thralls.

Lyra's soul was purer than theirs, and still, her goddess abandoned her.

The paladin screams as a female thrall crawls forth. The bodies of her massacred party surround her, a dozen dead and drained. Fangs—white in the evening light—dip to her throat as she screams.

"Help me!"

He feels the vampire lord's insidious enjoyment at her fall, as a single oath is broken and the enchantments fall away. Her irises turn crimson.

She still lives. The vampire is proud. *She will come to me in the end. A ribbon ready to be bound.*

And if you are freed? the man asks.

Cities, villages... you collect souls, necromancer. I prepare them.

The man nods. He may kill this one. He does not like degenerates, nor does he suffer them to live. There are those wealthy enough that have sought his services for sordid affairs. Their fates were far worse than their requests. The dead are tools at times, but they are not toys.

I will fell these three. The man stares in the psychic tunnel at the vampire. *If you do not deliver, I will house your soul in sunlight.*

A dark chuckle is the reply. *Free me, and it will be done.*

"Rayleth," the man whispers. He is surprised to see vapor pour from his own lungs. So much feeding as of late. He will need it for the journey.

The elf turns to him, eyes burning green. His soul is so

strong, the man has to use more force than controlling the bear.

"Fell them. Leave them alive."

Rayleth immediately walks through the padded snow. The moon is bright, and the man watches in lurid fascination. Deeper in his soul dungeon, he opens the wicket so Theris the Red can see their creation.

There are three Justicars of Selene. It is too cold to brave sleep, in case they will not wake.

"*Halt*!" a voice shouts.

The necromancer reaches out, battling with their divine influence. He cannot sever the link of their goddess, but he can fight it. It gives him pleasure as his blade ward charges into their midst, strangling the conduit of their faith.

Rayleth's skill is no longer impeded by self-preservation. A half-orc Justicar rises first, his mace flashing out in the night. Rayleth sidesteps it, rolling. Once he takes a sword from the human paladin, the end has already begun.

They shout for blessings. They shout for strength, but Selene's boons are a trickle. Rayleth is a blur. A flurry of steel and final strikes against banded metal armor.

The Justicars do their best. The man shudders when the first lifeblood paints the snow. The female drow kneels, grasping at a wound.

Both the human and the half-orc spread. The campfire flickers as they surround Rayleth. The elven swordsman seems to watch them without seeing, placing both of them in his blindspot.

The campfire turns to trampled combat. Breaths and shouts punctuated by the stamp of burning embers—as if these three fought in the forge of some smithy god.

The greenskin surges forward, growling with his shield. Rayleth plants a rotten boot on it, pivoting as if it were the ground itself. The human's sword slides underneath his spinning form, and the little blood in the necromancer quickens at the sight of such a glorious dance. In a flick, Rayleth cuts through bone and human palate.

The orc rebounds, trying to shield his fallen comrades. But Rayleth is there. His muscles gleam in the night, before embedding the longsword through the shifting split armor, puncturing a stomach in steel and acid.

Theris the Red grins from his prison. *Marvelous.*

The man agrees but shuts the wicket in response. The bargain has been made, and when the time comes, he may consider the blood mage's request.

Rayleth stands immobile, the sword gripped in his hands. When the necromancer approaches, he is rebinding the flesh of the paladins, staunching the more grievous of their wounds.

"Move them into the spire," the man orders.

Rayleth tenses as if he is not sure what he hears. He doesn't look at the man. The necromancer tightens the control over him, but as he reaches for those reins, he realizes something.

He is in Rayleth's blindspot.

The blade is a blink. It would sever his weakened neck. And the reattachment, while possible, would be quite the delay.

The blade hovers a grave's whisper from his throat. Rayleth's eyes are burning. So much ferocity. So much cunning. The dire bear screams in the distance. The man had released his control to stop his own demise.

"Inside," the man says again.

Rayleth stares at him. Then he drops the blade and bends low, a dreaming slave. He picks up the paladins and carries them to the cave.

That had been close. The man has spread his control too widely. Created too fine a weapon. The rivermen, the bear, Rayleth. He needs loyal servants.

Thank you for your offering. The vampire seethes with pleasure at his freedom.

The man follows when Rayleth brings the last of the Justicars. It is time to meet their host.

THE SPIRE IS A CAVERN, bringing a deep cold that gnaws at the necromancer's bones. But his are not the only bones here. The gnawed remains of a dozen thralls litter the ground in putrid decoration.

"What is your name?" the man asks.

A wet sound comes from the shadows, like a mouth too large opening. "I've had many names... bone mage." The accent is old. Too old for him to try to remember its origin.

The dark elf Justicar coughs, swinging from her chains. All that remains in this cavern are bones and chains. "Kraevor. He is Kraevor. Strike him down."

"Some call me that," the fiend admits. "But not those who truly know me."

Rayleth watches Kraevor in the shadows, tracking his movements.

"Your slave did magnificently." Kraevor is tall. The tallest vampire that the necromancer has seen. Something in his voice reminds the man of Theris the Red. This crimson-touched can change his appearance. His size, as well. Long black hair drifts down either side of his head. Hands with fingers too long. A wider face than expected, like a cave king of the Icelands.

Of the three mortals hanging before him, one is a half-orc male, another is a human male, and the one the fiend lingers most towards is the female drow.

"Selene will cast you down," she snarls from her chains.

The necromancer watches as Kraevor slips a claw into the

wound on her side that he recently closed. The paladin fills the cavern with screams.

The fiend sups at her side, groaning gutturally.

"Unchain this one for me." He pulls his long tongue from within her wound. "I would hear other noises from her mouth."

"You will hear your own," the necromancer warns. "There is game among these hills for you to drink."

It is taking a large amount of his power to counteract the divine blessings of Selene. At a nod from the man, Rayleth steps forward and raises the blade to Kraevor's neck.

The creature laughs, running his fingers over the sword. "Very well."

"You said you can sever them?" the necromancer asks, his voice cold and cutting. He feels the treachery of this one simmering beneath the surface.

The vampire grins, predatory and gleeful. "Thirst," he whispers. "Once the hand of their whore goddess falls from their shoulders, they will fill with sweet despair. Their souls will be yours to mold."

The man nods. *You mean yours to own.*

The necromancer does not have the patience for torture. The dead are to be respected, not played with. He could break the paladins himself, but it would take time —too much time. And time is something he does not have.

The vampire relents from his theatrics. His lip curls as he begins his darker work. He turns them, with fang and saliva, one by one. The process is as insidious as it is quick. Fever wracks their bodies. Blood and organs shift, trembling under the onslaught of unholy consummation. The cavern rattles with twitching chains.

They plead, and they cry out to their goddess for

vengeance, but she is silent. Like most paladial deities, she demands her followers find her; she does not come to them.

The necromancer watches their faiths fail with a hint of reverence.

We are all orphans, in the end.

Their prayers trail off after a time, their cries fading into soft, pitiful murmurs. Fangs lengthen in their mouths. This is interesting. The necromancer studies the half-orc's tusks as they fracture, twin holes forming to drink blood.

"Their transformation is beautiful," the vampire says behind him.

"It is an arcane infection," the necromancer counters.

"Blood," the half-orc murmurs. "Blood."

The vampire raises a long claw. "See his fall."

The man approaches, seeing the line of his tattooed oath broken. The fever and agony have done their work.

The gods do not deserve us.

The golden auras of their souls flicker and then finally extinguish. All that remains is the aura of blood-hunger, twisting them.

"Imbue them..." the vampire offers. "Turn them to what they might be."

The man hides his smile. *As if I would strengthen three of your followers.*

The necromancer has other plans. These bodies are prime conduits of the divine... and the profane. But to let these souls linger when tied to Kraevor? A fool's errand.

"A moment." The necromancer raises his hands. Solar light swirls between his hands, creating a barrier that backs Kraevor into the cave.

"What are you doing!"

"Keeping you there," the man says. But he realizes he isn't

speaking. He is receding...no, that isn't the right word. He is falling. Visiting a place most denigrated.

Himself.

THE MAN STRIDES. Here, within the confines of the fortress of his chest dungeon, he surveys the glimpse of the world that will be.

His chest dungeon is one of his greatest prides. He was not alone in its build or its design. The black fortress sits under an eternal dawn of violet and red light, swirling like rivers in the purest rivers of the Veil. Death is beautiful.

Let it never be forgotten.

The first soul he ever kept for himself was a master builder. The woman was both an engineer, a carpenter, and a visionary. For years he gave her what she needed—soul workers, laborers, profane overseers. Her fame of design wasn't influenced by landscape. Rather, she would sit in the mornings with kings and lords of old, studying them, and then set to task on building a keep that matched their very souls.

In his chest dungeon, she has done miraculously. You cannot enslave geniuses, not if you wish the true essence of their work. Her asking price had truly been a delight. She wished for the final stones in the spire to entomb her forever, embedding her into her masterpiece.

A necromancer is a bargainer above all else.

Now he walks within himself. He tries not to spend too much time here. It's too easy to forget your purpose when the sweet pillow of death is nearby. But as he sees the thousand souls sliding in the ethereal river, he takes a moment to watch the sunless world. A place without night or day.

You did well, Avaris.

Somewhere deep in the mortaring, she shrieks.

A multitude of souls rattle the doors of the chest dungeon below him, making sweet music of the mad and the hopeless. Every race is here—some long extinct. Creatures that defy logic. The stretched souls of shivering mages, still alive, sit pinioned in their eternal torment as he walks from the black spire.

He brings a lantern, casting the path beyond him in violet bobbing light. In the distance, he hears the thunder of hooves. There are those in his soul who think they are alive, and there are those who know they are dead.

But a select few know they *are* death.

He places the lantern on a single stone pillar, the impossibly high tower behind him stretching like a needle into the iris of himself.

Come, riders. Come, brothers of old.

Time does not truly exist in this place. It doesn't move. It lingers in pockets like gasps of air. He waits, skeletal hands crossed over his black rags.

A glint of white and yellow bone appears. The death knight is massive. He has grown in the untamed fields and plains around this castle. Once a warrior and renowned cleric of death.

"Too long have your banners been held by your hand alone." The man smiles at the Bone Knight. "There will be knights among your sortie, should you ride with me."

The Bone Knight stares at him from a helm of skull. Spikes and spindles and the yellow of ivory encase his massive form. His sword is the jawbone of a large beast, the teeth like serrated edges.

Yes.

The man is pleased. The Bone Knight moves a slow fist over

his unbeating heart, and in his jagged soul, there is a terrible hunger.

The next to appear is of glinting shadow. He is there, and then he is not. A shivering shadow stands before the man, twice as tall as a human. A spear of darkness is clamped in his gauntlets.

"I have such light for you to extinguish," the man offers. "For a year, I will free you from this place. I will support your form as you ride among the Lowlands, feasting on the lanterns and hearths of all."

There is no response. The Shadow Knight regards him for a moment before appearing behind him. Apparently, a deal has been struck.

The final visitor to appear doesn't arrive, so much as he rises. He has become the mortar of the fallen bastion. His form is the most humanoid. The reverence in his eyes is fanatical in the soft gelatin, as if they might wither from his eye sockets. A blade of rust is clasped in his hands.

The necromancer raises a hand at the Knight of Rot. The death knight does not move.

"Flesh, fear..." the man muses as he picks through the offerings to win this thing of decay. "I seek the bones of a fine warrior."

"Brides—" The Decay Knight's voice is a hoarse growl. "To wither."

The man considers this. The Knight of Rot would entomb them in decay. He thinks of the halfling cleric, so pure and devout to her goddess of love. He thinks of the Embriel warrioress and her never-aged flesh.

"As you desire," the man offers. "Never-aged flesh. Sanctified."

"Show me," the Knight of Rot demands.

The man bows and conjures a memory of the engraved man. Women around a tavern, smiling.

"Brides," the Knight of Rot confirms. He will not touch them. He will place them in his rotting keep. Guarding them for eternity.

Slowly, he walks forward and takes his place behind the man.

"Come, brothers." He turns and walks towards the castle. A drawbridge awaits, where the knights will ride their mounts into the shackled vessels of the sanctified Justicars.

"Bone," the necromancer declares, placing a hand on the human paladin's forehead.

The Knight of Bone emerges, manifesting into the material realm. The human's forehead cracks like porcelain as the death knight lays siege to him. He screams as his soul is trampled. The transformation is violent—his armor shifts, calcifying into bone, jagged and polished. The vampiric taint is eradicated, burned like rot from a wound.

"What are you doing?" Kraevor screeches from his prison of light.

"I do not need your weakness," the man hisses. "Only its use."

Turning to the half-orc, the necromancer speaks again. "Decay."

The Knight of Rot raises his putrid banner and rides forth. His armor is withered and rusted. The half-orc thrashes against his chains as the knight invades his soul. His tusks darken as they rot. The green flesh necrotizes into putrid shades of green and gray. The stench of the grave and rust fills the air as his once-sanctified armor flakes to the floor.

"Fool!" the vampire hisses behind him. He launches forward, but Rayleth is there. Weaving, spinning, striking back. Even for all his skill, the fiend will shred him apart eventually.

The Knight of Bone breaks free from his shackles. Beside him, the Knight of Decay opens his maw—a tongueless abyss. They lumber forward to join the melee behind the necromancer.

The drow woman stares at the necromancer. The exhaustion is so final in her eyes. If he had sympathy, he would give it to her. The pain of falling from her goddess.

"Rest now," the necromancer says as he touches her. "There is solace in *shadow*."

The woman's eyes go wide, blackening as her heart halts mid-beat. From the depths within him rides the Shadow Knight, its form a writhing void. Her soul is consumed utterly. It crashes over her like a black tide.

The necromancer turns, watching Kraevor leap from the stalagmites, battling his forces. Next to him, the Shadow Knight waits, seeking a command. With a wave of his hand, he could send his final knight against him and end this.

But the necromancer raises his hand, commanding his forces to cease their assault.

The vampire stares down at him from a crag of rock. For all his sinister desires, he is a creature. Nothing more, nothing less.

"Our bargain is complete."

Kraevor's grin widens. A terrible thing. A thing that belongs in the dark. "Fool." Then he launches himself in blinding speed at the necromancer's knights.

The Knight of Bone staggers, a ruinous gash cleaving from the shoulder to the dead pit of his chest. Bone and sinew splinter. The necromancer snarls, forcing the pieces to reknit.

Kraevor is already gone, his laughter trailing after him. Rayleth tenses, turning to give chase.

"Leave him."

Beyond the cave walls, out in the cold hunger of the world, the psychic presence fades. Kraevor flees into the night, seeking to consume the hundreds of miles towards the warmth of soft, living bodies.

The necromancer exhales.

It is time to go.

HIS THREE KNIGHTS and Rayleth follow him as he rides back to the edge of the glaciers. The knights make differing times. Blinking in and out of existence in wisps of shadow. Dragging their bone-feet across the snow. Rayleth is close by his side, the control in his dreaming mind back where it needs to be.

The man will need to be careful approaching him when the elf is in combat.

In the distance, his Midland oarsmen wait, their bodies twitching like black lines on the white horizon.

Yet something is amiss. The man's smile fades as his eyes follow the horizon, where his boat is but a dark speck adrift in the distant sea.

He feels his tethers of control over these Midland souls. One shines brightly, grinning in its defiance. The captain.

The man turns back to the drifting boat. "This is not ideal."

The captain's corpse eyes briefly spark with life. *We will not row.*

The thought reaches for him as if it were a blade, dripping with scorn. His own hand shifts, becoming a spectral claw.

He shatters the Midlander's soul with the swipe of his arm, silver wisps breaking apart like glass.

The client will not appreciate this delay. But the man is eager to move to the next chapter. He has had enough of ice. Enough of fiends lurking in caverns, and selling the souls within him.

Rayleth stares at him, green eyes flickering like distant lanterns. Lost in a dream. The man listens, and there it is—the campfire dream. While they stand at the edge of the world, Rayleth warms himself in the memories of friends long lost.

The soul stretched for communication within him vibrates. His client. He casts it into a nearby oarsman.

"What is it?" he asks the corpse.

"*They were seen in the city*," the corpse croaks. "*They left. We could not pursue; he would feel us. We only have days left.*"

The man shuts his eyes, feeling out into the world. The barest flicker of fever in Darkshire. A small flake of infection. Enough.

"I know where they are." He waves the soul back into its prison. The corpse collapses, truly dead. Somewhere in the icy distance, the psychic laughter of Kraevor echoes.

Days. He has only days now.

He needs speed. He needs something relentless.

He casts his senses outward. There is life beneath the black ocean. Large life.

A massive mammal churns beneath the waves. It has many names.

The Iceland tribes call them Wayfarers. That is foolish.

The Seavori elves hunt them with harpoons, dragging them to death on their ships. *Oil Dragons*. Also wrong.

The humans, even those who think they are fish, call them *Whales*. How appropriately incorrect.

But it will do.

The man gestures to the dark ocean depths. "Knights," he commands. "Bring us a mount worthy of our journey."

CHAPTER
THIRTEEN

"Whatever happens," Mara said as she fluffed her traveling pillow—those poor knights had probably left half their kit to carry comforts for this princess—"don't turn me into a frog. I promise to be a good hostage."

"You're safe with me." Karley winked at her. Then she realized the human couldn't see in the dark. They were alone in her traveling tent, and it was a damn nicer tent than what they had made the journey to Hollyhead in. Maybe guard duty wasn't so bad.

"I think you're the first woman wizard I've met." Mara sighed. She was lovely, filled with youth, and topped by brown hair and a pretty face. Nineteen maybe. Karley had always been good at guessing human ages.

All the years in the orphanage.

"I'm new to it." Karley smoothed out the plush bedroll. "I think you're the first... wait, what *are* you?"

Mara laughed. She seemed older than her age and barely recognizable from when she had come back with Brim and

Kardak. Poor thing had been starved. Karley never felt old, but around Mara, it felt tangible enough.

"My father is Lord Hamlin Sewell the Second. I'm simply Lady Mara, or in court, *Honorable*. I hate it." Mara shook her head and settled onto her pillow, staring at Karley.

It felt kind of nice to be around someone new. Someone who thought she was more than she was. It was like acting. That old ache seemed so smothered by the arcane now. The truth was she had been on stage for years, and her main audience was herself.

Karley grinned. "Very well, *Honorable* Mara."

Mara giggled. It was hard not to like this girl. For a highborn, she didn't act haughty. But then again, Karley hadn't really known any highborn.

"Do mages have titles?" Mara asked after a moment.

That was a good question. "I'm not sure."

Mara grinned, stuffing a hand under her pillow. "They should. I think it's exciting. What does magic feel like?"

That was also a good question. Mara seemed full of them. Her first touch with magic had almost killed her.

Until Davik saved her, of course.

Stay with me.

She had heard him, even in the grip of that dark fever. It wasn't something she would ever admit to him. That she had clung onto his voice. That she had felt him carrying her far across the world to save her. Somewhere in Stroudsburg, she owed the mage who saved her life a thank you, but she couldn't remember anything.

"It feels..." Karley felt for the right words. "Feels like you're waking up. Like you're *really* waking up."

"Oh, I might need some of that." Mara pushed a long lock of hair from her face. "Do you have a nightgown?"

"Uh, no." Karley looked around the tent. "I usually sleep a bit more bare."

"That's okay. Just us girls here. Not that strange gnome."

Karley laughed as she undid her belt. "He's not one you have to worry about. I can't speak for the wood elf."

Karley slid her pants off, bending to pull them from her legs. She felt hot, but she hoped that was just the day's ride. The magic she had let into her soul was like a bully looking for her in the orphanage, and she did what she always did. She kept her head down and hoped it moved on. Luckily this time, it felt like it had done just that.

"My goodness!" Mara laughed.

Karley turned around. "Huh?"

"Your underwear!" Mara whispered. Karley realized she wasn't being cruel. "I've never seen that! Is it... comfortable? Wedged like that?"

"Ah." Karley glanced down her own back. "Sorry. Didn't mean to moon you. Half-moon?"

Mara giggled and covered her mouth. "My sister and I used to moon each other. Our head of housekeeping was furious. She threatened to call for a cleric. *Women are sheaths to the Sword, destined for a single hip!*"

Karley slid the rest of her leggings down. It was cold out here at night.

Davik's probably warm as hell, got a woman for every limb.

"It's so lacy!" Mara laughed again.

Karley threw a pillow at her and smiled despite herself. "Careful, hostage, I can still turn you into a frog."

"Sorry, sorry." Mara threw the pillow back to her. "Just very bold. You have beautiful skin."

"*Bedwear* is a woman's gift to herself." Karley used the words the sultry saleswoman in Stroudsburg had said to her.

She had to admit there was something about good clothing that made you feel a bit different. A bit dangerous.

"I like that."

Karley pulled the bedroll blanket over herself. These highborn ones were stuffed with goose feathers. "Ah." Karley grimaced as a feather poked her thigh.

"They got you." Mara laughed. "My sister and I called it revenge of the goose."

"Pokey bastards." Karley settled into the roll.

Karley turned to rest on her side. In Oakshire, she would pile the blankets as heavy as she could until they felt like a great weight. Something to tether her, to keep her from running. There was comfort in that smothering feeling and the restraint...

"So, who are you going to marry?" Karley broke the silence.

"Oh, some ugly man, I'm sure." Mara's voice drifted towards sleep. "Maybe I'll wear underwear like yours on my wedding day. He'll die of shock when he sees my dress fall off."

"That's fucked."

Mara peered at her in the shadows. "What is?"

"Not picking who you marry. Seems strange. Is there someone you want to?"

Mara laughed. "That's all highborn maidens talk about. But with my sister's station, I've had to wait to be betrothed. What about you?"

"Never been married. What about Puris? He's your age."

"He *is* cuter than when he left. He seems different." Mara stared at her suddenly. "You can't tell him I said that."

Karley raised a hand in fealty, which she doubted Mara could see. "Drow's honor. Plus, I haven't spoken to him much. He seems attached to Eralt's hip. But I guess Davik and him used to know each other in that city."

"Rochdale." Mara's voice was wistful. "It's a sad story. My father wasn't among the banners that laid siege to it. But many were. They talk about them like they were traitors. And there was a mage family that was part of their ruling council. But all they did was rebuke tithes that my father says were unfair. He says they just wanted Rochdale for its wealth."

"Lowlanders are strange," Karley agreed. "I won't tell Puris. Who else?"

"Davik…"

When Mara spoke his name, Karley felt a pang of insane jealousy. That old, rotten feeling of another pretty human child being adopted before her. Mara was younger, but they married young in the Lowlands.

Of course, and why would he say no? What's another girl cutting in line?

Karley cleared her throat. "You like him?"

Mara shook her head. "Not at all. Not in that way. No offense to your friend. And I'll forever be grateful for what he did in Trinth… but you should've seen what he did. Do you know anything about his elven friend?"

"Not much." Karley rolled onto her back to hide her smile of relief. The last thing she needed was another innocent beauty batting their eyes at Davik. "But if he's Davik's friend… he's a killer."

"A handsome killer." Mara laughed. "Sit with me during the tourneys! There are burly knights coming to visit. I'm sure one will catch your eye."

Karley stared at the ceiling of the tent. "I don't think dark elves are on the desirables list, Mara."

"You're so beautiful. Just be careful. The Lowlands aren't full of very traveled people. They can be crass towards outsiders."

Outsiders was one word for it. One of the nicer ones.

"I'm a big girl. Don't worry."

The night fell on them like a soft hand coaxing them to sleep. But Mara interrupted the silence after a time.

"There were bodies everywhere."

Karley blinked. "Where?"

"In that dungeon with those men... Your friend had another man with him. They killed all the gaolers, except the jailor. I think they let him go once they made him carry the wounded man out. He scares me. I know he means well, and he saved Vorga, but your friend Davik scares me."

"It's okay," Karley reassured her. "Try to get some rest."

Mara did as Karley told her. As they fell asleep, a smile crept across Karley's lips.

Of course, he scares you. He isn't for people like you.

KARLEY WOKE in the middle of the night. Something churned inside her, somewhere deeper than her organs. Her mouth watered, filling with the saliva.

I have to cast.

She crawled forward from the tent flap, her darkvision adjusting to the brightness of the moonlight. Her stomach heaved again, and her bones ached like they would split. By luck, she found the spellbook in the tent as she knelt on the grass.

"Fuck." She coughed. It was happening again. It was happening again, and she hadn't even readied a spell. Felt like a bad joke. Her whole life she wanted to be picked, and now the Void had picked her. Her soul was a boiling tide. She held the book to her chest, trying to keep whatever was inside her contained as she stumbled along the grasses and out of sight.

She slumped onto her ass on a hillside. The grass was wet,

but she barely felt it. This had been a mistake. The tear was too wide. There was no going back.

Who would want her now?

Karley shivered. The taste of roses drenched in wine filled her mouth. Shadows swam at the edge of her vision. She was unbound. Falling apart. When she lifted the spellbook, it took every ounce of strength to place it on her lap and open the pages.

Fire.

It would need to be fire. Or light. Or anything to get this sensation out of her. Acid spurted up her throat. Every response her body could do to combat the unseen enemy inside her was coming to life. She needed to lie down. She needed to sprint into the hills. The urge to throw up or laugh was overwhelming.

When she peered at the spell page, the writing vibrated in her vision.

"Finum astis…" Karley muttered, but her teeth chattered too hard. The words had no meaning, they were just sounds.

Come on.

"Finananaumn—" she tried again. The edge of a cruel smile crept along her lips.

Couldn't even be this.

A demon walked towards her, but Karley was too tired to care. Figures danced on the horizon. If she focused on them, she knew their words would lead her astray.

The demon prowled closer. But as it came near, the shadows disappeared around it. He was like a torch in the fog, burning the darkness away. It curled off him in fearful whispers. Karley focused and saw Davik looking down at her, his face troubled.

Karley croaked out the words. "I can't… I can't read it."

Davik didn't say anything. He dropped his sheathed sword. Of course, he had heard her. Probably was writhing under a blanket of her friends.

He knelt down and sat behind her. Nothing felt better than his arms wrapping around her from behind, pulling her into the space between his legs. He could hold the pieces of her as they broke apart. Karley ran her hands along his arms as they crossed her chest. At least she would die with someone close.

"I've got you." His voice warmed her ear. Something felt contained now. Like the runes in him corralled the frothing power, pressurizing it. "Hold on."

Karley didn't answer more than a grunt.

Davik picked up her spellbook and tapped the page. He was so calm. How could he be this calm?

"Is it this one?"

Karley nodded. He held up the book, leaning his head on her shoulder. His left hand pressed on her stomach, guiding her.

"Breathe slowly," he urged her. "Say it slowly."

The small amount of moonlight lit the page for him. She felt more centered now with him around her. He slid his finger along the first line of the spell.

"Ignis." Karley fought to keep her teeth from chattering. "Et...et... fuck."

Davik moved his hand up to her face. He pressed on either side of her jaw, massaging the muscles before gripping her, commanding her like a horse with a bridle.

"Ignis," he whispered.

"Ignis." Karley fought a spasm running up her back.

"Et."

"Et."

"Finish it. You can do it," Davik held her face tighter, not wanting the final word of the first line to escape and be ruined. "Don't fight it."

"Umbra." Karley fell back into him. The void stopped churning. She felt it take form. Deiga had said this was the first part. The loading of the crossbow. Now it was time to release it.

"Good, you're doing good."

His voice. It was something other than soothing. The power stopped torturing her, and it sat poised like a dog waiting for her command. Her skin flushed. She rubbed her thighs together as the sensation danced along her flesh. The brink of death turning to that hungry place. There were flames in her soul, here bound in his arms, and she noticed just how good his hand felt on her throat.

"Consurge..."

When she spoke the final words, she didn't hear them as words—they were something truer. The true name of fire, consuming and unrelenting. The spell slithered within her, a roaring inferno that surged under her weak control. It was too much. A torrent she needed to purge. It felt like tipping back in a chair, that place between control and chaos. The pure density of it was beautiful.

I'm full of fire.

"Channel it." He squeezed her tight. He sounded like he was resisting something. Some urge to tear her apart. Her soul wrapped around the spell, guiding it. In that agonized mastery, she felt everything. She felt his skin on hers, his control. He didn't let her go.

Davik held her arm up, helping her spread the fingers of her clamped hand.

"Take it," he ordered like he was passing her the reins of a getaway cart.

When he released her, the spell hurtled forth. Terror and

exhilaration replaced the purging space of her soul. Sparks spiraled from her palm, reminding her of Aron's forge blazing against the dark. The fire roared, a twisting weave of heat and light stretching ten feet out. The flames scorched the damp grasses, turning dew to steam in a blistering echo of arcana.

Sweet nothingness. Like in her bedroom at night, hands between her legs. But this time she wasn't alone, Davik was here. Just like he had been behind the woodshed, bent over his lap. And in the alley, shrugging off her spell. Shrugging off her games like the distraction they were.

Karley slumped forward. Her palm still flittered with flames. Davik moved her flaming hand into his, quenching it and drinking her fire.

"Are you okay?" he asked.

Karley blinked, staring at the stars. She had wanted to see them so badly when she was a child. But she had never thought she would be alone when she did. Never thought about how alone they would make her feel, like she would tumble into the sky.

"Thanks," she whispered.

They both looked down and saw the long line of scorched grass.

Davik's voice was finality. "It isn't closing, is it?"

Karley shook her head. It wasn't, and it never would. Which meant she would never be the same. On the barge, he had said he didn't hate mages. How could that be true? She probably disgusted him now. He tolerated her, that was all.

But Davik pulled her back into his embrace, spreading the spellbook across her thighs. Power titillated her, and she felt every nerve ending in her body swirling like glowing plants in the Underdark. It felt like drinking a gallon of coffee. Her clit swelled, and she felt all too aware of the softness of the silk sliding across it. He didn't need to hold her. She could manage now.

"This one?" He turned to the ice spell.

Davik wrapped his arms around her again, pulling her into place. Felt too damn good, him holding her.

"Yeah." Karley settled back against him. "That one."

PART TWO

THE CASTLE

CHAPTER

FOURTEEN

Windpeak looked like it had the day I had first seen it. Only now instead of a crying daughter, I had Karley in my lap. The fortress sat against the sea, situated on a promontory with a now-burned port behind it. Eight battlements encircled it like uneven tent poles with high stone walls.

It was large and more imposing than the man and his family who ruled it. Large enough to hold multiple courtyards, a collection of rooms, as well as shelter the local villages and hamlets littered around it.

We rode through the nearby streets of a hamlet, villagers and villeins stopping to stare at our party. Aside from being a collection of races and species they rarely saw, we looked like a marauding warband. I had everyone do it up for our arrival. Reputations may proceed you, but it's best to reinforce them. I wanted to make one thing clear to any knights here.

Darkshire had arrived.

Sariel rode next to me in a trotting thump of plate armor. Below her stern eyes, the bottom half of her face was dabbed in

Embriel war paint. Her armor glittered in the dull sun, flanking me like a goddess of war.

Karley rode on my lap, her usually jagged makeup even more exaggerated this morning. Streaks of black curled up and down from her eyes, mimicking the voidsick eyes of warmages.

Tyra rode slowly atop Polly, her heavy crossbow resting on her hip. There wasn't a way to make Elina look more imposing, so Vorga sat next to her in the wagon with her spear held high, like a bodyguard for the cleric. Brim didn't need any help.

Even Trith wove twigs and thorns into his coppery hair, looking like a maddened wild sorcerer.

"Quite the proclamation, Davik." Puris grinned from his horse. The squire was loving this.

I nodded, steering the horse with Karley in my arms.

"How many houses will attend the gown tourney, Sir Eralt?" Elina called out.

"Four, my lady." Eralt motioned to the green banner flapping in the distance, camped outside the castle walls. "That is Springdall. Formerly under House Avelmont, until their demise."

Eralt and I shared a look. Prince Jame had been the heir to Avelmont, son of his feared father. Like most fierce political men, the garden shifted greatly when Ironclad died. I had heard about it before my last job in Swinford and raised a glass to his demise.

Springdall squires and attendants looked up at us as we rode past their camp. A tournament knight often needed upwards of six people to attend to him, along with men at arms and additional servants.

"My word." Sariel peered ahead at a mass of dead flesh ahead of the castle. "What is that?"

"Sir?" Puris looked at Eralt. The old knight's face darkened as we closed in on a giant mass of flesh, and the smell of blood filled the air.

"I'm sure they sought permission," Eralt grumbled.

We picked up the canter. The grasses here were cut low from grazing, exposing the dark soil.

A hundred feet from the castle barbican, several knights watched as a dozen villeins carved the carcass of a giant direboar. The sheer size of it was daunting. Almost twenty feet long. A thousand pounds. Twin tusks, now flecked in blood, curled from its deadened mouth.

Missiles with arrow thatching were piled next to it. Nearly as long as a lance and caked in gore.

"What kind of bow fires an arrow like that?" Karley wondered as we approached.

I gazed up at the battlement tower overlooking the field, seeing the contraption that had felled it. "Ballista."

Eralt steered his mount closer. "What is the meaning of this, Renrick Drakemoor?"

The name rang a memory for me. I remembered House Drakemoor in the war. One of the knight houses who had sat on the back lines. Late to the battles, early to the looting when the killing was done.

Renrick Drakemoor smiled up at our guide. "Ah, Sir Eralt the Unmarked! Good tidings. Lady Elyse mentioned meat was needed for the feast. My men and I were happy to oblige."

Puris was shocked. "These direboar are ancient to these lands. There are only several left!"

Renrick grinned. "It took some doing. Why don't you dismount, squire? Come give these men a hand?"

Puris glared at him. "You are not my liege."

"But I am your guest." Renrick's eyes flashed in warning. "My brother competes for the right to part your liege lady's thighs, does he not?"

Puris's hand slid to his sword, exactly as Renrick wanted. I had seen the dance of higher and lower houses in the war. Squires called out by experienced knights, bound by duty to defend the honor of their house. And I had seen them clutching grievous wounds, saved only by clerics from death. Drakemoor was a middling house but they had risen to great wealth after the war.

"Remember your manners on these lands." Eralt glared down at him menacingly.

Renrick laughed. He was young, strong, and surrounded by his men. He leaned over to stare at our collection. "Is this the entertainment, Eralt? Strange jugglers. Greenskins and gnomes? Lady Elyse needed assistance while you pretended to bring a dead legend back to life to stand as champion. Or do you have a dragon hidden back there?"

I steered my horse forward, parting Eralt and Puris.

"Did you ride the boar down yourself?" My voice cut through the bravado. "Or did your men hound it to the field while you sat atop the tower with the ballista?"

"Darkshire." Renrick's grin faltered. "It's true."

Karley straightened in my lap. I called out to the villeins carving the boar. "Farmer, did he pay you for the task?"

The middle-aged man looked up, elbows deep in blood. He didn't shake his head, but the fear in his eyes told me enough.

"Why didn't you gut it?" Vorga stood from the wagon. "You have to empty its entrails; otherwise, it'll rot."

A farmer doffed his cap. "We told them, my lady. But they were adamant to ready the finest pieces."

"For the castle, I've no doubt." I sneered. "While most of the carcass goes bad. Though Drakemoor always did have an eye for the best bits during the war."

Renrick stared up at me, reaching for anything to bolster himself in front of his men. "Would you care to be of help getting it to the castle, Darkshire? We have rope. I'd hate to spoil a team of horses when a magebreaker is more suited to the task."

I smiled. "My witch can assist."

"Davik?" Karley whispered.

"The spell you readied," I whispered to Karley. "Do it."

She looked back at me, fearful. "I don't know—"

"Yes, you do." I put a reassuring hand on her back. "You can."

Karley looked back at the boar. All eyes watched her, and I felt the pull on my runes as she readied herself.

"Hold me tight," Karley whispered, her voice settling into concentration. "It's easier when you hold me."

I slid my hand around her waist, feeling the frost spell she had studied that morning coming into the world.

Karley's voice echoed as she mirrored the void into this world. She stretched her hand out towards the direboar. "*Tenebris Glacius Alru!*"

Ice burst from her hand, slamming into the carcass and rocking the thousand-pound boar. Frost snapped across flesh as flies dropped like frozen rain on the frost-caked beast.

Renrick's party leapt backward. "Sorcery!"

"Had you ever graced the lines, it might not seem so strange to you." I nodded to the carcass. "That should keep your boon ready for the feast. Wouldn't you say, Eralt?"

"I would." Eralt motioned to the villeins. "Head to the courtyard for your coin. You are Lord Sewell's men, and Lord Sewell will see you paid. Puris, can the squire corps relocate this beast to the courtyard with a team of horses?"

"Oh yes," Puris said with a grin. "They'd be glad to."

I steered the horse forward. "I'm sure Lord Sewell will thank you for your hunt. If you'll excuse us."

Renrick grinned. "We already claimed the squire's

barracks, Darkshire. You'll have to join the squires sleeping in the courtyard."

"This party has accommodation within the castle." Eralt moved his horse. "As is Lord Sewell's wish."

Drakemoor's men traded glances. The farmers lowered their hats as we rode past, murmuring their thanks to Karley.

"Well done," I told her as we rode towards the open portcullis.

Karley shivered against me. "You put me on the spot."

"Only because I knew you could do it."

Karley sucked her teeth in irritation, but then she leaned back into me.

Tyra rode up next to us. "That was amazing! And after only a few lessons?"

Karley blushed in my arms. "Thanks. I think it might be here to stay."

"Just like you," Sariel said as she rode up next to us. "Don't worry, Karley."

Our conversation trailed off as we rode under the barbican, the teeth of the portcullis like black fangs above us. The dark stone of Windpeak was scarred white from the salt of the sea. A castle blacksmith worked his bellows under a thatched hut, and several squires turned to smile at Eralt and Puris' return.

"Should we get down?" Karley looked around.

"Just wait." I put a hand on her hip. "Here we go."

The doors to the main hall opened, situated between two towers that led towards the sea. The lord of the castle walked forth, flanked by men at arms. Lord Hamlin Sewell looked like twice the number of years had touched him since the last time I saw him.

"Well"—Lord Sewell looked at me with faded eyes—"you look the same as the day you came, Darkshire. Clad in black, with a rescued woman on your mount. Is this another one of mine you've saved?"

"I think not, Lord Sewell." I stared at the aging man. "I am here at your behest and because Sir Eralt swore us safe passage."

"It seems his oath did not deter you from requesting a hostage." Lord Sewell smiled and looked at his daughter, Mara. "Are you well, my dear?"

"Very well, father." Mara grinned from the wagon. "I promise, I wasn't captured again."

Guards and squires laughed around the courtyard.

Another figure drifted slowly from the opened doors of the castle. Though age had touched her, I recognized her immediately. Lady Elyse Sewell, the princess who never was.

Her hair had faded slightly, but she still walked with the calm authority of the highborn.

"Welcome to Windpeak, Davik." Elyse smiled at me. She always used my name during that year. She had been the only one who did. Where once she had been a spritely young beauty, that card had been shuffled to the bottom of the deck. She was heavier, as if she had armored herself against the world. Not as far as portliness but on the edge of it.

When she placed her hand on her father's back, he turned to her. "Oh, yes." Lord Sewell cleared his throat for his announcement. "These are guests of my house. Afford to them every courtesy and luxury as any of my bloodline. Protect them as my own flesh."

Heads bowed across the courtyard, surprising me.

"Have the servants show them to their rooms." Lord Sewell coughed, and the violence of it caused Elina to stand from the wagon, unsure if he needed help. Eralt was there first, sliding from his horse to hold Lord Sewell up.

"Quite alright—" Sewell wheezed. "I'm alright, Eralt."

"Herbs, my Lord." Eralt looked around. "Hot wine, perhaps?"

Sewell dabbed his mouth like a man grinning at death. His eyes floated back to me, full of purpose. "We are in the end, it seems. Perhaps the black rider waited until his herald arrived. I would speak with you, Darkshire, once you and your party are situated."

THE SERVANTS and chambermaids attended to our belongings, installing us in three grand rooms along the western portion of the castle. Windpeak was three stories, with the third belonging to the covered walkways and battlements atop.

"I've actually never stayed on this side!" Mara declared as she followed Karley and Vorga into a room. "It's lovely."

"They're already unpacking our things!" Vorga grinned.

Tyra wasn't impressed. The farther we entered the Lowlands, the more she drifted to my side. "That's what villeins do." Her eyes lingered on the chambermaids.

"Don't get any ideas, Sariel." Karley looked at Sariel. "We're not unpacking the guests' belongings in the tavern."

Sariel laughed. "Just taking notes."

I motioned Brim closer when the girls filtered into their rooms. "We'll move the wagon and two horses to a hamlet near here later. Until then, stay close to Mara. If anything happens, get them out."

Brim nodded and held up a pyrocrystal from his pocket. *Give girl?*

I shook my head. "No. Just keep an eye."

"Davik," Elina called me over. "Lord Sewell doesn't seem well. Could you offer my services if you think it would help?"

"I'll do that." I kissed the top of her head. "Keep them from wandering."

I doubted anyone would let Elina heal them. Lowlanders had their own clerics, few as they were.

Sariel, Trith, and I followed Elyse down the covered hallway, looking down at the garden in the smaller courtyard.

"My mother's pride," Elyse said without turning. "She spent much time there."

"It's lovely," Sariel offered. "A moon garden?"

"It is."

I hung back a step with Trith, placing a hand on his shoulder. "Spread some wine around tonight with the servants. I want to know every exit out of this place, how many people, and who sleeps where. These passages are a twisting nightmare."

"Should be easy," Trith answered. "What about the knights?"

"Do what you do," I told him. "Lose some gold, make some friends."

Trith nodded.

We followed Elyse to the main hall, where servants were lighting several hearths for the evening. An extensive set of tables was being prepared for a feast. Elyse led us up the carpeted stairs out of the main hall, where her father waited in a study. The shutters were opened to an expansive view of the sea.

Elyse floated to her father's side once we stood on his carpet.

"It appears," spoke the older man, "that it took more than my letter to assuage your fears in coming here. Eralt has told me of quite the bloody tale in Hollyhead."

I glanced at Eralt, who stood as a silent sentinel in the

background. "Your men did right by me and mine. Though it was Puris who persuaded me."

"The girl," Sewell said with a nod. "His sister. Eralt can take you to her."

"Which banner?" I looked at Sewell and his daughter. "To claim her hand?"

"Behind closed doors, we can stop pretending I am still lord of this castle." Sewell patted his daughter's hand. "Elyse has run things for years. There wasn't much else to do. But first, let's see this sorted."

Sewell nodded to a chest sitting in the corner. Eralt walked forward, lifting it. When he did, dull gold stared back at us.

I stared at the chest. "How much?"

"Five hundred gold pieces," Sewell said.

It was a fortune, to be sure. I cocked my head at him. "Not exactly *riches to fill me until my death*. Is it?"

Sewell grinned before sliding a roll of parchment out towards me. "But a taste, Darkshire."

"Don't call him—" Trith began, but I put a hand on his arm.

I looked down at the scroll. It was a contract, really, a fiefdom. But it wasn't lands or titles. It was fifteen percent in perpetuity for *Port Windpeak*.

I lowered the scroll and handed it to Sariel. When I looked past Sewell, down at the cliffside beach, the port was still a charred ruin. "Not exactly a center of great commerce."

"This wedding is important." Elyse turned around, her frame silhouetted by the seascape behind her. "Windpeak has been our cage since you slew Prince Jame. House Avelmont burned our port. We thought Jame's father would take the castle."

Lord Sewell nodded. "That we did."

Elyse stared at us. "But they laid siege with scandal and

word. First, it was my maidenhead in question. Then rumors I had paid you to kill Jame."

"And now knights battle for your hand." Sariel stared at her. "Isn't that a happy ending?"

"A dowry unlike any other drew them here." Sewell coughed. "A prize no one could refuse. And dealings to raise the port back to its former glory."

I nodded to the gold. "So, which knight?"

Elyse's eyes were still bright despite what the years had heaped upon her. "Highblade. Ettimer Highblade. A good and gentle man, I am told. His martial prowess is middling. The men who will compete here are rugged." And I saw it in her eyes when she held back. *Like you.* "Highblade isn't perfect. But he's the only one who won't bleed this house dry. I can live with that."

"Your house doesn't look so fallen," Sariel said.

"The coffers are strong," Elyse snapped. "But nothing compared to what these other houses command. We held the line after the war, our crops going unpurchased. Now, Lowland houses make their coin flooding food into Stroudsburg. The collegiates preserve it with spells and ship it all over the world. The port is our lifeline. Highblade will fund it, and we won't pay other houses to smuggle our crops with their own for a tenth of their worth. We live on a piece—of a piece—of a piece."

"Highblade," Sewell confirmed, "is our wish. He may not make it to the final bouts, but you will select him."

"And if he dies?" I asked. Tourneys were dangerous. The look on Sewell's face showed me they hadn't thought of that.

"Monks of the Sword will be present," Elyse answered me. "He won't die."

"And if my selection is challenged?" I looked around the room.

Sewell laughed. "Come now. Who will challenge Darkshire? This is theater! A story that soothes the Lowland soul. The man who murdered Elyse's first husband selects her second for his chivalry!"

"Highblade it is. When?" I asked.

Elyse walked from the window. "The tournament begins tomorrow, at midday. Followed by a lord's dinner."

Sewell regarded me. "Many travel to see you, Darkshire. Most of the squires here are survivors of Rochdale. They hold you in high regard. Now that you understand our position, there is the matter of Mara. I've pledged my men at arms to your protection. If you would consider—"

My answer was an axe. "Mara is our hostage until we leave your lands."

Elyse sighed. "She'll probably be delighted to hear that."

Sewell didn't like my answer, but he nodded. "So be it. I must rest before this evening."

As Lord Sewell walked out of the study, I stopped him. "I have a cleric with me. She has asked if she might tend to you."

Lord Hamlin Sewell smiled at me. The smile of a man with nothing left to lose. "Not even you can stop the *Rider*, Darkshire. Let him come."

Eralt followed his liege lord out. I put a hand on his arm. "I'd see Allie."

Sir Eralt nodded. "Meet me after. I have a request for you as well."

I let him go. Sariel sensed I had other questions for Elyse and touched my shoulder as she exited with Trith. "We'll be outside."

As they shut the door behind them, Elyse regarded me. "Many Lowland women would fear being in a room alone with Darkshire." Then her gaze softened. "Though many might secretly welcome it."

Elyse had spent more time alone with me than any Lowland woman. She had nothing to fear from me. My touch had been for helping her from carriages and gently placing her behind me when I escorted her somewhere.

"People love their stories."

"Oh, they do. Those stories ruined me. Who would wed the eldest daughter of a house who had lost her maidenhead to Prince Jame? And those who might have believed me would never have believed I remained untouched when you brought me back here."

"Never used to feel sorry for yourself," I noticed. Elyse wasn't a victim, she was a survivor. It was no task of mine to convince her of that. She could have had any life she wanted. But like most of us, she wanted what she couldn't have.

"Times change." Elyse stared me down. "I cursed your name for a long time, Davik. For the life you robbed me of."

I smirked. "Beautiful castle. Exquisite dresses. Nightly beatings?"

Elyse turned to view the burned port. "Each day has felt like a fist for years. Is it wrong to not wish for the rewards that would have come with the pain? I've stood in front of Mara's betrothal, a blemish on this house."

I joined her near the window railing, crossing my arms in a creak of leather and metal. "Is Highblade your wish?"

"He'll do..." Elyse shrugged. "Though I expect he'll be surprised that I'm untouched. Highblade sends their second son. Springdall has a brute of a knight. And then there's Drakemoor, always circling like vultures."

That was three houses. "The fourth?"

Elyse paused for a moment as if trying to remember. "Bronzefell, from the south. They haven't arrived; they might miss the lists. A decade ago, a gown-tourney for my hand would have had thirty knights entering the lists. House Avelmont sought to starve us out. But it seems Jame's father has finally loosened his grip on our throats."

I remembered Lord Elrick Avelmont, called Ironclad. He had been campaigning during my year of guarding his son, Prince Jame. Powerful men spawn spoiled lordlings. He felled nine Lowland banners, expanding his fiefdom in a push no one had seen in a long time. The song followed him across the Lowlands. Brutal as the battering rams he broke banners with.

The fields will burn, the skies will shake.
The lords will kneel, their dreams awake.
Fealty is due, and fealty is taken
No castle stands, no house untamed.
Knock! Knock! It's Ironclad!

"And why did he do that?" I asked. I knew he was dead, but I was interested if she had treated with him before that.

Elyse smiled. "Because he died. What else? Sickness last year. His ways were fading. Lowlanders sell crops to the mages they fought in the war. So will we."

"I see." I watched the sea churn around the burned port. The highborn were like birds in their beautiful nests, high above the rest of us. Their cries meant nothing to me when they tumbled down a branch or two—especially when someone like Tyra had been born at the bottom and clawed her way out.

"You keep intimidating company, Davik." Elyse regarded me. "Which one has taken your bed? The sorceress on your lap?"

"I'd keep my mind on your own bedroom, Lady Elyse."

"Mara said you worked in a tavern. I expected a single serving girl in your company." Bitterness crept into her voice. "Not such a coterie of flesh."

"Manners, Princess." I stood from the railing. "Otherwise, you might wound me."

CHAPTER

FIFTEEN

"Is that her?" Trith asked.

We stood on the outside of a small hamlet, a half mile north of Windpeak. Rather than a free-ranging village dedicated to farming, this was to support the estate. A mixture of castle servants and villeins moved from building to building, culling chickens from the coups and carrying laundry.

Allie walked with a woven basket, a dark red scrap of cloth over her hair. If I had passed her in the street, I wouldn't have recognized her. But with Puris pointing her out, I knew it was her. I hadn't come to Windpeak to fix Elyse Sewell's life or to fight knights in a tournament. I had come to see if the little girl who visited my fevered dreams was truly alive.

And maybe if I saw her here, she would leave my nightmares of that burning city.

Allie was a young girl now, walking with strong arms. For a moment, I could feel her on my shoulders in Rochdale. Laughing on the city walls, pointing.

Sheep!

"That's her," I said. Trith squeezed my shoulder. "That was... that's her."

Allie stopped, turning her head in confused curiosity at the strange man and elf next to her brother. When Puris waved to her, she rolled her eyes, lifting a few fingers from her basket in greeting as she walked to her task.

"She doesn't remember anything," Puris said. "Not the siege. Not our parents. When we hid in the cistern, I tried to cover her ears. But the echoes from the sacking..."

"You did well." I watched her disappear into a scullery.

Eralt cleared his throat behind us. "I have to check on a nearby camp. Farmers said the Springdall men poached a pig. Escort these two back to Windpeak when you're done here, squire."

"Yes, Sir Eralt." Puris bowed.

Eralt spurred his mount forward, its hooves thumping into the hills as he drifted into the horizon.

"Davik, do you want to speak to her?" Puris looked at me. "It's okay if you like. She's a good girl, stubborn now that she's older, but she's very kind. She might remember you?"

I watched her in the open door of the scullery. "It's best she doesn't remember me."

"She knows of you," Puris added. "Most do, here. But not your face."

"Let's keep it that way." I put my arm around Puris, and we turned back to our horses.

"Don't forget to bring your laundry!" Allie called behind us. "You always forget!"

"Okay!" Puris turned around.

I looked up to make sure Eralt was far over the hills. "You did well, Puris. And you were truthful."

"Of course." Puris smiled. We walked towards our horses.

Trith leapt onto his, steadying it. "I know you have reasons to be suspicious. But I hope you see now—"

Puris grunted as I slammed a fist into his gut, doubling over. Trith circled his horse to block the view from the hamlet.

"Sir—Davik!"

"Shh, squire." Trith slipped a halfling knife around his neck. His pleasant demeanor never faltered. "Don't move."

"What are you doing?" Puris stared at me as I took his swordbelt.

I didn't answer. I pulled a length of rope from my saddle and bound his hands and feet, trussing him like a pig. Then I threw a wheat bag over his head and hoisted him over the front of Trith's horse.

"If he tries to escape, kill him."

Trith snapped the reins, riding away quickly with Puris bouncing at the front of him.

WE RODE FOR A HALF HOUR. Away from the coastline and towards the forests. When I signaled Trith, he dumped the squire onto the ground with a thud. I felt rotten. I really did. He had told the truth about Allie.

"Davik!" Puris cried out through the bag.

"Quiet, friend." Trith climbed down. "Don't vex him."

I raised him to his knees and crouched next to him. "Listen close, Puris. I'm only going to say this once. You've done me a kindness, and Eralt as well."

"Whatever you think—" His voice cut off as I cuffed him on the ear.

"Tonight, you're going to get the key from Eralt, and you're going to let us into Lord Sewell's chambers."

"What!" The wheat bag turned up at my voice, shocked. "Why?"

"Because I'm going to kill him. And you're going to help me."

"I can't do that!"

"Can't?" Trith smiled down at the bound squire. "Or won't?"

"Please! Whatever you're thinking, Davik—it's different. No one here intends you any harm!"

"I know Sewell plans to do me in. I'm going to beat him to it. He's an old man, Puris. I have a vial I bought in Stroudsburg. He'll go in his sleep. All you have to do is unlock the door."

"Davik..." Puris's voice wasn't just shocked. It was disappointed. "Rochdale is over."

"Not for me," I declared. "Not for you now, either."

"Come on, kid." Trith nudged him with a boot. "How many years does he have, anyway? Just give us the key, quick and quiet. No one will ever know."

Puris's trembling ceased; his ragged breaths moved the bag in and out over his mouth. "I would know."

"The key, Puris." I stood up, guilt flooding my heart. This wasn't something I wanted to do.

Puris shook his head. "I can't do that... I won't."

Trith sighed, never one who enjoyed violence. He'd rather we were in the castle, making the rounds and trading stories. I spun my sword from the scabbard. Puris had a stout heart. He didn't flinch when I rested it against the back of his neck.

"You ever see a beheading with a sword?" I stared at the young man who had helped me. "Takes a few swings."

Puris didn't respond. A small prayer slipped from his lips.

"Not here." I nodded to Trith. "Up the hill."

"Come on." Trith grabbed the teenager's arms and lifted him, guiding him gently.

"Sword, give me strength," Puris intoned.

"That's good," I told them. "Kneel, Puris. I'll do my best to make it quick."

"You aren't my liege," Puris's voice was steel. "I don't kneel to you."

"So be it. A squire dies tonight." I hefted the blade back, and he stood straighter, trying to stare at me through the bag. My sword shimmered with torchlight.

Then I ripped the bag from his head.

"So a knight can be born."

Puris blinked, trying to make sense of what he saw.

The entirety of the squire corps stood in two ceremonial lines, leading up to a thick tree. Eralt stood at the end of a tunnel of torches and steel like some Lowland legend. His face was stern, his gauntleted hands resting on the hilt of a sword pointed at the ground.

Puris looked at me in disbelief. "I was right," he whispered.

"Did we give it away?" I asked.

Puris shook his head. "I was right about you, Davik."

Among the gathering, Sariel, Brim, Elyse, and all the girls waited on the right-hand side, smiling.

The squires wore ceremonial white tabards for the occasion. I fell back as Eralt called to his squire. "Come forward."

We joined our group. Torches sputtered bravely in the failing light. I felt Tyra and Karley drifting next to me. Brim craned his neck to see, until Trith swept him onto his shoulder, eliciting a grin.

Tyra squeezed my hand when Puris walked forward, kneeling before Sir Eralt. Giving him a scare and a mock execution was the last thing I wanted, but Eralt had asked it of me.

"It's called the Trial of the Keys," Vorga whispered to me. "It's an old legend of the Sword."

"An orphan without legacy or liege." Eralt intoned as the

torches lowered. "Found in the crippled streets of Rochdale. A fine squire, and while forgetful at times—"

Laughs came from his comrades.

"Never wavered in his duty. Battle touched his youth before the path to knighthood. He stood atop the walls of Rochdale. A city—A city I was ashamed to lay siege to."

The words shook me. Eralt the Unmarked had left the service of his liege after Rochdale, eventually finding his way to Jame.

Heads bowed across the squire corps. Rochdale faces softened in memory and understanding. For the first time since I had known Eralt, I heard his voice waver. "Where I—I was unworthy. After the fall of the city, he protected his sister, Allison. Ever her steward."

Eralt turned to me, eyes glistening with torches. "He has proven himself steadfast and true. A knight unlike any other."

Tears slid down Puris's face as he stared up at Eralt. Next to me, Elina and Vorga wiped their eyes.

"To say I found a lost boy would be a lie," Eralt declared. "For I was lost, without house or sigil, and the Sword seemed so far away. He found me. He has proven his valor without weapons, proven his temperance in the midst of temptation, and never wavered."

Eralt raised the sword. "I knight thee, Sir Puris of Windpeak. Puris the Bladeless. Commander of the Squire Corps. I bequeath to you all that I own. Little as it is." Eralt removed the sword. "Rise, knight of Windpeak. Rise, brother. Rise... my son."

Cheers broke across the crowd. And several heads hung to wipe the tears from their eyes. Puris threw his arms around Sir Eralt, clasping him tightly and weeping into his shoulder.

"He earned it," Sariel said with a smile. When she turned to me, my heart melted when she kissed my hand.

Did good, ugly-man. Brim's voice echoed in my mind.

Trith turned to me, holding Brim up on his shoulder. "Nice to act that out for once, isn't it?"

I watched the squires crowd around Puris. "It is."

I KNOCKED on the door to Karley's chamber. Tonight's theater required her at my side and I was looking forward to it.

Mara waited down the hall with Sariel and Tyra while the last of the girls got ready. Trith was already at the feast, making nice with the knights and sourcing the information I had asked for.

"Come in."

I walked into the bedchamber. Unlike the usual chaos of multiple women sharing a room together, Karley had kept hers orderly. Everything was calculated. The small tins of makeup sat in specific succession on the vanity.

"Almost ready." Karley ran a pencil under her eye. "Luckily for me, the light in this castle is awful."

Black lipstick matched her eyeliner, and a cloud of rouge drifted around her eyes. She looked like a witch in a dark coven. A woman you'd lose your sanity and life to and not even regret it. There was a surety within her now, as if she had come to terms with what she was becoming.

"There we go." Karley set the pencil down and peered in the mirror. Everything about her was premeditated. What she wanted the world to see. What she wanted herself to see.

Violet legs, smoothed by soft spidersilk nylon—ended at the tops of her thighs. A dancer's body. Lithe, porcelain-smooth, and tight. A smudged eye of twinkling darkness glanced at me.

Karley stood and turned. "How's this for your sorceress, Darkshire?"

Her dark panties were as thin as mist, the glint of her flesh behind the crackling fabric. She was all edge. And that edge pointed at me.

"Dangerous."

Karley watched me as she stepped into the dress she had gotten in Stroudsburg. Eighty gold pieces were never so well spent when she lifted it up. Black and purple Dridersilk encased her, replete with white feathers on her shoulders that matched her hair.

"Got the idea from your pauldron." Karley smoothed one of the feathers. "Breaks up the black."

"Need a hand?" I offered.

Karley turned, and I buttoned up the back of her dress. When I finished, she walked to the bed and slid on two fishnet gloves.

I leaned over, seeing a strip of black leather with a chain, the same I had seen in Elina's dressing room. "Is that your jewelry?"

Karley might have blushed before, but now she smiled and picked it up. She opened the strip and held it around her neck, the chain slinking to the floor. "They tell stories about Darkshire keeping a sorcerer in a chest. Perhaps a witch on a leash would be... fitting."

The dark elf stared at me, holding the collar as if waiting for my command.

"Might be too much," I admitted.

She nodded as if I just answered a question. "You're right. When we stop at Stroudsburg again, I can see if they'll take it back and—"

"The chain." I reached up and undid the fastener. "Not the collar."

Karley bit back a smile. Without the chain, the collar looked like an elegant choker.

I poured the chain into my pocket. "I'll hold on to it."

Karley bit her lip. "For safekeeping?"

"You never know." I smiled.

Silence fell like a blade between us. But it couldn't touch the delicious tension, the attraction between my runes and her arcana. Karley had run like she always did, but I was the only one to catch her. I had wanted it to be somewhere like this. Not in an alley, and not in the cellar of the tavern. I had seen the softness in her in Tawney, dressed up, dancing, all eyes on her and me.

"Glad I could play this role for you," she whispered. "Actress and all."

"I am, too." I offered her my arm. "Shall we?"

Karley smiled as sharp as a knife, slipping her hand over mine. "Careful, Davik, you might enjoy keeping me too much. Like those falcons they have here, perched on your arm."

"Well," I said as we walked down the hall to the rest of the group, "your feathers *are* better."

CHAPTER

SIXTEEN

hree Monks of the Sword were present at the feasting
hall for Puris's knighthood. Lord Sewell joined us,
flanked by Elyse at the high table. Eralt sat at his liege's right
hand. Springdall and Highblade were given seats of honor. I
noticed that Renrick Drakemoor and his men were not.

I had wanted Mara seated with our group, so she was still
within our grasp. I could protect Karley if something came. I
wanted everyone else to be near our hostage. Then Puris asked
me if she could be at the table for his feast. When I saw the
look in his eye, I agreed.

Now Karley sat next to me, a witch for all to see.

"How we doing?" I asked under my breath, staring at the
three long tables filling the hall. Our group kept smiling at us.
And I saw Trith doing what I had asked, going and making
friends.

"They light another fireplace," Karley said without moving
her mouth, "and this makeup is going to pour off me like a
waterfall."

Lord Sewell stood slowly, raising his hands for attention.

"Rarely do we have a knight joining our ranks who has passed the Trial of the Keys. And I would say"—he glanced at me sitting with Karley at his table—"we are lucky that our Gown Champion was not serious in his request. He seems to have changed his ways."

Laughs came around the hall. Brim cackled louder than anyone.

Ugly-man at table.

Sewell continued, "We are fortunate to have Puris. As well as so many boys who Eralt trained from Rochdale. Young men, please stand—those of you from the city."

Several squires slowly lowered the spoons they held like vipers so as not to stain their ceremonial dress. Fifteen of them stood, looking around the hall.

"Once enemies of certain houses and now friends." Lord Sewell smiled at them. "I thank you for your virtue. I believe one of the brothers of the Sword has something for your new commander."

Three monks bowed from their seats, pushing away their free meals. I stopped myself from sucking on my teeth at the sight of them.

Never liked Monks of the Sword. And I had seen plenty of those grey-robed bastards blessing men before they sacked Rochdale, absolving them of the crimes they were about to commit.

But for Puris, I kept a neutral face.

The brothers came forward and presented a painted shield with a coat of arms on it. "The squires guided our brushes."

It was the elder brightberry tree of Hollyhead, bisected by lightning and a blade. As the monks handed it to Puris, he looked down and smiled. "Thank you, thank you all."

"*Hell of a thing, drawing a knighthood fighting wingers!*" a drunken voice cut through the crowd.

The squire corps snapped their heads over. I saw a smile stifled by the Lord of Springdall. And in that shifting crowd, where armed men drink and tensions shimmer, I saw Tyra's face go cold. Like the term had just confirmed something for her.

"What a cunt." Karley hissed next to me.

Sewell peered into the crowd until Renrick Drakemoor stood and bowed. "My apologies, Lord Sewell. One of my servants is in his cups."

"I'd see him removed," Eralt growled from his seat. "Lest we trim names from the tourney lists."

Renrick grinned a shit-eating smile and bowed deeper. "I will attend to it. My apologies."

Lord Sewell smiled pleasantly. "Please do. This feast is in honor of the squire corps."

Puris glanced at Mara to my left. I saw Sariel and Elina grinning. Then I locked eyes with Vorga, giving her a soft nod.

The Brother of the Sword turned as Vorga walked forth to hand him a scroll. "What is this?"

When my voice cut across the room, everyone quieted. "His entry."

"These are usually penned by those familiar with..." The monk turned to me. When he saw my eyes boring into him, he stopped. "I'd be glad to read it."

Eralt leaned over from the end of the table, glancing down at me. I gave him a shrug.

The monk cleared his throat. "*Puris the Bladeless, who leapt into a cavern of unknown danger, with enemy beyond counting.*

In the service of his liege lord, he traveled across the Midlands to the faen vineyards. Whilst there, he defended the townspeople of Hollyhead against forces of far greater number, felling many men and saving many more. Not once did he falter. Passed the Trial of the Keys, and when shown his own death, he did not waver.

Knighted by Sir Eralt the Unmarked, on the eve of the gown tourney for Elyse Sewell, Lady of Windpeak. Witnessed by his liege and comrades and the traveling companions he had made.

In attendance was the brigand known as Darkshire. Friend and comrade to this young knight."

Shouts came from the squire corps as the monk closed the scroll. Fists banged rapidly on the tables. Puris walked forward and accepted the scroll, holding it up in thanks to Vorga and Sariel.

Before Vorga went back to her table, she grinned at me.

I raised an eyebrow. "Brigand?"

"Suits you." Vorga laughed. "And your witch-queen."

"That was so lovely!" Mara declared next to me. "And penned by your hand? I thought those stuffy monks were going to keel over!"

"I'm glad you liked it." Vorga smiled. "Come join us when you can!"

"Thank you again for coming, Davik." Puris walked up to us. "It means a lot."

I stood up, aware of every eye on us that pretended not to be. I clasped arms with him. "Happy for you, Sir Puris."

"Thank you, commander." The once-squire grinned as he used my title in Rochdale. As he walked away to his seat, Mara leaned over.

"Is that true? What Vorga said?"

"More than true," Karley answered. "Puris spilled blood in Hollyhead. Even before that, he leapt into a pit of feral goblins with nothing but Eralt and a shield to save Davik."

"Really?" Mara looked over at the new knight as he sat down. "Saved... Davik?"

I whispered in Karley's ear. "Seems you left out the part where I leapt in to save you."

"Shh." Karley peered at me. "Dangerous witches don't need saving."

Once the fanfare died down a bit, and Lord Sewell spoke along the high table to my left with the Lords of Springdall and Highblade, the merriment began. Two jugglers walked the halls, tossing half a dozen balls in the air while spinning and tumbling. Mara eventually drifted off to the table to sit with Vorga, Sariel, and the others.

I looked at Karley. "You might be the finest actress I've ever hired."

Karley blushed for a moment, hiding it with a raised goblet. "Think the show will catch on?"

It took quite a bit of me not to kiss her right there. The way she looked at me. I leaned over, my hand grasping her thigh. "I want to show you something, after this."

Her nose slid across mine as she looked at me. The weight in her voice made my cock ache. "Have I seen it before?"

"Not properly." I squeezed her leg. "Not in the way you deserve."

"I'd like to take a closer look." Karley shuddered, grabbing my hand and sliding it up her leg. "Davik, when you carried me from Hollyhead, I heard your—"

"Must be nice, Davik." The words tore the moment like a page as Elyse leaned over the absent seat of her sister. "Getting to sit at one of these."

"What do you mean?" Karley asked.

"Davik's been to plenty of feasts." Elyse wavered a bit as if the heat and wine she had imbibed were getting to her. "But he used to stand in the corner, watching the whole time."

Here we go.

Elyse's voice picked up an octave. "We felt bad! I asked Jame if he minded if we brought him scraps from the table. From the nicer selections. He was my sworn blade, after all." Elyse raised her wine chalice, smiling into it. "Maybe he took his job too seriously. The man meant for my bed couldn't even get past his guard in the end."

Karley's gripped my forearm.

I smirked. We all tell ourselves what we like to believe. But I remembered Elyse's trembling hands when I found her in her chambers. The dark bruises dotted her like she had fallen asleep under a ripe plum tree. The way she had cried in my arms when I carried her out, looking away as I slew two gatemen.

Elyse shot a look at Karley. "Only he had a key to my chamber, you know."

Karley slipped her arm from mine.

Before I could respond, the hall crier stamped a long staff with a bell on top. "*House Bronzefell!*"

Heads turned as the last house arrived for the tournament, their knighthood retinue over fifteen strong. The brothers of the Sword bowed as a tall man in bronze-colored armor strode in, his face concealed behind a barbute visor.

Lord Sewell stood as the Bronzefell party bowed before him. "Welcome!"

"Our apologies," the lead knight said to Lord Sewell. "Rains delayed us. We bid you and Lady Elyse well, and thank you for your hospitality."

"What is that?" Karley asked, staring at the silent helmed warrior.

"A Helmed." I kept my eyes on him. "Trained in the monasteries. Not quite a paladin, not quite a cleric. Enchanted armor. Strong."

Elyse grinned and rose, holding out her hand.

The leader of the Bronzefell party—a handsome enough blond man who had the lookings of a man who had been in the field—kissed her ring. "My lady. It is our honor to enter the lists for your hand."

"You've brought so many knights, Sir Hewer." Elyse was practically melting. Down the table, I saw Ettimer Highblade turning red while he sat far from a place of honor.

Interesting.

"You know our champion?" Elyse turned and gestured at me. I didn't stand. Sir Hewer looked at me, nodding in anything but greeting.

"Many do." His eyes floated to Karley and then turned to the table of Sariel and the girls. "It seems the gown tourney has brought many... outsiders to visit."

I had never heard of House Bronzefell, but apparently, they had heard of me. The Helmed warrior behind Hewer turned his helmet in a grind of metal, regarding me from the dark crevices. The dark slits made my hand itch for my warhammer.

"Your quarters are ready." Elyse smiled. "Would you sup with us? Before the tilts on the morrow?"

"Ugh." Karley groaned next to me. "She bats those eyelashes any faster, she'll float away."

Sir Hewer inclined his head. "Some, perhaps. We thank you."

Lord Sewell waved an exasperated hand forward for one of his personal attendants. "Take them to their quarters in the south wing."

"*As you wish, sir.*"

As the knights in bronze took their leave, one among them stayed. The squires corps craned their necks to see the famed tourney knight and swordsman. Even Puris looked enamored when he recognized the man smiling at me.

"Hail, Darkshire." Serlo grinned. He didn't wear the colors of House Bronzefell.

I stood with a smile and walked around the table as Trith

came to join us across the hall. "Serlo the Loner, keeping company as usual. Good to see you."

We clasped arms. "Glad I'm not the only name they bought for this tournament."

When Trith walked up, the swordsman turned with a grin. "You! The dice sorcerer! You almost left me naked on my return!"

Trith grinned. "You were a chatty captive."

"Captive?" Sariel joined us from their table.

Serlo nodded. "I was hired to hunt these two and their band after Rochdale. I woke up one evening with a rope around my neck. Next thing I know, I'm on my knees while a dark cleric rolls the bones of my black deeds!"

"Anyone here you haven't kidnapped?" Sariel smirked at me.

Serlo continued, "They ransomed me back, thankfully. But not before Valek and Trith had won everything from me, save my sword."

When the shadow passed over my face, Serlo cleared his throat.

"I'm sorry, Davik. I spoke for Valek when they captured him. I offered a duel to settle his fate. But the Lowland houses..."

"We know," Trith said softly. When we found Valek's body and what they had done to him, Trith had left less than a week later.

"I need to worry about you?" I grinned.

Serlo held up his hands. "I think not. Bronzefell hired me. They ride, but they need someone in the melee."

I glanced back at the high table, where Elyse had taken my seat and was leaning over to speak to Karley. I gave her a quick smile. She could handle herself.

"Do us a favor." I turned back and put a hand on Serlo's

shoulder. "Go make the rounds with Puris and that group of squires. Otherwise, they'll break their necks tomorrow trying to impress you."

Serlo laughed, then clasped a fist on his banded plate. "As you wish."

"I like this better, Davik." Trith smiled. "Eating at a feast, instead of sneaking past it or robbing it."

Sariel leaned back, staring at the high table. "Looks like the bride-to-be had too much wine."

When I looked, Elyse walked with her servants off to her bedchambers. As they led her across the hall, a smirk was planted on her face.

Karley stared into the crowded hall, smoothing her dress absentmindedly.

"I'll get back to it." Trith clapped me on the shoulder. *"Brim! Come here! Meet these fellows."*

"Dice?" Brim asked.

Trith winked as he walked away. "Oh, maybe a game or two."

"She okay, Davik?" Sariel noticed Karley.

"I'll find out. You heading back?"

"Think it's bedtime for us all." Sariel leaned forward and kissed my cheek. "I'll be the responsible one and watch Mara tonight. Love you."

"Love you, too," I said.

But something was wrong as I approached Karley. To my right, Lord Sewell spoke with his guests, while Serlo and Puris spoke excitedly, slowly being surrounded by more boys from the squire corps.

"The moon garden," I said to Karley as I walked up. "Thought we might take a look?"

"No thanks." Karley stood up, smoothing her gown with

one closed hand that held something. "Wouldn't want to delay you."

"What's that mean?"

The drow snorted like it was my first day in the tavern again. "Here. She left this for you. Guess she thought I wouldn't mind—with your habits and all."

Karley dropped a heavy iron key into my hand.

I looked up at her. "Elyse?"

"She said midnight still works." Karley turned from the table, trying to hide her anger. "Like all the other times."

I curled my fingers around the key, strangling it as I saw Elyse smirking as her servants followed her upstairs to her chambers. Too far for a biting mark, and in this tilt, she had won.

When I turned, Karley was already halfway to the door, Tyra falling into step beside her.

"What's wrong?" Tyra called after her.

But Karley was already through the hallway doors. Running, like she always did. Unchained and uncertain to return.

CHAPTER
SEVENTEEN

I slipped from our room close to midnight. The fire had long gone out, and the storm battered on the windows. I pulled the covers up over Tyra and Vorga as they slept. When I had come back from the feast, I had found them asleep while Elina and Sariel watched Mara in the secondary room.

"Everything alright?" Trith asked me in the hallway.

"Just got to check on something. Everything good here?"

Trith nodded in the shadowy corridor. "Quiet. Eralt's men are guarding the other door. Hold on, I'll wake Brim and come with you."

"Going alone on this one." I turned down the hall. "Don't wait for me."

Trith chuckled behind me. "You know I will."

Windpeak was a large castle, but its vast estate—once a sign of supremacy—had become more of a burden than anything. Had Lord Hamlin and Elyse had more sense, they would have abandoned this place and rebuilt something more suited to their station. But we all hold on to the past, as real as the key in my hand.

As I pushed the doors open to the hall, two Rochdale squires stood armed with halberds.

"Evening," I said and shut the door behind me.

"Commander."

When I turned around, the teenage men smiled at me. A stout one spoke up first. "My father was on the walls with you. Remember seeing you with him as a boy. Died when the gates opened."

I'd buried too many fathers at Rochdale... and after. Now their sons stood before me.

"What was his name?"

"Ekyll Thatcher." The youth inclined his head.

"And yours?"

The muscled squire smiled. "The same. I carry his name."

"Mine was in the hills with you," the skinnier boy said. Where his partner was brimming with bravado, this one seemed quieter. Not shy but sure of himself. "Name was Royce. Joined the rebels after my ma and brother fell."

"I remember your father," I said. "Leatherworker. Good fighter."

The teenager didn't smile. "Axe was his favorite, wasn't it?"

"It was." An axe meant for wood felling had become an executioner's weapon in the man's hands. Royce had been one of many Rochdale men, lost in the dark tunnels of vengeance. Tunnels guided by my torched hand. "He slew several knights."

The boy nodded as if he already knew this. "Before they hanged him."

"That's right."

"Will you fight tomorrow?" Ekyll asked. "Springdall was at Rochdale."

I shook my head, disappointing the two of them. "Fighting's a young man's game. I'm just to stand as champion." I watched the two of them. "What about you two?"

"First squire tilts." Ekyll grinned. "Against a Drakemoor."

I looked at the quiet one. "You?"

A smile crept across his lips. "Squire's melee."

"Luka's a good fighter," his friend added. "Our best."

"I look forward to your victories." I nodded to them. "Excuse me."

It was close to midnight, and I had somewhere to be. I crept through the castle, retracing the portions I had memorized. The call of a woman is a funny thing. My runes were empty after a long day, the healing spells from Elina long eroded now. Yet there was an eagerness in me as I stole into the shadows.

Elyse's bedchamber would be unlocked. The doors, no doubt, freshly oiled. And within it would be a highborn woman, waiting for me to claim her. The wronger something is, the more some men are drawn to it. Ruin lies in the winks of women.

The wrong women.

I found her on the battlements braving the rain. Her voice was a knife when I climbed up into the cold air. "Elyse must be underwhelmed at such a short visit."

"Very disappointed." I shut the trapdoor under me.

The rain fell in sheets around us, so thick it was like flaps of a tent around the cocoon of the guard tower.

Karley's sneer was half-hidden in shadow.

"You just take what's offered wherever you go, don't you?"

"Do I?"

"My boss. My friends."

I took a step towards her. "Didn't take you, once."

The mage's face curled into rage. There was a new spell in her, something intricate and higher-level. Consumed from her spellbook in the rage of the evening. "That wasn't offered. You think I care if you visit her bedchamber?"

"I do." I took another step. "And I didn't. Not now, nor then."

Karley watched me, weighing if I was lying or not. "Doesn't matter. I'm leaving after this."

"I know."

There were words in her she wanted to say, like a spell. And I stood there as I had a thousand times, waiting for a mage to make their mark. "I'll join the Severed in Stroudsburg. They're taking people back."

"No," I said slowly as I stepped closer to her. Our whispers seemed to thrum in the echo of the tower. "That's not where you're going."

"No?" Karley gritted her teeth. "Where am I going? Tell me, busboy."

"Where you belong." I slid my hand along the hard mortar. Smooth one moment, jagged the next. "Wherever I am."

"Lucky me." Karley's chest heaved. "Last one in the tavern to be picked."

"Not last." She was so close. I was a squire trying to capture his first goshawk, trying not to startle it. "Next. Felt right, didn't it? You and I together?"

She stared at me, her voice quivering like a crossbow's cord. "We were just pretending."

I watched the dark elf's face. "I wasn't."

Thunder rumbled overhead. But all I felt was the spell locked in her soul. I didn't smell the petrichor of rain on stone. I smelled the crushed roses of the perfume she dabbed on her neck.

I was made to kill her. To rend her body apart until her soul followed. But before that, I was an orphan—just like her. And when there's no one left to pick you, and you're alone, the only thing you want is what you can't have.

"Davik," Karley whispered. "I always—"

"I chose you." I pulled on her cloak string, drawing it slowly until the knot came loose. The cloth parted, revealing her dress underneath. "Not a princess. Not a castle. You."

Karley exhaled, almost trembling. "You going to keep chasing me?"

"No." I leaned forward, my hand sliding along her hip. The same as that dance long ago in Tawney. "I've caught you."

It happened in that timeless space, where the distance between your lips and the woman you want seems to vanish. All those days in the tavern, the teasing, the running. It ended now, as her black lipstick stained my flesh, and a whimper of relief sounded from her throat.

Everything between us had been a duel. A duel now that neither of us wanted to win because surrender was the real victory.

I felt the silk of her dress as I backed her into a parapet. How many mages had I felled with steel? With my bare hands? Countless.

Not enough.

Karley backed into the stone, sitting on the ledge as she wrapped her legs around me, nylons sliding across my hips.

"I knew it," she whispered as I tasted her neck. "The day I saw you standing there outside the tavern. Watching you with Sariel. I knew—" She gasped as I slid my hands up, feeling the edge of her hips.

"Tired of you," I whispered in her ear. "Just watching."

Karley's nails dug into my neck like spurs on a destrier, urging me on. Her breath was hot in my ear. "I was never so wet as the day you grabbed me behind the woodpile..."

I stared into her eyes, taking my time as I lifted her dress, sliding my hands between her widening thighs. I coaxed her panties aside, feeling the treasure they guarded. "Prove it."

"Ugh," Karley groaned, gripping my forearm as I teased her.

My runes were a line of war drums, demanding her death. They wanted her thrown on the table behind us, rutting into her like a slum alley whore.

But I had never chosen my runes. I had been strapped to a table, subject to the whims of the world. What mattered more was what we wanted. Not just the scarred flesh of what life subjected us to.

When I stared at her, feeling her thighs clamp around my hand, I saw a lost woman, now found. Not mine to own, but mine to claim. And the difference was a promise. One that men had vowed for centuries.

"I'll always protect you," I whispered.

"Yes," Karley whispered as she writhed onto my touch. "You will."

I kissed her, lifting her by her hips and writhing against her. Karley moaned as I ground against her. She grasped at my armor buckles, undoing them. "Take it off," she ordered. "I want to feel all of you."

Karley's eyes drank me in.

When I tugged my shirt off, she met me halfway, lips crashing into mine. Her nails raked down my back in slow, deliberate trails, then swept across my chest like she was claiming me.

A boy kisses a girl in the dark corner of a castle. It's a story as old as time.

One worth repeating.

I sank to my knees, pulling her panties down. Karley hitched her dress. Dridersilk spread like a curtain as I slid my tongue up. When I reached my prize, I inhaled the scent of her. Sultry musk, bare and ready. I gripped her hips and pulled her onto my mouth.

Karley shuddered, head arching towards the storm. "Ugh, Davik— Oh, fuck."

I filled my mouth with sweet drow flesh. I slid my hands lower, burying my face into her. I drowned myself in her, sliding up, watching her fall as I locked onto her clit and sucked.

"Fucking—" Karley spasmed, pressing into me. "Davik…"

I tasted her slowly. Flicking my tongue like a slow lash against a slave. I slid lower, entering my tongue into her. Karley's feet slid on either side of my neck, her legs spreading as she slid against me, gripping my hair.

"Come here." She pulled me up, reaching for my belt with a huff. "I've seen it… but I've never"—she gripped me with a groan—"had it for myself."

Karley tugged on my cock, leading me towards her.

"I've wanted you," I groaned.

The sensation of her was intoxicating. Being so close to her arcane soul, I felt like I could rip through the mortar. I held the back of her neck, staring into her eyes as I slid my cock against her. Cold rain drenched us.

"Please, Davik. Take me—" Karley pulled on my hips.

When I entered her, it was like quenching hot steel. Karley's mouth opened in an unbelieving whimper. Her quim was so tight, but she lifted her hips, straining for more. When she welcomed me, I groaned, taking her slowly, watching her face as she surrendered to what we were now.

"Oh gods, Davik." Karley shuddered. I felt the arcane power in her, submitting and spreading. Making way for me. "I feel you."

"I've thought about you." I huffed as I sank further into her.

"It's like"—Karley groaned, pulling me in—"you're in my soul. Don't stop. Don't ever stop."

I wrapped my arms around her, pressing our bodies together. Rain danced on our faces as I bucked up.

"Give me all of it." Her voice melted. "I want to feel you, Davik."

"You've been thinking about this," I whispered into her ear. "About us."

"Yes," Karley moaned.

Lightning flashed across the sky. Hairless, violet flesh filled with the magic I was made to destroy shuddered as I lost myself in her.

When she swelled around me, coming, her eyes flared violet. I plunged ahead, burying myself to the hilt, barely escaping before I burrowed within in her, over and over.

"I didn't take stillseed—" She groaned.

I slid back from her, teetering.

Then she hefted her legs around me, pleading.

"Don't go," she whispered. "I want it. I want you there."

The begging in her voice felled any last sense I had. I fell into her with abandon. We were two people who finally had one another. Both jagged, aligned to where we fit. I watched the shudder of her flat chest, the sweet flesh of her stretching and taking me.

"Yes," Karley moaned. "Yes I want to—"

When I came, she arched back. Her eyes flared violet, the spell in her soul breaking forth, curling around our pressed souls.

She groaned as I shot line after shivering line into her. As wild as the storm around us, lancing like the lightning that cut through it. My cock spasmed as I filled her. The agony of it was exquisite and so very final.

We froze, locked together as the rain flared through the opening, breath steadying.

Her heartbeat thrummed through her, pulsing into the core of me. Its steady beat fell, resting in my hands.

Where it belonged.

～

KARLEY SHIFTED in the shadows of our room. We had fallen asleep briefly but woke in a cuddle. Now she was wrapped around me, burrowing under my arm and laying her head on my chest.

"Really? Before the haircut?" I teased, feeling her smirk against my chest. "You don't even grow body hair; I figured beards wouldn't be your thing."

"Liked you all rugged when you first showed up." Karley slid her head up and smiled at me. "You looked like the kind of human we used to tell stories about. Made me scared of you. That was until I saw you with Sariel that day."

"I remember that," I said with a smile. "You standing in that doorway. What was your plan?"

Karley tucked herself tighter against me, her skin cool where mine burned. It was a contrast I never wanted to let go of. "Didn't have a plan. Just was a little...wound up. Wanted to see the free show. But... when I saw you and her. Sariel's so beautiful, I almost ran out of the room. Guess I wanted to see if you'd still pick me."

"That I did." I kissed her. "And that I have."

Karley laughed and laid her head back down. "Had been seeing Elina for a bit. Trying to understand facets and what she meant. Honestly, I just needed someone to talk to, but it was strange talking to one of your lovers about you."

"What did you learn about your secret facet?"

Karley chuckled and slapped me gently on my stomach. "I

used to feel ashamed because I'd have different urges for things I'd never done but thought of. They came out more when you arrived. Darker, I thought. But Elina told me they're not dark. That a hand on some women's throats feels as good as being held. That maybe because I had drifted so long like a ship, I craved the ropes and sails of structure. Then she told me that touching myself wasn't shameful, and I laughed so hard I ran out of the temple."

I ran a hand down her back. Does anything feel so good as when a woman stops being a stranger and lies naked under the sheets with you?

"You're my first..." Karley uttered the words. When she looked up at me, I smiled at her. "And that didn't come easy. I used to tease people at the tavern and leave them waiting when the night came. I don't know."

I heard the fear in her voice. When someone who runs their whole life finally stands still, the worst thing they dread is being left behind.

"Not just your first"—I leaned down—"your last."

"That so?" Karley grinned up at me. "Room around your campfire for Karley the bartender?"

"There's been room for you in my life the whole time." I slid my lips against hers, sliding down the mattress. We lay facing one another.

Karley slipped her hands under her cheek, blinking at me. "Well, at least I didn't have to learn to make a love potion."

"Wouldn't have worked on me, anyway."

"Are they real?"

"No idea."

Karley shifted her hand down my stomach, teasing me. She inhaled sharply. "I can't seem to get enough of you, busboy."

"Don't you worry. You'll be sick of me in no time."

"No." She blinked. The way her face shifted, it was the most vulnerable I'd ever seen. Her next breath felt like a vow. "I don't think I will..."

I pulled her closer to me, running my hands over the flesh that housed the arcane in her. I would always be aware of her, and in time, I would become used to that feeling. I'd always be able to find her. "Me either."

Karley ran her hands over my chest, tracing in lazy circles. "There's something I want to show you..."

"Can I get more water first?"

The drow chuckled and slid up from the sheets. "Not that. Stay here."

She drifted from the bed, her lithe body padding barefoot on the floor. When she returned, she held the spellbook that had almost ended her life. The one Vilas had given her.

"I don't remember much from being a kid. Sometimes, I'm not sure if it's a dream or a memory." Karley sat down next to me, opening the book. I sat up, feeling honored to be shown something so intimate from her.

In the dark, I could barely make out the neat lines of writing. It wasn't chaotic, but there were paragraphs written horizontally and vertically. I leaned down to squint.

"Ah, hold on." Karley leaned over and grabbed the dwindling candle from the bedside. As she held it over the pages, her finger went through the different patches of notes.

"This is drow?"

Karley looked up at me. "I think it was my mother." Her finger fell on a paragraph. *"Evsha' nurit hisk para tum."*

"What's it mean?"

Karley smiled. "I used to have this dream, where I was a little girl walking in the Underdark. In the orphanage, we called them *orphan dreams*. But I was following someone. We would always walk to this little cliff where none of the glowing vines or flora would be. And I would just hear someone shout, '*Evsha! Watch!*'"

She shrugged next to me. "Always thought it was just an orphan dream. But I remember looking down at my feet. I had socks and shoes on, my legs swinging over the edge of the cliff, watching flashes of light. And someone had their arm around me." Karley looked at me. "I felt safer than I ever have. Until now."

I leaned forward and put my arm around her.

Karley looked back at the book splayed across her thighs. "Vilas said this was my parent's book. That they wrote it. If he were telling the truth, they were both drow mages in a certain enclave. *Evsharen.* The book is spells, really powerful ones. But it's also about when they met." She flipped the page. "When I was born. How they wanted more children, but the collegiates had entered the Underdark. There's talk about the Severing."

"Is it them, you think?" I stared down at it.

Karley smiled, staring at the pages. Then she flipped to one that she had marked with a long ribbon. It wasn't a spell. It was a little inscription.

"Didn't think so until I read this. *Took the stars to the dark, and when I cast for it, the star melted.*"

Karley looked at me. "*Evsha* means stars." A tremor crawled into her throat, and her face froze as she strained not to cry. I'd seen Karley run. I'd seen her fight for her life. But I'd never seen her afraid of hope. "It wasn't a dream, Davik. My parents called me their *stars.*"

I held her as the book slid from her.

Karley's voice was ragged. "They didn't abandon me. They saved me. There were too many spies from the collegiates after the Severing, working for the mages, infiltrating the enclaves. I think they did it to save me."

I slid back, holding her chin. "They did what they should have. They loved you."

Karley sighed. "You think they're alive?"

I wouldn't lie to her. "Maybe. If Vilas said an enclave was looking for you, that might be why. We can find out in Strouds-burg when we head back. Why didn't you tell me sooner?"

Karley laughed silently. "Hells, Davik, I'm still translating it." She ran her hand lovingly over the page as if trying to reach her parents through it. "Figured that part out last day of Stroudsburg. I thought it was about same spell I almost died trying to cast, but I didn't realize I was what they meant."

"I'm proud of you," I told her. "And you impress the hell out of me, bartender."

Karley shut the book and curled into me. "You, too. I know Windpeak—and finding Puris's sister alive—meant a lot to you. Even if some of the people here were your enemies. But I think I like the story of the bartender and the busboy more than Darkshire and his witch."

I pulled her into me as we drifted into the shadows behind our eyelids. "Me too."

CHAPTER

EIGHTEEN

I t had been a nearly sleepless night, but my runes woke me
with a soft pull as they sensed Karley's shifting soul. As I
creaked my eyes open, dawn threatened the window with
predawn light. It was the first day of the tournament, and I
thanked the gods my only role was ceremonial.

Before me, Karley lay prone on the bed, wearing only her
underwear as she studied the spellbook Deiga had given her.
Her ghost-white hair was pulled into a short ponytail, and
each foot swung back and forth like two pendulums passing
one another. When she heard me wake, she swung a foot back,
nestling it between my legs.

"Good morning, gown-champion."

"Good morning," I said with a grin. *"Evsha."*

Karley turned her head with a smile. "I like that. Am I your
stars, too?"

"That you are." I glanced at her ass, reaching up to tease
her through her panties. "How can it be morning when this
moon is still out?"

Karley bit her lip as I circled my finger over her quim, teasing the hot silk. "Again? Should I get my collar and leash?"

"Keep studying." I spanked her, drawing a little moan from her lips.

The dark elf wriggled against my touch. "Hard to concentrate..." When she spun around, crawling towards me, she slid the covers down on my lap. "Felt selfish to keep you to myself. And since I tore you away from Tyra in Hollyhead..."

"Yeah?" I leaned back, watching her lips hover over my freed cock. Karley ran her tongue down my length, torturing me while she tightened her grip.

"I ordered you breakfast..." she whispered wetly.

The door opened, followed by as a mass of red hair slipping into the room. Tyra's shock quickly turned into a hungry grin. "You greedy drow."

Karley turned her head with a smile. "Just preparing for you."

Tyra's eyes fell on mine. "I was hoping you'd say that." She walked forward, already unhitching something behind her back as her blouse came loose. As she approached the bed, my two newest lovers shyly glanced at each other.

But any inhibitions fell away as I pulled Tyra onto the bed and she straddled my chest. "Is she taking good care of you, Davik?" Then she unhitched her blouse, freeing her heavy, sparkling breasts.

I stared up at Tyra as I put her nipple in my mouth. Behind her, Karley groaned as she took me into her throat. There is something so tantalizing about a woman's eagerness for you that makes her inexperience inconsequential. I groaned as Karley's tongue circled the head of my cock.

"You forgot the door," I whispered and slid my hand around Tyra's skirt.

Tyra shuddered, her faen imbuement flowing into me. Karley moaned as the sensation coursed through my body.

"I felt that..." she whispered before covering me in the warmth of her moaning mouth.

"Did I?" Tyra grinned down at me. Then I heard someone else slip into the room.

When I leaned over, I saw Vorga drifting towards the bed after shutting the door behind her. The most-orc smiled at me. "We decided that you need to be nice and relaxed for the tournament today."

"Safer for everyone. Making sure you're not pent up." Tyra settled her crotch against my abdomen.

Vorga undid her dress and stepped out of it. Karley squealed as she received a swift spank from her. Tyra sank lower, sliding from me to join Karley's efforts from the other side. They both looked at each other, my cock between their faces.

"This is strange," Tyra giggled. Then she reached forward, taking her place to wrap her lips around the other side of me. "But he's addictive, isn't he?"

Vorga walked on the bed before sliding to sit behind me as I leaned up. She wrapped her arms and legs around me, and her hands drifted to my shoulders, kneading the muscles there. Her voice slid into my ear as Tyra and Karley's giggles slowly turned more illicit, each of them warring for space.

"I love you, Davik." Vorga kissed my neck. "And I love you being loved."

"I love you." I ran my hands down her calves. She enveloped me from behind, and my world was the heat and scent of three women adoring me. This strange but beautiful dance of finding space for one another. Not shared, like a meal, but celebrated.

Karley stared up at the two of us like an actress on the

stage. Her head drifted lower, hot breath and tongue tracing down until she was sucking on my balls. Tyra reached up to Vorga's leg as she slurped on my tip, both her and Karley's hands churning my cock like a butter churn.

"Mmm," Vorga writhed behind me as Tyra shared the sensation. "That tickles."

Karley pressed herself back onto my fingers, her breath a hushed whisper. "So who gets it?"

Tyra squeezed my cock longingly. "I think you're in for a surprise. He can satisfy all of us."

Vorga teased me with her tongue down my neck. "We have an hour until Sariel and Elina are done watching Mara... And Elina says she wants to bless us all before the tournament with some divine charm."

Tyra looked at Karley. "It was strange for me at first, in front of others. There can be collisions, but nobody has developed new tastes for anything but him. Vorga can be naked around anyone. I saw her and Sariel with him on the way to the festival last year. But I joined her and Davik in the shower in Stroudsburg."

Vorga giggled behind me. "She's the greedy one! Hogs the soap too."

Tyra slapped her leg before turning back to Karley. "But if you want to go last, or for us to leave—"

Karley slid up instantly, straddling me as her answer. Tyra crawled under my arm, nestling close to me. The three of us watched Karley bite her lip, both Tyra and Vorga teasing me with their mouths on my neck and chest.

"Every actress," Karley exhaled as she sat lower, enveloping me. The violet grip of her quim spread as she strained, joining with me. "Needs an audience."

"How is it feeling?" Elina looked at us as we walked the makeshift stalls towards the tourney grounds near Windpeak later that morning.

"Still oily," I said. The spell *felt* like I was coated in clinging oil, causing me to keep glancing at my flesh.

"It's strange." Tyra looked at her. "I keep wiping my arms, but there's nothing there."

"Protection from poison spell," Elina said with a proud smile. "Just in case anyone gets any ideas to fell our gown-champion."

"The way that castle food tastes," Tyra said with a smirk, "we'll need it."

I laughed and pulled the faen under my arm. "Ready to head home?"

"Aye," Tyra said and winked at me. "Though I've enjoyed the mornings here, as of late."

"Mmm," Sariel said and turned around in her plate armor, smiling through her war paint. She bit into a meat pasty as we walked under lines of multicolored flags. The people of the hamlets were out in force today, bringing their children to see the tournament's first day. "This is pretty good. You should try one."

"Not better than mine!" Tyra reached forward, her red hair a blur, and snatched it from her. As she chewed and slid back next to me, she shook her head. "Ugh. Gamey mutton."

Brim and Trith were each holding horns of spring ale, walking on our left. A game of chance in a colored tent started to draw them in until I motioned at them. "After, fellas."

Brim scowled. *Quick game, ugly-man.*

I laughed. "There are no quick games with you."

Trith pulled him along, looking around at the small city of tents and stalls set up. "This is the big affair?"

"Bloodsport," Tyra answered. "Chance to see your landlord break his neck on a horse? Who wouldn't flock to see that?"

Elina pushed her short legs to catch up with us. "This mud! This isn't a street. I swear by the Mistress if I— Oh!" She laughed when I picked her up and sat her on my left shoulder. "I seemed to have found my mount."

I patted her on her hip, looking up at her. "Hey."

Elina grinned down at me, her cheeks slumping over my pauldron. "Hello, lover."

Tyra pulled my right arm around her as we walked. Of all of us, she and I looked most at home in the Lowlands, which explained our lack of amazement. Elina sat on my shoulder, and Karley grasped my left arm. Each time she squeezed it, we traded grins.

"Can see so much up here," Elina mused. "Flags, horses, villeins... and a new facet settling in."

"Careful," Karley warned her. "I can turn you into a sheep now, Elina."

The cleric giggled. "I'd hate to be *chained* so. *Bound* in such a smothering feel of wool."

"I'm never going to your temple again." Karley blushed.

Elina reached down, squeezing her shoulder. "I'm glad you enjoyed my presents. You looked fabulous in them."

"That you did," I agreed.

Tyra's voice mimicked the store woman in Stroudsburg. *"Bedwear is a woman's gift to herself!"*

"Best place to see it—" Elina began.

Sariel raised her glass of wine as we walked. "Is on the floor!"

I'll kill you, ugly man, Brim mentally whispered as we walked.

"You know," I said, "lots of betting goes on at the tournament."

Brim's head snapped over. "Rahh?"

"Oh, indeed." I turned around, holding Elina up. Vorga was quiet behind us. Not upset, but lost in thought. After our tender morning, while everyone got ready, she dove back into the books I had given her. I practically had to pull her away to come to the tournament. "You still thinking about it?"

Vorga looked up at me. "I swear I saw it! *Bronzefell.* It's nowhere in the histories of the Lowlands."

"It was written before they formed, is my guess."

Vorga caught up, linking arms with Tyra to slide closer to me. "I know. But I swear I read Bronzefell somewhere. That's why it's driving me crazy."

"We'll figure it out." I winked at her and pulled her under my arm. "Why don't you come on the dais with me, take a closer look today?"

Vorga grinned. "Yeah?"

"Can't be a gown-champion without you protecting me."

It felt strange, being near a tourney ground again. I remembered being a boy and coming to one with my parents. It had been the first time we'd seen a potato—as strange and rare to us then as a dragon before the crop became popular.

My mother loved a good tourney. It meant the day off, and it meant seeing those who wrote the laws we obeyed carried to the medicae.

I kept a careful eye on everyone. This felt better—moving among the villagers and villeins, inspecting wares and seeing jugglers—than being in the stuffy castle. The rain wasn't as heavy as the evening, but as thunder rumbled above us, I doubted the affair would last long.

"I could get used to this." Elina laughed as I carried her. "I'm like one of the trays in the tavern!"

Sariel put a friendly hand on Mara, who wore a plain dress in an attempt to blend in. But every eye was on us as we walked the streets of the small fair, crusted around the edges of the tourney grounds in anticipation of bloodshed. Many doffed their caps as she passed.

"Guess my disguise isn't working." Mara laughed.

"Don't worry." Sariel handed her a glass of wine. "I'll put some warpaint on you."

"Karley"—Vorga hid under my arm from the rain—"did you learn any spells yet that keep us dry?"

A smile crept along the drow's mouth. "Have been pretty wet lately, haven't we?"

"Oh gods." Tyra laughed. "There's the snark."

When we got to the stands, Windpeak men bowed and let us pass through the gates. Sariel turned, giving me a quick kiss. "I'll be watching you, my love. Don't go jumping into this tournament."

Everyone save Vorga and Karley filtered off. I guided them in front of me as we stepped through the mud, over towards the entrance for the highborn.

"I can't believe we're going to see a joust!" Vorga laughed. "It's like those stories, Davik. Remember?"

"I do." And I'd rather Vorga was reading them to me while I split lumber than being here.

As we approached the entrance, the Windpeak men at arms nodded. "Hail, Darkshire."

"Darkshire walks with his witch queen and orc huntress," Vorga mused aloud. Then she shot a look at Karley. "But sleep was scarce, as the moans of the dark elf echoed through the castle walls the night prior."

Karley turned away in shame.

Vorga looked mortified. "No! I didn't mean it in a bad way." She walked forward, taking Karley's arm. "If you want to know who gets loud, Elina can say some—"

Then Karley grinned. "Got you."

215

Vorga laughed and slapped her on the shoulder. "You keep at it! I'm going to write a play, and you'll have to be in it!"

"Davik!" Puris called to me as we entered the area. "How did my squires do last night on guard duty?"

"Disappeared when they needed to," Karley said with a smirk. Both girls looked over, where the higher born knights, several attendants, and lords floated within a bank of food up for grabs. Roast chickens, snap peas, and the waft of dishes simmered in wine punched through the air.

"Let's get the others some food." Vorga pulled Karley along. "We'll pass it from the stands to everyone."

"Vorga, you're so damn strong!" Karley laughed, and I broke my gaze from Puris to watch her face turn in delight, smiling after me.

"Stay where I can see you," I called after them, then turned back to the new knight. "Ready for today?"

"I am. It's my first tournament. I hope to do Eralt proud." Puris looked around. "Is Mara not with you?"

"Ah." I grinned. "You didn't even miss me? I feel used, Puris."

The young man smiled. "If I win, I plan to ask her favor. She came, correct?"

I nodded, patting him on the pauldron. It was heavy stuff, heavier than war plate, but he was strong. "She's in the stands just to our right with everyone."

Puris nodded, exhaling. "I'm nervous."

"Well, it isn't goblins."

"That it isn't." Puris gave me a brief bow. "See you out there."

"Puris," I called to him when he turned. The young knight looked at me, and for a moment, I saw him as I had years ago, standing on top of Rochdale. Some of these same houses

216

competing today had been among those that were our enemies.

"Yes, Davik?"

"Win or lose," I told him, "ask for her favor. If you don't, that's true loss."

The young man smiled. "You might be right. See you, Davik."

As he walked back towards the tourney grounds, I saw a sight that made my blood churn. Vorga stood with a large plate of food, Karley, next to her. But her face was shocked, too shocked to say anything, as a monk of the Sword stood in front of her, wagging his finger in her face.

I saw Sir Hewer of Bronzefell looking on in amusement, along with several Springdall knights.

When I approached, his words fell on my ears.

"I'm not sure how things work... where you come from. But you take as much for yourself, not your entire day."

"I'm sorry," Vorga's voice fell. "I just wanted to give some—"

"Don't put it back!" The monk jabbed a finger, barely touching her dress. "No one wants to eat what your hands have touched! They don't have manners where you come from?"

Vorga's face burned as she looked around, unsure what to do.

I approached the monk from behind. I felt the eyes of lords and knights on me. They were eager to see if Darkshire was just a story or something else.

The words felt like acid when I hissed them, "They don't have fistfights where you come from?"

The monk turned, surprised. He was younger than the other two I'd seen in the halls. I saw several lords smirking.

"Gown champion, I was just telling this greenskin here—well, instructing—"

"And who are you"—I stared down at him—"to instruct my retinue in anything?"

Vorga grabbed Karley by the arm, pulling her away.

"Manners are important." The monk spat. "Chivalry, such things. Ransoming captured knights *alive*. Rochdale forgot their manners, forgot their place."

I nodded slowly, feeling the slow pulse of violence in me. "My mother always said manners weren't knowing which fork to select. But pretending not to notice when your company didn't. Did they not teach you that in the monastery?"

The monk sucked his teeth. "Never thought I'd see the day when a greenskin and a shadow elf desecrated a lord's dais." He looked around at the lords. "Two whores straddling their pimp."

The tent shifted, every eye and head turning to us.

"Not to worry." I smiled. "You won't."

Two teeth flew from his mouth when my fist slid up, knocking his head skyward. A groaning scream echoed from him as I grabbed his bundled robes. "Fucking monk," I hissed as I drove my fist into his soft little gut, plied with free food and wine, leaving him to collapse on the ground.

No one moved, not a knight, not a lord. I looked around the tent. The monk shuddered with broken teeth, before vomiting a belly of wine at my boots.

"Darkshire?" Eralt stepped into the tent. His tone wasn't angry, but there was a note of exasperation.

He took in the scene. The monk curled on the ground. The teeth. The lords doing their best impression of statues. Tension settling like dust in a quarry.

Eralt sighed through his nose.

I let my gaze travel the tent, meeting every pair of eyes. If they thought they could test me, they were mistaken. I had waged war on these cunts before. My people were not to be touched. "This brother has fallen ill, Sir Eralt. He needs the medicae."

"Ekyll!" Eralt growled. "Bring Luka, and take this monk to the medicae. Tell his brothers he needs their help."

Two squires yelped a confirmation. When I turned back to Vorga and Karley, they were both grinning. "Shall we, my ladies?"

"I think so." Karley drifted towards me, playing the role of the witch. "Do you have enough, Vorga?"

"Oh yes," Vorga said with a smirk as we stepped around the shivering man. Before we left, I leaned over and grabbed an entire roast chicken as the conversation picked back up around us.

Sir Hewer's face darkened, and he turned from the tent without a word.

Silas Drakemoor stifled a laugh. "What fool put him up to that? Testing Darkshire?"

Renrick Drakemoor gulped a glass of wine, glancing at Sir Hewer. "Blond is my guess."

"This way, Davik." Eralt nodded to the stairs to the Lord's dais. "I would also appreciate if you need something from the tent, could you ask the attendants?"

"Sure." I followed Eralt. When Luka and Ekyll, the squires who had guarded the hallway, saw me, they grinned. I tossed the chicken to them.

As we trailed up the steps, Karley and Vorga giggled once we were out of sight.

"Is it bad I liked that?" Karley asked.

"Might need that drying spell after all." Vorga laughed. Then she squeezed my rear as I climbed above her. "Saved by a warrior in dark armor."

I stood on the Lord's dais, sheltered from the drizzling rain under a canopy. My seat of honor was filled by Vorga and Karley.

The first tilts were among the squires. I recognized Ekyll, and the crowd murmured its disappointment when he fell against a Drakemoor squire after two runs.

"You've done so well training them, Sir Eralt," Elyse said behind me. "Truly impressive."

"My thanks, Lady Elyse." Eralt inclined his head. "They are here to do you honor."

"What's taking so long?" Elyse looked around from her seat. "The last bout ended some time ago."

Eralt inclined his head. "Tourney plate weighs much more than standard war plate, my lady. It takes some doing to get the men onto their mounts."

Lord Hamlin waved a fly away. "Avelmont had a pulley of sorts." Now that the rain was falling, the insects were taking refuge under the covered dais. "Seven tourneys a year. They made a profit from it, if I recall."

"Indeed, Lord Hamlin."

I glanced over at the crowded seats next to us, watching our group.

"Must be hard to keep an eye on your flock, Davik." Elyse sipped her wine. "Numerous as they are."

"I have sharp eyes," I answered her.

Sariel and Elina sat in the front row, with Trith and Brim two pews above them. Between all of them was Mara, our hostage, speaking excitedly with Tyra.

"Knights are much the same." Elyse set her cup down. "A war horse and tourney horse. A traveler and trotter. Is there a particular way you select which to ride?"

Before I could respond, Karley cut in. "He rides them all. Daily."

Vorga laughed. "*Stop it.*"

"Such a man of endurance." Elyse stared at the tourney grounds as the next knights took their positions. "Though my father said Magebreakers were always good for that. There were some here after the war, skinny things. We gave them food but had no work for them. Hard to imagine Davik so skinny, isn't it, girls?"

"What's that?" Lord Hamlin leaned forward. "Horses?"

"Nothing, Father." Elyse patted his hand. "Let's watch and see who your new son-in-law is."

If Elyse thought she would get under my skin, she'd have to try harder. But when I gazed back at Vorga, I saw her cheek darkening. I held out my hand. "Come here, my love."

Vorga floated next to me. "This castle isn't exactly what I thought it'd be," she muttered.

I slid an arm over her shoulder. "I love you, you know."

She smiled. "You better. Did you see jousts when you were younger?"

"Once." I turned to look at the field. "They rode in groups then, as was the fashion. No fence in the middle."

"A sortie," Eralt said from behind Lord Sewell. "Was the term. I preferred it."

"So it was." I smiled and turned back to Vorga. "But in the war, knights would bring their tourney armor. They'd put on a show sometimes in the camps. Coins clinking everywhere."

"*Sir Hewer of Bronzefell!*" the crier announced. Every head turned in the rain to see the Springdall knight, clad in burnished bronze. The caparison gripped his mount from the rain. I was surprised they hadn't called the tournament for the weather, but I suppose they had a schedule to keep.

"*Sir Silas Drakemoor!*" Heads turned to see Renrick Drakemoor's brother.

"Who do you think will win, Sir Eralt?" Vorga looked at the knight.

"I wish them both good fortune." Eralt inclined his head, but as Vorga stared at him, he broke into a smile. Vorga could bring the soft spot out of most gruff men. "I've heard some knights are wagering strongly on Sir Silas, my lady."

Black and red colors, with a long cape, followed Silas Drakemoor. From the camps behind Bronzefell, I saw the figure of Serlo the Loner speaking to someone in bronze armor.

Both riders spurred their horses forward. Hewer rode well, like a soldier. Not light in the saddle. His lance was a spiral of painted ashwood, his shield a curved rectangle. But Silas Drakemoor rode like a druid, one with his mount.

"Holy hells." Karley leapt up behind me.

Rain slid from both knights as they rode towards one another. Mud splashed on hooves as the thunder in the ground matched the aching sky.

The crowd roared when Drakemoor's lance split on the Bronzefell shield. The collective roar of the crowd echoed the splitting wood. But Hewer was strong and stayed in his saddle.

"Lean away," Eralt muttered. I cast an eye over to him. He was ready to leap into the grounds and show them how to do it himself.

"It's like Hollyhead..." Vorga whispered as Silas Drakemoor took another lance from his squire. The tips were blunted, made to shatter on steel, but those splinters could find their way into a gorget or an eye-slit.

Both Karley and Vorga gripped my forearms as the knights rode each other down, now coming wide and circling in.

"Too wide," I found myself saying. But I was right. They were moving diagonally towards one another, not parallel enough. Silas Drakemoor saw what I did, and in an insane bout of bravery and stupidity, he dropped his shield and steadied his lance with two hands as they closed on one another.

Hewer's hit clipped his shoulder. But Silas leaned from his saddle, trying to muscle the unwieldy length of ash. The tip bobbed wildly, but the timing was incredible. It surged up as Hewer's horse's head dipped down, crashing into the hips of the knight and blasting him from the saddle.

Eralt surged forward to the edge of the dais, his gauntleted fist ripping into the air. "That's a win!"

The crowd surged to its feet. I felt the old Lowland ways working their way into me.

Look at me, Ma. Up here with the lords on the dais. Not on your shoulders in the field.

"Is he alright, Eralt?" Elyse asked.

Squires ran out to Sir Hewer. Two Monks of the Sword came as well, bending low to tend to the man. Then one of them waved with a smile at the crowd.

"It appears so, my lady." Eralt composed himself again.

I grinned at him. "You know, Eralt. I've a horse you can borrow if you wish."

"Quite alright." Eralt shook his head. The old fellow was enjoying himself. "Just damn fine jousting. Damn fine."

Silas Drakemoor raised his hand to the crowd, trotting around the arena until he sauntered over to the dais and unhelmed himself.

"A step closer to your hand, Lady Elyse." Silas Drakemoor bowed from his horse.

"It would seem so. Well ridden!" Elyse smiled at him.

Silas raised an eyebrow. "Could I beg your favor, perhaps?"

Elyse laughed. "Let's wait until after the second rounds. We can't be showing favorites, can we?"

"She's loving this," Vorga said when she turned back to me. "So many men fighting over her."

"Refreshments?" A servant walked up and held a pitcher of wine. After she refilled Elyse's, the girls took two pewter cups.

I watched Elyse, sitting on her small little chair, watching the show that would determine her future. Despite her attempt at cutting remarks, I was glad to see her enjoy what little she could of this spectacle. The years hadn't been kind to her, but the bright girl I guarded years ago was still there.

The next two tilts brought swift victories to House Bronzefell, felling one of Eralt's men and a Springdall knight who flew through the air in a tumble of white and green. It took two Monks of the Sword to help him regain consciousness.

"These are skilled men," I noted, watching the Bronzefell knight return to his side. "War seasoned."

"Highly proficient," Eralt said, somewhat confused.

Vorga took the chance to pry further. "Sir Eralt, where is Bronzefell?"

"They're a newer house," Lord Sewell cut in. "Far south."

"Prized armor for such new blood." Eralt looked at them.

"Hmm." Lord Hamlin stared into the crowds. "Sir Eralt, is Puris up soon?"

"He is, my lord."

"Go give him a word of encouragement from me, would you?"

"I'd be glad." Eralt bowed and walked from the dais.

"I love your dress, Vorga," Elyse said behind us. "It's quite lovely."

Vorga smiled. "Thank you. We had it fitted in Stroudsburg."

"Quite lovely." Lord Hamlin nodded without looking. "Ah, here comes Sir Puris."

"You did such a good job on his chronicle." I squeezed Vorga's shoulder. When I looked past Karley to my right, Sariel and Elina were sharing a baked treat from a vendor in the crowd. Brim was betting gold with a group of other Lowlanders, wagering heavily on Puris. Trith leaned forward to throw his coin on top of Brim's.

Tyra and Mara smiled up at me, giving me a small wave.

"Sir Puris the Bladeless!" the crier announced. Most of the crowd didn't realize it was a Windpeak knight. But the squire corps followed him out as he wore plain tourney plate, hefting an unpainted brown lance.

"Puris looks great," I said as the squire trotted out, steadying his horse.

His opponent was a Highblade knight. Ettimer Highblade. The man I was supposed to choose for Elyse. His yellow armor was freshly painted, and he looked like he didn't know how to move in it.

Worse than that, I realized as I stared at him, trying to steady the horse. I looked over in the pew next to us, and Tyra saw what I did. She looked at me to confirm what she saw.

Ettimer Highblade barely knew how to ride.

"Oh dear." Lord Sewell shook his head. "I'm afraid you'll have your work cut out for you, Darkshire."

That much was true. There was no bell to begin. Puris raised his lance in a salute, and Ettimer did the same.

Puris thundered towards him on a palfrey. He had skipped the caparison for his first bout as a knight. Ettimer Highblade's horse nearly reared itself until a squire behind him gave it a push-slap, and he began his uneasy gallop towards Puris.

He made it barely three strides, his lance still waving haphazardly, when Puris hit him square on the chest, toppling him violently over like a cup.

The crowd roared as loud as they had for Silas Drakemoor. Elyse let out a long sigh. "Not even halfway down the field..."

Puris raised his broken lance and trotted around the stands, the distant mountains and long green grasses of the

Lowlands framing behind him like a painting, smudged with rain. I heard Brim and Trith's shouts in the air. Karley and Vorga clapped next to me.

"Good for him!" Vorga laughed.

The young knight rode steadily around the arena before slowing and sauntering towards the dais. Puris removed his helmet and smiled at Lord Hamlin.

"Well struck, Sir Puris!" Lord Sewell announced.

"Thank you, Lord." Puris smiled, the smile of youth and victory. The whole world was in front of him at that moment, and I felt privileged to see it. The shy squire was beaming, reborn as a knight. He had penned the first line of his new tale himself, and the victory was written in ink. "If amenable, I'd seek your daughter's favor."

"You are free to seek." Lord Sewell laughed. "But the granting is not up to me."

Elyse stood up a bit straighter in her seat, holding back a smile. But Puris bowed to her and moved his horse over to the stands next to us, stopping to stare at Mara.

"My lady?" Puris smiled at Mara.

Mara blushed as the crowd applauded, but her eyes were for Puris. She stood and pulled a ribbon of silk from her dress, pale orange, and draped it over Puris's broken lance.

"Ah, to be young." Lord Hamlin chuckled. When I looked back, Elyse's face looked darker by the moment.

The crowd began to laugh at the flailing Ettimer High-blade. This man had no chance to finish the tournament, much less win it.

"That's hard to watch." Karley shuddered next to me. "Getting wet out here even with this canopy."

"Go stand near the brazier," I whispered. "Warm yourself up."

The drow grinned at me. "I think I'll stay right here."

The squires' melee was set to start. Young men from four different banners walked into the field while the workers took the jousting post away. But the crowd began to shift as the rain fell harder.

"Can they fight in this?" Vorga asked.

No one responded to her. When I turned around to eye Elyse, she gestured back at me. "You're the gown-champion, Davik. If they fight in this deluge, it's your command."

Eralt rejoined us, beaming at Puris's victory. He looked at everyone. "Are we retiring?"

It wasn't going to be a pretty bout, with the grounds turning into pure mud. But no one had asked us in the war if the weather was ever to our liking.

I looked over at the collection of Windpeak squires. Ekyll was there, seemingly entering the bout. He spoke excitedly to his other armored comrades, replete with hauberks and a collection of weapons.

Then I saw that quieter squire, Luka. Smaller than his friends. Bronzefell and Highblade both fielded their squires across the field. Luka stood still in the rain, his gauntlet flexing around the handle of a blunted war axe.

An orphan like me. I saw him staring at me when Spring-dall entered. The crowd chanted for more action before the day was done, and I'm sure every vendor with a stall was begging for the festivities to continue. There would be no more jousts. No knight with their head on straight would risk a horse in this weather.

The crowd quieted when I raised the hammer. I kept my eyes on Luka. How many of those squires fathers had I known? How many had stood in the rains of Rochdale before me?

I watched Luka, and I knew the melody of his soul. What it was to lose your family. To warm yourself in hate every day, praying for revenge. And the fear that something so small as

227

rain might take it from you. Or worse, that when you finally get it, it changes nothing.

What would I tell him, that taverns of beautiful women can fix you? Would they have done anything for me when I was freed from the camps? I had lived to see the fear in mage's eyes before I snatched the light from them like a candle. When your life is defined by what's been taken, sometimes all you need is to hurt something. We get what we need or what we want. Rarely both. And one is usually worse for us than the other.

"Begin!" I shouted.

The crowd roared. The knights of four houses pushed the squires forward, small collections of men in differing colors, bent on attacking one not like their own. The terrain was awful, slick with mud. When they started hammering and bashing each other, it was the din of clinched combat and broken jaws.

The onlookers loved it. A Springdall squire slumped when Luka crashed an axe into his gut. Another squire, in a tabard too dirty to signify his house, slipped and thrashed under a storm of steel boots.

The crowd turned into a breathless mob, bellowing into the storm as they watched men battle. But they weren't men. They were teenage boys trying to kill each other in the mud.

Same as any war.

CHAPTER

NINETEEN

Dinner that evening was a sparser affair. Moods were lowered now that the gown-jousts were delayed. The question hung on everyone's mind—how long would they wait? As I moved among the hall to find my place, I overhead several knights talking about their chances. The Windpeak squires had won the melee. Now they manned the walls outside in the storm, doing honor to their guests.

Elyse waved to me when I entered the hall. There was no high table this evening. The storm battered the fortress.

"Davik, please join us. The gown champion should preside."

I glanced at the table where the rest of the group sat, save for Vorga. I felt better about keeping my eye on them, and I had kept my armor on when coming here. Brim nodded to me from a long line of the girls.

I am watching, ugly-man.

Knights in a feasting hall and Elyse Sewell; it was like I was traveling back in time. I sat down on the bench. When I glanced down the table, Trith joked with several Springdall knights he had gotten friendly with. Sir Hewer walked back from the privy, taking his place across from me.

"Sir Hewer," Elyse noted as the Bronzefell man sat down, "your men wear your armor to dinner?"

"As does our guest." His eyes settled on me. "Seemed prudent, considering the company."

"A fine gown-champion." Lord Hamlin Sewell nodded, hoping to move the conversation along.

The second course was the direboar, simmered in mushrooms. I had seen the carcass of the beast now rotting in the rains outside the castle, moved outside for local villagers to take a carving from if they wished.

"I, for one," a Springdall knight said as he raised his goblet, "welcome our new friends. Too long have we held grudges against the mages after the war. Now they flood our country with coin. Whether for crops or tumbling dice!"

Trith smiled. "Not of the collegiates, sir. Never was in the Summoner War."

"All the same!" The knight grinned around the table eagerly. "Welcome!"

Silas Drakemoor chuckled next to his brother. "You just like him because you win money from him."

"That, too!"

Vorga came in from the hallway, smiling as she walked. I leaned back and beckoned her over.

"Don't want you wandering around alone," I whispered. "Okay?"

"Sorry. I figured it out, by the way." Vorga smiled. "It wasn't Bronzefell. I kept looking at those three books you gave me. It was in the book we got in Stroudsburg on Lowland legends. House Whitmer of Bronze*fall*."

I raised an eyebrow at her. "What was the story?"

"About a man who faked his death to collect taxes from his

subjects who feigned poverty." Vorga kissed my ear. "Love you."

"Love you, too," I murmured as she walked back to the table. Vorga grinned as she plopped down next to Mara, and they began giggling.

Two seats down from me, far from a seat of honor, Ettimer Highblade seemed lost in his soup.

Does he even know? He must, that he's already chosen for her hand.

Maybe that was it. He had embarrassed himself greatly.

"Rough ride today, Sir Highblade," I offered. "The rain did you no favors."

Ettimer snorted like a man used to chastising himself. Perhaps Elyse was right to choose him for his gentler nature. Though I suspected he seemed a finer puppet than a lover. "That armor was so damn heavy."

I nodded. "Tourney plate is like that. You should have your blacksmith see to a training set."

Highblade grimaced as he muttered, "Bronzefell loaned it to me. Could never afford plate like that. Excuse me." The knight pushed himself up from the table to wander towards the privy.

Karley and Tyra smiled at me between the shifting men across from me. I felt the pang to return to Oakshire. We'd get through tomorrow, and then we'd be on our way. I expected harder jousts, fiercer melees, and then we'd move on after the wedding ceremony.

The rain crested on the roof of the castle like a thousand fingertips on a single drum. For all their preparation, Windpeak couldn't control the weather.

Never afford plate like that.

Ettimer's words circled like a cold knife around my mind.

Highblade was supposed to fund the rebuilding of the port. That was why he was here.

Several servants swapped out buckets to repair the water coming in through the roof. In the light of the fireplaces, the drift of deteriorating tapestries wafted down like a foul mist.

Never afford plate like that.

"You keep sipping at that cup," Renrick Drakemoor chastised his younger brother, "and you'll sleep through your chance to win the dowry."

Sir Silas grinned. "I ride better hungover. The dowry will be secure."

The conversations seemed far away suddenly. And what was Elyse's dowry? The castle needed mortaring. The tapestries were threadbare. Yet, they hadn't blinked when they slid a coffer of coin towards me. What knight would want a seat at Windpeak? It was akin to buying a sinking ship. What did they have to offer?

Lord Sewell's words came back to me.

A prize no one could refuse.

Me.

Bile rose in my throat. Sariel saw my face from her table. Her smile fell slowly as I locked eyes with her. I cocked my head to the side. She set her napkin on the table, not betraying anything, a signal that we had worked out that she had understood.

"No minstrels tonight?" Renrick Drakemoor looked around.

"We thought it best to give our people a chance to keep warm in the rains." Lord Sewell smiled down the table.

Sariel and the girls stood up, excusing themselves, taking Mara with them.

Elyse noticed and reached out to her. "Sister, won't you come join us for a moment?"

"I will when we return." Mara grinned. "There's something we forgot to bring."

"Nonsense." Elyse pulled her. "Davik can keep an eye on you."

My stomach twisted as I looked around the room. Why? Why would Elyse bring me here? What could she possibly gain from my death? Jame was gone, as was his father, Ironclad. If anything, these houses would be glad his shadow no longer controlled them. No knight here would risk their life to slay me for the favor of a poor house.

"Sir Drakemoor"—Elyse twisted her goblet—"how do you favor your chances tomorrow?"

"Well enough, my lady." Silas bowed his head. "Luckily, I'm the only brother who rides well."

As the doors closed behind the girls, the wind caught it and slammed it shut. I saw the Helmed warrior shift suddenly near the wall, startled by the sound.

I looked up and stared at those blackened eye-slits. A tall man. Tall like—

It's about a man who faked his death.

"Sir Hewer," I cut into the conversation, "does your Helmed brother not eat?"

"Only in prayer." Hewer smirked. "He fears for my safety in your company. I'm sure you understand."

"Those days are gone." Elyse smiled at the group. "Thankfully."

"Good bodyguards are so hard to find." I looked at the Helmed man. "But I suppose Prince Jame knew that even better than I."

Silence fell like a corpse dropped from the rafters.

"Too much wine." Elyse smiled weakly. "This new stock is so sweet, it's easy to overindulge."

"I don't think I've had enough." I stared at my cup.

"Allow me." The same Springdall knight who had toasted to Trith stood up quickly. Far too quickly.

Both Elyse and her father froze in their seats as he walked towards me.

I didn't dare give it away with Trith.

You fools. You impatient fools. The girl is right next to me.

He bent over and poured a freshly opened bottle into my cup. "The past is easy to latch onto. To new beginnings!" I never took my eyes from Elyse and her father, who turned paler and paler, as if the wine entering my cup was blood from their own bodies.

I swirled the chalice. Trith stared at me from down the table, watching me intently. When I swallowed the wine, I felt Elina's protective spell churn inside me. Waves of black nausea cascaded up my gullet. I gritted my teeth as divine magic shimmered faintly around me. My stomach heaved as the poison was counteracted.

Eralt looked at me in concern from his place on the wall. "Davik, are you unwell?"

He didn't know. Puris hadn't either. I was right to trust them.

But wrong to not question their trust.

Every Springdall and Bronzefell eye watched me like hunters waiting for their quarry to bleed out. Silas and Renrick continued, oblivious. The buckets filled with the drip from the rooftop. The fire crackled on wet wood.

I exhaled, still alive. I stared up at Sir Hewer. "Bit bitter for my taste."

Eyes began to shift. There were twenty knights at this table, and more around it. The quiet kiss of steel sliding against itself. Something hadn't gone according to plan.

All we had to do was get through dinner. Grab the girls. Escape.

Trith's looked at the Springdall knight he had joked with moments ago, his voice flat as it cut through the silence.

"You just tried to poison my friend."

The knight turned to him. "What? Come now—"

Trith emptied a wand through his breastplate in a flash of white heat. Blood and bone burst through his back in a sickening crunch.

The remaining Springdall knights rose from their seats. Trith stood at the same time I did, both of us throwing the table over for cover. Food and wine smashed onto the floor as roars filled the air. On our side stood Drakemoor and Highblade men. The Bronzefell knights drew hidden daggers and swords, including their servants, who were no servants at all.

"Stop this!" Eralt shouted.

"Not yet!" Lord Hamlin screamed. "He has my daughter!"

Yet.

"Come." Elyse pulled Mara away, grasping for Lord Sewell. "Come, Father."

"Lord?" Eralt's voice was devastated. "What have you done?"

"Davik?" Mara looked at me.

The knights waited, clinching together. Sir Hewer shook his head. "We tried to settle this in the lists... but now it must be this hall."

But he wasn't speaking to me. He was speaking to his lord. The lord of a house risen from the dead.

The Helmed warrior removed his helmet slowly as if he were savoring this moment.

Ice blue eyes stared at me, the same as his son's when they looked up at me from that bloodstained desk.

Lord Elrick Avelmont. Father to Prince Jame.

Ironclad.

There was no smile from him. He was here to collect his tax

of vengeance. For a moment, all I heard was the crackling of the fireplaces.

I grabbed Mara, wrenching her in front of me. I slipped the dirk from my hip and placed it between my hand and her throat. "Don't move," I warned her.

Elyse was mortified. Trith circled to my right, unsure if Drakemoor or Highblade were enemy or foe. We'd been here before. My brother knew the plan. Survive and escape. That was victory this night.

"I'll open her throat," I warned Ironclad.

The old conqueror smiled coolly at me. "So open it."

I slid the blade. Blood pooled down her neck; the only sound from Mara was a gurgled gasp as my fingers dug into her throat.

"I'll finish her," I warned and wrenched her towards me. Mara couldn't speak as I squeezed her throat. "Talk some sense into your guest, Sewell!"

It was an old trick, one I had used before. Put the blade to their throat and hold your hand over it. When they move, draw it across your palm while you choke them, and hope they don't notice.

"Mara!" Sewell screamed. When I eyed him, he turned back to Ironclad. "Stop this! It wasn't supposed to be like this. You said you would wait!"

I hated this part. The moment they didn't know if you were bluffing or a monster.

Lord Elrick Avelmont watched me. "I've waited long enough."

The Springdall knights seemed unsure of what to do.

"Just a moment!" Sewell screamed. "Eralt! Grab the women from his chambers! We'll trade, and then we'll have him."

Eralt locked eyes with me. Then his gaze fell to my fingers.

A cascade of emotions covered his face as he looked back at Lord Sewell.

The final one was outrage.

He drew his sword, angling it at both his liege lord and Ironclad. "You treacherous dogs!"

A knight made a break for the door behind us. Trith blew his face away with a wand. "Nobody leaves this hall," he hissed and backed up with me.

"Too true." Ironclad weighed the life of the girl in my hands.

Bodies shifted, closing in. Then Ironclad spoke.

"Kill him."

TWENTY

"What's a sword?" Rayleth asked me long ago.

"A weapon."

The elf looked at me. "Is it a weapon when it's on the ground, thirty feet from you?"

"It's just metal."

The rain drenched us both. We stood on a cliffside path, and our path was blocked. Trith and Eron panted behind us. The agony of our climb hadn't done their wounds any good, nor the creeping fevers their casting had just bought them.

"It's an edge," Rayleth whispered. "For all its gold and finery, all the hammer blows that forge it, it's an edge. An introduction into what can be. A defiance against what could happen. But it's nothing without the arm that wields it."

A profane cleric walked back and forth ahead of us, sword glimmering with otherworldly power. Something evil that lived on this peak—without reason or purpose. The rain hissed into bouts of steam every time a raindrop touched the metal of his cursed blade. His antlered helm stared at me. It seemed as if the metal was molded to his flesh.

We had been separated from Brightplate and the others in Daggar. They had the scroll and the names. But they couldn't do the job without us.

Trith coughed behind me. Whatever spells had lived in their souls were empty now. All they had were Trith's bandoliers. Eron needed shelter, too, a fire, and a bottle of hot wine.

"What's fighting?" Rayleth asked me.

I stared at the enemy blocking our way. It stopped walking and stared at me. The steam stank of metal and terrible power. "Exertion."

My friend pressed his shoulder into mine as he stood next to me. The only warmth in this shivering deluge.

"Show me."

TABLES SPLIT UNDER ARCANE BLASTS. Trith spun as a sword crossed his chest, his arcane armor glowing gold next to me. He slammed his spear against a knight's head, lightning crackling, illuminating us as the man's brain boiled solid.

"Bastards!" Trith screamed and flung the remaining sorcery from the staff, where it danced across four more approaching figures.

I booted a knight from me. I had flung Mara towards her sister—the treacherous bitch. They had disappeared up to the rooms. Somewhere in the confusion, Ironclad's men slew Lord Hamlin Sewell.

Almost every candle had burned out, and our figures were lit by the faraway hearths. Now we fought in the near dark. Like the war. Unsure if the man near you was your enemy or your friend, and both were just as confused and dangerous enough to kill you.

"Silas!" Renrick screamed near me. When I turned, I saw the man's brother mortally wounded, clutching his belly.

There were almost thirty armed men in the hall. A third of them were Highblade's men, standing in paralyzed shock at the onslaught. Betrayal, hate, aggression—this was my domain. If they wanted Darkshire dead—they'd have to meet him first. I killed anything with a green or bronze tabard.

"Fucking cunt!" I head-butted a Springdall knight's nose to mush. When I dropped him to the ground, his comrade swung a longsword at me. I caught the blade with the ridged edges of my left arm. Something I used as a shield when I didn't have one.

Or a snare.

He tried to wrench the blade free, but he was too slow. Steel trapped in black iron. My hand clamped down on his forearm—twisting until the bones split from his elbow. The pop sounded like ripping a drumstick from a chicken's carcass.

His comrade flinched when I turned.

I tilted my head as I put the dirk in my left hand, giving him a heartbeat to wonder if he was next. Then my sword spun from its scabbard across his face.

Trith circled towards me, both hands on his spear. His casting needed time to replenish. Two knights broke apart his sorcerous armor in a flash of golden light. They'd been in the war, they knew there were limits. I grabbed him and spun him behind me. A blade snaked from the shadows, cold steel parting something in my jaw.

"Bring him down!" Ironclad screamed.

I surged towards the two knights. It was too dark to see the color of their tabards, but they'd be red in a moment.

My boot found his knee, and the joint folded sideways with a wet *pop*. His scream barely left his throat before my elbow shattered his jaw, teeth snapping loose like dice on a tavern table. He choked, trying to spit blood, but my boot came down before he had the chance. The skull beneath my heel gave like rotten fruit, and the spray painted my legs. I snarled, already hunting the next knight.

"Davik—" Trith said in a tone I knew well.

The knight backed up, stumbling over a table. To our right, Ettimer Highblade and his men looked on in paralyzed shock.

I wove in, blade coming down high. The knight slid for a riposte. Our steel danced. I felt impatient as I hurtled through his guard. I wanted my mace. I wanted my hammer and dented breastplates.

I felt Trith cast from his soul. An orb the size of an apple glowed red hot on the knight's cuirass—all Trith could manage—but it was enough.

My sword plunged through the steel like soft cheese. He gasped, looking down at the blade that ended his life. I ripped it free, his blood bubbling and hissing on hot metal. I ran the hardening steel from the blade along my catch-sleeve.

Trith sent a blast of wind at the knights attacking Eralt, hurtling them back several feet.

I breathed the acid from my lungs. Something flapped on my face, but I was too wrathful to feel it yet. I pointed my dirk at Ettimer Highblade and his men in warning. "Stay there."

Elina's healing spell slid from a rune in my shoulder, sliding up my neck to weave my flesh back together like a clicking spider. Highblade's eyes looked like he saw a devil.

"Sword damn you all!" Eralt roared up the hall. "Show yourself, Avelmont!"

Ironclad did just that. Nearly every knight in the hall fell back near the lit fireplace.

I walked past Renrick Drakemoor, crouched over Silas. "Brother... stay with me."

Trith flocked to my side as we moved towards the gathering knights. His face was grim, lit by the crystal tip of his spear, his eyes already stained with voidsickness. He pulled a wand from his chest and sent another arcane missile toward Ironclad. The ball of energy broke apart on his armor.

"Fucking enchanted." Trith shifted his spear.

I glanced at a monk of the Sword, eyes darting between us and the path to Bronzefell. He dropped a bloody dagger he had slain a Windpeak man with as if his sin could be cast away.

"*He's* not."

Trith snapped a wand from his hip and grunted. The monk's leg disappeared in a crunch of red mist and wet slapping sounds. When he fell screaming, I silenced him with a sword through his chest, eyes locked on Ironclad.

The lord in hiding, now free to taste his vengeance, stared at me. "You lived too long."

Eralt and his man circled from the other side.

The fire crackled.

Ironclad gazed around the hall, unbothered. He pushed through his group of knights, raising a blade at Eralt's man at arms.

"No!" Eralt shouted. But it was too late. The soldier leapt forwards, ready to strike the head from the snake.

Ironclad stepped towards him.

One stroke.

The man's helm clattered to the floor before his body did.

"The girls," I whispered to Trith. Then I looked at Eralt. "Get over here."

Now that the slaughter had stilled, we could hear the war beyond these walls—steel against steel. The melody of treachery.

Eralt glanced towards the feast hall door, where his squires and men were locked in battle.

Trith grabbed Renrick Drakemoor by the back of his tabard. "Let's go."

Highblade knights looked back and forth between our two parties. Ettimer Highblade's face was pale. Ironclad turned to regard him.

"Make your choice."

Highblade swallowed. He had eight knights with him. "Aid Lord Avelmont."

Silas Drakemoor gurgled what sounded like his last words as his brother dragged him towards us. "Craven."

"Let's go." I snarled and backed into the hallway towards the girls. Trith followed, and Eralt helped Renrick drag his dying brother with us.

Ironclad slid his helmet back into place, his voice a death knell. "I'll drown your whores in your own blood, Darkshire. And when I'm done, I'll raise a cup to my son."

"Your son died with a whimper." I spat on the ground, blade pointed at him. "His bladder stained my boots before his blood did."

Ironclad's sword wavered a fraction, just a hair, but I saw it. His gauntlet flexed against the grip in a whine of metal.

Got you.

Eralt and Trith slammed the doors shut as I backed into the hallway. We looked around for a brace.

"What have you got?" I looked at Trith.

He was already pulling a scroll from his belt. "Ice."

I stood back as he recited the words. A foot of ice spread from the floor, crawling up the hallway doors, splintering and freezing the wood and metal underneath it. The scroll fell to ashes in Trith's hands as he grabbed his spear. "There goes a hundred gold."

. . .

Sariel yanked the door open the moment I knocked, pulling us inside before slamming it shut and barring it. The thunder outside nearly drowned out the sound of steel hacking against ice.

Renrick and Eralt dragged Silas toward the cleric as she crouched over him.

"Elina!" I barked. "Help him."

"I felt it in my ring." Sariel grabbed me, turning me toward her. Her hands were steady, but her eyes were searching. "Are you hurt?"

I shook my head. That ice wall wouldn't last forever, but with the storm outside, we had a window. "I'm fine. We need to go."

"Davik," Tyra approached, voice low. "Are you sure?"

"What happened?" Vorga asked. "Where's Mara?"

"She's with her sister." I exhaled, steadying myself. "She's fine. We need to move. Grab only what you can carry."

Trith slumped against the wall, exhaustion pulling him downward. He reached into his vest, thumbed a stopper loose, and drained a small vial. The color barely returned to his face.

I took stock of the room—Silas bleeding out on the floor, Elina's fluttering tattoos illuminating as she checked him. A terrible stillness settled over her features before she looked up at me.

"Davik..." Her voice was tight. "He's—"

"Can you help him?" Renrick pleaded.

I met the knight's wide, desperate eyes. "He's gone, Renrick."

"No!" The highborn's voice broke, his hands trembling as he clutched at his brother's cooling body. "No! He was just—"

Eralt placed a bloody gauntlet on his shoulder. "He was valiant, Renrick. Truly."

"Can't you bring him back?" the knight begged Elina. "You have power. Just bring him back."

"I'm sorry." Regret filled her voice. "Your brother has passed."

Renrick collapsed over Silas's body. The sound that tore from him was something primal, something worse than a scream. Sariel and Tyra pulled Karley and Vorga away, trying to give the grieving man space. But there was so little to give.

I thought no less of him. I had sounded that same cry before—until the cord had been plucked too many times.

Brim caught my attention from the window.

Ugly-man. Come here.

I crossed the room, stepping onto a chair beside him. Outside, the storm was relentless—sheets of rain hammering against the stone, the wind howling like a hungry beast.

"What is it?"

Brim raised a hand, pushing the raindrops aside with a psionic ripple. *Something's in the mist.*

I set a hand on his shoulder. "I need you protecting them."

When I turned back, Tyra was tightening the drawstring on a crossbow, her red hair tied back. "I'm not dying in the Lowlands."

"No one's..." I started to say, but my gaze landed on Renrick.

Sariel looked to Eralt. "Where are your men? Where's Puris?"

Eralt shook his head. "They barred the feast hall. The storm muffled the fighting." His gaze flicked to me. "Davik, if we make it to the courtyard, we can rally them."

The steady chop of steel against ice pounded through the walls.

Trith pushed himself upright, his hands shaking as he gripped his spear. "It won't last much longer."

"Wait," I told him.

"I've got a featherfall wand," he said. "And darkness. We can slip down the castle walls and run for the hills."

I shook my head. "They'll run us down with horses. We need those mounts."

I swept my gaze over the room, noting every face. Sariel's jaw was set, her willingness to do whatever it took already carved into her stance. Elina looked caught between thought and prayer, the weight of everything she believed in cracking under the reality of our situation.

Tyra met my eyes, crossbow at the ready. She didn't look surprised that we were being hunted.

Vorga stood by my side, shaking her head. Karley slid towards me, her face a question.

How much death had I dragged these women into?

Didn't matter. None of it did. Only getting them out alive mattered.

And if we ran? Ironclad had pull. He had wealth. Worse, he had patience. A man who could fake his death for a year wasn't the kind to let prey slip away.

I thought back to my last words to Vilas.

Let them come.

No more running. I'd finish this now.

Karley locked eyes with me, sensing the shift. "What is it?"

"Get your spellbook."

CHAPTER

TWENTY-ONE

P uris walked among the courtyard battlements. Eralt had told him he would be welcome at tonight's feast, but it seemed important to be here, braving the rains with his men.

"Too good to share wine with us, Sir Puris?" Ekyll grinned at him from the brazier. Half his face was swollen from the melee. Luka stood next to him, quiet. But then again, Luka was always quiet.

"Never." Puris smiled and took the flagon. "But as your commander, I'll have to confiscate this."

"You rode well today." Luka inclined his head. His father's axe hung on his back. Puris had seen him in the melee, and by the time he emerged, the tourney axe had resembled flag iron. Without Luka's relentless fury, Windpeak wouldn't have won.

"You fought well," Puris responded. "Those squires were grown men."

Ekyll grinned. "Didn't matter much in the end, did it?"

"No," Luka whispered. His canine tooth was newly shattered like a wolf that had bitten onto plate armor. "It didn't."

Even now, with the knighthood and the new mantle, he

felt the distance from his brothers. The Squires of Eralt were the true family he had been given after Rochdale.

"Sir Highblade did not ride well, unfortunately." Puris tipped the wine back. Normally, he would chastise them, but he wanted one last moment with his brothers.

Strange how I feel far from them now. I cannot wait for them to be knighted, so we are brothers again.

Puris held out the wineskin to Luka, but the squire shook his head.

Ekyll was stronger, the strongest really. But Luka was the greatest fighter in the squire corps. He fought like Davik did, moving from opponent to opponent as if each were a dish he had to devour. Eralt once said that Luka looked for something that was no longer there, and the reality of it put darkness in his heart.

"Can we see it?" Ekyll asked after a moment.

Puris reached into his pocket and withdrew Mara's favor, holding it out for them. Both squires stared at it, neither reaching towards it as if they would taint it.

"Looks soft," Ekyll said. "Has she said anything?"

Puris smiled at the cloth. "Not yet." Eralt taught them that there was nothing more chivalrous than burning for a woman you couldn't have, but that would not be his fate. Lord Sewell was a kind enough man, but it was plain his daughters ran him.

"Lady Elyse wouldn't mind if you married Mara, I bet." Luka tried to smile, the expression unnatural on his face. "You aren't highborn."

"She does get jealous," Ekyll agreed. "Those women with Darkshire, are they all his?"

Puris sighed and looked out the castle walls. "Davik looks after them. That's all I'll say on the matter."

"How did he fight when you saw it?" Luka edged forward. "Is it like they say?"

Puris nodded. "It's more. I walked through a tavern he cleared. The wounds I saw on men... it looked like a devil came from hell. Then later..."

He didn't share that story of Davik on the ship. It wasn't one any man would believe. The way he had drank power from that mage before leaping from the bow and severing a ship in half. Then the murder—the butchery in the river? Every time Puris had looked up from the oars, Davik was slaying another man, rending them apart with arcane blows.

When he had fought that giant man on the ship, he hadn't seen it, but he heard the ring of steel like a storm.

"Later, what?" Luka asked.

Puris smiled faintly. "Nothing. He's a tremendous fighter. But he's cunning. He slew the man who opened the gates at Rochdale in Hollyhead."

Ekyll's voice was a dare to himself. "Slew him how?"

Puris remembered the stoneskin body falling into the river when the ship finally caved in. "Took his head."

"Give me that." Luka snatched the wine. "If I drink to anything, I'll drink to that."

"*Commander!*" one of his squires called out from the western wall.

"I'll be a moment." Puris handed the wine to his friends. Yet when he held the skin out, he was greeted with grins.

"We'll escort you." Ekyll winked. "Keep you safe."

As they walked, a fog fell down on them through the rain. The braziers flickered, smothered in an almost dust-like substance.

"The hell's that?" Luka looked around.

Puris looked at his gloved fingers, rubbing them. The fog had small particles. When he looked up to the sky, he saw dark clouds forming, somehow separate from the storm clouds. Darker than any cloud he had ever seen. The three of them picked up the pace, jogging in their half-plate.

Goodwyn Cobbler, a squire of fifteen, held a torch up to the black mist. He pointed to the burned-out port. "Something's washed ashore, Puris!"

"*Sir* Puris, you dolt." Luka shoved the other squire aside. "Lower your torch so we can see."

"The hells is that?" Ekyll peered ahead.

Puris leaned forward. Something sloshed on the beach. Something large. It was hard to tell in the rain and damned fog, which shouldn't exist but—

Lightning flashed in the distance. Illuminating the circle of storm above the castle. It was a beached whale. The largest he had ever seen—or even heard of.

"Look at the size of it!" Ekyll cried out. "The storm must've blown it on—"

"Shut up." Puris squinted. He counted the flash of lightning between heartbeats. The only sound was the rain on their armor, twinkling wet metal. A slice of green light flashed on the beach.

The lightning cracked through the sky again.

He saw a robed figure standing on top of the mass of flesh, holding something glowing like tethers sliding into its head.

"Sword..." Goodwyn whispered.

The skin of the beached beast rippled, muscles flexing in ways no corpse should. Then its jaw sagged open—not rotting, but reshaped—like something was moving inside. Pushing, parting it like a mare birthing a foal.

The maw of the whale opened, rippling in green light. Figures out of a dream stepped from it. Not men. Large and inhuman. They looked like sketches of knights that Allie would draw, too hard with the charcoal. Sharp angles.

The figure on top of the whale raised its green hands. So bright, he could see them from here. He was pointing at the castle.

One figure walked forth, lumbering and grotesque, carrying a heavy blade. Followed by another, holding something that looked like a jawbone or a tree branch.

"The size of it..." Ekyll whispered.

The third figure blinked in and out of existence, dotting in black shadow up the beach. Puris felt his stomach churn. The same way it had in the cavern with those goblins.

Somewhere behind the four teenagers, a bell rang over and over. But their mouths were open, their faces lit green and smudged in shadow.

A fourth figure, the size of a man, walked from the glowing mouth of the whale. It didn't approach like the other three.

"Sound the alarm," Puris mumbled. But when he turned around, he saw now. The alarm was already being rung. Windpeak squires and men at arms were fighting in the courtyard. One archer held his neck, while a Bronzefell servant and a Springdall soldier looked up from his dying body. Figures moved all over the courtyard, white tabards staining themselves red.

We are betrayed.

Shadows of death and bone stalked towards them from the beach. Man fought man within the castle walls. The servants and attendants of houses who were no servants at all stabbed workers. Henri the blacksmith lay slumped over his anvil, blood trickling down the dark iron.

"To arms!" Puris shouted, shaking each of his friends. "We are betrayed! Close the portcullis!"

"The—the..." Goodwyn looked at Puris until he slapped him across the mouth. Something came roaring out of him. Traitors first. Then the nightmares.

"Close the portcullis on your *life*." Puris nudged Luka and Ekyll and stared down at the growing battle. "You two, with me."

I HEFTED THE WARHAMMER, squeezing the steel until my glove creaked. The hallway was the best chokepoint we had. Rain thundered down to our right, flooding the moon garden below.

"Can I tell you a secret, Davik?" Trith stared at the torchlit figures chopping through the ice.

"Sure."

The ice wall shook.

"I don't like Windpeak very much."

"Me either."

We are ready, ugly-man, Brim whispered in my mind. *When Karley returns, I'll lock the door.*

Renrick was a quiet mess, but he clutched a longsword and stared at the ice.

Eralt braced next to me, ready to retake the castle from invaders. His lord and his lady had failed him. All he had were the boys in the courtyard and the guests he had sworn to protect.

"Why did you leave service after Rochdale?" I asked him.

The old knight glowered at the figures through the ice. "Now isn't the time..."

There's a stillness before chaos. And when Eralt saw me waiting for him in it, he relented.

"I saw anointed knights betray their oaths in slaughter and sacking. Men I had trained became beasts in the streets. I stopped what I could, but there was so much I didn't. I was ashamed."

"Price of being a good man," I offered.

A block of ice fell from the top of the barrier. The first mortar in a siege wall, about to come down.

Eralt locked eyes with me. "When I went to my liege to protest, he said he had encouraged it. A reward. His heraldry disgusted me. I vowed not to wear it."

"They killed my brother," Renrick whispered next to us, lost in his own world.

"Springdall first," I reminded the men around me. "They've no enchantments."

Trith sneered, his eyes glowing with power.

There was only the feel of my brother next to me, as he had been my entire life. I was where I needed to be, standing between death and the friends and women I loved.

Sariel stood twenty feet behind us, her sword leaning against the railing to the garden below. Her bow was nocked and ready. Karley stood next to her, shivering from the spell she had gorged on.

The ice wall came loose, slabs of white-blue frost falling as men surged out of it. That thing—that old and terrible thing—came forth in me. No longer restrained. Coaxed forward. Derision filled me, as it had so many times in my life.

Ironclad was in their rear. The first Springdall knight stumbled through the ice, collapsing on all fours. When he gazed skyward, I hissed and brought the hammer down.

His helm was crushed with a spark. No magic here, just the ancient spell of one man making another disappear. Blood splattered my face, but I was already turning. Already raising the hammer—

"No!" Another Springdall knight raised his hands, forgetting the sword in them. The weight of the hammer flowed back, then forward as I urged it over my shoulder. I caved in his breastplate, sending the blood from his chest exploding out of his mouth.

Swords and pikes came at us. Trith roared, sending out his sorcery. Eralt and Renrick parried men who tried to get past me.

Lightning, old-terrible lightning, erupted from Trith's staff. I screamed when it struck me, my runes drinking it in, breaking it, but the pain was terrible. I wasn't here. I was back in the war. Pulling a cart. Slapped with a riding crop.

Wars we wage'em!

Crackling energy echoed through the hammer as a High-blade man lunged forward. They were holding a line, keeping me at bay with pikes they had found in the castle.

"Forward!" Ironclad ordered.

A barb slammed into my gut, needling through the metal plates.

A Highblade knight tried to slip past my right to Trith.

Mages we slay 'em!

I crumpled him to his knees and turned towards the wall of spikes, roaring at the men pressing towards us.

Trith seized the kneeling knight's helm, jammed a wand in his mouth, and snarled—"Fuck *you!*"

Thorns erupted through the helmet, and then he sent a blast of cold at the knights, coating them in frost.

Days we save 'em! Oh!

It was carnage. There were no other words to describe the butchery. I had a warhammer, I had my armor, and I had my brother next to me. Sariel's bow slipped between our weaving heads. Fletchings crashed into necks and eyes like sparrows flocking to their nests.

Trith cooked men to death with a raised fist, their unenchanted armor glowing red hot before they fell to the ground like hissing roasts, writhing under liquid metal.

I dug in, flooding my cresting wounds with two healing runes from Elina, a berserker let loose on the front lines.

Thirty knights turned into twenty-two. Eralt half-sworded a man through the eyes, twisting his blade free. He taught boys how to fight. Now, he taught men how to die.

I reared the hammer. I had no shield, only its horrid weight. A man slammed into the wall as I tore him from the line and swung, embedding him into the mortar.

Renrick snarled—any chance of swordwork gone in his grief. He simply plunged ahead, shouldering through the blocks of ice to stab steel. A hooked halberd cracked him across the head.

"Drakemoor!" Eralt tried to get at him, but the line of knights consumed him, their blades like the legs of a spider as they drew him forth to die. He screamed his brother's name until Ironclad silenced him with a swing of his enchanted sword.

I thundered forward. A knight fell to Sariel's arrow. Then another. My hammer was caught in a crumple of steel and bone that had been a man, wedged between the ice. I snarled, hefting it forward as Sir Hewer brought his blade down on me.

Trith emptied a wand, all charges let loose in a cone of acid. Sir Hewer's face and arms hissed and bubbled, the acid spraying both of us but only eating him. Two more knights fell to the ground behind him, clawing at their exposed skulls.

Ironclad wavered, seeing his line about to fall. It was too cramped, the weapons too long for the hallway. "Back!" he ordered. The Bronzefell knights around him fell back steadily, trained men able to stay calm.

Springdall didn't listen. They slipped and fell. I slew one, then another, the maul head of my weapon caked in skull and steel. I treated them like tent spikes, sinking them with a single swing at a time.

Karley screamed her spell as our enemies fell into the darkened feasting hall. *Revelus Ist Natum!*

255

The arcane power poured from her, parting around me. The softest chimes twinkled around the Bronzefell knights.

"Man the line, you currs!" Ironclad ordered Ettimer Highblade and his men.

Eralt, Trith, and I walked steadily forward. My body ached, and my bones hummed from the concussion of strikes. Trith pointed a wand at the last fireplace burning, a black twig of creaking shadow.

Darkness encased the feasting hall like cold mist. Every brazier, every hearth twinkled dark. Highblade fell back, walking slowly towards the rooms where Elyse and Mara hid. Ten men can break a line of a hundred. All it takes is fear and the reminder that the next death might be your own.

"To me," Ironclad grunted as his men fanned out around him.

"Sir..." one whispered as he looked down.

As they fell into the darkness, Karley's spell became more apparent. The armor was enchanted by Monks of the Sword to save them from sorcery, to make them stronger and their blades sharper.

Now they glowed with the detection of magic. Something so simple that we had used to find enchanted artifacts in a dark dungeon.

Blades and armor glowed with faint blue light. They couldn't see us, but we could see them. We had moments before Trith's darkness spell ended.

It was like fighting ghosts in the dark. Except now we were the wraiths.

Sariel and I sprinted forward, our bodies tuning for a darker dance. I slew a man in glowing armor, his face turning to horror as his armor illuminated the last face he saw.

Sariel severed a man's neck. I couldn't see her, but I heard her near me, the soft grunt of her throat as her blade whirred.

Ironclad, massive in his form, backed towards the dark hearth as his glowing men fell like trampled flowers in the Underdark.

Every kill felt closer to victory. I swung overhand and crumpled a man, his skull and spine crushed between his legs like a broken hinge.

Trith hissed in the dark, his spear jutting into the mouth of a man. When a blade came across him, his new mage armor illuminated us all for a moment. Sariel's eyes were slitted as she killed. I wove in, smashing men, dashing teeth from mouths. Eralt dueled in the dark.

Trith killed another knight, one of his dwindling wands blasting him apart in a burst of crimson energy.

I pulled my hammer from a mound of gurgling meat. When I turned—as the darkness spell receded—I saw my world about to come apart.

Ironclad knew his cause was lost, so he would carve from me what I had taken from him. Sariel battled him in a roar of Embriel curses.

I saw it coming—as Rayleth had taught me long ago. As certain as sunset, Sariel's death waited in two more swings. She was good, but Ironclad was stronger. He was faster, aided by magic and hate. He had carved his fiefdoms from a warhorse saddle.

"Davik!" Trith screamed, but I was already moving. Sariel riposted Ironclad's enchanted blade. Their footwork matched, but he pivoted.

Ironclad's sword descended, promising to cleave my heart in two. All the light in my world was about to vanish.

Sariel's face never changed; she never stopped fighting.

I reached out too late. Too short. I couldn't parry the blade. So I took it.

It was like our dance in Tawney as I held her shoulders. The sword crashed into my head, splitting my scalp. Enchanted steel dulled against my fortified skull.

Sariel stared at me—shocked—as blood crashed over my face like a burst egg.

My vision flickered for a moment. The hammer slipped from my hand as a tremor raced down my arm.

"Davik," she whispered.

As the blade was wrenched from my skull, Ironclad said something. Trith shouted my name. Eralt sprinted from the final knight he had slain as Highblade's men looked on in morbid shock.

"Long have I wished for this." Ironclad raised the blade, hefting it down again.

Right into my blindspot.

The steel broke across my ridged arm as I turned, catching it. The sliver of the blade sliced through my face, parting a nostril, splitting my two lips into four.

My hands found his chest plate. That old, awful strength he and his kind had engraved in me surged forward, wrenching him down. I slapped the sword from his grip and seized his throat, pushing him to his knees.

Ironclad gasped, struggling against my hands, the enchanted steel useless against the force strangling the life from him.

Elina's healing spell whispered my flesh back together. I tasted blood.

But not enough.

The great Lord Elrick Avelmont clawed at my wrists, and I squeezed tighter. His lips moved, but no words could slip past my grip. His face darkened as I squeezed, watching his veins bulge.

"Be careful what you wish for, Lord," I hissed, watching the fear in his dimming eyes.

His hands fell limp like swinging bells. The final gurgle from his throat—the last chime.

I let him go. Dropping another corpse to the floor with a thump.

Eralt stood, staring down at our vanquished enemy. All four of us looked at Ettimer Highblade, the supposed new groom to this castle.

"We need Elina." I breathed the words as we walked towards the hallway. "Then we'll take the courtyard."

As we walked, a darkness so thick and black you could feel it encased the hall. I looked around. "Trith?"

"Wasn't me," he hissed, pointing his spear-staff ahead of us.

"*What is that?*" a Highblade man yelled.

"*It's his witch!*"

Then I felt it, the soul of a mage but stranger—far stranger—approaching the castle.

Lord Ironclad rose like a puppet pulled by sorcerous strings, his grey face lit by the light of Trith's spear. The dead Bronzefell knights twitched around us, deadened lungs wheezing like broken bellows.

"Sword save us..." the words fell from Eralt's bloody face. "Protect us from evil."

A dry, grating sound rasped through the darkness. Every head turned as the corpse of Lord Avelmont pointed a finger at me.

"*Knock...*" The corpse of Ironclad wheezed. "*Knock...*"

Then the roar of a tusked beast, long dead, screamed on severed vocal cords from far outside. Followed by a thump of dead meat on iron.

CHAPTER

TWENTY-TWO

When the darkness crashed over the library, Karley couldn't see it, but she felt it. The spells inside her responded, recognizing its kinship.

Something like her was here.

"What is that?" Tyra whispered. She turned in the shadows, hefting her crossbow. The slow clap of the frying pan hung on a loop on her hip.

"Do you think they're done?" Vorga glanced at the barricaded door.

"Girls," Elina said as she backed toward a wall. "Come here."

They inched towards Elina's voice. Karley wished in that moment she knew a light spell for them.

This was bad. This wasn't knights.

Brim growled somewhere in the darkness.

"Brim," Karley called between the bookstacks, "get over here!"

"Mistress," Elina murmured, her tattoos flaring to life. "Look over your daughters. Protect them from the profane."

Karley turned, following a shadow that crept along the wall. How could there be a shadow in the dark?

It dripped down the wall. A splotch of twitching oil pooling on the floor.

"Oh... fuck..." Karley whispered.

"What is it?" Vorga squinted.

The shadow pooled on the floor, growing in size until the twitching outline of a ten-foot knight, thin as a dream and jagged as a nightmare, emerged. Its helm was shadow as it turned and regarded Karley.

Elina shouted her prayer, encircling them with a protective shield. Karley squinted against its glare, blinded by its golden light.

Vorga's voice was an echo. "We need to move!"

Tyra was eerily calm. Karley felt a pang of jealousy at that. There was a toughness to Tyra. She didn't pretend to be something, she just was.

Old fear, born of years in an orphanage, thrummed through Karley as the shadow being twitched forward.

Not now. Not now, I can't be afraid now.

The flickering knight slid towards them, hefting a spear of shadow. It held out its hand, beckoning them forth.

Not them.

Her.

Tyra gripped Karley's hand, leveling her crossbow at the thing. The shield flickered as the monstrosity ran a claw down it.

"Slowly," Elina said through the effort of concentration. "Walk together."

It didn't follow as they stepped inside. Their shoes knocked together, then slid across the floor, veering away from the door and toward the shelves. Karley caught a glimpse of Brim moving silently along the far wall, his fist clenched around a pouch of powder.

They stumbled, and Karley fell forward.

Tyra grabbed the back of her dress. "No, you don't."

"Thanks," was all Karley could manage to say.

The urge to run screaming from the library was overwhelming. Vorga slid a hand up Karley's back as she guided them forward. She couldn't run now, not with her friends here. Even Elina—whom she looked at like a too-kind elder cousin—depended on her.

They couldn't see, and she could.

"What's it look like?" Elina whispered.

Like a shadow that eats other shadows. Like someone took a knife to reality and carved it into the room with us.

"It's just dark," Karley murmured.

As they inched past the tall bookcase, the shield shimmered faintly, its edge brushing the carved wood like oil on glass.

"Shit," Tyra gasped. Karley could almost hear the sweat dripping from where she gripped the crossbow. "Can you make it smaller?"

Elina shut her eyes. "Trying."

Black shadow flickered before them, bending down to peer at them like gifts in a glass bowl.

"Oh, fuck!" Tyra screamed.

It didn't move. It just *writhed.*

"Back up," Vorga swallowed. "We'll just back up."

Karley gulped, her eyes watching the humming borders of this dark thing. It was like a man but not. As they slipped back, the shadow vanished.

"That's good, right?" Vorga looked around in the darkness. "Right?"

No one said anything. They turned together, four women

trying to maneuver like a unit. The only door was barred, and all they could do was move away from this thing. Vorga stumbled over someone. When she fell on all fours, a strand of her dark hair fell from the shield.

"Elina, don't move!" Tyra turned slowly, trying to stay within the shield.

The cleric shuddered, and she murmured something, lighting their way with her glowing tattoos.

Vorga's hair lifted, twirling in the air. When Karley focused, she saw the creature holding a strand of it.

"Oh gods, oh my gods," Karley whispered as she saw Vorga's hair lifting.

The firmness in Elina's voice was an order. "Run for the doors when I say."

It shamed Karley how relieved she was to hear that. And in that moment, she felt lesser. Still a child squinting in the orphanage, pretending the light didn't bother her.

I've pretended my whole life.

She was just a girl. A dumb girl who had dabbled in magic that had almost killed her. The weight of that spell—she had known how dangerous it was. Starfall. But the book had said it was her mother's favorite.

Why did you throw me away?

Elina wasn't a girl. She was a woman. The priestess saw people healed. She comforted the grieving and the dying. She brought babies into the world and had held her own in Hollyhead, powering a divine shield until blood ran down her nose.

Tyra dropped the crossbow and grabbed Vorga as the thing tried to pull her. "Get away from her!"

All Karley could do was grab Vorga. The shadow knight shrieked above them. Its spiked helm wanted to consume them in a darkness so bleak, a drow like her would be blind in it—wandering forever.

"Girls..." Elina warned. Her chest heaved, her amber eyes focused in a strange finality.

She's going to fight it. She's going to fight it and die.

Of all things, Vorga called to her, "Karley it's *got* me!"

Tyra fell to the floor, holding Vorga's legs as the shadow tried to pluck her from the shield.

A flash of chemical light blinded them.

"Gabya-hee!" Brim screamed as he hurtled forth. Trails of glowing dust flitted from his fingers.

They hurtled back from the psionic blow. The shadow knight reeled from the light, swiping at Brim with its spear. Their tavern dishwasher rolled and cursed at it. His voice thundered into all their minds.

Run.

The shield blinked out of existence as the four of them toppled over each other.

Karley looked up, seeing the shadow-thing battling with Brim. Every time it reached for him, he pushed it back. But each pulse of psionic energy seemed to grow weaker and weaker.

Tyra's skirt had blown up over her waist as they pushed themselves up. Karley, in a moment of insanity, almost gave her a spank on her meaty ass.

There's a moon Davik chased and caught.

Brim backed against a wall, feinting and pushing. The spear plunged towards him, and he pushed it away with psionic power.

"Go, girls." Elina pushed herself up, blood trickling from one nostril. "Find Davik."

The spell inside her whispered to Karley. It promised her things. She had studied it after Elyse had played with her mind. The same spell that had almost killed her. She pretended to be many things, but Karley was a mage now. A good one, a poor one, it didn't matter.

Some portion of her soul broke loose, like a door she had held shut. And as the magic melded with her, she saw how wrong she was to be afraid of it. How dismissive it had been.

The spell tasted what she felt and purified it.

Fear turned to power, and worry turned to surety. For a single moment, she was what she always wanted to be.

Sure.

"Brim!" Karley walked towards the knight. "Get over here!"

The gnome limped over as the shadow ignored him. It wasn't here for a dishwasher.

It was here for her.

"Astralis," Karley muttered. Hot blood flowed through her, causing her to clench her fists.

The shadow knight raised its spear, writhing in a form only she could see.

"Ecta." Karley stared up at it as the weapon reared back.

Elina pushed the shield spell back into existence, raising a single hand as her tattoos glowed behind Karley. Somehow, she pushed Elina's shield away with a flick of her mind. An arcane hand denying its divine protection. Karley was meant for darkness, for shadows.

They made the light more beautiful.

She sneered at the shadow thing. Arcane power throttled through her, and she welcomed it. The same spell had torn a hole in her soul, but she saw now, as the last word hurtled out of her—how wrong she had been to fear it.

The stars came forth, streaming from the ceiling— borrowed from another plane. Burning streams crashed down in hurtles, destroying the bookshelves in blinding astral light. Celestial bliss streamed through her, bathing her in starlight. She wished Davik were here to see this. To see her cast it.

The shadow knight screamed, turning to flee. But

anywhere it slipped, her eyes followed, and the stars crashed into it. Blobs of pure star, not heat but gorgeous *light*. The shadow bubbled, splashing like a puddle in the rain. Missile after missile smashed into it, cratering its helm. Denting its soul.

I'm full of stars...

The most wondrous emotion beckoned her. Karley leaned back, surrendering to the cosmos pouring through her. Her eyes glowed violet-bright as a piece of the spell fell into her outstretched hand. It should have burned through her. But she only marveled at it, holding the beating heart of the heavens.

I am the stars.

The knight clawed towards her. Karley held the glowing starfall in front of it, and it recoiled. It shivered in shame and awe. Pure, invigorating power cascaded through her, and she plunged her molten star-fist into its chest, burning away the shadow of its heart.

It broke apart in whispers, flooding the room with its absence.

When the spell left her, she felt like weeping.

I love you, Mom.

The dead rose around us, twitching and shaking in the feasting hall.

"Can't see a thing," I whispered as an arcane darkness choked the hall.

A door creaked open on the upper banister.

"*Eralt?*" Mara's voice called out.

"Close your door, my lady!" The old knight spun, watching the bodies rise. "Bar the door!"

"*Get back in here!*" Elyse screamed, and all we heard was the echo of a door shutting.

Thanks for the invitation, Elyse.

More banging came from the courtyard. Further than that. The front portcullis.

"There's a caster here," I warned Trith and Sariel. "Outside the gates."

Sariel gasped when she backed into an undead knight. The corpse was still wet with the blood she had spilled from it.

Trith's voice dripped with hatred. "Necromancer."

I gripped my warhammer. This was a problem, one Trith and I had seen before. Some undead were nothing more than drunks that bumped into one another. Others moved like packs of wolves.

Some even ate people.

Ironclad's body groaned on broken vocal cords. The dead moved in unison towards us and the Highblade men.

Heads and mouths moved, powered by unseen strings. "*The drow. The lost daughter. Bring her to me... unharmed.*" The voice filled the hall. "*Open the gates and bring her to me. And the Darkshire.*"

My runes felt out, feeling the caster beyond the walls. But it was hard to pinpoint him. Something was wrong with his soul. Behind me, I felt Karley's soul flash—an ache in my bones.

Eralt held his sword up. "Darkshire, my men are out there."

"We have to fall back," Sariel whispered.

A voice cut through the groan of rising corpses. "And if we do?"

We turned, seeing Ettimer Highblade staring at the corpse of Ironclad.

"*Safe passage...*" the voice hissed. "*Only then... the dead will rest.*"

"Ettimer," Eralt warned him. "Help us clear this hall. We can take the castle."

But the young lord swallowed, and his eyes kept floating to the hallway where Karley and the girls were. I saw the gears in his head turn. Grabbing a girl was much easier than killing men who rose from the dead. They'd leave us to be overrun.

For every step we took, the dead took two, and Highblade took three. It felt so unfair after taking the corridor and the feasting hall.

"They're in the library," Ettimer whispered to his men, gripping his sword.

"You go for that library"—I stared at him in the choking darkness—"and I'll feed you that fucking sword."

Sariel sneered and turned, weaving her blade between our enemies.

"Hey," Trith called to a knight next to Ettimer. He palmed a particular wand from his hip. "Don't try it."

Nine men, hell-bent on living, stepped towards the path to our people. The hall filled with the slow creak of armor shifting.

The dead clinched around us, choking the air with death and ruptured flesh.

"Now," I ordered.

Sariel and Eralt were closer to the hall than Trith and me. Every person, living and dead, broke for the corridor we had just retaken. The dead screeched, but not in pain. It was the sound of metal scraping metal, of enslaved lungs trying to suck air they no longer needed. Their motion was instant, like strings yanked tight.

There was no combat, just pure flight as we ran for our lives. Sariel grabbed Eralt, dragging him behind her to keep pace as they outran Highblade who pursued. Trith sprinted, glancing back at me as I brought a tide of teeming dead. I knew the look he gave me.

"Do it," I grunted, sliding the warhammer into the brace on my back. Somewhere behind me, a rotten hand reached for it.

Trith blasted the knights ahead of us with his wand. A cone of arcana slowed the air ahead of us, filling with the drift of arcane feathers.

Featherfall.

Highblade ran straight into it. Some leapt; some stumbled. Ettimer was in their rear, but they were all caught in the spell's effects. I knew it well, because I had once cursed Trith for a week when he pulled me out a window and cast it, and my body crashed right through it onto the cobblestones.

When we hit the spell, Trith looked like he was caught in a wall of invisible gelatin. I tackled him mid-sprint, driving him through it. It was like wading through waist-deep mud. Trith's body dragged in my grip, his limbs slow, his eyes flicking to me in a bemused panic. The spell warped the air, thick and syrupy —but my runes burned hot, unraveling a path.

The dead followed me.

Ettimer Highblade turned as I passed him, his panic-stricken eyes meeting mine. His lips formed a plea, but the sound died in the thickened air. The first clawed hand found Ettimer's wrist.

His scream came in broken syllables, warped by magic. Another bony hand clamped onto his jaw, wrenching his head back.

I dropped Trith to find his feet on the other side of the spell. When we turned to see the horde behind us, the knights twitched like flies in a web. Blood moved in slow ribbons, drawn by clawed hands and clacking jaws, like a painter spreading his reds. Ettimer Highblade's silent screams were drowned in slow bloodshed. A single begging eye stared at us, pleading for someone—anything—to remove the jaws burrowing into his opened gut.

He was still reaching for us when we turned away.

As we limped toward the library, our ragged breaths trailing behind us, Sariel reached out and grabbed my hand.

"It's not Avelmont," Sariel whispered. "That caster wants Karley. And you."

I glanced behind us, seeing the dead slowed by the spell. "Someone Vilas spoke to."

Eralt bent over, racked by a fit of coughing until Trith helped him up.

"Could it be him?" Sariel asked.

I squeezed her hand. "There's no coming back from what I did to him. This is something else."

Sariel's face was bruised, and the sight of it landed like a mark on my own heart. I knew her; I had learned the ministrations of her soul. That's what happens when you sleep next to someone, breathing the same air, building a life. Our true home was in each other, in the girls and Brim, the ones we walked toward.

She was a battle commander. A victorious one. Sariel knew what it was to fight the living.

But we were in the realm that Trith and I knew too well. Where strange things stepped forth from the shadows of the world. Where paladins had burning swords that cleaved steel, and the entities of other planes raised the dead as puppets.

When we reached the library, Elina opened it at our approach. It reeked of arcane combat and singed paper. I took in the sight of our group.

"We're okay," Elina declared. "Karley saved us."

Brim growled in agreement. *Fuck this wedding.*

Trith slumped down next to Brim, joining him in exhaustion. I walked forward and held Tyra and Vorga, curling the two of them under my arm.

"Are you okay?"

Tyra shook her head. "This is bad, Davik." She glanced back at the window, where the mist circled the castle, punctuated by flashes of green light. "What is that?"

I stared through the frosted glass, listening to the hiss of ethereal energies. "Spirits. Summoned entities."

"Death magic," Trith coughed from the corner.

Sariel put on her best face, stuffing the fear of losing anyone down. "Come here, girls. Let me check you over."

Karley was the only one who didn't look petrified or exhausted. When she approached me, there was a fire in her. Her fingers curled into my coif, her breath warm and wild. The blood from my armor soaked her dress, but she pressed harder as if daring it to matter.

"It wants me..." she whispered. "Doesn't it?"

"Doesn't matter," I said. "You aren't going anywhere."

Elina turned from the window and walked towards me. "Davik. That mist. We could get through it with my barrier."

"Are we fighting?" Tyra looked at me. Her red hair hung limply around her. Vorga glanced up, waiting for my answer. We were in one of her storybooks now, and we desperately wanted the ending.

Trith kept his eyes shut, leaning against the wall. His soul was ravaged from our combat. From retaking the feast hall—all for nothing. Giving bodies to something more sinister.

"Fighting..." I said, tasting the word. But it felt like a lie. I looked between my friends and the five women dear to me. Retake the castle?

You don't hold five eggs in your hand and try to fight your way through a food riot.

"We're leaving." I looked at Eralt. "Can you get us to the servant's tunnels, out to the beach?"

The old knight nodded. "I'll take you there."

"We can barely see," Vorga whispered. "The torches don't do anything."

I reassured her. "Karley can see for us."

The spell in the hallway broke loose. The dead surged forward, the trample of their ruined armor filling the darkness beyond us. Everyone held their breath as they branched out and began to slide among the corridors outside.

"I need time," Elina whispered to me. "To pray."

I walked to my pack that Brim had brought in here. It was time to regroup, rearm, and ready for the final push out of this nightmare.

Tyra slipped next to me. When she touched my arm, I felt the flow of resolve.

"Don't waste time reloading if you can't." I handed her a bundle of bolts. "Use the pan."

My fingers touched the wood of Searlus's mace I had brought with me. When I withdrew it, Tyra peered at it. "A cudgel? Is it magic?"

"No." I turned the weapon in my hand, remembering what I had been told about it. And the hellish strike of it when it struck me on that bridge. "Something else."

Brim's psychic voice whispered in my mind.

The dead are spreading, ugly-man.

Sariel cocked her head. "They've stopped moving."

"Are they waiting for us?" Vorga turned to the door.

"Not for us. Something is coming." I looked at Elina. "Say your prayers."

CHAPTER
TWENTY-THREE

Puris wove his blade back and forth, parrying two Springdall men. They wore servant's clothes, but they were gruff men, familiar with violence.

Yet, they were not knights.

Both hacked at him with long cleavers. Once he had hated the rigorous training Eralt put them through. Now as he parried, defending himself on the rain-slick battlements, he could have kissed the old knight for his lessons.

Eralt favored half-swording, believing in the grip and leverage of a plunging weapon. But against two unarmored men, it wasn't necessary now.

The courtyard teetered towards chaos. All three knights of Windpeak had been killed first, their bodies collecting ragged pools in the rain.

We are betrayed.

The man on his right gasped when Puris wove the tip of the longsword through his gut, gripping the hilt to plunge and pull it away. When his body fell from the rampart, his comrade never slowed. The man was older, stronger, but he was tired and it showed.

The cleaver scraped across his breastplate. Puris turned and ripped his blade across his neck. When his hand went to the wound reflexively, Puris snarled and planted a boot in his gut, sending him from the battlement. The cut had been shallow, but the fall killed him.

He kept moving.

A churning pit of loss threatened to overtake him. This was Rochdale. This was the nightmare of the walls coming back to haunt him. Several of his brothers—no, his squires—had tried to fall back inside the keep. Orphans who had become brothers.

Now their bodies littered the front of Windpeak's grand hall doors. Their path had been barred from within. Treachery had already infected the castle.

Somewhere in there was Mara. His heart longed to find her, but his place was here. There was no time to tell these men of what nightmares walked towards Windpeak.

Goodwyn had closed the portcullis, at least. When Puris ran to the top of the battlement, ignoring the growing cloud of darkness spilling over the castle, he called to the figure hunched in the mist and rain.

"Is it locked?"

Goodwyn didn't release his hands from the iron lever. As Puris stepped forward, he saw lifeblood dripping down the chains that powered the iron gate.

"Sword welcome you," Puris whispered.

We are betrayed. And for what?

Springdall and Bronzefell men lay dead in long lines. For every two or three, a Windpeak man lay between them. Brave men at arms who had never abandoned their post. Squires, some little more than twelve—their faces pale and so much more childlike now that death had them. He watched their faces obscure in the strange darkness that fell over them like snowfall.

"To me!" Puris called out. Hoping for a voice. A brother. For anything. "Rally to me!"

"*Open up!*" voices called from the other side.

When Puris looked over, he saw Bronzefell and Springdall men waiting, looking around as they held torches.

A legend's voice slithered towards him. "You should listen to them, son."

Puris spun, holding his blade out.

Serlo the Loner regarded him sadly, holding a blade caked with Windpeak blood. "Undo the lock and surrender. Your castle has fallen."

"Not while I stand." Puris hefted the blade. He felt like screaming. Like crying. "Not while I breathe."

The famed swordsman, once his hero, took a step closer. "This is the way of war. There is mercy, ransom—even service after defeat. Eralt knew that."

Fear crawled through him. "Is this you? This sorcery?"

Serlo held a gloved hand up, examining the mist. "Not I, Sir Puris. Perhaps our master had other weapons. Open the gates. Let the men in."

"Lord Sewell won't fall," Puris warned him. Somewhere in the darkening mists, he heard the jog of half-plate. He hoped dearly it was his brothers.

Or am I truly orphaned once more?

Serlo seemed melancholy when he answered him. "Lord Sewell was to give the order to stand down. But it wasn't to happen tonight. He knows, Puris. Step away."

"You lie!" Puris snarled. "You are a false knight."

"On that, we can agree." Serlo inclined his head. "I'd not take your life."

"Nor will you." Puris crouched, preparing to lunge. He was going to die. He was going to die at the end of Serlo's blade, but at least he would die true.

Screams came from outside the castle walls. For a heartbeat, both he and Serlo shifted. It wasn't the combat of men.

"A moment," the swordsman whispered and leaned over.

Now. Darkshire would do it now.

Puris lunged, stabbing at the man. Serlo seemed to parry Puris without even looking. The blade slid along his as Serlo tripped him and sent him sprawling.

Before he could even rise, cold steel touched his throat in warning.

"Yield, Sir Puris."

Rain flitted down on them, as cold as the treachery that had killed his brothers. The walkways shined with braziers, illuminating steel in a molten red. But near the crenellation, horrifying sounds widened Serlo's distracted gaze.

"By the gods," Serlo remarked.

Puris didn't look. If he was about to die, he would savor every moment. He reached into his pocket, feeling the silk of Mara's scarf. When the castle fell... it would be like Rochdale. At least Eralt had found him... given him a family. Taught him his letters. Taught him what a knight could be.

As he gazed up at Serlo the Loner, he saw what most were.

Luka and Ekyll emerged through the black fog.

"Lower your blade!" Luka called out.

Serlo's blade dipped. His breath left him in a sigh. "Something else comes." A gust of wind—wrong, thick, and too warm—rushed past them.

Then the screaming began in earnest.

Puris looked down and saw, for the first time in his life, something worse than Rochdale.

The invading force was nearly twenty-strong. Men

masquerading as camp attendants of visiting houses were rent apart. The nightmares from the beach approached, save for the blinking figure of darkness.

Puris felt his heart turn to stone. *It's probably in the castle. It's near Mara.*

A figure in dark robes walked forth, and men seemed to split and wither when he raised hands. No, Puris realized. Not hands. Glowing *claws*, emerald in the night. The tents in the distance sounded like pure carnage.

A monstrosity of pale bone strode toward the betrayers. Luka's voice was in his ear. Puris had been too shocked to notice his approach.

The bone monster raised its sword in salute, like a king of old. Then it swung.

A man split in half, metal and meat ringing in the pissing rain. Its master looked on from his shadowed cowl. Traitors died without even raising their weapons. Fates so grim, men turning to carcasses, that even Puris wouldn't have wished them on them.

"Run!" Serlo screamed down to the men, but the assassins needed no spurring. They broke for their camps. Now that the monster was closer, Puris saw—it was a knight. A knight from another realm of existence, where graves and crypts were ruled over instead of lands and people.

The bone knight plunged his sword into the earth. It looked like a vine of bones spiraling out, erupting from the mud with a hard *snap!*

"Sword save us..." Luka uttered the first prayer Puris had ever heard from him.

Knights howled. Torches fell to the mud, illuminating a twitching bushel of men impaled on skeletal thorns.

The monster walked toward them, rain falling from its bone helmet.

This isn't real. This can't be real.

Men shrieked as their bones betrayed them. The creature's porcelain snare shifted, goading the skeletons to rip themselves like freed passengers, crawling in bone-pink shrieks to the feet of their new master. Offering themselves as they joined with his armor.

"*Good,*" a voice from hell whispered through the mists. How could the cloaked thing whisper so loudly?

"That's a wizard," Serlo warned them. "A mage unlike any I've seen..."

As if to punctuate his point, the dark-cowled mage turned and gestured at the rotting direboar. The beast had been dead for days, yet its flesh rippled, its eyes snapping open, glowing green as it rose.

With a flick of his fingers, the caster sent it lurching toward the gate. The reanimated prize of Windpeak let out a deafening scream and slammed into the portcullis.

Vibration thrummed through them. Stone shifted. The boar reared back, thousands of pounds of rotting flesh quivering, then charged again, screaming.

"It'll hold," Puris stood, shaking off the webs of despair. "If anything does, it'll be that gate."

Somewhere behind them in the courtyard, squires called up to him, trying to find them in the darkness.

The boar rammed over and over, vibrating the castle wall.

A slim figure in a rotten shirt stared up at them, an elf, from next to the dark-robed mage. When the boar finally crumpled its own skull into the portcullis, it twitched and died for the final time.

It can't function without the brain. It's the axle to all the wheels.

"*Rot.*" The dark cowled creature's voice didn't miss a beat. "*Raise the gate. Keep it intact.*"

They smelled it before they saw it. Ekyll retched next to him, and his vomit was a relief compared to the stench that slid up to them. It looked like a knight made of rust and rotten meat, encased in steel so putrid it appeared gelatinous.

"Get inside," Serlo whispered, his eyes never leaving the nightmare that approached the portcullis.

The last of Puris's squires ran below them, moving through the dark mist. He could only see them because they found torches somewhere. "*To the gate!*"

"No!" Puris cried out. "Get back!"

But they were Squires of Eralt, set on valor.

The rotten knight grasped both gauntlets around the iron of the portcullis. The castle blacksmith had told Puris about the gate a hundred times. That even the famed Ironclad's battering ram would take a day to get through it.

"He's lifting it!" Ekyll wiped the sick from his mouth. They all turned to see the lock scream behind them, struggling against the brute strength.

"Get up here!" Puris shouted at his men. "Now!"

"No time. I'll hold them." Serlo jammed his boot back down on the lock lever. Then he looked at Puris. "You have somewhere to be, Sir Puris."

"*Them,*" the otherworldly voice hissed.

The elf—sickly gold, too fast, too fluid—vaulted over the rotting horror and scaled the gate. His limbs moved like a whisper. Outpacing the straining iron. Scrambling up the stones to them.

Serlo leaned back. "Go, boys. Get your lord and his daughters out of here."

Luka and Ekyll grabbed Puris, pulling him towards the tower.

The elf landed lightly atop the battlement, barely stirring the rain-slick stone. A plain longsword pointed at the famed knight, as if declaring who would die next. Its eyes gleamed like emeralds, reading Serlo's stance before he even moved. Puris saw Serlo's grip shift. For the first time, he looked unsure.

The elf flowed forward, an unspoken executioner.

Serlo gave ground immediately. The man who could have cut the three of them down fought for his life. It was the finest swordwork Puris knew he would ever see, and as the world collapsed around him, and the gate creaked with the sound of metal snapping, he knew they were lost.

Serlo parried and defended. High, low, pivoting like the expert he was. A talent so exquisite that the world seemed not to know what to do with him. He roared, but the elf was preternatural. He fought without looking. His strikes weren't just swift, they thundered. Denting rivets into Serlo's blade.

"Come on!" Luka grabbed him and pushed. Then he shouted down to the squires in the courtyard, as the portcullis was raised. He saw his brothers wither in their armor from an outstretched hand, the steel slipping from them, shattering when it struck the soft mud as if it were made from a thousand-year-old dream.

Puris looked back at the battlement.

Serlo knelt, one hand fumbling at the blade buried from his shoulder to his heart—as if he could still pull victory from it.

The elf wrenched the blade free, his glowing eyes following Puris.

"Keep"—Ekyll grunted as they raced towards the tower door—"moving."

The dead bodies in the courtyard rose, turning their heads to follow their path. Too many dead men were standing.

"Fucking hells," Luka hissed as they slammed the tower door open. They could take the ladder into the castle, but it seemed not to matter. Nothing would matter soon.

The three of them barred the door, closing it like a coffin lid.

Luka collapsed against the tower door. Ekyll shook, muttering to himself. Slowly, the three friends looked at each other, knowing the path ahead to secure their lord and his daughters might be worse. But in each other's eyes, they saw the first taste of duty failed.

The courtyard was lost.

TWENTY-FOUR

W e slipped through the hallways of choking darkness, a chain of bodies moving as one. Nine people held their breath, guided by Karley who led us through the gloom with her darkvision. A drow threading a needle of people between the dead.

Each person gripped the shoulder ahead of them, moving blindly. Tyra's emotion bled through the link—fear, outrage, a pulse of raw faen imbuement settling deep into our bones.

Above the moon garden, the sky was void-black, broken by the flash of hissing spirits, their flickering mouths stretched in torment. The dead shifted along the corridors above, swaying like ships moored in a harbor.

Karley's grip tightened on my hand in warning. Then she tapped me twice. Two undead ahead. Easy to dispatch but impossible to do so without bringing three times our number down on us.

The air reeked of unlit torches soaked in pilfered lamp oil. The necromancer's presence pressed against my runes. Not like a mage. Not like a man. He wasn't just beyond the walls. He was in them. Pushing against the stone, squeezing from the shadow.

One step, then another—living bodies slipping past the dead. At the eastern stairs, we fanned out before our descent.

"Slowly," I murmured. "Hands on the wall."

We moved down, planning to cross the moon garden and get to the servant's quarters beneath the castle. Of all the dead we'd seen, none bore Windpeak's colors.

Step by step, we descended to the ground floor. The cool air of the garden welcomed us—a warped reflection of the night.

"This way," Eralt said, leading us left. His eyes continually shifted towards the courtyard, hearing the silence of defeat.

The rot hit first—thick, suffocating. Decay so strong that Vorga gagged next to me.

"What's wrong?" I held her. She shook her head, trying not to retch.

"That smell..." Trith coughed. "That's not—"

The avalanche we had been avoiding melted. Above. Behind. All at once. Powered corpses collapsed in heaps of metal—thirty gongs ringing through the night.

"They're not moving," Karley whispered, barely a breath. A hint of hope crept into her voice. "Maybe they've—"

A gust swept through the moon garden as the door beyond opened, carrying the breath of something ancient. The profane darkness finally parted, bowing to what had arrived.

A figure stepped forward. Larger than a man. A sickening pantomime of a knight. Rusted armor cloaked his body. His eyes were dull lanterns in the fog. He lingered as he moved. Patient. Inevitable. A gauntleted hand rose towards us.

"*Wither.*"

The command rippled towards us. Stone cracked above, blackening under its own weight. The entire walkway shifted, our path breaking like a snapped bridge.

"To the tunnel!" I barked.

The others broke into motion, running. Brim hurled mortar from above Karley, Tyra, and Vorga. Eralt fell, diving from the debris, but a pillar trapped his leg.

The death knight strode towards me, armor rattling with each cursed step. I remembered the dark cleric on the cliffside so long ago, and Rayleth's voice echoed in my mind.

Show me.

Grass wilted under his approaching step. The air soured further, tinged with decay. My runes flared as I stepped towards him, carving a curtain of protection against his corruption like mist. His gaze dragged over me—assessing, dismissing—before settling on Sariel and Elina.

His voice was curdled blood. *"Brides..."*

A sneer curled on my lips as I hefted the hammer. Brim and the girls scrambled to free Eralt from the rubble.

The rotten knight raised his hand, sending a wave of arcana towards me. My skin prickled. My teeth ached, begging to shatter. I could always feel the spells. It was always just enough to drive you mad. My runes broke his curse, but in breaking it, they echoed it back.

The hammer darkened, corrosion creeping along its head like rust eating iron. The knight chuckled like bubbling tar.

Sariel fired an arrow into his exposed flesh. It would have punched through a boar, but it simply stuck, sinking like thick honey. Trith unleashed a blast of wind magic, and raw force punched into him. The metal absorbed it. *Swallowed* it.

I roared and swung. Each impact shaved flakes from my eroding hammer.

"Sir Eralt!" Tyra shouted behind us.

"Stay with us!" Vorga grunted as she pulled a stone loose.

My hammer embedded into the knight's side, but as I

wrenched it back, it wouldn't move. He raised a blade of rust, the corroded edge poised to split my throat.

Trith slammed into him with a crash of sorcery. Lightning and wind howled from his spear-staff, shattering the rusted sword.

"No," I whispered as the monstrosity raised Trith's flailing form by the neck.

Decay surged into him. His boots darkened. Then they fell from his feet as if they had aged a hundred years in an instant. His never-aged flesh turned gray. His sorcery—wild and alive —battled in blind reflex against the corruption. The wands along his chest split, rotting like driftwood.

"Dav—" Trith gurgled, eyes bulging. "Run..."

Trith was sacrificing himself, my one last brother.

And to an orphan, that meant everything.

I plunged my hands forward, punching into the rotting knight. Rage tempered my wrath as his other hand clamped around my throat, dragging me closer, smothering me in rot, and slicing my face with jagged metal.

It was like fighting Kardak while paralyzed. I seethed, arching up. I had broken the backs of horned princes. Heard their howls in caverns as I wrenched their spine apart. But the profane were near impossible to kill from force alone.

You needed light magic. Or a strong paladin.

Or a cleric.

"Mistress—" Elina's voice rang with divine certainty. "Guide your daughter."

The knight turned, dropping Trith as Elina stepped forward. A predator drawn to prey. Sariel loosed another arrow with a curse, and it withered against his crown.

Elina's fingers curled in a sacred gesture. She reached out, tattoos flaring with her goddess's power as she healed the monster I struggled with.

The knight recoiled. For the first time, he hesitated. Sariel's arrow struck home this time, staggering him. He braced, taking a single step toward Elina.

"The fuck are you going?" I snarled, gripping the solidifying bones in his chest.

Trith, coughing blood, grasped his spear-staff. Elina met the knight's lifeless gaze.

"*To wither...*" he croaked.

"To grow," she countered, lowering her hand. Flesh bloomed along his rotting leg. Trith plunged his spear between the greaves, bringing us both to our knees.

I surged forward, plunging my arm deeper up to the elbow. Elina stepped closer. A cleric of love, resting her small hand on my shoulder as if selecting a suitor who had won her heart. Her amber eyes glowed with furious love. Divine power crashed into me—a rushing river, sifting through my runes, defying everything unholy.

I clenched my jaw, willing them to tip forward through my hand like offensive spellfire. My hands sifted through ribs of soft, wet rot.

Elina's gaze never wavered. Her tattoos flared, the story of us, of all of us, etched in moon ink on a moonless night.

The healing spell trickled from my fingertips, coaxing the deadened heart of a monster to life.

The death knight shuddered, morphing back to whatever it had been. I saw the rotten stump of tusks. The pointed ear under his helm. A half-orc, once. His armor turned from flaked rust to brittle steel, corruption and vitality warring in his form.

My fingers closed around his heart. Imbuing it.

"Fucking..." I growled, pushing forward into him.

I felt his heart beat once. A single, shuddering throb in my grip.

"Die."

I crushed it as it came to life. The knight sank down, the rot flowing from him like a foul dam let forth. Trith and I both turned to stare at Elina.

"My love," Elina whispered. For a single moment, in this garden, it felt like we were in Oakshire. That she was looking up at me from that bench in the garden of her temple, her legs swinging underneath. "I'm so happy I found you."

Then she collapsed.

"WHAT OF ERALT?" Ekyll asked Puris.

They walked slowly through the upper area of the feasting hall. When Puris looked down, seeing the smoking tables, he knew Davik had been here.

"Eralt will do his duty." Puris moved with his longsword. Below them, the feast hall doors had been opened. The beast of rot had walked through the hallway, following the surging dead.

Luka limped down the stairs, too wounded to move silently. Something had torn in his knee, and Puris saw the wince of pain every time he moved.

"It's Lord Sewell," his whisper crawled up the feast hall towards them. "His head is broken apart."

"Sword save him," Ekyll muttered next to him.

Serlo had said he had known. That he had orchestrated this. But that couldn't be true...

A muffle of noise came from one of the bedchambers. Puris raised his blade and crept forward. Ekyll shifted behind him, and Luka crept up the steps to rejoin them.

"Do you have a key?" Luka looked at the door.

"No." Puris gritted his teeth. "Get behind me."

As they approached the door, more dead rose from the

courtyard and surged through the feasting hall. They were after something.

"My lady?" Puris whispered into the thick wood. "My lady... it's Puris."

"*Don't open it.*" A voice sliced into his ear.

"*It's Puris!*"

Elyse and Mara. Puris thanked the gods they were unharmed.

But when Mara went to the door, he could hear Elyse slam into it. The noise echoed through the hall.

"Oh fuck." Ekyll groaned.

Luka shook his head. "She always was loud."

Ten undead traitors and comrades jerked their heads up from the feasting hall. Their eyes glowed faintly for a moment. That dark cowled puppeteer had pulled on their strings.

"Open the door, Mara." Puris twisted back to face the approaching mass.

"*It's a trick!*"

"It's no trick!" Luka shouted as the first undead touched the steps. "Open the fucking door!"

The sound of muffled sibling combat scrambled behind them. Finally, the door unbolted and swung open. "Puris!" Mara beckoned him.

Too late.

The dead had reached the top of the stairwell.

Puris hissed and grabbed Luka, but his squire shrugged him off.

"Get inside!"

"Secure them, Sir Puris," Ekyll grunted as he toppled a corpse down. "We'll be fine."

Before Puris could surge forward, Luka spun.

"For Rochdale," Luka whispered. Then he booted Puris through the door.

Mara and Elyse grabbed Puris as he staggered back, slamming the door shut on his brothers.

"No!" he screamed.

"I order you to remain," Elyse glared at him. "Do your duty."

"*Lead them this way!*" Luka roared through the door. "*So they might escape!*"

It felt like the last candle in his heart blew out. He stood there for a breath, listening to the dead take everything that remained. His brothers would fall back to the tower.

Where they'll be overrun and die. And return. If I see their corpses in that multitude...

Puris looked around, stifling the urge to scream. "We must head to the servants' tunnels, take any survivors, and find our way out."

"No." Elyse shook her head. "We remain here. My father will come. Lord Avel—"

"What?" Puris cut her off. "Avelmont?"

Mara had been crying. But the rage in her voice made Puris feel ill. "She colluded with them—with Ironclad! They *are* Bronzefell. Father is dead."

"You don't know that for certain," Elyse's voice held the first tinge of panic. "You can't."

"I can. He's dead." Puris realized he was shouting, but he didn't care. "This dark wizard—this was your doing?"

Elyse rolled her eyes. "You have no idea what you're speaking of."

"Puris," Mara begged him. "Put that away."

He looked down, realizing he was pointing his bloody sword at Elyse. But he didn't move it. "Speak plainly, Elyse."

The lady of the castle's mouth fell into a flat line. "You don't give me orders!"

Puris stepped towards her. All his friends, all his brothers...

"Puris." Mara put a hand on him. "We have to escape. We can get to your friends."

"My *friends*." Puris sneered at Elyse. "My *brothers* are dying for you. They died because of you. For what? To curry favor with the father of your abuser?"

Something terrible swelled in him. He had killed men in that frantic feel of combat. But this hatred...

This is how Darkshire feels. This is what warped him, and Serlo —and so many others. But Eralt would have me cling to the Sword. Only my fondness for him will save her life.

"I'm going to escort the lady of the castle to safety." Puris dropped the blade point downwards. "And the servants hiding in their corridors—from this doom you've brought upon us. And when we're safe, Lady Elyse, you'll take holy orders of the Sheath."

Elyse's face twisted into a rage. "A nunnery! I'll do no such thing."

"You will," Puris vowed. "And Mara will rule. You've orphaned her this night."

She stared at him, aghast, as if only now seeing him for what he was. A peasant, an orphan, giving her orders. But the world had changed, and her name meant nothing to the teeming dead.

The words came from his torn heart, and it was almost as if Darkshire spoke through him. "Now walk, or I'll turn her into an only child."

CHAPTER
TWENTY-FIVE

I cradled Elina in my arms, shielding her face from the rain. Her body was too cold.

"Hey," I whispered, "stay with me."

Sariel's face broke when she came forward. "Elina? Elina! Wake up!"

All I felt was the rain on my face and the coldness of it. I held her close. Tyra's hand slid over her own mouth in disbelief.

"Davik..." Trith's voice filled with sorrow next to me. He reached for the vial of his potion.

Brim stood, his face shocked. *Ugly-man... she's...*

"No." I turned away.

It was just the rain, that was why she was cold. That was the only reason. Just the rain and the mist above us. If I set her down, she'd be closer to the ground, and she didn't belong there. That's where you bury people, and Elina would outlive me. She'd live forever. The people you love have to live forever.

I knelt under the walkway, cradling her drenched body in my arms. We all have our pride and what we think we deserve.

Little is more sacrilege than a man like me asking gods for anything. And nothing is more honest than knowing you don't deserve it.

Please...

I felt the strand woven from my heart into hers. And it hung, slack and tetherless. She was a facet of my soul, and I couldn't stand a life without her. People you love are things you live for, and they can destroy you.

Please...

Then I felt a single pluck on the strand between us. Like a harpist reminding their instrument of what it was.

Elina groaned in my arms, the sweetest sound I'd ever heard. "Davik..."

"I'm here." I hefted her up. She was so small, so fragile. "I'm right here."

The barest slit of gold, the only light in this dark place, peeked through her eyelids. "Love it... when you hold me."

Her tattoos glowed faintly. I looked up and took the small vial from Trith. It was a healing draught. Would it help her? Would it calm the strain on her soul?

Trith forced the glass into my hands, his grip strong despite the way his whole body trembled. "Do it," he rasped. "She's still with us."

Karley turned away, wiping her eyes as Vorga embraced her.

Eralt limped forward, tugging on his necklace. "I have more."

She opened her lips as I tipped the glass upwards. It took her a moment to swallow. Then she nodded. "Just need to rest, love. Just take me to bed."

"I'll take you to bed," I promised. "You hear me?"

Elina nodded, turning into my chest. Her sandals had slipped away, and I hefted her bare feet. When I turned back,

Vorga and Karley sobbed into each other's arms in relief. Tyra sat down in the rain, blinking at nothing.

I looked at Sariel. "We have to go."

Brim picked up my hammer from the pile of sludge that had been our enemy. Its head was gone and most of the handle.

Sariel inhaled sharply, nodding to me. What we had nearly lost hadn't been worth it. The stakes were too high.

It was time to stop playing.

"This way," Eralt beckoned. He limped, his movements stiff with pain.

Trith caught up to him, slipping an arm around his waist to help him walk. "Lead the way, old man."

The elf steadied him, then shot me a tired but relieved smile. "And when we get out of here, find us some damn sausage sandwiches."

I looked up as I carried Elina. All I had now was my sword and Searlus's mace. But it didn't matter. It was time to put the leather on our feet to use and leave this fucking castle. The darkness lifted as the black mist cleared. I knew it was only the tide of horror receding, readying to crash over us with something else.

We walked in muffled silence. I carried Elina as we descended past the garden, through the pantry, and deeper into the servant's tunnels.

I watched the people of my life as we moved. Brim's quick breaths as he powered his legs. Vorga continually looking back, not to make sure I was there but to understand the grim look on my face. Tyra hefted the frying pan, her crossbow lost in the rubble. A beautiful faen cook, so far from her stove. Karley moved quickly, keeping pace with Sariel, both of them scanning the distance ahead for danger.

Above us, the lilt of the dead rose.

293

"Hurry," I told the group. We stepped deeper into the earth, the tunnels narrowing.

Vorga raised her torch when we came across the servant's quarters, looking through the wickets. "They're all empty."

"Hopefully, they fled…" Eralt grunted. You could hear the lancing pain in his voice. I knew he had his own healing draught, and I admired him for not using it until we absolutely needed it.

As we walked through the underground passage, we heard the trudge of metal ahead of us.

"I'll take her." Vorga turned to me with a smile. "It's okay, my love."

I handed Elina to her. Vorga. Shy, sweet Vorga. I still had the book she had written me in my pocket. The pages stamped with her declaration. She lifted Elina gently, her face barely straining.

"What now?" Sariel muttered at the noise as she hefted her sword. I walked up next to her, drawing my blade and keeping Karley behind us. Above us, the dead surged somewhere else. Hunting other prey.

There was no torch ahead, only the sound of panicked bodies moving. Corpses likely—risen and eager for mayhem. Then the movement slowed, and a voice quested out.

"*Eralt?*"

It was Puris.

The old knight limped forward. "Puris! Is that you?"

A scrape of flint sounded ahead, followed by a torch flickering to life. The young knight walked forward, followed by a mass of Windpeak servants looking furtively around.

Tyra lowered her frying pan and leaned on me for support. "Davik, please get me out of the Lowlands. I don't care how fancy the next wedding is going to be. Let's not come back."

I agreed. "Rather we stayed in Hollyhead, drinking imbued wine with you."

"Ah, and those pastries." Tyra shut her eyes. "And naps in tangled sheets."

"Thank the Sword it's you," Puris said with an exhausted grin as he approached. He looked as if he had barely made it out alive. "The mist is clearing. We can get to the beach and then the hamlet close to here where Allie is."

Puris shifted, revealing a familiar figure in the torchlight—Mara, wide-eyed and unharmed. Vorga's relief was audible as she held Elina. "Mara!"

But then I saw her. Elyse Sewell, the pen behind this entire ordeal, watching us like we were ghosts.

"You."

Sariel stood straighter, realizing who we had with us. It might have been the most murderous look on her face I'd ever seen.

Puris turned, then looked back at me. "Davik."

But I barely heard him. I walked forward, the sword clenched in my hand. Even with the dead overtaking the castle, two-dozen servants shrank back, from the lady of Windpeak to my wrath.

"Go ahead." Elyse had steel in her voice. Then she gazed back at our group behind us. "I didn't bring evil here. You did. Go ahead, Davik. You've killed women before, haven't you?"

"Many," I admitted, my eyes tunneling into her. I thought of that feasting hall, the dead Windpeak squires, and Elina limp in Vorga's arms. "But they all wielded a sword or sorcery. Yet, none were as dangerous as you."

"Davik," Puris begged me. I looked at him, seeing the battle he had fought to get here. Seeing the girl he loved and the predicament he was in with her older sister as a traitor.

I could have done it. Cut her down in the dirt and walked away without a second thought. It would have been easy.

And worth nothing.

"Let's get to the hamlet."

THE MAN STANDS, feeling the fall of the Knight of Rot. No longer will the decayed spirit roam the cryptlands around his soul dungeon. In his eagerness, he had brought his own ruin and goaded their prey further from them.

It doesn't matter. The pieces are moving. The drow girl will be easy, a fruit plucked from a rotting branch. He could snatch her now and deliver her to the prattling mages in Stroudsburg. They'll give him what he needs—the entrance to the Void itself.

But he wants those engraved bones.

Rayleth stands motionless next to him, eyes blazing in the night. The necromancer calls his moat of souls back into him, dispelling the shadows encasing the castle. It's time to drown the Darkshire's soul. Submerge it in torment and memory until it gasps, ready for a new vessel.

A corpse twitches next to him, powered by the incessant tug of his clients. He sneers and casts the tethered soul to it. *"Do you have her?"*

The man sneers. "Nearly."

"Three days... We must have her in three days," the corpse warns.

The man severs the soul connection. Mages. No one is patient any longer.

Deep inside the dungeon of his soul, he feels Theris the Red laughing. *You are losing, little necromancer. You don't have time. Bones or bartenders? You'll need to choose.*

"You are welcome to your mistaken thoughts." He shuts the wicket on Theris's dungeon.

Lure isn't the right word for what he's about to do. It's too simple. But it will do.

He turns to Rayleth. "Go meet your friend."

The elf doesn't bow. He wakes from his dream-cage and sprints into the castle.

Below him, the Knight of Bones wanders around the courtyard, absorbing skeletons from the corpses. Ruining them.

"Cease," the man growls.

The knight turns, its boned helm staring up at him. Once they are done here, he will fief this castle to him. Allow him to grow an empire of bone and corpses, before the clerics and paladins of the world come to fell him in holy battle.

Such is the nature of things.

But it is time for his work. He tasted the fevered dreams of the Darkshire in his little town. He turned the pages of his memory. It's time to rip them out and decorate the castle.

The man reaches out. He sends his consciousness into the castle, feeling along the corpses. Waking them. Using them as channels as they spew his illusions to life. The dreams of the Darkshire drape the castle, curling in fevered energy. It is time to bring the audience to the stage.

A castle is never just a castle. It is a bastion of battle. And every battle turns into a graveyard.

He leaps from corpse to corpse, moving like the notes of a song. Seeing stone, then corridors.

Then mud.

CHAPTER

TWENTY-SIX

It was a slow descent into the castle's exit. Every step deeper was a stutter, paused by those who survived the castle and feared every noise. Terrified horse grooms and whimpering chambermaids swelled our collection. The tunnels trembled with the surge of bodies, so very close to panic. I held Elina in my arms again, marching steadily behind the group.

"Davik," she whispered, smiling up at me, "are you okay?"

I laughed, the first smile cracking on my face in a long time. "I've been better."

"You should do it, you know."

"Do what?" I slowed down as an older maid fell, allowing her friends to lift her up. Far ahead of us, Puris led the path out of here through the twisting tunnels.

"We need to move faster!" Karley called ahead.

"No shit!" Tyra gasped.

"You can't," Elina whispered in my arms.

"Can't?" I glanced down at her as the crowd of people moved through the tunnel.

Ahead of us, Puris led the group left. People were clinging to those with torches as if the light would save them. Or maybe they just didn't want to die in the dark.

"Can't always go alone, my love." Elina shifted in my arms. Her robes were stained from the blood on my armor, but I held her close, cradling a flame I didn't want to be blown out.

"Let's leave the mindreading to Brim."

She coughed. "Your facets are here to give you strength. And growth."

My facets are flesh and blood women, and I have to keep one inside the other.

"Just rest," I told her. This wasn't Oakshire. This wasn't people smiling and drifting towards one another in a tavern. Nor was it the dungeons and keeps of my former career. I wasn't prowling in a mage's tower with ten other professionals.

Too soft, Darkshire. Too many pillows and pretty girls.

"You should tell her yes," Elina whispered. "Tell Sariel yes."

"Yes to what?"

Elina grinned up at me. "Her question. She wants a baby with you. We should all... have babies."

The crowd slowed as we came to a turn. "This way!" Puris shouted back.

"Don't wait, Davik." Elina shuddered in my arms. "You take on so much by yourself, but your facets are here to help you."

I looked up at Sariel, jogging relentlessly. There was an iron in her I knew well. Born of endless marches, where you look back and see a man fallen. And if the lash or the arm of his brother can't get him up, that's where he'll die.

As the mass of people slowed, I looked back at the dark tunnel behind us. The sift of soil hummed through the hall.

"Why are we stopping?" I called ahead.

299

Puris turned from an iron door, raising his hand. "Davik..."

I walked through the press of bodies, handing Elina to Sariel. We shared a look as I approached Puris and Eralt.

"What is it?"

Puris nodded to the iron door. "This leads towards the beach, but that's where they came from. I saw it. If there's a barrier... something arcane?"

The crowd of two dozen servants stirred. Eyes glanced everywhere as our torches burned low.

"Let's just go!" a chambermaid yelled.

I nodded to the door. "Open it. I'll go."

Brim growled. *I come, ugly-man.*

"Me, too." Karley slipped through the crowd. "You'll need my eyes."

Trith nodded to me, letting me know he'd stay behind to guard the group. I looked back at the sea of terrified faces. "I'll be right back."

The door squealed open on grating hinges, growling into the night. As we slipped from the choked tunnel, fresh sea air greeted us, punctuated by a waning rainfall. I saw the beach, where the corpse of a whale slowly churned, the tide trying to pull its mass back to sea.

We walked slowly, stepping over an old ruined pathway. When I looked behind and up, I saw the peaks that gave the castle its name, shimmering with rainfall on rock.

Brim sneered as we walked, sucking his teeth. Then he raised a hand, lining up the path to the hamlet some miles away. *It's that way.*

"Anything?" I looked at Karley.

The dark elf shook her head as she turned. "Nothing."

Brim stopped to feel the soil of the unfinished path.

"What is it?" I watched him.

The dishwasher shut his eyes, sensing the soil.

The castle groans.

Screams echoed behind us and the pierce of cast iron striking metal.

Tyra's pan.

We turned and raced back to the open door, and what we walked into was a living nightmare. The tunnels had been clear. But now, they were filled with teeming dead. Old skeletons clawed through the tunnels.

"They're coming out of the walls!" Tyra screamed.

The servants panicked, pushing past Eralt and Puris, blocking them from fighting the dead coming from every angle.

"Move!" I shoved a servant aside. But it was too much. It was a stampede of bodies. Even if I slew them, it was too tightly packed.

Puris and Eralt struggled from the wall, dead hands grappling them.

Vorga hefted her crossbow, using it as a bludgeon as the dead erupted from the soil, smashing rotten bones that belonged to hissing skeletons. Trith spun, struggling as half a dozen corpses grabbed him, pulling his staff away.

They had waited until I left. Nothing was over. I pressed through the bodies, living and dead, pushing people out of the exit where Brim was still stuck.

Tyra fought like a red-haired lioness, swinging her frying pan savagely, shattering bone and caving in undead skulls. Every impact sent a flash of arcane fire licking along the iron, the air thick with the scent of scorched flesh and blackened marrow.

Karley surged forward behind me, her scream cutting through the chaos as people shoved past in blind terror. She grabbed Sariel, who crouched protectively over Elina, shielding her from the stampede.

"Come on!" Karley shouted, hoisting Sariel to her feet.

"Back!" I bellowed to Sariel and picked Elina up, handing her over. "Get out!"

The dead swarmed, their clawing hands grasping at me, but I pushed forward. I reached for Trith, his form barely visible through the roiling bodies.

The tunnel cleared as people scrambled through the metal door, pouring onto the beach in a tide of panicked breath and stumbling limbs.

A faen scream ripped through the crush of bodies.

"Tyra!" I roared. I heard her, her voice raw with effort, her struggle lost in the mass of pressing undead.

Then the tide surged, shoving us backward, forcing us out into the night rain. Cold air slapped against my skin, the sky a churn of storm and twilight. The dead poured out after us, and I rose to fight.

Then—stillness.

The horde halted in eerie unison, frozen mid-motion as if a puppeteer had pulled their strings. In their center, Tyra writhed, caught in their unyielding grip.

I stepped forward, my breath ragged, my hands clenched around my blade.

Behind me, the surviving servants fled into the hills, their screams fading into the night. Somewhere in that stampede, Elyse ran with them.

But I wasn't looking at them. I was looking at the dead— silent, waiting. Holding Tyra like an offering.

"Davik..." Elina whispered from the ground.

When I glanced back, Trith's mouth was open in shock. At first, I thought he'd been struck.

Then I saw it.

Sariel stood with a sword to her throat, her own disarmed

at her feet. A lone figure held the blade. One ear mangled down to nothing but a hole in his head, clad in sickly golden skin.

When he turned his head, I saw the face I had known for years with blazing green eyes.

Trith moaned the name in my mind. "Rayleth..."

Rayleth stared at me without a flicker of recognition. This wasn't an enslaved corpse—the necromancer had created something else.

The dead opened their mouths in unison. "*The dark elf. The Karley.*"

Vorga bent to reload a crossbow, but the claw at Tyra's throat dug deeper, making her squeal in the grip of the horde.

"Don't!" Elina screeched in a hoarse whisper. She struggled to push herself up.

Brim prowled a step closer. "Tyra."

I tore my eyes from Rayleth's revived form. We were in the Lowlands, where chess was a game played often. Never had the taste for it, but I'd watched it often during the war. You think you're still in control, right until the last move is made.

Checkmate.

"Let her go." Karley's voice cut through the silence. Then she looked up at the thing that was Rayleth. "Both of them."

Tyra winced as the claws bit into her skin, her breath hitching.

The dead echoed in unison, "*Come, lost daughter. Come willingly.*"

"No." I stepped between Karley and the horde of dead. "Release them first."

Karley smiled sadly at me, her pearly white hair blown back by the storm. "Can't run forever, Davik." She pressed lips near me, her whisper parting as she passed. "But you can always find me."

Karley walked into the crowd of dead, their bodies parting as she approached. She stood still for a moment.

I looked back at Rayleth, or what looked like him, as he slowly removed the edge of the sword from Sariel's neck. Her breastplate and greave were battered from a duel that looked like it had lasted half a moment.

The corpses released Tyra. When she stumbled forward, Karley caught her.

"Karley," Tyra choked. "Don't do this—"

"It's okay." The calmness in her voice was a vow. "It's all going to be okay."

Then the dark elf walked into the crowd of dead as they pressed around her, slowly marching backward. Unharmed had been the order earlier, and it still stood.

Karley's eyes found mine as the dead pressed around her.

Then she was gone, swallowed by the shifting tide of death.

Rayleth left in a sprint, cresting up the peaks. Not climbing —gliding. His bones too loose, his movements too perfect. More agile than he had been in life, his sickly gold flesh like a maggot worming its way up the side of the cliffside. When he reached the highest portion, he turned, twin green eyes staring down at me in challenge.

An ethereal voice whispered from the castle walls. I saw Brim wince, holding his skull.

Come, Darkshire.

Bring me your bones.

"They're running." Vorga's voice was the amused fascination of shock as she stared at the servants fleeing over the hills.

We stood there, amputated, missing someone.

"Not all." Mara emerged from a clump of stone. "How can I help?"

Sariel rose unsteadily, limping. I knew Rayleth's swordwork. I knew his ferocity. Even an Embriel battle commander had been nothing to him.

"He stole him, Davik." Trith was blank-faced, as if he couldn't believe what we had just seen. "He went north and *stole* him. Why?"

"It's just his body," I said, more to myself than him. But it hadn't seemed that way. That was my old friend, under some dark charm. "We have to go get Karley."

"Let's go, now." Sariel grunted through the pain. When I saw the look on her face, I knew there was no talking her out of it.

Eralt and Puris came forward. The younger knight inclined his head. "We'll help you, Davik. There's another monstrosity in the courtyard. A thing made of bone."

I fished the mace from my hip, handing it to Puris. "Take this. It's enchanted... or disenchanted."

"Why don't you?" Puris peered at the weapon.

"It'll be dead in his hand," Trith groaned and stood shakily from the crag.

"Puris—" Mara whispered.

But the knight turned to her, smiling. "She's our guest, Mara."

Elina reached for Vorga. "I can go, just help me."

I looked at the exhausted people with me. Tyra and Vorga grabbed their items, and Elina could barely stand.

When I walked up to the both of them, I shook my head. "Help Elina. Keep her safe."

Vorga threw her arms around me. "I love you, Davik of Oakshire."

I shut my eyes. "I love you, too." Then I turned to Tyra, inspecting the wound on her neck.

"You come back." Tyra stripped the amber necklace from her neck and slid it into my hand. It had just now started returning to its normal color. "You get Karley, and you come back."

When Tyra kissed me, it felt like standing in an orchard when the sun rose. I held her close, and I didn't respond. I wasn't going to make a promise I couldn't keep.

"Take them to the hamlet," I told Brim. "We'll meet you there."

He hesitated, his eyes questing into the tunnel. I knelt down and grasped his arm. "You can't come this time."

Brim stared up at me, finally nodding. *I'll look after them, ugly-man.*

"Elina..." Sariel put a hand on the cleric as she tried to rise. "You're too weak."

"No," Elina said. "I can go. Just—"

I kissed Elina on the top of her head. "Not losing you again."

Puris lit a torch, leading Eralt back into the tunnel.

Trith raised his spear in farewell to everyone, limping towards the metal door.

"Trith." I motioned at him. His eyes were darkening with voidsickness.

The spellslinger walked ahead. "Not happening."

Sariel picked up her fallen sword, wincing from a broken rib.

"Sariel, you're hurt!" Tyra said. "You can't."

"We'll be back soon," she promised them. It was her first mistake because she was wrong and didn't know it. She wouldn't be coming back. Her face split into a grin. "And then we're never leaving Oakshire."

Sariel fell in behind me as I walked back through the tunnel door. It was a time for killers, and that's what we were.

"Can't live with it," Sariel whispered my own thoughts out loud. "Leaving her."

The words were dry in my mouth. "Me either."

As we entered the tunnel, I turned to her. "You know I love you. More than anything."

"I know." She smiled. Then she leaned forward, and we kissed, standing between darkness and the rain outside. I held her face, staring at it. Trying to burn it into my memory.

"I'm so sorry," I whispered, savoring the feel of her.

When she looked up, confused, I shoved her back and shut the door on her.

"Davik! What are you doing!" Sariel screamed through the iron wicket. Sariel wasn't coming back, because she wasn't leaving.

A lump rose in my throat. "Couldn't live with it."

"Don't do this," she pleaded, her breath catching. "Davik, please—Don't leave me."

Tears streamed from her eyes. She didn't hear me. She pulled on the door. Then she started kicking it. But the bolt was locked, and it flared briefly as Trith heated the metal, warping it. Sealing my choice in metal.

"Hey." I met her eyes through the wicket, forcing her to see me, to hear me. "It would've been yes."

Sariel clawed at the door. "Yes?"

A strange serenity filled me. It would have been selfish to have her come die with us. It wasn't about what men could do and women couldn't. There are some treasures you don't risk, even if they might save you.

"The answer to your question," I said.

Her eyes widened in understanding. "Davik—"

I smiled at a piece of my own heart. "It would've been yes."

Then I shut the wicket.

TWENTY-SEVEN

A long time ago, in a city called Runethor, two elves and a human had run out of wine.

I lifted Rayleth up the steps and threw a glance at Trith.

"What?" The sorcerer laughed, pointing at me with a sausage sandwich. It had become our ritual on nights out. "You lift tree trunks when we camp, but I'm supposed to help you carry *him*?"

"Over here." Rayleth nodded, reeking of wine. It's no issue carrying a drunk elf... until they think they can walk. We leaned over the railing, staring out at that city of sorcerers. Energy whipped through the towers of the collegiates.

"Hate this place," Trith said. "But these bastards pay well."

"Money," Rayleth slurred. "Money, money, money. What good is it?"

I laughed. I had warmed up to these two this last year. "Helps buy things."

"Does it? How many towns have we passed through where they won't even trade bread for it?" Rayleth leaned forward, threatening to topple over the balcony. He had demanded we come up here, and looking at the brooding exiled royal, he was going to be in rough shape tomorrow. "It's just metal."

I sighed and leaned onto the railing. Runethor was a bad place. I'm sure in the eyes of mages, it was the first chapter of a new world. But there were other cities I preferred. Cities that had gone dark, taken over by a strange unnamed group. For some reason, it had the mages scared.

We had passed through a town that woke up one morning, half their guards missing, their mayor vanished, and new banners flying over their walls. New ordnances hammered on the town square without warning.

Absolute control. Faceless and relentless.

It was there we saw a faen hanged. His crime? Unknown. They dropped him, but he was winged. Hands bound behind his back, he fluttered for almost half an hour, until finally bouncing like a corked bottle thrown in the bay.

"Wish we had another sausage sandwich." Rayleth coughed, shaking his long hair. "Bread tastes better when you're drunk."

Trith smirked, producing a pipe. "Davik's got some bread."

My face froze. It wasn't something I hid, how I kept it stuffed in my pocket. But I didn't announce it either. I felt wrong if it wasn't there. Sometimes I heard the sign from the prison camps clacking in the wind, and it only stilled when I touched it.

Rayleth turned his head. "That's *his* bread. Don't do that."

"It's alright." I put a hand on Rayleth to steady him.

"Sorry." Trith inclined his head. "Didn't mean nothing by it."

We stared at the collegiate towers, swirling with power. Tomorrow, we'd leave the city, heading off to find something or someone. Bring it to the mages. Rinse and repeat.

"Give us a show, Trith." Rayleth spread his hands towards the sky. "Show these wizards what it's all about."

Trith and I grinned at each other. Seeing Rayleth like this was a rare pleasure.

"Just for you." Trith pulled a wand from his chest. He pointed it at the sky and emptied it into the air. We looked up as a flare rose, lighting the night with soft orange tendrils.

"There we go." Rayleth exhaled as he stared up. As the light cascaded down, I saw the carved ruin of Rayleth's missing ear. The slippery knife work that had maimed him.

"Not bad." Trith lit his pipe with a flash of sorcery and looked up.

"You like my sword, don't you, Davik?" Rayleth said.

"Don't like it when we fence, that's for certain."

Rayleth laughed. He clicked it from his belt and turned to me, one eye half-opened. "This was my father's. He gave it to me."

I stared down at the masterwork. "It's beautiful."

Rayleth shrugged in that over-exaggerated way of the drunken. "It's just metal. Tell you the truth, I hate it."

Trith puffed on his pipe behind him. "Why carry it, then?"

Rayleth's head bobbed back and forth, his eyes swirling in memory. "Because it's the blade that killed him. It's... a prom-ise. My brother Venthren did it. And I—I couldn't kill him." He looked up at me. "I loved him. His mother had other children with other men. Little merchants and sorcerers so lowborn they couldn't come to court... Valas or something... but him I loved. And I hesitated."

I stared down at the sword. "A promise of what?"

Rayleth smirked, his eyes growing dark. Gone was the reserved warrior who bested me continually, his eternal skill a whetstone for my brutality to become something else. "Never hesitate. When a man intends to do you harm... he's not your brother."

I nodded, not wanting to interrupt him.

"You take this if I die, Davik. You take it. Be careful, because Venthren wants it. But he'll get it." A dark smile crept across his lips.

I made no move to touch the sword. "I think I'll be dead long before you."

The elven exile laughed. "That's because you're young."

Rayleth clipped the blade back onto his hip. It looked like stars wrapped in steel. As we leaned back on the railing, the moment was heavy with Rayleth's admission.

"You two are my brothers now," Rayleth vowed.

It was the last time I ever carried bread in my pocket—that night. I pulled it out, breaking it apart and passing it down to the two of them. Both of them took a piece with a hint of deference, the agreement unspoken between us. We stared at the city, chewing stale bread.

"Thank you," Trith whispered. "Brother."

"You gonna tell me who the woman is?" I reloaded the crossbow and handed it to Trith. "Or am I going to die without knowing?"

Trith swallowed in the chapel hall. We had taken a twisting way back up to the castle, coming from the rear. Void-sickness was going to be on him soon. He knew it, and I knew it. Of the dozens of wands that had encased his body, none remained.

"You knew her." Trith shrugged.

We hadn't been attacked on our way in. Rather, the castle had turned into some strange theater. Energy poured everywhere. Shadows, light, strange noises. Behind us, the dead moved in sequence. Their long chant echoed after us.

"*Wars we wage 'em...*" the chorus moaned, each note sounding from differing throats. "*Mages we slay 'em. Days we ... save... 'em...*"

I popped up and fired a crossbow. It rattled through two rotting heads. The dead turned, shambling towards me.

"Why are these ones slower?" Puris asked.

Trith answered. "Because he pulled them from the ground. They're rotten."

We fell onto the shambling dead. Claws raked our chests and arms. I broke them apart with the hilt of my scabbard and the fist of my glove. The stained-glass windows pulsed with violet, profane light.

Puris surged ahead, hacking the dead apart. When we had crossed the hallway we had retaken, we stopped for Eralt and Puris to don the Bronzefell enchanted armor and take their blades. Now they walked, reeking of death.

Eralt limped forward.

"Eralt," I began. "You can barely—"

The old knight snorted. "This is my castle, Darkshire. I'll be present when it's retaken."

"Why are they singing your marching song, Davik?" Trith looked around as we walked.

I watched the choir of undead wound up like little time-pieces, knocking into things. "Asshole thinks it'll rattle me."

As we crept farther into the castle, illusions danced in the corridors. And my stomach churned as I saw they were all for me. I was glad the girls weren't here to see them. No matter what was shown here, I could follow the pull of Karley's arcane soul.

We passed by an open chamber, once an armory. A man sat there, rocking under a thin blanket. He was surrounded by wire. My heart stopped when I saw the enclosure that used to haunt my dreams. The wind knocked harshly, rattling a blurred wooden sign.

I watched myself in Darkshire. It was towards the end, when the snows had melted.

Trith stared at it, his voice a thing of grief. "Is that..."

"Yeah." I looked away. "Keep moving."

More illusions waited. Each one pulled at me. I saw Lonny, smiling at me from atop a pile of frozen dead. Eralt and Puris fell silent, trying in that awkward way to make it seem like they didn't notice.

"*Get your hands out of me!*" a too-familiar voice echoed down the hall. "*Fucking bastards!*"

A man struggled on a rack in a thaumaturge's tent. When I looked within, I saw my body as it had been before the engraving. Muscles straining against leather I could later snap within a heartbeat. The warlock looked back and forth from a book while his assistant held a long blade for him to take.

"Davik—" Trith's voice was hollow. When he stared at me, he looked like he was about to weep. "Is that what they did to you?"

I held his look. He was my brother, in the most important way. He knew my past, but knowing and seeing were two different things. "That's over." You can look at the past, but I had stopped staring long ago.

Eralt shook his head. "This is... performative."

I felt Karley ahead in the courtyard. Her soul was still there, still intact. How this bastard mage knew my dreams and memories, I didn't know.

It didn't matter.

The hallways flickered for a moment, causing us to spin. Searlus's mace swung on Puris's hip dangerously close to me.

"Careful with that," I hissed. "Don't know what it does, but it hits like a bugbear."

Then the hallway morphed. It wasn't a castle. It was a Lowland forest. Knights hung by their necks by the dozen, the illusion draping over us like vines as we walked. Their eyes bulged, following us in the creak of rope.

"What is this?" Puris whispered.

But Eralt knew the answer, same as Trith and I. "The knights they hung, squire. The sorcerer shows them to us."

"But, why?" Puris wondered. When he reached out to touch the boot of one man, his hand slipped through the illusion.

"To shake you," Trith answered as we walked.

"Are these memories?" Puris looked around.

I looked up at the knight hanging near us. He struggled continually on his rope, but the heraldry on his armor was a blur. "Dreams."

Puris shook his head. "I've never had dreams like this."

My voice was dry in my throat. "Nightmares are dreams, too."

At the end of the hallway, I watched myself, more than a decade younger, sparring with Rayleth in a forest clearing.

"You have to learn to feel it," my old friend said to me.

Trith bowed his head. "Never a finer friend or finer swordsman."

I watched him, moving. Leaves shifted around us as we snaked the blades together. My hand went to the sword that was in his hand.

Trith saw me gripping it. "We did right by him, in the end. He wanted you to have it."

I watched him. "Still died."

There are people who leave you, that you would give anything to spend another day with. Rayleth was one of them.

Never was the swordsman he was, I lacked the artistry. Once he died, I never practiced again. Never honed my skills. I went back to being a killer of killers.

Yet I still carried it.

We heard the last illusion before we saw it. It sounded like a howling animal, strangely familiar, in the way you hear your own voice in an echo.

We stopped and stared. It was the peak of an ancient citadel, a lone crag of mountain in an icy wasteland.

I held Rayleth's body, limp in my arms. Eron was there, and Brightplate, and Trith and the others. Mercenaries and adventurers who had stumbled into something so much bigger than our own growing legends.

They stared mutely as my voice cracked, shattered in an open wail. Raw as the wound in my heart that day. Hadn't shed a single tear the whole way there. Not when we slew those red paladins and fetched his body back. Not when we rode there, to a place where he could at least see the sky. Not left inside some dungeon.

But when I saw where we would bury him, it was too real. The period at the end of a sentence I couldn't bear to pen.

Eron the mage bent forward, a man I had hated and later called brother. He placed a hand on my shoulder. Trith inhaled sharply next to me.

"We have to bury him, Davik."

The illusion kept starting anew. The details were wrong—constructed. My hair hadn't been that long that day. My armor had had more blood on it. The necromancer took his liberties.

But he got the gist of it.

A coldness came over me as I stared at the moment that had hurt me the most since the camps. I could feel the wind of that peak without the illusion. The harrowing feeling of being so alone. Outrage pulsed through me, seeing this moment laid bare like theater.

"This way." I turned towards the feast hall.

As we approached the courtyard, the doors were closed.

"Deiga," Trith blurted out.

I turned, not understanding.

His face broke into a sheepish grin. "It's Deiga. The woman."

The insanity of the revelation threw me. Despite everything, I laughed. "Rayleth's sister? She's an elf. What happened to *humans only*?"

Trith laughed. "Just kind of happened... when I went to Stroudsburg. We had... dinner. She stabbed me." Then his face grew alarmed, like a man who realized he had just ingested poison. "Think I love her. But, felt guilty. Rayleth and all."

"Well"—I stared at the doors—"you'll have the chance to ask for his blessing here in a moment."

Trith's voice fell. "It didn't seem like just his body, Davik."

"No," I answered. "It didn't."

I couldn't think about that. I couldn't divert my attention. This entire drama, these memories—all designed to throw me off. But my friend had died long ago, giving his life for us. And if the necromancer went through this trouble, it meant he feared me.

And he should.

Eralt drew his sword. "The elf... Rayleth. Is that Rayleth the Half-Heard?"

"That was one of his names." I inhaled, savoring the moment before hell was about to break loose.

"Was he famed?" Puris asked.

Trith chuckled. "You really are young, aren't you?"

I held back a smile. "You ever hear of Dain Ironsoul?"

Puris blinked. "He was *real*?"

"He was, as was his glowing blade." I tightened the strap on my left vambrace, an old habit coming to life. "Until he met Rayleth."

"Why does the death mage want you, Davik?" Puris asked.

"Doesn't matter." I slid my hands up the feast hall doors.

I stared at the doors, feeling the storm outside beyond. Karley was so close, I could almost smell the crushed roses of her perfume.

Eralt nodded when I looked at him. "I'm with you, Darkshire."

Felt like a prayer when I answered, "And I, you."

We hit the courtyard with a swagger. Nearly dead men come to battle already dead ones. Sometimes, attitude is everything. It's the difference between digging yourself out of a hole instead of filling in your own grave. The rain poured down in sheets, slapping stone and ramparts of the castle. An eerie green glow cascaded from the top of the portcullis gate.

Karley was there, a crumpled heap on the ground, and it looked like she was fighting to stay awake. Tendrils of green energy circled her hands and legs, trussed up like a pig for delivery. But she looked unharmed.

I saw the haunted figure next to her, his hands like growing green claws. Lightning flared, and the face of a dead man stared down at us.

It was the corpse in Oakshire. Marked from the Halls of Neythra. I had already buried him once.

Eralt and Puris shifted in the enchanted Bronzefell armor. The necromancer reached out, and I smiled as his sorcery broke apart on me. Trith's mage armor flickered. The sound of grinding steel filled the air, as what would have been death wounds carved deep grooves on Puris's breastplate.

His soul was concentrated now. I felt him; every rune inside me demanded his demise.

The voice emanated like a rushed whisper from the necromancer above. *"Bring me his bones."*

Our eyes floated down to the monstrosity that lumbered forward. It gasped, hefting a jawbone for a blade. Every part of it was encased in bone half a foot thick.

"Wish your hammer didn't break," Trith said as we walked forward.

"Me, too." I raised the sword and charged ahead.

Trith's lightning arced from the forge of his soul. This was the monstrosity Puris had described. The lightning hissed through the air, the mere sight of it setting my heart into madness. I hated it, and in that hatred, I channeled it forth.

The abomination roared as it swung its jawbone sword in a whir. I dropped into the mud as mortar exploded from the stone next to me. Rising, I swung at its weapon. It was like trying to fight a block of stone with a dinner knife. The elven blade had felled everything that walked on two legs, and some on several more, but it was just a blade.

I held it two-handed, bracing as the sword throttled back toward me. When I caught the blade with my own, I slid back in the mud. Trith pushed forward, an arcane blast whining from his spear. Eralt put his strength against Trith's, holding the thing's two arms apart.

"Now," I grunted as I slid back. The molars of some long-dead beast ground against the silver-blue steel. I truly, in that moment, wished Kardak was here. The minotaur would have done wonderfully. "Would be the time!"

Puris raced forward, Searlus's mace held high in his hand. The death knight's head turned, regarding this new attacker. The newly anointed knight brought it down across his bone helmet.

It sounded like a god swinging a hammer. The knight's

head broke apart like chalk dust, and a long roar echoed from the thing as we fell against the walls.

This, an ethereal voice said around us, *is not ideal.*

I blinked, looking up in the rain. As we stood, Puris grinned at me, holding the weapon. Every inch of his face looked like a teenager asking *can I keep this?*

The bone knight exploded. Spikes jutted forth like a rose bush coaxed to rapid life from a druid. Bone spindles and jagged spikes punched out. They weren't magic; they were reality. I rolled back on instinct, my death following me. Trith did the same.

Eralt didn't.

A long spike of bone anchored itself in his chest. The old knight stood upright, his tiptoes barely touching the mud.

"Eralt!" Puris screamed and fell forward. I saw a hideous collection of bone breaking through his armor, and one thorn had punched through his hand. The shock of the moment was the only thing keeping him conscious.

Eralt wheezed a death rattle. Thick globs of blood streamed from his mouth, caking his chin in red vomit. Puris walked through a thornbush of bone, bending and hacking. But the bone knight was dead, as was the magic protecting him. The mace was just a mace.

I hammered the bone out of the way with a fist, making a path. Puris fell in behind me, tears streaking down his face.

Eralt gasped, struggling to hold on.

"Sir Eralt..." Puris sobbed. "Sir. Give me your draught, we can... fix you."

Eralt was doing everything he could not to die, and I knew why. He focused his fading eyes on the squire. "Puris..."

"Give it to me." The knight wept. "Your draught!"

But Eralt shook his head, a small smile forming on his bearded mouth. "I am...proud of you... my son."

"Eralt!" Puris screamed. "Please! Don't leave. The castle needs you. It needs a commander."

"It"—Eralt smiled red—"has one."

Puris sobbed as Trith pulled him back, locking eyes with me, knowing what needed to be done.

I hefted the sword in my hand and looked him in the eye. "Wish it had been you who found me."

"You'd have been a fine knight... Davik." The old knight gasped, struggling against the hideous wound that pinned him. "Do it. Don't make him... fight me."

He held his chin high, as he deserved to. The only true knight I'd ever known.

I cleaved down, severing his head from his shoulders. Puris tried to turn, but Trith held him. Some things are better left unseen.

I reached forward, as I had a thousand times in my life, and looted a corpse. Eralt's health draught hung in a slim vial around his neck. It had cost as much as a castle.

And so had he.

"Sword keep you," I whispered. Then I turned away before I could feel anything at all.

Puris broke from Trith's grasp, running towards me. I grabbed him, holding the draught up. "Take this, Commander."

When he tried to look at Eralt, I stopped him. "Get to that ballista, load it, fire it."

"Okay..." Puris croaked the words.

"Say it to me."

"Load it, fire it."

He nodded, trying not to weep. Trith came forward.

"Melt the head of that thing and buy him time," I told him. "Stick the mace on the end of it. You get a shot, take it."

"I'll hold him off." Trith looked up at the caster.

We both watched Rayleth emerge over the castle walls, his sword primed in his hand. His stance was perfect. Too perfect. The fluidity of a swordsman honed over a lifetime—yet his eyes were molten emeralds, waiting to cool.

Trith stared at what had become of our best friend. "Did you ever best him, Davik?"

I gripped his old sword in my hand. "Never."

CHAPTER
TWENTY-EIGHT

After Daggar but before Rochdale, we took a simple job from an elven prince. We were tasked to find an heirloom and bring it to him.

I crept along the hallway of the elven prince's summer home. The job was done, and he had been so pleased with our progress that he invited us to stay for the week—to use his smiths and enjoy the crafts of his leatherworkers.

Rushe met me in the hallway, protected by darkness that Trith tucked back into his vest. The three of us shared a cold look, and I saw down the hallway the bodies of two guards, their elven armor draped in the blood of knife work.

"Easy now." Rushe smiled as he knelt before the lock. I stared down at the little thief. It had surprised me, him agreeing to this. He never put his neck on the line if it didn't suit him. But Rayleth had been by my side when we rescued him from that lord's courtyard.

Debts are a funny thing. They don't vanish when the man you owe them to passes.

Trith's face was unusually dark. He hadn't smiled the entire time we'd been here.

Rushe moved his lock picks, unlocking the door and standing. "I'll keep watch."

"It'll wear off by now," Trith whispered. We had slipped something into Venthren's wine that night.

"Good." I pressed the door handle. We had waited until the deep night, so he'd be able to wake. The plan had simply been to poison him and slip away, but when we saw his drunken glee at receiving Rayleth's sword and his boasting, our intentions had turned darker.

The door opened under Rushe's touch. A fine desk littered with papers and scrolls—the debris of managing a minor fiefdom of the high elves—sat empty. Outside, the forest was dark, shielding our movement.

Venthren slept, the sword clutched in his drugged fingers. He stirred when I grasped it from his hands. I fought the urge to run a rag over it, to remove his touch from my brother's blade.

"Wha—?" The prince blinked.

Trith bent over and slapped him across the face, waking him as I drew the blade. Promises either meant something or they didn't. Just because our brother had died, it didn't mean he didn't deserve his vengeance.

"Wake up," Trith spat. When Venthren tried to rise, the wood elf shoved him down.

I pressed the blade against his chest. Trith slowly released him as our client stared up at us.

"What is this?" Venthren hissed. "Are you mad?"

"Oh yes," Trith sneered. "After Daggar, everything *has* felt a little funny."

I stared down at him. "Those red paladins. You paid them for his body."

"We killed a lot of them to get him back." Trith stared at Venthren. "And we buried him proper. The world was going to end, and you put a bounty on Rayleth's corpse?"

"We can speak." Venthren raised his hands. He glanced around, hoping for a guard. "There's so much more I can give you."

I smiled. It wasn't my revenge, but it still tasted wondrous. "Like what?"

"Anything!" Venthren pleaded. "You knew my brother, I understand. But this is old. This is the way of the courts. You don't understand. My brother—"

"Wasn't your brother," Trith denied him. "He was ours."

I pressed the sword a minuscule deeper into his chest, the point of it pinning his shirt into him. Another breath, and I'd plunge it through his sternum.

"Anything you want," Venthren pleaded. "Whatever you want, it's yours."

I locked eyes with him. His widened in realization, then in horror as he understood there was no bargain to make. He opened his mouth, maybe to beg again, to lie, to curse us. But the blade took his words, and I twisted it, pinning him to his own bed.

"I want this," I whispered.

～

RAIN SLID ALONG EVERYTHING, turning the world wet. Puris and Trith were on the ballista, and I saw the ember glow of hot metal as he heated the barbed head, nestling the mace at the end of a loaded missile.

Karley lay bound, thrashing against her restraints beside the necromancer. He flicked his gaze to Trith and Puris and, with a sharp gesture, unleashed a lancing bolt of sorcery. Trith snapped his spear-staff up, deflecting the attack in a crackling burst.

Rayleth stepped towards me, his blazing eyes trailing along the sword in my hands.

"Venthren..." He hissed the only words he had spoken.

Had I seen him before this, it would have broken my heart. Maybe I would've tried to reason with him. But he was lost, trapped inside his own mind. I had no words for his dreams.

We shouted in steel.

He lunged in a blink. His footing was impeccable. It was like fighting a whisper. Anything I knew about true swordwork had come from his tutelage—and the lessons had been far from over when he died.

We fought viciously. I swung, never hesitating when he was within my grasp. He parried, but somehow—like always —he was on the offensive. Braziers howled under the onslaught of rain, and we battled. He was cold precision; he was a hundred years of practice.

Our blades never locked. He was that good. Behind every swing, my arms howled. He was as fast as he'd ever been, as skilled, and stronger.

We pressed back and forth. His blade slipped along my forehead, sending blood down my eye before I felt it. I riposted, crashing a masterwork of smithing against cheap steel. But you don't fight the sword, you fight the swordsman.

High, low, it didn't matter. Anything I had left, I poured it into my body. For every strike I delivered, it was met with steel and answered twice. Like trying to outclap an applauding crowd.

"You killed our father." He glared at me as we circled.

I spat blood on the wet ground. "Killed your fucking brother for you." If I could get through him, I could get to the necromancer. "You stubborn bastard."

I looked over and saw Trith battling the dark figure. Storms of green energy battled wild magic, and the spellslinger had no wands to sling now. He shouted over the storm, deflecting whipcrack after whipcrack of arcane energy. A tail of it deflected from Trith's staff, chipping the crystal. The energy rebounded, breaking the handles of the ballista and throwing Puris back, toppling from the tower to the close cliffside below.

There went that idea.

Rayleth nearly took my head off. I twisted my blade just in time. As we riposted, sliding away from one another, I felt something trace up my leg. The bastard had cut three inches of my old incision scar there.

Bring me his bones.

He wasn't fighting me. He was dissecting me.

I shook my head, trying to get to Karley. "I'm going to send you home, brother."

Rayleth dipped, moving through the rain. When he fell on me, it was with such havoc that I fell back. I swung, sliding steel with him. If I could get close to him, I could grab him.

But this was his domain. This slither of bladework. Not the swing and the lunge, but the strategy of slipping blades. When I pivoted, half-swording to bring my blade across his chest, he leapt back. Then he delivered a sword blow to the side of my head like a fucking battering ram.

My skull kissed his blade before the force threw me to the ground.

I saw Karley and pushed myself up.

A kick met my upturned face, bashing my head into the battlement. I saw stars in a starless sky. I nearly bit my tongue in half, filling my mouth with hot blood. And it tasted like defeat. Like the truest realization I had ever known. Just like every time I had fought him.

I was going to lose.

I coughed, and he plunged the blade into my side. Only my armor saved me, catching it for a moment. I spun on my knees, bringing a fist into his gut. It didn't drop him. He danced back.

Behind him, along the spitting braziers, Trith channeled the void, orange light crashing against tendrils of green. But he was losing, just like me.

I pushed myself up. "You one-eared fuck..."

For a moment, his sneer flickered. Eyebrows bending in memory. But the moment slipped away, replaced by another boot to my face. If my neck could have broken, it would have.

"Rayleth—"

The sword came down in a killing blow.

I raised my arm, using the bones like a shield as the blade sank into me. My skin split. I felt so little. Not from rage. Not from the power to see it through, to get to Karley. But from the cold call of my own grave.

Rayleth hefted again, striking me over and over. Hacking at my arm. It reminded me of the first time a guard beat me with a cudgel for begging.

I released the final rune of Elina's healing spell. Even if she'd been well, I wouldn't have brought more than that. The more I had in me, the less my runes would work against magic.

Trith roared behind me, burning his soul to keep the necromancer at bay. He was holding out for me to make the killing blow.

I raised my blade, feeling my left arm wrap together. Wounds half-healing, spiraling pink and raw.

Rayleth sneered. *"I've waited a long time for this."*

Legends had died on the end of his blade. Maybe it was time for one more. I saw the necromancer turn, leaving Trith where he was. Collapsed and on his way to death.

"Open him."

Rayleth flicked his blade out, cutting my world in half. I

reached up, feeling the split jelly of my eye. It hadn't even hurt, but that feeling... the running of it was like a yolk down my face, the rain taking it away before I could even notice it missing.

The one-eared elf, the first friend I had made after the war, shifted. I wavered, forcing my lungs to suck in more air. For the first time maybe, I knew what he felt. Much had been taken from me in the war, but never a piece of my body.

I turned, dropping into the stance he used to make me practice over and over. But instead of the blade facing him, I tapped it on my own shoulder in a grim salute.

"Focus."

His face morphed, aching in memory.

I fell into him, slipping and feeling. I let go of everything, every reaction. I stopped trying to chase his strikes, and I simply met them. For the first time, as I warred with one hand, I had to be precise. Blind and tactile.

His blade waved past my face. I spun, hearing Karley's scream when she saw the state of me. Rayleth walked into my blindspot.

And I saw it—in that blind, perfect way. I knew it was the finest swordwork I would ever do, and if he could have, he'd have been proud.

His blade slipped down my back, curling grooves through the leather. He was so pinpoint, so perfect, that he opened my armor where the seam met under the reinforced spine.

The kiss of the blade found me, so much like the thaumaturge years ago. Old scars reopened, and then his boot kicked out.

But I wasn't there.

The sword that had slain his father, and later his brother, was buried to the hilt in his lung. A wheeze crept from him. I didn't hesitate and withdrew the blade, slapping his from his hand.

As he stumbled back, I lunged forward, but he twisted, driving a kick into my wrist and knocking my blade free.

How do you beat the best swordsman you've ever known? Someone far better than you?

Not with a sword.

I punched him in the face, all my might hurling forward. My boot twisted; my right eye was absent. But I felt him there. The snap of his head to the side. He wasn't alive, and he wasn't dead. The normal rules didn't apply here.

He struck me back. The necromancer watched in grim boredom. Our swords were clattered beneath us, but we fought. I was stronger than him then, and much more now.

Every time I struck him, his eyes flickered like a storm lamp. I held his shirt, swinging my fist into his side over and over. He jabbed at me, then when I had him in a bear hug, I pulled his head into my shoulder.

"*Peel him,*" a dark voice commanded.

Rayleth reached back, fingers sliding into the opened incision on my back. I howled like I hadn't in a decade—not since the surgery table—the terrible feeling of someone *opening* you.

I headbutted him, caking his golden face with the blood of my eye socket. We lurched together, exhausted, two prize-fighters dying for a single viewer. His lesson came back to me.

You can't batter your way through every man.

But some, you could.

I picked him up and twisted, throwing the elf over my head and slamming him onto the stone. We both hurtled in the air, the breath driven from us as I embedded us into the mortar.

Rayleth blinked. I spit blood from my mouth, pushing myself up, wincing as the slice up my back nearly killed me with pain.

I looked down as I crawled over him.

"Davik..." he whispered.

I realized that my arms were on either side of his head. The runes were blocking the control the necromancer had on him.

"Hey, Leth'."

A smile crept across his mouth. "We should get sausage sandwiches."

The necromancer turned to approach us with something like a sigh wheezing from his throat.

When I started to push myself up, Rayleth grabbed my arm. His face contorted in concentration, like a man trying to stay awake at the wagon reins.

"Go home, Davik."

Then he left me for the final time.

All I could do was turn from where I collapsed. His old sword was in his left hand as he ran like a man escaping death. Trying to shovel himself into a furnace that threatened to swallow us both.

My good eye was filled with blood and rain. Just enough to see him, like staring through warped glass. The defiance of it, the will, when the green spectral tethers reactivated, and he threw himself at the necromancer who had stolen him from his grave. A shout—so alive.

"No..." I groaned.

His sword was in the air above him. The caster stepped back. With a flick of his glowing claw, something broke apart. And my friend died for the final time.

Go home, Davik.

I rose.

The necromancer turned, his hands like green claws. Rage wasn't the word for what I felt. It was pure grief. It was Renrick Drakemoor howling over his brother. I stumbled forward, teeth gnashed. It was like so many years ago when he fell. Only

330

now there was no one holding me back from joining him in death.

The necromancer turned, seeing me. His face was a corpse, beyond the gray of death. Karley's bonds shimmered with witchlight. He moved like an old man, creaking. And I was on him before he could kill her.

I threw him from the parapet. He was so light, and I wished he were heavier to feel his fall.

He crashed onto the ground, his legs breaking far below me.

His cowl fell back, a head with several strands of hair turned. The necromancer looked up at me, green light pulsing in his eyes as his legs knitted.

I limped forward, hitting the release on the portcullis, slamming it shut.

"Stay right there," I said with a mouthful of blood.

Karley coughed as her bonds shimmered out of existence. When I bent over her, I felt her pulse. Her hand reached up to me, and I felt the spell wrapping her soul.

"He... put me to sleep." She smiled, already falling back under. "But I heard you. I always... hear you."

Mage armor glittered over her, and I looked up and saw Trith lowering his hand. It looked like the last spell he would ever cast.

I limped towards Trith, moving along the crenelations for support. One, two, then the next. I couldn't descend the stairs, I knew I would die before I got to the bottom. My body was undone, bleeding in shallow rivets. I had wounds that were given a tenth of the healing they needed. The last rune of Elina's spell wouldn't save me, just buy me time. It felt like the bridge to the afterlife as I stumbled towards him.

Trith looked up at me, breath rattling. I saw Eralt's draught near him, its chain broken from where it had fallen from Puris.

"He broke the fucking draw wheel," Trith coughed.

I blinked and stumbled behind the ballista where the end of Searlus's mace protruded from the head of the bolt.

"Davik..." Trith groaned. But I wasn't listening.

I spun the ballista, staring with one eye. The cut on my back opened like a smile, rattling a seething groan from my lips.

The cord was spun steel. The draw weight? You'd need a team of horses. A winch a foot thick with a man on either side spinning it back.

Or a Magebreaker.

The necromancer raised the gate slowly, his hands glowing with power.

"Fucker." Trith coughed wetly. "Takes his sweet time."

I leaned over the ballista, my split hands wrapping around the steel cord. I gripped as hard as I could and leaned back, my boots slipping until I dug the spiked one into the wooden base, stapled into the tower rookery.

Trith pushed himself up to help me, then he collapsed again.

I heaved back, every portion of air slipping from my lungs. The muscles in my neck locked, but the cord retreated an inch. And then another. My fingers split like sausages left in the pan too long. The pain felt distant, and I knew I was like the braziers flickering out of existence around us.

One last time.

Behind me, the crunch of metal on stone sounded. Puris ascending maybe, but he was too late.

The gate raised, and I saw the necromancer walk forward. I groaned as Trith stared up in amazement as I spun the wheel, turning the weapon towards him. My blood slipped down the ballista. It took everything I had—everything I could ever have

—to hold the wire back. My teeth smashed together. My one eye bulged from its socket.

I blinked, my vision turning blurry.

"Lower," Trith wheezed. "A bit lower."

The string came fully back as I jerked, hefting. It felt like my organs shifted. Something pressed in my groin, a strangling sensation. I was in too much agony to breathe.

The dark figure turned, regarding me.

I wavered, my eyesight shimmered as my muscles locked. A tendon split, severed by the garrote I held in my hands. I wasn't holding it with my fingers, I was holding it with the scrape of fingerbones. One finger sprang free, no longer under my control.

I couldn't see. I heard trudging metal in the rain, like armor. The march of a war long gone. I wondered in that insane moment if hell would just be the war all over again.

"I've got you," a voice whispered in my ear. I couldn't see her, but I could smell Sariel. Her hands wrapped around mine, chest pressed against my back to guide me. Giving me what I was missing, as we always had to each other.

I held it as she turned the weapon. Sariel's face pressed against mine, staring down the sight.

"There," she whispered like a kiss.

I let go.

CHAPTER
TWENTY-NINE

T he man falls.

It is not the first time, but it is close. All he hears is laughter when the Darkshire flings him from the castle wall. The mud welcomes him as he crashes into it. His legs snap. The laughter grows louder and he realizes it is Theris the Red.

"*Greedy...*" the dark elf cackles deep within him.

The man coaxes his legs to straighten. He sees the Darkshire walking towards the dying wood elf. He reaches out, seeing what corpses are nearby to aid him, but none remain. His target sits atop the wall, fighting the spell of harmonious sleep.

It will do.

When the gate slams shut, he feels a flicker of something. Panic? Fear? They are just words.

Concern is the right one.

The engraved man limps towards his friend. The necromancer watches for a moment. The Darkshire is close to death... those bones are so close. But he needs them alive for the ritual. To transfer one soul into another... he will have to wait. He has waited before. He is patient—as he was taught to be. Another year. Another ten. It doesn't matter.

A tendril of a soul pulls at him as he stands. He sucks his deadened teeth. Failure is thick in the air, and his nostrils can smell it. The knights of bone, shadow, rot... and his blade ward are gone. But there are so many more delicious minions in his chest dungeon.

The stretched soul quivers inside him. No, that is not the right word. It is a *yank*. Like a spoiled child tugging on his sleeve, demanding his attention.

His patience finally erodes. He shuts his deadened eyes, reaching through with the glory of the profane along the tethered soul to his clients. He sees them as he travels the expanse of space, slipping along a soul as thin as a cleaved hair.

Veilwalker... a voice calls to him. *Time runs short.* He surges towards it, pouring the power of his soul, draining the moats around his chest dungeon in a furious charge.

The four dark elves are gathered around a scrying table. Spies and exiles from their underground kingdom.

The room is in Stroudsburg. The table is runemade and enchanted. They look young, but their coven is old and like him, they are the last of it.

The three males and one female are thrown backward when he breaks the crystal and reaches forth with a snarl. It has been over a century since he lost his temper, and the effects of that still linger in that little city.

What is life without minor indulgences? What is death without the same?

Mages. Freed from the underdark, playing their little games. Bothering him for what? For power? For grudges? To barter a little bartender back to her family and open the tunnels under the world?

No. He smiles as he grasps their souls—burning so

335

brightly, tinged with arcana. They struggle, but they are in his world, the place of souls and ether. They reel from him, but his grip is absolute. He will find the path into the void itself and coax their lore from their tortured souls.

The dark elves don't die. They simply fall, limp from their chairs like the bags of meat they are. Their souls scream in his claws as he recedes back to himself, ripping them from their bodies, and turning their heads to stare at the blinking darkness he covets. The great veil of death.

He slams them into his soul dungeon with such force that doors break. It is no matter. He will tend to it later. It isn't enough damage to wake the builder, so it will be fine.

The man opens his eyes. There are secrets within him now. Four little dark elves howl deep within the caverns of his chest dungeon. And their screams are such sweet music.

He raises his claws as he opens his eyes. His body is stronger than it has been, but it is still slow. Power curls around him as he draws from his collection, raising the portcullis with hissing spells. Prying the mouth of this castle open so he can walk forth.

He turns his head, still grinning from his indulgence. Thaumaturges, mages... no one is patient any longer. Why should he be?

The engraved man has the Embriel behind him. They are pointing the ballista at him. His lips curl into a sneer as his left hand crackles with power.

The bolt releases, hurtling towards him. He can see it tunneling through the rain. A projectile. A missile. Those are the right words.

He draws his power, ready to turn it to kindling. He'll kill the Embriel for this, just to wound the Darkshire a *little* more. If he lives, his soul will be ripe for the plucking.

He raises his hand, profane power glittering, and casts.

Nothing happens.

Something like a sneer slithers into his mind. Theris the Red is loose. The blood mage grins thickly as he sits atop the necromancer's soul, subduing it. The door to his cell is wide open, holding only empty chains.

As if he could have freed himself at any time.

"Did you really think." Theris grips his arm, stifling his power. True surprise strikes him for the first time in decades. Windpeak wasn't the only castle with an invader this night. *"I would let you destroy the beauty of the arcane? The finest love I've ever known?"*

The man thrashes. His feet are planted to the ground. His body is frozen. No, not frozen—stolen. His own limbs, twisted against him. His power is wrenched from his fingers. He has never felt this before. He has never—

Something is stuck on the end of the projectile, and Theris turns him to face it. His power is incredible. All these years waiting in his soul dungeon. Letting him get closer to his goal, only to rip it from him.

The missile crashes into him. Somewhere, in the caverns of his chest dungeon, the violet skies darken as an obelisk hurtles down. It is the cataclysm of his soul. The ruination of all. The shattering of spirits, and secrets, and himself.

The man screams.

CHAPTER

THIRTY

The bolt slammed into the necromancer, stapling him to the wood of the blacksmith's hut. I fell into Sariel's waiting arms; the momentum crashed us against the tower wall next to Trith.

The three of us stared at the explosion of profane power.

Green wraiths rose from the ruined body—a thousand souls, maybe more. Many were inhuman. Many were things none of us had ever heard of before. A spiral of energy whipped through the storm, shrieking in celebration as it rose from the corpse.

"Good shot," Trith rasped.

My head slumped forward as Sariel held me. I couldn't see her, but I could smell her. Around us, the freed souls wafted over the castle before hissing into the sky. The stormy night flashed with emerald defiance before they poured off to whatever fate awaited them.

Sariel moved from behind me. Her hands were bloody from the climb up the peak, half of her armor discarded. "Hold still, my love." She bound a wound on my leg I hadn't even noticed.

"Puris is okay—he's on the crag below the tower. Broke his collarbone, so he couldn't climb."

"Good," I groaned. "Get to Karley. Make sure she's alright."

Sariel stared into my one good eye. The look on her face made me turn the ruined one away—not in shame, but to spare her from seeing it.

The souls continued to pour from the necromancer's corpse, curling up like steam from a green cauldron.

We looked up as a single specter stepped slowly along the walkway—this one not in a hurry to rush to whatever lay beyond. Where the others hummed with green power, this one shone silver, tinged with red. A dark elf.

Sariel drew her sword and walked along the parapet. But the spirit didn't harm Karley as she regained consciousness. The wraith of a dark elf raised his hand, an almost gentle look on his cruel face. Even in death, his power was palpable—a mage, long vanquished, now freed.

Karley shifted, coughing. She stared up at the figure, blinking in the rain. He placed a hand over his heart and bowed. A single word echoed from a voice as old as the written word:

Descendant.

Then he was gone.

Sariel crouched and pulled Karley up, holding her steady. Behind Trith and me, the rattle of armor sounded in the storm as Puris tried to climb his way up.

Pain pulsed through my body, dull and numbing. I rolled towards Trith as the candle of my life burned low. He was too exhausted, too close to death himself, to do anything but shift his eyes onto me as I held Eralt's draught up to him.

"Drink it," I wheezed. The muscles in my body ceased their hum, the final tones of struck chimes growing still. "And look after—"

Trith pushed the draught away. "Fuck off."

"Stop," I choked out, spitting blood. "Come here."

With the last of his strength, Trith slapped the draught from my hand. I glared at him with the only eye I had left.

Trith shrugged, his copper hair limp against his head. "I'm coming with you."

We ceased our final duel, lying against the tower walls. I watched as Sariel helped Karley up, both of them shuffling toward us. The braziers no longer burned in the night. The fires had done their job. Rayleth's body lay supine ahead of us.

"Should've been this way," I whispered.

A vibration hummed in my pocket, making Trith turn his head. "What's that?"

I pulled the small scroll out, blinking to bring it into focus. I had had it in my pack, but collegiate contracts always had a way of ending up where they wanted to be.

"Evior's offer."

"Let's see it. I wonder who"—his voice broke as he coughed—"the hell he wanted."

I summoned the last of my strength to break the wax seal. I unfurled the contract, peering at it. It was the same as always. A name. A location.

I laughed as I dropped it onto my chest. A single line began to bisect the words.

"What's it say?" Trith looked over.

I turned it so he could see the words.

Kill the necromancer. Windpeak.

My eye socket was a carved cavern, and my back screamed with pain as I laughed, louder and louder, until Trith's cackling joined mine.

The door to the tower broke open in a heave of anguish. Two wounded squires emerged, bearing torches. I saw Vorga and Tyra holding Elina, helping her walk. The frying pan on

Tyra's side was caked in bone and seared flesh from their battle here. Brim walked ahead of them, hurrying towards us.

We were still laughing when they approached, the scroll sitting between us in the rain. I was sure we looked like madmen as they gathered around us, our faces lit by the glow of Elina's flaring tattoos.

～

THREE DAYS LATER, the castle had been cleared by the returning servants. Most of the deaths had come from the squires and men at arms, along with Lord Hamlin Sewell. I was too weak to attend Eralt's burial, but Puris and the remaining squires had put him to rest with honors near the knighting tree.

People returned to what they knew after calamity. Tanners tanned, and cooks and laundresses shifted back into the castle.

Elina's power had saved me, and Trith had drunk the draught in the end, only after he was sure I wouldn't perish. The priestess had kept me from the brink of death, but by the time she could cast again, my eye was gone.

When a man loses an arm in a dungeon and a cleric heals it, it doesn't grow back. It closes the wound. Too much of my eye was gone. My back was closed, my muscles restored, but there was a deep exhaustion in me. I stayed in bed for three days.

Half my world had been taken away. But I still marveled at what my life was now.

Vorga shifted her hips as she straddled me, taking her time. As she writhed, she reached out to clasp her hands into mine. "I had to sneak in. Sariel's been"—Vorga shuddered as she spasmed around me—"hogging you."

I groaned as I released inside her.

Vorga fell into my arms with a sigh. "That was nice."

341

"Yes, it was." I held her tighter.

Karley traced a nail across my chest, kissing my ear where she lay nude next to us.

Vorga turned her head in a grin. "He's mine right now. Do you have any... you know? Mine's in the other room."

Karley laughed, reaching over to the nightstand. "Here, have some of mine."

Vorga sat back with me still inside her, her pert breasts shining with sweat. The room smelled of hot stew as Tyra's makeshift stove bubbled in the corner. She wore an apron and nothing else. Her plump cheeks shifted as she stirred, and she bit her lip. "Food's almost ready."

"Ugh," Karley groaned. "Can't believe you're using that frying pan after what was on it."

"I washed it!" Tyra turned. "And scrubbed, scalded, and left it in a fire. It's clean!"

"I'll still eat it," I said with a grin. I held Vorga's hips as she raised off of me, my cock sliding from her spreading lips until warm seed poured over me.

"Sorry," Vorga whispered with a grin. "Price of me being on top. I'll get a rag."

"Don't bother," Karley's voice was heavy as Vorga crawled to my side. She bent over me, kissing down my chest. Her dark lipstick stained me as she locked eyes with me, holding her ass in the air as she cleaned me with her mouth.

"Mmm," Vorga whispered, running a hand over my chest. "Sariel usually does that. Looks like she has competition."

I shuddered as Karley sucked on my softening cock.

"Hey, now," Tyra called over, pointing with a wooden spoon. "Food first. He needs his strength."

Karley released me from her mouth and grinned. "Sorry."

Vorga held up the small pouch Karley had handed her. "This is your stillseed, Karley?"

"It's Sariel's," Tyra said across the room as she stirred. She had placed a pot on top of the frying pan, using it as a heat source. "She gave it to her. Guess Davik made her a promise."

I smiled. "That I did."

"That's why she's been all over you!" Vorga laughed. "She kicked me out last night. Very feisty."

The door opened, and I sighed in relief that it wasn't a servant. Elina and Sariel both smiled when they walked in.

"I go take a bath for a single hour"—Sariel looked at the two women in bed with me—"and look what I come back to."

"You love it!" Vorga laughed and pulled the sheets to cover herself.

Karley slid from the bed and slipped her robe on. "Careful, Sariel. I can cast a sleep spell on you and steal him."

"Mmm," Sariel whispered, her eyes drifting over me. She had been fraught with worry for my health, but once I recovered enough, she had really shown her fury. Our lovemaking was usually sultry, punctuated by her innate demurity.

But that first day there had been no mercy. She had mounted me like a vanquished enemy, galloping on me with determination in her silver eyes.

Don't you ever do that again, you hear me? Now give me your seed. Give me all of it.

Over and over, until we both grasped one another, and I delivered on my promise. Elina had said a union between us would take time as we were different species, and Sariel was determined to surmount it at every chance.

Elina walked forward, checking the bandages over my eye. "The more facets around him, the better his recovery." She kissed my lips. "Make sure you're napping, my love. All these lovely women might put you into a coma."

I bit her lip for a moment, making her giggle. Then she

slapped my hand playfully. "Let me change your bandage. Are your runes still full of my healing spell?"

I nodded as she undid the cloth around my head, the air of the room hitting my eye. The eyelid had come back together from her divine healing, but it had nothing to protect any longer.

"I think it looks good." Karley smiled at me. But we both knew the truth about my appearance. "Suits him."

She walked past Tyra at the stove, snatching a piece of bread and dipping it into the pot. Tyra snapped her spoon out, striking her with a swift smack on the ass.

"Ow!" Karley yelped.

Tyra pointed at her. "Not so fun when it's not Davik doing it, is it?"

Karley took a bite of her bread and bowed. "You win."

Elina replaced the bandage around my head. "We just have to give your body time. You're healed, but your mind has to adjust. Let's make sure you walk today."

I shuddered as Sariel started kissing my stomach, replacing where Karley had been. I couldn't see on that side of the room, but I heard Tyra sigh, exasperated.

"Sariel! We're about to eat!"

"So eat," the Embriel responded between kisses. I felt her trace down, her nose sliding across my waist as she gripped my rising cock. "He can eat while I sit on it."

"It's a stew!" Tyra cried out. "The sheets!"

"All your facets," Elina whispered as she pulled my bandage tight across my head. "Adore you, my love."

I slid my arm around Elina as I turned my head. It was the one habit I found most annoying about losing my vision. Having to crane my neck everywhere.

Tyra threw her dish rag down next to her pot, shaking her

head as she came forward. She bent down, taking the other side of Sariel. "I was next. Let me have him first."

Sariel grinned and gripped my cock. "Fine. Help me get him—"

A knock came on the door. "*Davik?*"

"Go away!" I shouted as the girls giggled. Tyra ran her lips along the other side of my cock, joining Sariel. "This part of the tower is under construction!"

But the voice came through the door even louder. It was Puris, and even after everything, I heard the shy, halting tone in his voice. "*You said you wanted to be told when they arrived.*"

We all looked at each other. Some things were worth interrupting.

I watched from the balcony overlooking the courtyard. The sun was stronger the last two days, turning the mud into soft soil. As I looked down from the parapet, Puris stood with Mara, their arms around one another. Last night, he had knighted his two squires. Sir Ekyll was to be commander of the guard, and Sir Luka was to lead and train the Order of Eralt.

Only one monk of the Sword was among the arriving party. The rest were sisters of the Sheath, the holy order of nuns for the old Lowland religion.

The girls waved up at me from the courtyard.

Elyse Sewell stood, resigned to her fate. As the sisters came forward, they traded words.

"Lady Mara." One bowed. "We hope you are well."

"Thank you," Mara said with a smile. "This is Sir Puris. Soon to be Lord Puris—when summer allows."

The lead sister looked at him. "Sword guide you, Sir Puris."

The young knight inclined his head.

The older woman looked up around the courtyard. "The sisterhood is always glad for more faithful. Are you ready, Lady Elyse?"

Elyse Sewell looked anything but. Everyone knew of her treachery and what had led to so much slaughter in the hall, as well as Lord Sewell's cowardice.

This day, a new Lowlands would come forth. Elyse embraced her sister Mara before joining her new coven, where her title would be stripped, and she'd spend her days in holy contemplation and doing good works. She looked up at the parapet and met my eye.

There was no hate there. Only resignation, and at that moment, I respected her for her accountability. She had chosen, and she had lost. Our roles were reversed from when I had first seen her years ago, arriving at Prince Jame's castle and seeing the girl who I'd guard on a parapet.

I nodded to her, inclining my head once. Elyse did the same, seemingly agreeing with herself. Then she turned to join her new family. It would save her honor and her life. Maybe there was happiness for her in the future, but it wasn't my business.

A servant moved along the walkway behind me. My runes tingled in recognition. "Wine, sir?"

When I turned to look at him, he looked like an older human male. "You know I can tell it's you."

The illusion vanished, and Evior stepped towards the parapet to watch the procession with me. "That was always your gift, wasn't it?"

I stood there, looking down at the proceedings with the collegiate master. A collegiate of spies, saboteurs, and turn-cloaks. "Felt you when you snuck in the with the nuns ten minutes ago. Do you have something for me?"

"That's usually my question." The half-elf mage smiled in

the soft sunlight. "The coven was a group of dark elf collegiate sympathizers. They craved the reopening of the underdark, and they wanted your friend Karley as leverage. Her mother and father are... good friends of ours. We've fed them information for years on their enemies, but this was the last way to flush out the lingering traitors in their midst."

"And this coven?" I stared at Karley, laughing with Vorga and Tyra in the courtyard.

"Funny thing." Evior lit a pipe that appeared in his hands. "The landlord who let them the building found them the other day, dead on the floor. Souls ripped out of them. The last of their members fled the city. But they never made the gates."

I reached into my pocket and slid the contract scroll out, leaving it on the wall between us. "Very funny."

Evior picked up the scroll and slipped it away. "Nothing funny about it. That's a name we've tried to cross off for a long time. The coven hired him, as many desperate do. But his ultimate goal was something we couldn't allow."

Or perhaps Evior's collegiate had done the hiring. In his world, friend and enemy were interchangeable. And in typical fashion, the answer I sought was the very task he had given me to uncover it.

"Terrible thing, losing an eye." Evior puffed on his pipe before offering it to me.

I shook my head. "No thanks."

"You should try this mixture, Davik. A good friend of mine grows it. It has wonderful properties." The collegiate master smiled at me, and for a moment, his eye flashed silver. "It helps. Trust me."

I took it. If he truly wanted me dead, it wouldn't be something I could stop. The smoke was acrid, but it wasn't tobacco. My runes pulsed as I inhaled. It tasted the way sunflowers smelled.

347

"We were very lucky you happened this way," Evior said.

"Pure coincidence, I'm sure." I handed him the pipe back. "How's the currency of my favor now?"

Evior looked over his shoulder at the ocean. "Well, you own part of that port, don't you? We like Windpeak, Davik. They have a progressive mindset. Ironclad was too stingy with crops. Hated mages and trading with them. Certain collegiates are going to arrive here soon, looking for new trading partners in Stroudsburg. I think the young engaged couple have quite a rich future ahead of them."

"Funny how things turn out." I turned to face him. "And the names Vilas mentioned?"

The half-elf nodded, growing serious. "Done for now. But you never know. You've done us a great favor, Davik. As you have in the past—whether you knew it or not. What would you wish?"

I looked back at Karley in the courtyard. The underdark would remain sealed for now. "Could a conversation be arranged?"

Evior took my meaning. "Her parents have cleansed their kingdom of collegiate agents for almost two decades. But they knew if the Severing was lifted too soon, they'd be infiltrated again. The covens of mages in the underdark want to open it and bring their people home, reestablish, but on their timeline."

"You have a habit of not answering a question. Do you know that?"

The spymaster laughed. "A conversation can be arranged." Then I felt his soul shift, casting a spell silently. My flesh tingled, every capillary in my lungs flaring for a moment.

Something solidified within my skull. Not the divine healing of Elina but something *crafted*. Something made from the basest construction of magic—pure arcane precision. So slight that it slipped past my runes. The sensation was unnerving, making me grip the parapet as vitality churned through my body. It wasn't painful, but it was one of the strangest sensations I'd ever experienced.

Evior turned, shifting his glammer back into a servant. "A man should have both eyes when he sees his first child. We owe you, Darkshire." Then he walked away.

I pulled the bandage from my face, blinking as I stared at the courtyard with two eyes. The miracle of the moment stifled by Evior's trickery.

"Fucking wizards."

When I looked down at the girls, everyone was laughing and joking now that Elyse was gone. They all turned to smile up at me.

It was the perfect moment, as Brim and Trith looked up from their dice game, and all the women in my life regarded me. The castle had been won. The enemy was gone.

Elina waved, her curls shaking in the air. Tyra stared at me, biting her lip. Vorga swayed in her dress and mouthed the words *I love you.*

Karley's soul pulsed, her magic yearning for me. I stared into the eyes of my new lover.

Sariel smiled at me, surrounded by the family we had fought to protect. I smiled back.

Then her face grew alarmed. I leaned over the balcony, seeing if she saw something. But then the color drained from her face.

"Sariel?" Elina put a hand on her back. "Are you well?"

"What's wrong?" Tyra asked.

A grin broke across the silver-eyed beauty as sweat climbed up her forehead. She locked eyes with me, a delight there she wanted me to see.

Then she vomited onto the ground.

PART THREE
THE TOWN

CHAPTER
THIRTY-ONE

That summer, Tyra and I walked in the fields near Oakshire, watching the river slide by as summer reigned around us. The herbs we hunted were called mortroot.

The faen redhead crouched down, grasping two more strands of the white petaled stuff. "This should do it. Though the morning sickness has passed, we should keep it stocked up."

I bent over and grabbed one to add to Tyra's collection basket. "Elina says we have almost two years."

"Isn't that strange?" Tyra giggled. "Embriel and other high elves gestate for over three years. I can't imagine being so uncomfortable. At least since you're human, it'll be shorter.."

"Well, they live pretty much forever. Plus, Sariel isn't going to show for a while." I wiped my hands. Sariel's morning sickness had been almost instant after conception—something to do with carrying a half-human according to Elina.

Tyra lifted her basket. "And I'm going to feed her the best things. Keep the kitchen stocked for cravings."

We walked over to the set of trees where I had taught her to ride Polly. Tyra spread her skirts, sat down on a small picnic stool, and sprinkled the mortroot into a mortar bowl.

"Petals are so thin," Tyra murmured, her blue eyes bright. "The oil dries. Have to grind it up quick to keep it in there."

She shifted, grinding the herbs. With the valley behind her, she looked like any shepherd girl in a village. Beautiful, young, but with sparkling flesh. The air smelled of warm wheat grass and river water under the cool shade of the tree.

Tyra's loosely tied blouse slipped down, her long cleavage jiggling as she ground the petals. Her bare feet were planted in the earth, her skirts sliding up her thighs while she worked.

"Hey." I grinned.

Tyra looked up, slowing her grind. "See something you like, you fruitful man?"

"Matter of fact." I stepped closer. "Wondering if you needed another riding lesson?"

I had already had her this morning, over the stove. But even still...

"You're insatiable since we've come back to Oakshire," she teased me. But her breath hitched in her voice. I stared down, taking in the sight of her. You can keep your castles and your cities. I'll take an Oakshire tavern girl any day.

Tyra's fingers left the mortar and pestle, climbing up my trousers. She looked up at me, chin resting on me. "The bright-berry wine got to us last night."

"Got to you." I smiled and reached down, freeing a heavy breast from her blouse. I wanted to see it while she worked me. "And don't blame the imbuing."

"Mmm, guess the secret's out." Tyra pulled me from my trousers, holding up my half-hard manhood and giving it a single stroke. "You felt so good back there. I was surprised."

"The wine leads us to new places," I whispered.

Tyra kissed my length slowly, each touch sending a jolt of

her faen connection into me. It's one thing to see a woman's eyes glaze when they give themselves to you completely. It's another to feel it echo from her soul.

"Poor baby," Tyra whispered as she held my cock. "You need relief already." Then she wrapped her lips around my head, flicking her tongue against it. Embers of lustful imbuement drifted into me, as I hardened in her mouth.

I gripped her fiery red hair. "You know I'm going to take you again."

Tyra moaned in agreement, bobbing her head to take me deeper into her throat.

The air sounded of the river and the ministrations of her mouth as the stool creaked under her devotion. When she pulled her mouth away, she looked up at me in adoration and slapped my manhood against her tongue. "That a promise?"

Tyra yelped when I pushed her down into the grasses. I hefted her skirt up, revealing her beautiful, thick ass. Pale cheeks sparkled back at me, shifting as she raised her hips, revealing the pink glint of her quim.

I slid my cock up and down against her, causing her to moan.

"I think," I whispered as I kissed the back of her neck, "you're the insatiable one."

She reached back, grasping at my cock, trying to pull me in. "Yeah?"

"That's right." I sank into her. She groaned as wet warmth coated me, the tight grip of her fueling my plunge as I slipped home.

"Holy hells," Tyra gripped the grass. "Oh—Davik."

Nothing felt as good as those cheeks pressed against me, and her magical body shuddering under mine. Her faen eyes fluttered with pleasure, but they never stopped watching me.

We fucked until she was a moaning mess. I writhed into

her, our lust punctuated by the steady slap of my hips on her cheeks—until I plunged deeper. I cradled Tyra's chin as she sucked my finger. Spiraling tendrils of desire cascaded into me, telling me how close she was. Her body begged me every place we touched as we imbued one another.

"Davik..." But she didn't need to say anything, I could feel her need. How she wanted me pressing her into the soil beneath us.

"You want it, don't you?" I whispered as I rutted her. I looked down to see her plump cheeks rolling, her bare feet sliding over the back of my calves.

"I want it." Tyra slipped her mouth from my finger. She craned her neck to turn to me, and I leaned over. "Look into my eyes, Davik—I'm, oh fucking hells—I'm coming all over your cock."

She clamped down, milking me. Tyra groaned in slow agony as she came, her body fluttering in a tidal wave of sensation. It was like lying on top of a soft storm. The purest need floated from her. Not a request for confirmation but affirmation—that she was mine.

I held her tight, lost in the kissing of her neck and below her ear. When I felt myself breaking, I slid my tongue onto hers, both of us rebounding our feelings from one another. She grasped my neck, tethering me close as I broke and filled her.

We lay like that for a while, breathing, casting looks at each other. Tyra squeezed her quim around me, biting her lip. "I love it, you know. Being your woman." Then she grinned. "What's it like, knowing Sariel is carrying your child?"

I laughed and slid from her. We turned, and she rested in the crook of my arm. The soft light of the day filtered through the tree above us, highlighting parts of her like a painter's brush, making her sparkle. "It's surprising. Elina said half-elves usually take a bit of time to make."

Tyra giggled, her face flushed. "Maybe it's about quality more than quantity. A baby conceived in Windpeak. Does that make her a Lowlander?"

"Gods, I hope not." I raised an eyebrow. "*Her*?"

Tyra shrugged, pushing her skirts back down. "I'd be a good girl-aunt, is all." She reached out and slid my hand under her breast, helping me feel the thump of her heart. It felt like Polly when she galloped in the grasses here. "Be good at other things, too."

I rolled over, kissing her. "I've no doubt."

Tyra smiled wryly. "But I think we have a lot more time in the kitchen... before anything gets put in the oven." Then she stared up at me, those blue eyes like icy lakes I could fall forever into. "I... want you to know that—"

I slid my hand up her face. "I love you."

ELINA RODE on my shoulders that afternoon, waving to the townspeople of Oakshire as I carried both her and her things.

"You know, you seem to enjoy this." I shifted her bag to my other hand and held her thigh as we broke off the town road, walking down towards the house.

"Davik!" Silvus waved as he hop-jumped up the field with a few other Hollyhead faen. His green cap was never absent from his head. "You working tonight?"

"Yes, he is!" Elina announced. "We'll see you at the performance!"

Silvus tipped his hat. He and several others had come down with the newest shipment of faen wines and meads, among a few sacks of imbued sugar for the cafe. Tyra's only demand was that the baker had to make some cider rings.

As we walked down the green hill, Elina shielded her face with the blade of her hand. I looked up at her. "Hey, lover."

"Hello, Davik." She wriggled against the back of my neck. Then she leaned down, bending over to kiss me. For a moment, her long curls blotted the summer sun out before she righted herself again.

As we walked, I felt power flow through her as she whispered her prayers and cold energy whipped down my back, filling my runes. Her power had continued to grow. She could heal at a distance now, and the expectant mothers of the valley had an even greater love for her.

"Agh!" I laughed at the sensation. "It's so much stronger now. You fill my runes every time you see me now."

Elina chuckled, lacing her fingers into my hair like the mane of a horse. "I have a theory, that's all. Besides, it's always good to be prepared."

As we walked, skirting around the pond towards the house, I felt her combing my hair with her nails, inspecting something. "Don't tell me I have lice."

"Oh, no," Elina said with a laugh. "Never you, my dear. The man who owns the bathhouse is the cleanest one in the valley."

"Why don't you flip around and sit the proper way?"

Elina looked puzzled, then understood. "You brute!"

I picked up speed, jogging as she bounced on my back. "What did you call me?"

"A brute!" Elina's laugh broke into a giggle. Her thighs clamped around my neck as I ran, and her dress flew back. "Davik! My rear is exposed!"

"Can't hear you!" I grinned and sprinted faster. "Just a brute!"

Elina cackled as we slowed next to the house. When we looked at the treated lumber and boards for the expansion—

along with tool pails left for tomorrow's continuation—she took in a sharp breath. "Wow. They work so fast."

"Norsuid Wrathforge and his friends are worth every penny." I looked at the beams that would hold up the renovation. "I trust a timber dwarf over me any day."

"Hmm," Elina mused. "I heard you built something recently, for a certain mage and actress."

I grinned, dropping her bag near the front porch. "Well, I couldn't have someone else build that. Besides, I'm told my poor workmanship adds to the appeal. More draconic."

Elina sighed pleasantly. "Karley has such a wonderful facet. Tender, needful, and the love of restraint and your dominion."

"My brutishness, you mean." I ducked so she wouldn't hit her head on the framed beams.

Elina looked up at the framed room above us. "This looks wonderful! A nursery?"

"Maybe," I replied. "We're adding a few rooms. This will be a nursery." I dipped low, walking to the farthest framed room. "Little widow's walk here. Same as the one they're putting on the tavern. This will be a study or examination room. Everyone gets a little balcony now."

Elina nodded, taking it in. "It's going to be beautiful. You're all going to have more room. I'm so glad you didn't tear it down, just added to it."

"Oh, I could never tear this house down." I squatted and returned to another room next to Sariel's on the second floor. "This is a bedroom, too. Going to put another floor heating system in before they board it up."

"Another!" Elina laughed and looked down at me. "Are you seducing another woman into your coterie, Davik? Does your facet know no limits?"

My smile faded. I had wanted to be the one to show her, and it wasn't often the house was empty. "It's your room."

Elina stared down from my shoulders. "*Mine?*"

"That's right. Well, yours and mine. You're here half the time, anyway. Going to make it permanent. I dug up the fallen stones from your temple, and we're going to adorn part of the wall with it."

"Davik..." I heard the longing in her voice as she stared up at it. "It's just that—"

"You're the facet of my soul, Elina. You belong with me. With us. Once the baby comes, you'll be here, regardless."

I lifted her up, turning her so she was facing me. Elina yelped as her thighs parted before my face, and I pressed her against the wall underneath the room she would move into.

"You're asking me to move in?" Elina's voice floated down to me.

I held her up. Each kiss along her thigh was like undoing the teeth of a lock, causing her to slowly widen them. "I wasn't asking. Just showing you where you'll be living. Besides, these lengthy sleepovers have people not sure where to find you."

Elina exhaled, spreading her legs. I kissed her dark brown flesh, hiding in the shadows between her legs. "How will I get to the temple?"

The twenty-minute walk, which for a halfling was closer to forty, was no small feat. Nor was it insurmountable. "I'm going to buy you a pony. We'll keep him here."

I looked up, seeing her amber eyes staring down at me. When I pulled her panties to the side, kissing her sweet quim, she gripped my hair and arched against the side of the house. Elina slid either leg down my back, gripping a beam for support. But it wasn't necessary. I had her.

I slid my tongue into her, burying my nose against her clit. "Oh, Davik—" Elina groaned, gyrating against my mouth.

I stopped, looking up at her. The cleric of love who had saved my life in more ways than anyone didn't need a posting. She needed a home. The words were true and therefore right when I spoke them. "I want you here. I want your facet close to mine."

Elina blinked as I slid her down from my shoulders, holding her around my waist. Her skirt trailed loose behind her. One small hand held onto the beam of what would be her home. "Yes."

We kissed as she curled her legs around me, and I pressed her into the foundation. I slid myself free from my pants, aching for her. My runes hummed with divine healing, but everything was sunlit, and nothing needed tending. It felt like an abundance as I welcomed her here.

"I love you, you brute," Elina whispered as I slid her down, teasing myself against her. I wouldn't let her touch the ground.

"I want you to think of this," I whispered as I entered her, eliciting a pleasant gasp. "Every time you go in this room."

The beams creaked as we joined, grasping and pulling. I buried myself into her divine flesh, the strand between our hearts humming, placed there so long ago by her goddess when we bound to one another. Her tattoos fluttered, and I knew somehow they would grow from this. Another line added to our story. As strong as the creaking foundation around us, meant to be built upon.

THIRTY-TWO

"This was a mistake," Vorga murmured, staring at the shifting crowd. We had cleared out the back of the tavern, relocated the woodpiles, and trimmed the errant grass with scythes. I even covered the outside of the outhouse with boards that we painted to look like the remnants of a castle tower.

I slipped in next to her, putting an arm around her waist. "No time like now."

Her nervousness was plain on her face. "Before the Autumn festival? I was crazy. Maybe we should—"

Tyra poked her head out from the back of the tavern. "We're ready!"

"Okay." Vorga exhaled. "Just..." She shuffled a wad of pages lined with her notes.

"Hey." I nudged her. "After what we did at Windpeak, why would you be nervous about this?"

Vorga blushed. "Do you see how many *people* are out there?"

"Not every day a play comes to Oakshire. Even less when it's made here."

"Agh, why did I want to do this?"

"Because it's the second-best thing you've ever written." I patted the notebook she had given me. It lived eternally in my back pocket. "And... well, the second thing you've written. Karley's the one with all the lines."

"A book isn't a play—maybe it shouldn't be one." Vorga peered past the edge of the bathhouse at the crowd. The seats were full, and the members of the valley piled in around the edges.

I had it easy. I was a tree and helping the girls change their costumes. "Can I give you some advice?"

Vorga nodded.

"Never." I slid my hands along her hips, turning her to me. "Be afraid of what you want."

Vorga smiled and nestled closer to me. "I might take you up on that."

"Vorga!" Tyra called again from the back of the tavern.

"Here we go." Vorga grinned. "Love you."

"Love you, too."

I watched her walk towards out to the makeshift stage. Norsuid and his son had hammered it together, and the same lumber would later be dismantled and used for the expansion of the house.

The last patrons took their reserved seats. I spotted Lyra walking with Mabel, lending her the strength of her arm while they approached their seats from the front. As they passed through the crowd, Mabel stopped to regard Trith where he sat with Deiga. They had been renting one of the rooms in the tavern for a week now.

"Aren't you a pretty man." Mabel smiled.

Trith stood and bowed. "A pleasure to meet you."

"Meet, eh." Mabel cackled. "Did you ever attend the play-house in Stroudsburg some years back?"

Trith blinked. "I did. Have you been?"

"Oh," Mabel said with a grin, "just for an evening." Then her eyes floated over to Deiga. "Enjoy your evening. Your friend here is quite the morsel."

Deiga's scarred face morphed into confusion. "Thank you."

Mabel turned and shot me a wry grin as she followed Lyra to their seat. Trith sat down, an uncertain look cresting across his face. When Deiga asked him something, he shook his head. My attention was drawn away by Lyra, who raised her pale fingers at me in greeting. I gave her a brief bow in rustling leaves.

Sariel took the stage, resplendent in one of her dresses. This evening, she had selected a deep blue for the nature of the play. "Thank you all for coming. We know the autumn festival is soon, but a bit of entertainment was due."

She looked over at Vorga, who stood at the side of the stage. "I've known Vorga for quite a few years. If you know her, you've probably waved to her plenty of times. But she likely didn't return it since her nose was in a book."

Laughs came through the crowd. Helena, the bookstore owner, called out, "You should just drop her pay off at my doorstep!"

Sariel grinned. "Perhaps. She's the mind behind all of this tonight. But we have two talents to showcase. Your favorite bartender is the star of the production. So, without further delay, let the show begin!"

Brim walked forward and clapped his hands together, sending a psionic blow through the crowd. I felt Karley dip into her arcana behind the stage, and when she walked out in her dark dridersilk dress, the crowd gasped at her pale makeup and smudged eyeshadow. Dark mist, born from a spell she had prepared, whispered out from her palms above the crowd, smothering the lanterns in the haunting dark.

Behind the stage, Brim blasted sheets of hammered tin, echoing a storm.

Vorga smiled at the audience, and her hands stopped shaking. "It was a dark and stormy night..."

THE PLAY WENT OVER FANTASTICALLY. I moved through the tavern, eying any errant cups that could be returned like downed soldiers to the back line. The tavern was as full as it had ever been, and we shut down the stoves for the event. All we had working besides the bar was Brim at the dishwashing station.

"Brim!" I yelled back as I carried an armful of glasses.

He still wore his goblin outfit. I set the glasses down next to him.

Busy night, ugly-man.

"That it is." I leaned against the cold stove. Tyra was out on the floor, taking drink orders and running them back to the bar. "Probably not going to finish washing those for another hour, huh?"

The gnome sneered over his shoulder. My own costume hung in tatters around me. Trees are important, and my time splitting lumber had suited me to the role of being one of the moving pieces of background.

"Hell of a dice game going out there," I continued.

I'll kill you, ugly-man.

"I know you will." I stepped forward and clapped him on the shoulder. Then I lifted him off his stool and set him on the ground. Brim glared up at me.

"Kitchen's closed." I rolled up my sleeves. "Can't be back here."

Realization broke on his face, and he smiled as he flung his dish rag to me.

Maybe it was the full house tonight, or the play and the subject matter within—a story about a lost dark elf princess, guarded by goblins in a castle, but Brim had come back for me time and time again. When Luka and Ekyll had found their way to the metal entrance to the beach at Windpeak, they had pried the door while Brim blew it open, causing him a severe nosebleed from the exertion.

"Hey, Brim," I said as he neared the door to the front of the house.

The gnome turned. *Ugly-man?*

I looked at him. "Would've done the same for you."

Brim nodded slowly. For a moment, I saw the glint of the gnome stone in his front pocket as he patted it once.

I know.

He left me with the fifty cups to empty and clean. I set to work, listening to the sounds of a tavern filled with celebration. Oakshire was like any village. They had their pride and their rivalries. Those had only grown since the brawl here with the girls from Tawney. Now, Vorga had put on a play.

The clink of glasses and laughter were like the waves of some beach, massaging the clenched fist that had been Windpeak open in me. On our return, all of us could have kissed the ground when we came back to Oakshire.

"Davik!" Silvus yelled through the doorway. "You almost done?"

"Not nearly." I grinned at the faen hop-scout. "Give me a bit."

"Aye." He raised a cup at me and wandered back out.

I scrubbed the last glasses. Then my runes shifted, sensing a spell. I turned, just in time to catch the soft glow of Karley's magic filling the tavern—mist curling through the air, drinks shimmering in hues of orange and green. The crowd roared in approval, and Deiga, watching from the corner, smiled at her student.

Tyra passed me on my way out, holding several mugs. "You go! I've got these." She giggled as she passed. Then she gave me a quick squeeze on the ass and rushed past.

I slid behind the bar, wrapping a quick arm around Sariel. "How are we feeling?"

She smirked as I slid my hand over her belly. "You keep asking me that. It'll be months until I'm showing. No one can even tell."

I kissed her behind her ear. "I can."

She swatted me with a dish towel while pouring a glass of wine. "Hop to, busboy. You're not the one who has to swear off wine for almost two years."

"Other ways to relax." I pinched her rear gently, feeling her press back to me.

Sariel laughed. "Relaxing got us into this."

Karley still had her costume on from the show, looking like a witch queen from the underworld. Vorga had been the pen and voice, but she had been the star who brought it to life. When I walked behind her, she was chatting with two tavern-goers who were raving about her performance.

"Need a keg changed, guy." Karley didn't look back at me.

"No, please?" I asked as she pressed back against me.

Karley grinned and kept talking. It was crowded, and there were eyes everywhere. Her smile turned into a mask of surprise when I gave her a swift spank on her ass.

"Something wrong?" I murmured as I cleared away an empty wine bottle next to her.

"Just that keg... might need to be tapped." Karley turned from her patrons. "You'll have time for that?"

I nodded while looking at the crowd. "Might do. Have something to show you later."

Karley's eyes slid to the trap door that led to the cellar. "Did you finish building it?"

I moved my rag to the other shoulder. "That? Oh, yes. But this is different. I'll show you after we close up."

Before Karley could respond, I kissed her, drawing several claps from the shifting crowd. She blushed and turned away.

"Careful, lad!" Rober blocked my way out of the bar by barreling into it. His cheeks were rosy, and he held two empty glasses. "That witch will turn you into a frog if you're not careful."

Karley snatched the glasses away to refill them. "Or worse. More of the same, Mayor?"

"Aye, more of the same." Rober smiled. He looked up and around the tavern. "Nice draw that little play Vorga put on. Just what our place needs."

"I thought you'd be busy running the town and such?" I grinned at him.

"Herding disputes and nonsense!" Rober cackled. "So... what do you say? You think on what we talked about?"

"I did. Let's move ahead."

"That's the spirit!" Rober snatched the mug of beer Karley sat down as soon as it touched the bar, raising it to me. "Gonna be a fine expansion!"

"Outdoor seats." Karley grunted. "Wow. What will you two think of next? Sunshades?"

"Nah, come now!" Rober grinned at her. "There'll be a pass-through for food. Outdoor stove maybe? Smokers, of course, for the fish race!"

When he yelled it, half the crowd echoed it back. *Fish race!*

Karley sighed. "That term really caught on."

"Not just seats, you know." I held her eye. Since our return, the more bratty she acted, the more I knew she wanted me to chase her down. Open her door at night.

"No?" Karley laughed. Then she blew a spell into a glass, holding it up like a lantern. "Gonna have little strings of lights?"

"Course we are," Rober sipped his beer, then turned to wave at Linnie to let her know he'd be back at their table shortly. "Otherwise, the damn stage is in the dark."

Karley's grin faltered. "Stage?"

I slipped away while Rober continued, "Ah hells, Karley! Davik made me and the carpenters redraw the whole damn thing! Place is centered around the stage back there. Said it's for musicians and the plays you'll be in."

I met her eyes through the shift of the crowd. Little is better than truly surprising a woman.

"Rooms all good?" I asked Trith and Deiga at their table. Next to them, six men were rolling dice with Brim, and Trith had a stake in there.

"They are, thank you, Davik." Deiga smiled up at me. There was still a coldness between us, but it had lessened when we brought Rayleth's body back to her. That old wound, finally given permission to close. In the end, we buried him properly outside the city.

"How's Karley's progress?"

"Oh"—Deiga leaned over and put her head on Trith's back—"she'd put a sorcerer to shame. Thank you again for the rooms. It was out of our way, but we wanted to stop here before our trip."

"Thank *you*." I offered her my hand. The scarred elf took it, shaking it slowly. "For what you brought for Karley. Silvus and his men gave me a hand putting it up there."

"She'll love it." Deiga nudged Trith to turn from his dice game.

"Davik! You are a marvelous tree!" Trith stood and threw his arms around me.

We chuckled for a moment, but when I went to let him go, he held on. "Love you, brother."

I shut my eyes, seeing him dying next to me on that parapet in the rain. *I'm going with you.*

"Love you, too."

When we slid back, Trith wiped his eye. "Fucking smoky in here! Shall we drink to the father-to-be?"

"Tomorrow." I grinned at him. "Tonight's for the play. What's this trip?"

Trith grinned and looked down at Deiga. "Heading to see my folks... Figure might as well give them another heart attack." Then he grabbed my shoulder. "I won't be there long. Deiga's reopening classes in Stroudsburg, but we've talked about moving around. Maybe taking students out here for part of the year."

"You're always welcome." I blinked at him as the tavern bustled around us. "How did we end up here, Trith?"

Trith raised a glass. "Stuck together, that's how."

"Damn right." I clapped him on the shoulder and slipped away. Trith was a friend I could not see for years and then spend night after night out until the sun rose. That was the blessing of an elven friend. They don't get old on you.

I ducked through the crowd, honing in on Vorga.

"I was scared! Honestly!" Helena laughed with her. "The mists and fog were great, but the story! My gods. I'll never go down into a cellar again in case goblins are waiting for me."

"Not that goblins are uh"—an Oakshire man tried to navigate the conversation—"well, bad..."

I slipped next to her. "Orcs and goblins are different species. A man who studied mushrooms told me that once."

The man nodded, thankful for a lifeline from tripping over his tongue. "Of course! Of course they are."

"And those were feral goblins in the story." Vorga turned to give me a quick kiss on the cheek. "Like this one here. Can't let him get out of your sight."

Helena smiled and put a hand on Vorga's shoulder. "Well, it was *wonderful*. Karley did such a fantastic job, but I could feel your hand behind every line!"

"What about me?" I asked. "Wasn't I a good tree?"

Helena didn't let me off the hook. "You shifted too much! There's no breeze underground."

"It's all that brawn," Vorga said as she gripped my hand. "Too burly of a tree."

"Well, I think it's going to do fabulously at the Autumn festival." Helena smiled at the two of us. "And a much bigger crowd."

"I don't know..." Vorga murmured. "It would mean a bigger vendor lot..."

"It'll pay for itself." I kissed her on the cheek. "Plus, I bet your bookstore will pick up."

"You mean Helena's bookstore." Vorga laughed until she saw Helena and me regarding her. "What did you do, Davik?"

"Oh, nothing too major." Helena smiled, smoothing her braid. "Davik bought you into the store—an eighth. Nothing crazy."

"You did what?" Vorga looked at me in bewilderment. Then her voice fell. "I don't want to leave the tavern..."

"You won't," I promised her. "But Helena's going to buy some new books. She'll need a good acquisition specialist, reading them, seeing what'll sell. You think you can manage that?"

Vorga looked down as Helena slipped a key out and held it out to her. "I could use your help, Vorga. You're in there all the time, anyway. Besides, the copies of your play here are going to be quite popular. Two scribes in Tawney are hard at work. They should be arriving soon."

Vorga blinked. "Copies?"

I smiled. "To sell at the Autumn festival. Seeing a play's one thing, but people want to hold a piece of a story in their hands."

"I'll leave you to it. Lots of fans to greet." Helena winked and walked away.

Vorga held up the key, staring at me. "Davik... you didn't have to do this. After what we spent on the play..."

Aside from the gold Puris insisted we were paid from Windpeak, I now owned part of their growing port. The first payment had arrived, transferred to Lord Mirrimer and given to Silvus. Audrey hadn't been able to visit this round of deliveries, with the vineyards reopening, but if what arrived was just the start, we'd be quite situated.

"If it was up to me, I'd keep you to myself." The tavern crowd pressed around us, pressing us closer. "But I wouldn't deny the world your voice, even in ink. When I'm splitting wood and you're reading to me, it's some of my favorite times."

Her eyes smoldered as she slipped the key away. Vorga wasn't a big drinker, but she was two glasses deep tonight. "What can I do to make this up to you?"

I leaned forward. "You really want to know?"

Brown eyes, nestled in soft green freckled skin, regarded me. "Yes."

She yelped when I hoisted her on my shoulder, causing a few inches of wine to drip to the ground. "You can sing for me."

"No, Davik!" Vorga laughed and struggled. But the crowd turned, raising their glasses and calling out.

Song! Song!

"Come on," I said up to her. "You know I love it."

She smiled down at me, lips spreading behind her two short tusks. Then Vorga raised her cup to the crowd. When her voice came through the room, every eye turned, and the warble of her voice sounded like home.

"The fields are wet, the fields are dry,
Riches promised, riches lie.
I've seen castles grand and towers tall,
Yet none mean a thing when night does fall.

Bound for home, I am,
Bound for home, I am,
Back to your waiting arms.

Through battle's dust and hallowed halls,
Warring drums, lost to all.
Through faen orchards, berries bright,
None called me home like your voice tonight.

Bound for home, I am,
Bound for home, I am,
Back to your waiting arms.

No king nor crown could steal my way,
No storm nor sword could make me stay.
For what is gold, and what is pride,
When all I crave is by your side?

Bound for home, I am,
Bound for home, I am,
Back to your waiting arms,
Where I belong."

The crowd broke into raucous applause. I spotted Rober drying his eyes, and Brim leapt up onto the dice game table and shouted something. Vorga laughed, covering her mouth in embarrassment. Tyra and Elina smiled up at her, and Karley flicked a spell across the bar, filling the room with golden light.

Sariel walked forward, holding up a bottle of sparkling brightberry wine Silvus and his people had brought from Hollyhead. She slid a knife along the neck once—sending the glass-wrapped cork across the room in a loud *pop!* The wine flowed and frothed as she raised it to Vorga, who took it and brought it to her lips, her eyes never leaving mine.

CHAPTER

THIRTY-THREE

O nce the tavern shut for the evening, and all our guests
passed out in their rooms upstairs, I slipped out to the
bathhouse as requested.

I sank back into the swirling waters, sighing from the
efforts of the day. I kept a few lanterns in here but hadn't both-
ered to light them tonight. A small sliver of summer moonlight
slipped through the opening of the door until it shifted with
someone's approach.

Vorga kicked the door open, grinning at me in the moonlight. The bottle of sparkling wine was gripped in her hand.
"Hey, you."

"Right where you told me." I rose from the water to help
her, but she threw a fistful of dust into the swirling liquid. For
a moment, it flickered before it lit the clouded waters in swirls
of glowing blue.

"Glowstone dust." Vorga giggled. "Deiga gave us
some."

I'd never seen her this into her cups. But her step was
steady as she slipped her dress off. As she wandered around

374

the edge of the pool, she looked down at me. "You're my favorite tree, you know."

"Is that so?" I took in the sight of her body.

"Mmhmm," Vorga whispered. "Big roots." I watched her pert green breasts and sultry hips. Vorga stepped gingerly around the pool, beckoning me with the bottle.

"Will you help me with this? I'm already drunk and I— I can't drink more."

"Sure." I reached up to take the bottle, but she held it away.

Vorga grinned menacingly, face lit by flashes of blue light. She stepped on either side of my shoulders as she poured the wine down her chest, letting it drip in slow, frothing rivers into my waiting mouth.

Brightberry wine, imbued with the feeling of celebration, coursed into my body. Vorga grinned, feeling bold from its effects. Until I pulled her down, feeding that pouting mound of green flesh into my mouth.

The bottle rolled on the ground as she squatted over my face, feet flexing against the edge of the pool as she gripped my shoulders for support.

"Davik..." she breathed the words. "I love it when you kiss me like that."

I swirled my tongue slowly. It had been an active day, but Tyra had been right. Ever since returning, I'd been insatiable for these women. Not just their flesh but their company. The sound of their voices, the smell of their hair... it was all I wanted. Maybe the journey back into the world, in all its bleak fatality, had made me appreciate this place even more. But it was just a place. It was the people in it I loved.

"Ugh," Vorga groaned, flexing against my mouth.

I broke my mouth from her, not wanting her to fall into the water. I took her in my arms and turned around as she wrapped her legs around me.

My cock slid underneath her spread cheeks as we kissed. I held her to me, legs sliding with glowing water. Vorga sucked on my tongue, holding my face.

"You've given me the perfect night," she whispered. "I love you."

I smiled, feeling her melt into me. "I love you."

Vorga smiled and reached back, angling me against the heat of her entrance. "I need you." She huffed, the touch of the wine making her words more illicit than usual. "I love you stretching my tight green pussy."

I bucked into her, feeling the grip of her hot flesh spreading around me. It wasn't the best leverage point, but I knew Vorga loved being pressed against me.

"Yes," she whispered in my ear. "It's always yes, Davik."

We surged against the edge of the pool, our wet flesh punctuating the air in steady slaps. This wasn't a rapid onslaught, it was a slow churn. I wanted her. All of her. I held her cheeks in my hands, plunging into her like a captured prize. When I slid my finger along her asshole, she moaned and dug her tusk gently into my neck.

"I'm going to—Oh, Davik, right there." Vorga's head fell back, tusks jutting into the air as I powered into her, racing to batter her defenses down. When she came, her entire body clenched. Shy, bookish girl or not, she still had the strength of a most-orc, and I loved it.

"Remember the field?" Vorga moaned. "On the way to the castle?"

"I think about it all the time," I whispered as I sank into her. "Tell me again."

Vorga moaned the words as I took her. "I love you, I love you." Her hands dug into my back, shaking against me. "I love you."

"Oh, hells," I moaned as she clamped down around me.

"Give me all of it," she whimpered. "I want it."

I couldn't speak. My cock was a bar of throbbing iron, hot from the forge. She quenched it, gripping me tight as I broke, spasming line after trembling line of seed into her. For a moment, I saw the shifting grasses—her face when she told me.

You know I'm in love with you, right? I can't not be.

So far from the girl reading on the porch of the tavern, but still, so much the same. I held her close as we fell into the water, still joined, surrounded by glowing heat.

"Amazing," Vorga whispered as she settled around me.

"It was—"

"You," Vorga said with a smile. "You're amazing." The heat rose from the depths, igniting the inebriation in us both. "Buying me bookstores. But all I want is this, forever."

I sank lower into the heat, holding her up. "Just part of one."

Vorga nestled into my neck, resting her tusk on my shoulder. "Part of forever is enough."

I SLID the covers over Vorga in her bedroom. It was a warm night, and I didn't need to light her small stove. She burrowed deeper into the pillow, and I set a glass of water next to her. It was going to be a harsh morning for her. Bubbled wine does that—certain as sunrise and much less pleasant.

When I slipped out of her room, Sariel waited for me in the hallway, wearing her bathrobe. "Tonight was wonderful."

"Many more to come." I slid my arms around her, giving her a kiss. "Need me to put you to bed?"

Sariel raised my hand to her mouth, kissing it. "Elina had a little too much wine, and she's asleep in our bed. I don't want to disturb her. But why don't you wake us up when you get back? I know you want to show Karley now that it's done."

"Alright, lock up behind me."

Sariel winked. "Always. Goodnight, my love."

I walked back to the tavern, staring at the stars. No clouds tonight, meaning what I had planned would be perfect. I repositioned the dirk in my belt. Ever since Windpeak, I'd been keeping it close. Most of Vilas's dice were done rolling for us. His threats against Sariel were moot, and we knew about Lyra's fiend that had turned her. Justicars of Selene still hunted him.

"Evening, Davik." Lyra nodded to me as I passed her near the tavern. Now that it was deep night, her cloak hood was down.

"Constable." I stopped, regarding her. Her hair had grown slightly longer in our absence, and her eyes were dull red from recently feeding on my donated blood. "Everything good?"

She nodded. "I may need a delivery by tomorrow. Is that alright?"

"Everything okay?" I asked, gauging her.

Lyra nodded. Such pale flesh marred by her affliction. "Comes in waves sometimes, my thirst."

"Elina says you've been attending sermons at the temple."

The vampire regarded me. Two dangerous things, staring at one another in the night. We were lucky she was on our side, for now. "Nice to see belief, is all. I feel almost... at ease there."

"I'll drop some off tomorrow for you."

Lyra bowed slightly, shifting her longsword. "Thank you. The evening is fine." Her eyes slid over me. She had drank my blood for the better part of a year now. And the more she did, the more I saw her watching me. Not like a predator, but like the faces of my youth, reflected in a shop window for the things we could never afford.

"Goodnight, Lyra."

"Goodnight."

The night constable walked off. As I curled around the front of the street, I saw Kardak's place was the only building with candles lit, and in the night, the sound of glasses clinking with Brim wafted towards me.

Karley looked up as she scrubbed the bar, half her makeup gone from the sweaty evening. "Look who decided to show up."

"Better late than never." I gave into my runes, drawn towards her by her arcane soul. It would never not be this way, me wanting to pursue her.

The dark elf looked up, black, smudged lips shifting in anticipation. "What did you want to show me?"

I slid a hand over hers, stopping her. "Come with me."

This was our way since we had returned. She enjoyed being guided or told what to do. But no matter how tight the bindings around her wrists and ankles, or my hand on her throat, afterward we always lay in one another's arms, speaking gently. A hard spank, or a yank on her hair could drench her thighs. But those soft moments after were what we both craved. Two people with needs, or as Elina would say—facets, rough and edged—seeking to smooth one another.

Don't ever question your luck. Just thank the unseen hand that gave it to you.

I'd asked Evior for a conversation to be arranged with her family, and he would deliver. A message had come to Oakshire from that strange invisible collegiate, the small contract scroll disintegrating as soon as she and I had read it. Giving us a location and time of year—some months from now.

Outside, I lifted her to the overhang above where the wood was once piled. Karley climbed up, her tight leggings hugging her plump little ass as she clambered upwards. I didn't blame her for getting out of her costume. I leapt up after her, boots scraping softly on the roof tiles.

We held hands as I guided her around the second-story windows, coming towards the chimney.

"Deiga brought the last pieces, and Norsuid gave me a hand," I told her and stepped aside on the uneven roof.

Karley's eyes softened as she stared at the small telescope. We had built her a little observatory, with a flat platform that was six feet up from the roof of the tavern. You couldn't see it from the street, only if you came down from the east. It was nestled between the peaks of the tavern.

"You once told me the sun was too bright," I turned to her. "But the stars never let you down."

She slid a strand of pearly hair behind her ear. "You made this... for me."

It wasn't a question. "Thought this could be our place. Maybe you could teach me."

Karley hid her smile as she glanced at the small ladder leading up to the platform. "That stable?"

I bowed. "One way to find out."

I went up first, and it was a solid platform when I stood atop it. Norsuid's workmanship couldn't be denied. Karley climbed up after me, and I pulled her up and into my arms.

"Wow," Karley whispered.

The telescope was a foot in diameter at its widest, creaking down in tightening metal tubes. "The lenses are gnomish. Deiga inspected them. The gears are, too. I'm not sure what the markings mean on the gears."

Karley squatted down, spinning a dial that shifted the telescope. "Coordinates, for astronomers." She glanced up, peering at the sky with a smile. It filled my heart to see her so taken with it. "It's summer, so"—she bit her lip as she calculated—"this should do it."

The telescope stopped moving, pointing to the sky. She removed the front cap, tossing it on the cover that was tied to the base. It was weather-treated, but like most things, we'd still need to protect it from the worst of the elements.

"Go ahead." I stood back. "See how you like it."

Her eye filled with the light of the moon and stars above us. I saw her smile as she stared. "That's amazing." She turned away. "I want you to see, too."

I bent down, seeing the shift of an amplified image. I saw the hairs of my own eyelashes reflected back at me until I relaxed my eye and stared at a twinkling star shifting in blue pulses. "What is it?"

"It's all alone." Karley's voice filled with weight. "They call it orphan's star."

I turned from the viewing lens. "Do they?"

The dark elf took a step closer to me. "They say it's bad luck to look at it alone..."

In that moment, we were just two people staring at something miraculous. It didn't matter how many times I'd saved her. She'd stopped running, and if she ever did again, it would only be towards me.

Her lips tasted like plum, and her tongue held the spice of cider as we embraced. I curled my arms around her, smothering her arcane soul with my runes. Karley pressed against me, dark eyes looking up into mine, reflecting the cosmos. We stood like that for a long time, holding one another, until we seemed like one thing. Like two orphans grown up who had found one another.

The End.

EPILOGUE

I woke in Karley's bed, still hours before sunrise. Despite the celebration of the evening, I felt renewed. My arcane lover shifted next to me, spread out on the mattress.

"You hog the sheets, you know." I slipped down, untying the silken ropes that hung from her wrists and ankles. After the evening, we had just untied them from the bedposts and fallen asleep in one another's arms.

"Mmm," Karley murmured in her sleep. "Gonna sleep in today."

I kissed her cheek. "You've earned it."

She crawled under the covers when I rose, hoisting them around herself in a little cocoon. Her pale hair floated down around her head.

The house was quiet as I closed her door. When I opened Sariel's and my bedroom, only Elina was in there, snoring gently under the covers. I walked back in the hallway, going downstairs as the smell of the morning hearth wafted up to me.

"Did you sleep?" I asked Sariel when I found her on the couch.

"I did." She handed a cup of tea to me. "But got a little heartburn."

I drank from her cup, watching the first portions of flames leaping up over the logs as she laid her head in my lap. When I slid my hand over her belly, she held it there.

"Going to be awhile until we can feel it," she whispered.

"Are you scared?"

Sariel shook her head. "Never with you around."

As I shifted my hand along hers, I felt for her ring.

"Where's your ring?"

Sariel grinned in my lap. "Felt a bit hypocritical to wear it, after what we did in Windpeak. Now I just keep it close so I know when you're up to your old tricks."

"I think we're safe to put it away for now."

"I thought after Hollyhead and Windpeak... it would bother me more." She held her hand out, staring at where the ring was absent. "But once I felt... felt your child inside of me, I didn't mind. All I care about is our family. I just want to be a mother to our child." Then her voice hardened. "And keep everyone safe here."

"Oh, I can't wait to see how protective you are." I sipped her tea and set it down on the table ahead of us.

Sariel giggled. "Elves take a long time to bear children. It's probably part of why we live so long. Our little half-elf is going to take his sweet time."

I looked down. "His?"

Sariel shrugged. "Depends on the day. Sometimes it's him, and sometimes it's her. What do you think it'll be?"

"If the gods have a sense of humor, which they do, it'll be a little hellion."

Sariel nestled closer in my lap. We sat there together in the pre-dawn light as the fireplace crackled. "I don't want anything to change because of this."

I laughed. "I think *everything's* going to change."

Sariel slid a hand up my leg, teasing me. "I mean... are you still going to want me when I'm all bloated, leaking milk?"

"Are you crazy? How could I not?"

Sariel turned with a grin, her robe hanging low. "Even when I'm eating pastries all day?"

"Especially then."

Sariel sat up, the soft cloth of her robe parting. She was one of the most buxom women I'd known. As I slid my hand into her robe, feeling the heavy weight of her breast, she shuddered. "They're already growing. Can you tell?"

I nodded, feeling her soft flesh. Changing from our union, her body responding and morphing to do what it was designed to. There was a soft delight to her now. When I watched her and she thought no one was looking, she would slide her hand to her abdomen, and the most satisfied look would crest her face. The first place she would look afterward would always be at me.

"Good, because..." Sariel shifted in her robe, pulling my fly apart. When she reached into my pants and pulled my cock out, she gripped it eagerly. "I still love you returning to me. Now that Karley's in the mixture... I was thinking about you all day. You slept with all of them, didn't you?"

I shuddered as her hand churned down. "I did. Must be you being pregnant."

Sariel kissed me again. "Maybe..." I groaned as she pressed me against her quim. "Or maybe Elina keeps filling your runes for a reason."

"What?"

But she slid my hand up her chest as she spread her robe,

letting it billow down her shoulders. "I don't want you to think it'll hurt the baby."

I pressed up as she slid me along her cleft. She was already so wet, but when I entered her, the heat of her body was like a furnace.

"Holy hells," I said with gritted teeth. "You're so warm inside."

Sariel kissed my neck, easing down and grinding onto me. "I'm making you something, that's why. Tyra says the best roasts in the oven"—she moaned as she took me to the hilt— "are well-basted."

I held her hands for a moment. "What did you mean by Elina filling my runes?"

But Sariel didn't slow down. She writhed onto me, leaning back and holding my legs. "Just a theory, my love. You can't reverse some rivers, but you might be able to slow their flow."

I pulled her onto me, moving forward on the couch. That explained Elina pouring so much healing into me each day. I doubted it would make a difference, but I wouldn't stop their little experiment.

Sariel's stomach pressed against mine, and I kissed up her neck, feeling the heft of her ass as she ground onto me.

"Promise you'll always want me?" Sariel whispered, bathing me in fiery heat. The fire crackled behind us, its soft warmth nothing compared to the fiery core of her changing body.

"I promise."

Sariel wrapped her arms around me, pulling my head into her chest.

As her fingers sifted through my hair, she whispered, "I love how dark your hair is getting."

∽

"NO FIGHTING!" Deiga warned the group of us as we gathered on the street. The mage had warmed up well to the group in the tavern who stood around her.

"Oh, they'll be good." Sariel smiled from the railing. "The father of my child wouldn't dare risk landing in a lockup."

Vorga ran out of the front of the tavern, holding a knapsack. "For the road!"

"Thanks." I took the sandwiches. "Be back tomorrow. Promise to be good."

"Not too good." Karley winked at me. She was back in her old attire, but she wore the choker she had donned in Windpeak—an affectation and talisman of us being together. "Otherwise, I'll put you in the stocks."

Vorga looked over. "There aren't stocks in Oakshire."

"You haven't been in the cellar lately, have you?" Tyra snickered. Then the faen leaned over the railing. "Kiss me, you dashing human."

I obliged. Behind us, Trith and Norsuid, along with Brim, Kardak, and Silvus, waited in Rober's wagon.

Tyra ran a hand down my face. "Have fun on your stag party thing."

"It's a sire party!" Trith raised a bottle of beer. "King's march. Man expects a child. He's gotta make the rounds."

"Mmhmm." Elina stepped down from the railing. "No hangover cures for any of you tomorrow."

"Rahh," Brim responded.

"Love you, cleric of Oakshire." I held her for a moment.

"Love you, too." Elina laughed. "Alright, off you go!"

I climbed aboard the wagon. Kardak had taken the day off, with several of Silvus's people agreeing to take up his post so he could get away. The girls waved to us as we set down the road to Tawney. Kardak walked next to the wagon, too heavy to be pulled alongside it.

"You let us know when you need a break," I told him as Trith handed me a beer.

"I can flit around a bit, lessen the load," Silvus offered.

Kardak dipped his banded horns. "I am sturdy, breaker." Then his bovine eyes twinkled. "You're all too weak to make the journey on hoof."

Rober hiccupped from the front of the wagon, already flushed from starting the day early. "When I was a lad, we'd walk to Tawney and back in a single day."

As the wagon settled down the road, and the bright sunshine and drinks hit our gullets, we all looked at each other.

"Wager?" Norsuid asked, his dwarven voice lilting.

"Rahh." Brim agreed.

"Do you see it?" Trith held a hand up to his forehead. The wager had quickly parlayed into a drinking game. Norsuid split a barrel of beer, letting it trail behind the wagon. A faen, a wood elf, two humans, a gnome, and a minotaur had trailed after it, filling their beer, running to the back of the line, and then finishing it before it was their turn again.

"It's fuckin'"—Silvus wavered, his wings flitting randomly —"up there somewhere."

"My horses won't go far without me," Rober vowed. "We're a family."

"They went far without you," Kardak's voice rumbled.

"Horsey," Brim agreed.

Kardak and I were the only ones not stumbling. Brim lit a pipe of sweetvine, and before I could tell him it would slow our group down, it was already being passed around.

We found the wagon after three hours. The horses had

simply slowed, cresting up into a hill. It had given us time to sober up.

"Finally," I breathed. "Let's take it easy for a bit until we get to Tawney."

I heard the *thunk* of an axe and looked over to see Norsuid and Trith grinning over another barrel.

"Just a cup!" Trith laughed. "Thirsty business, chasing this wagon."

Once we had fed and watered the horses, making sure they were cool enough to travel, I climbed into the driver's seat. We set back off the road. It was impossible to stave off the mugs of drinks being shoved into my hands or poured into my mouth as we drove. The chant around the group every time a drink was passed to me was:

Davik's having a baby!

I don't remember much, from the journey to Tawney. The first tavern we walked into, we were kicked out after an hour. Something about parking our wagon.

"You're talking crazy," Trith told the town constable in the middle of the bar. "This is Davik."

The constable looked less than pleased. "Yes, you keep telling me that. Davik is having a baby."

"Tha's right!" Rober jabbed a finger at him. "Having a damn baby! And you're talking to us about wagons? Did the wagon have a baby?" Rober looked around, knowing his point was irrefutable.

Silvus burped. "It didn't."

"There ya go! No baby!" He turned away.

The constable sighed and looked at me. "Can you come outside?"

When I did, I saw the problem. The wagon's two front wheels were parked on top of the walkway. The horses couldn't move because Kardak was passed out in the back of it, tilting the wagon back.

"We were afraid to wake him," the constable explained.

"He's a constable, too! He's guarding it!" Trith burst through the doors behind us. "Where's Brim?"

Norsuid wandered down the street, holding up bundles of food in wax paper. "They got fried fish!"

The constable turned to me. "Can you move this wagon?"

"Sure," I slurred. "Trith, unhitch the horses."

"Come on," Trith called to Norsuid. "We have to hitch the horses."

"Unhitch!" I yelled.

A crowd started to gather. Norsuid was a bit more sober, but not by much. He left the food in the back of the wagon next to Kardak. When they undid the horses and led them away, I walked up to the hitch and lifted it, drawing murmurs from the crowd.

"Oakshire!" Silvus yelled drunkenly, gesturing at the crowd.

I pushed the wagon back onto the street. When I set it down, I turned to the constable, almost falling. "Good?"

The man nodded. "Thank you. Do you mind giving the tavern a rest for a bit?"

"Oakshire trash!" a man in the growing crowd yelled.

Silvus wandered down the steps, his wings fluttering. "Who said that? I'm a proud Oakshire man."

"You're not from Oakshire," I mumbled at him.

Norsuid and Trith looked over after tying up the horses. I raised my hands, trying to calm the growing crowd. "Just a bit of fun. Come on now."

When I turned to regard Silvus, something crashed into my head. I blinked, looking at a bewildered man holding his aching fist.

"Did you just hit me?" I wasn't being coy. I really did want to know.

"Come on!" Norsuid roared, raising his fists. "You sons of whores."

It was at least two dozen Tawney men—grain silo workers it looked like. I wavered a bit from the drink, peering at the young man who'd struck me. Then I raised a finger at him. "Wait! You're one of the servants from what's-his-name? Ruthmad."

"Ruthlad," the man sneered.

"That's it," I nodded.

Rober burst from the tavern doors, eyes blazing. "Davik is my baby!"

I watched in the drunken slowness of the too-inebriated as the mayor of Oakshire stumbled down the steps and planted a fist into the man's head. They toppled over. Brim came flying out behind him, leaping into the air.

"Gabya-hee!" he screamed. I'm not sure where he was aiming, or if old instincts gave in, but his fist slammed into my ribs, powered by a psionic blow.

"Ow!" I yelled as I was knocked to the ground. "You fucking missed!"

"Rahh!" Brim growled from the dirt.

The four of us looked up as the crowd circled in on us, all bearing Ruthlad's colors. Norsuid and Trith had the shirts of two men over their heads, striking them repeatedly.

"Stop this!" the constable yelled. But Silvus had already leapt from the railing, flying drunkenly and crashing into Trith in an effort to help him.

The brawl began until a heavy roar sounded from the back of the wagon. Everyone stopped, looking over as Kardak raised his banded horns, creeping like a beast from the depths. His eyes were bloodshot and crazed.

Then all hell broke loose.

~

WE MADE it halfway back to Oakshire before we camped for the night. Trith lit the fire, and we sat around it, eating food we'd somehow negotiated in exchange for us leaving Tawney with the constable.

"They make a fine fish." Rober raised his meal. His eye was already turning dark with a bruise.

Norsuid groaned. "Scrappy, those men. Are we out of drink?"

"Yes," I answered him for the dozenth time. "Just water. Probably for the best."

Brim grinned and raised a cup. *To the ugly-man. Soon to be ugly-dad.*

"Cheers, Davik," Kardak rumbled, wiping the crumbs from his meal away. "Best if Lyra didn't hear about this."

"Ah!" Silvus waved his hat. "Fuck 'em! Just a little dust-up."

It had been a long time since I'd had a proper outing with a group like this. "Have to admit, it was nice to break away. Wish we had another barrel of beer."

"Any sweetvine left?" Silvus looked up, but both Trith and Brim shook their heads.

I finished my fried fish and mushrooms, wincing against a lance of bitterness in the flavor.

Trith raised a fist. "Break out the mushrooms, Brim."

Rober chuckled. "Oh, I haven't done that in ages."

I looked at Trith. "Your fish didn't have any?"

"Mine did." Silvus looked around. Then his eyes settled on Brim, who stood up and held up an empty sack.

"What's that?" I asked.

Mushrooms. Brim grinned. *All gone.*

391

We all blinked at him. I felt my stomach lurch as it devoured what I had just put inside of it. Rober started laughing, and Trith joined him.

Silvus looked around in horror. "Brim... you didn't."

"I don't want to alarm any of you," Norsuid called out as he returned from the treeline, buttoning up his fly. I didn't even remember him leaving. "But the damned ground is breathing!"

IN THE MORNING, I woke with a headache designed to fell a god. "Oh, fuck."

Trith groaned across from me. We were three hundred feet from the camp. "Turn the sun down, Davik."

I sat up, blinking. Rober, Silvus, and Norsuid were passed out around the fire. Brim whistled as he moved among the camp, unrolling the sandwiches Vorga had packed for us.

Trith sat up across from me, his face covered in streaks of mud and a bewildered look on his face.

There was a fallen tree between us and the camp. A big heavy one, and I saw an axe sticking out of its chewed stump.

"The hell happened there?" I asked.

The wood elf rubbed his eyes. "I don't know..." Then his gaze lifted, and something clicked. "Oh, shit. Do you remember?" He turned to me, a flicker of wild nostalgia in his eyes. "Kardak climbed up there and wouldn't come down. Said he was afraid he'd fall into the sky."

"Where is he?" I looked around.

Trith's voice was tinged with laughter. "You cut him down."

I stood shakily. There are hangovers, and there was whatever sordid thing had a grip on me. I would have given anything for a single touch of Elina's healing spell.

We walked over to the tree, and for a moment, I thought Kardak was dead. He was snout-down in the dirt, his horns planted into the earth. Then he gave out a long, rasping breath and pushed himself up.

"Breaker," he rumbled.

"How we doing?" I crouched down, fighting the urge to vomit. The edge of my vision danced with moving foliage, and there was no breeze. But one problem at a time.

The minotaur grinned. "Don't have more baby parties for a long time."

"Come on, big guy." Trith pulled at his back. "We're late."

We were in sorry-ass shape when we returned to Oakshire. Every man among us stumbled, wavered, and threw up once on the ride back. Silvus couldn't stand the wagon, so he hop-jumped to keep up with us. Somehow, we had gotten turned around and came up through the south of the valley.

"My blood is half wine," Trith groaned as the wagon rumbled.

"Shit!" I looked up. "Let me off here." I had forgotten to drop Lyra off my blood.

Rober slowed the team, and I climbed down. My sire party group smiled back at me with bloodshot eyes, bruises, and filthy clothing.

Brim grinned at me. *Good party, ugly-man.*

"See you at the tavern"—Trith hiccupped—"Davik."

"Thanks." I smiled at all of them. "This was something."

As Rober clicked his team back into a stride, up towards the town to drop everyone off, he waved back at me.

"What's the occasion, boys?"

The echo followed me as I stumbled towards Mabel's house. *Davik's having a baby!*

I kept my eyes on the ground, not wanting to look at the sky. The clouds had a habit of swirling when I did. The cool shade under Mabel's porch was a relief as I rested my head against the door, knocking softly.

Mabel opened the door. "Oh, hells! You look like shit. Get in here."

I nodded and followed her into the house. "You always keep it too hot in here."

But Mabel wasn't in a joking mood. My business partner grabbed my shoulders, steadying me. "Davik, something's off with Lyra."

"I didn't drop blood off yesterday." I looked up at her. "Probably hungry."

Mabel shook her head. "Not that. I had a reserve saved that I gave her. If she drank from you right now, she'd probably be drunker than an ox. Go check on her. I haven't been able to get her to answer."

The old woman stuck a cup of water in my hand, forcing me to drink it before I walked down the hall. I'd never been in this part of the house, but I knew where Lyra's room was. Thankfully for my pounding skull, the shades were drawn to block out the sun.

"Lyra?" I knocked gently on the door.

A moan of anguish came through the door. I made sure my dirk was still on my belt and entered.

When I walked into her room, it was nearly pitch black. But I saw Lyra's pale flesh trembling as she knelt alongside her bed, nude—her armor discarded next to her.

A small book was on the bed, and I recognized the emblem of the Mistress. Her scarred back shifted as I approached, and it sounded like she was weeping as she inhaled.

"Lyra?" I whispered.

Her bare feet shifted, her rear rising from her heels as she turned to me. But it wasn't hunger in her eyes, madness, or falling to her affliction. She winced as pain seemed to tunnel through her skull.

"Davik..." she murmured my name, blinking as she focused on me.

I knelt down. I didn't know if my runes would help, but I slid my hands on either side of her head. The fallen paladin's expression softened—either from the effect or my touch, I didn't know. "Is it him? The one who turned you?" She had told me his voice haunted her in the wind sometimes but had lessened. *They hunt him even now.*

The vampire looked up at me. It wasn't a revelation. It was a realization as she spoke. "He's free. He's free, Davik. They failed to slay him."

I stared at her, cold realization dripping down my fevered body. "Is he close? Is he coming here?"

Lyra shook her head. "He's moved far from here. He seeks to renew himself. To grow. It'll take time. I saw a city... but he calls to me." Then her cold flesh pressed against mine as she threw her arms around me. It was the most vulnerable I'd ever seen her. "He keeps calling to me."

"What's he saying?" I demanded. "What's he saying, Lyra?"

Lyra's voice was dry in her throat, the creak of it like the sway of a hanged man.

"He's laughing."

WHERE TO FIND ME

Thanks for checking out *Magebreaker 2*! If you've enjoyed the book, please consider leaving a review.

To learn about new upcoming projects, get early previews on Magebreaker 3, or just to show support—be sure to sign up for my Patreon! (patreon.com/c/DeclanCourt) Any support goes a long way. There is a free tier if you want to stay updated.

To keep in touch with new updates you can join my newsletter — (http://subscribepage.io/declan-court-newsletter)

ABOUT THE AUTHOR

Declan Court pens tales of fantasy, speculative fiction, romance, and asshole gnomes.

He lived in Seoul after college to teach students the finer points of English and what a hungover American looks like. He returned to the states to grab an MFA.

Currently he spends his time in the southwest writing.

ACKNOWLEDGMENTS

Firstly, thank you to my supporters on Patreon.

Especially:

Juan for his fervent generosity and service.

Julie for her astounding support.

Will B. for his early support and kind words.

Ashford, Joseph Murray, Scott, Oscar, Version93, Colten and Daniella Warvel, Molecule, Jeremy M. And Seth L. for thir patronage.

A big thanks to Jessica at Royal Guard Publishing, and Marcus Sloss who does so much for this genre. Thanks for being great to work with on the audiobook project. And to the narrators Melisandre Verte and Patrick Dubois— thank you for your passion and outstanding work on Magebreaker 1 and 2.

Lastly, thank you to the readers and those who have supported and reviewed Magebreaker. Your support and word of mouth have meant the world to me. I hope to always be worthy of it.

Made in the USA
Columbia, SC
27 May 2025

58450509R00250